Angel Of The Tsar

With Love We Live Forever

Part 1 of:

"The Gemstone Angel Trilogy"

By

Marlene Christian

iUniverse, Inc.
Bloomington

Angel of the Tsar
The Gemstone Angel Trilogy, Part 1

iUniverse books may be ordered through booksellers or by contacting:

iUniverse
1663 Liberty Drive
Bloomington, IN 47403
www.iuniverse.com
1-800-Authors (1-800-288-4677)

Because of the dynamic nature of the Internet, any Web addresses or links contained in this book may have changed since publication and may no longer be valid. The views expressed in this work are solely those of the author and do not necessarily reflect the views of the publisher, and the publisher hereby disclaims any responsibility for them.

ISBN: 978-1-4401-6345-6 (sc)
ISBN: 978-1-4401-6346-3 (e)
ISBN: 978-1-4401-6347-0 (dj)

Printed in the United States of America

iUniverse rev. date: 8/8/2011

Table of Contents

Part 4 - "The Light of The Goddess"

This book is dedicated to the Creator of the Universe,
The Holy Mother and to all of the Angels that assist them.

It is also dedicated to my mother. As a child, you were my life and I have loved you all of my life. And to my father, who gave me life, I will love you forever daddy.

88888888

The day is thine. The night also is thine.
Thou hast prepared the light and the sun.
Thou hast set all the borders of the earth.
Thou hast made summer and winter.

88888888

What is man that thou art
Mindful of him?
And the son of man
That thou visiteth him?
For thou hast made him
A little lower than the angels
And hast crowned him
In glory and honor.

Psalm 8

88888888

Introduction

In Russia there is folklore of a sacred healing stone that was handed down throughout the centuries to the descendants of the Tsars. It was called Angel of the Tsar.

In April 1998, Canadian journalist Angelique Laird is couriered a package stamped with a curious Russian insignia. Within are an antique diary and an ornate filigree pendant encasing a luminous gemstone. Unbeknownst to her, this gemstone of Russia would be the key to Angelique's mysterious past ... and also to her destiny.

****

Prologue

The Russian Royal Winter Palace - April 4, 1834

"Alex, you must hurry! It is your birthday and there are more presents waiting to be opened!"

His childhood friend Larissa stood in the doorway of the nursery where Alexander was positioned splayed out on the floor intent on a game of soldiers. His new clothes were crumpling under his weight as he lay flat on his belly. Alexander was intently focused on charging his front line up and over the hill and then into the lake that stood between victory and defeat for his troops. The "war field", as he called it, took up a quarter of the large nursery and had been Alexander's passion since he first received it at the age of six from his father.

A good scholar with a kind heart, Alexander was defined by his teachers and mentors as "an old soul" and possessed a fine sense of his own destiny in his future role as the next Tsar of all the Russias. However, at this point in his life, Tsarovich Alexander Romanov II enjoyed just being a boy.

"In a minute Larissa" Alexander sighed. He was dragging his troops through the lake on the "war field" and if he could just take them a few feet further...

"Alexander!" It was the voice of his mother, the Empress. The former Princess Charlotte of Prussia was a regal and self-possessed woman. It was her stern tone that Alexander recognized and when she used 'that voice' he knew better than to dally.

"Yes mama!" Alexander jumped up smartly and, after looking down at his clothing, tucked in his silk shirt and straightened his royal blue velvet jacket.

"Your father wants you to come to the main salon *immediately.*" After expressing her veiled command, his mother turned regally, lifting up the side of her elegant silk gown to engage the turn more gracefully.

"There is a very important gift awaiting you, Alexander. One you will be well pleased to receive." Alexander thought his mother added the last comment with a tone of mystery and it did indeed tweak his curiosity, as his mother knew it would. Alexander had always been a curious boy, forever wanting to learn and understand ideas and issues far beyond the scope of a twelve year old boy.

Alexander strode smartly to the Tsarina's side and walked with her to the main salon where celebrations of his birthday were concluding. The wrappings of his gifts were left in a pile on the marble floor by the fireplace. Alexander was perplexed as he had already opened all the gifts that had been presented to him that day, or so he thought.

"Ah, Alexander …" His father, Tsar Nicolas I, held out his arm to encourage the boy to come hither.

"A very special gift has come to you from the Urals. They have named it the Gemstone Angel." His father smiled encouragement to his son and nodded to Alexander to explore it.

Upon a narrow golden table beside his father sat a small red velvet box. Alexander felt instantly drawn to the object even before his father finished his introduction and ran to the table to lift the lid off the velvet box to explore its contents. Within the box, sitting on a tiny white satin cushion, was the most beautiful object Alexander had ever seen. It quite took his breath away. A luminous rose hued stone seemed to glow out specifically in his direction and beckoned his touch. Alexander lifted the gemstone and held it in the palm of his hand.

Immediately upon holding it, Alexander felt the energy of the gemstone wrap around him and pull him into its core, where he was encircled by a pale golden mist. There was an explosion of light and an elegant luminous angel appeared before him. The angel took his hand and led him through the mist. Alexander understood that he was about to be shown his future.

Alexander stood motionless as he viewed visual images of the life that lay before him. Like newsreels, the images started at a certain 'scene' or age of his life, stopped and began anew with another scene and another and another. He viewed the reforms he would make as Tsar that would leave him the legacy of 'The Liberator Tsar' for freeing the serfs. The angel also allowed him to see the lovely family he would produce and his happiness with them.

As he followed the angel further, the mist deepened in color and begot a more ominous energy. Alexander was then shown two assassination attempts upon his life as the Tsar and his survival of both.

The angel then turned and spoke to Alexander. "There will be, in total, three assassination attempts upon your life. It is necessary for you to carry this gemstone always, for your protection. Your very life will depend upon it."

The angel made one more comment that was more like a prediction. "The power of the gemstone is only for the descendants of the Romanovs and those chosen by them. If placed in the wrong hands, it could bring great tragedy."

The vision of the angel began to break up into what appeared to be tiny particles of stardust and then dissipated into a fine mist before disappearing altogether.

Alexander felt himself pop back into his body in the main salon of the Winter Palace.

"Alexander!" He could hear his father's urgent voice calling out to him.

He shook his head clear and answered his father. "Yes papa?"

"You have been staring at that gemstone for half an hour. What is fascinating you so?"

"The stone spoke to me!" Alexander exclaimed.

The Tsar and Tsarina exchanged glances with one another and then looked over to their son.

"What did the gemstone say to you, Alexander?" his father asked.

Viewing the iridescent Gemstone Angel as he held it close to his face, Alexander voiced quietly, "It told me of the man I will become."

Tsar Alexander Romanov II, Emperor of all the Russias, kept the Gemstone Angel in his private keeping all of his reigning life and never left the palace or travelled without it, wearing it contained in a golden pendant beneath his clothing. He referred to it as his Angel of Peace and Protection and put away his "war field" forever after receiving it.

Tsar Alexander II concentrated on bringing peace and reform to his reign as Emperor and became known as the Liberator Tsar, freeing the serfs and encouraging self development for his people until his death.

Tsar Alexander II was assassinated in front of a church in 1881 after having just signed a document that would have helped deliver the very people who killed him. In his haste to attend a church service, he had left his Gemstone Angel on the very desk upon which he had signed the document.

After the death of Tsar Alexander II, the Gemstone Angel mysteriously disappeared for over sixty years, reappearing just prior to the Russian Revolution.

This book is a continuation of its story.

Part I

"The Bringer Of The Grail"

Chapter 1 – "The Seventh Diary"

10:30 A.M., April 7ᵗʰ, 1998

My fingers almost set the package into flight as my excitement carried it and me up the stairs to my second floor pied a terre.

"Oh!" Remembering my manners, I turned around and hollered down the staircase to the bemused mail courier, "Thank you very much!"

"That's okay mam', just doin' my job. So enjoy and have a good day, hey?"

Thankful for my foresight in putting on my stretch jeans that morning, I maneuvered up my back stairs two at a time as I couldn't get through my door fast enough to open the package.

"Oops! Come on Fluffy, back in the house", I called to my Himalayan as he attempted his usual dash through the open door. My right foot halted his bolt so with a quick twist of dexterity, which I often admired him for, he jumped up in the air and turned himself inward. Picking him up, I carried him over to the chintz sofa, marveling at how light he was for all that fur.

"They certainly wrapped it up well enough, didn't they Fluff?"

I was used to including Fluff in my daily conversations with myself. He was a wonderful listener and also my best editor. When I wanted to know if my articles were a bit too long or not of sufficient or captive interest, I'd read them aloud to Fluff. If he fidgeted, the words needed work. If, on the other hand, he sat and fixed his brilliant lapis orbs on me, the story was a winner as he was right a hundred per cent of the time. "Fluff, you're my best critic!" I would tell him.

The stern twine on the package was tricky to cut away. While figuring out a method of attack, my vision caught and stopped at the label on the front of the package.

Mille Angelique Alexandra Christina Laird
The Old Mill Condominiums
Unit E
Toronto, Ontario

"Hmm… You know, that's strange, Fluff. No one has used my full name like that since high school. And 'mademoiselle'! They must think I'm a teenager!"

In truth, Angelique was the original spelling of my first name and the correct one on my birth certificate, but it had always been pronounced *An-gel-ee-ka*, taken from the French pronunciation and then bastardized by my Scottish uncle Cecil who gave it a Celtic flare and it stuck. Everyone assumed I was named after the actress Angelica Huston. Interestingly enough, she had inherited the same cultural heritage as my own; Russian mother and Celtic father, although her father (director John Huston) being of Irish descent to my father's Scottish one.

There seemed to be no return address on the label, save for a tiny gold insignia that appeared to have been stamped onto the upper left hand corner. There was an inconsistency here. Although the package was of that ordinary brown parcel post species, the label was of parchment, very fine and of the palest lavender hue. The label was hand written with a fountain pen in dark blue ink, the letters and numbers scripted in calligraphy; an art seldom used now, unfortunately.

On closer inspection I discovered the insignia was shaped like a small crown but not a familiar one. It was almost structured like a samovar (an intricately designed ornate container usually made of silver and used for holding hot water to make Russian tea).

While examining the crown more closely, something startled me. I stood up suddenly and surveyed the room. There was an eerie sense of not being alone. Settling back down on the sofa, still holding the as yet unopened package, I felt the tremendous urge to fold my arms over it and hold it to my chest, close my eyes and cradle it like a small child. For several moments I sat quietly and meditatively. Then I heard her.

"The secret is in your name. Anya…"

The voice was soft and feminine with a slight refined European accent and seemed to come from within me rather than from outside of me.

"Who is Anya?" I wondered out loud.

The voice spoke again. *"The secret is in your name… votre nom… votre nom…"*

The words 'votre nom' echoed in my mind as I opened my eyes; the package still in my arms. 'Votre nom' was very formal French, almost never used in modern French language, with the exception of professional business or legal documents. 'Tu' was normally substituted, especially during personal and intimate conversations and this woman's voice was *very* intimate. It was another inconsistency. The biggest inconsistencies however were; from where had the package come and from whom?

9:05 A.M. (Earlier that morning)

The ringing of the telephone woke me from a very sound and much needed sleep, having just returned very early that morning on the last flight out of Vancouver. Although it was a four and a half hour flight, there was also a time change of three hours so arrival time in Toronto was 3:30 A.M. By the time I got home it was 4:35 A.M.

"Hello", I answered, as articulately as could be managed.

"Ms. Laird? Ms. uh…An…gel…ee…" the young woman's high pitched voice stumbled out.

"Angelica" I offered. This was not unusual. People were always mispronouncing my name.

"Oh…Yes. Ms. Laird", she proceeded. "This is International Courier Services. We have a package for you here that we attempted to deliver a few days ago but there was no response at your building. It's marked an urgent express parcel and we did leave a notice in your mailbox."

"I have been away for several weeks and only just returned *extremely* early this morning" I explained, exaggerating the word extremely.

"*So* sorry to disturb you. As I mentioned, however, the parcel is marked 'very urgent' and it was directed to be delivered to you as soon as possible. Will you be available today to take the delivery?"

"Yes, I will be here". She was verging on becoming irritating. "By the way, where is the parcel from..?" She had already hung up.

After sitting up and pulling the duvet back down the bed, I covered my bare toes, which often get cold in the warmest of weather, with the lace hem of my favorite Laura Ashley nightgown. It felt comforting to be back in my own home again, the pastel color scheme throughout creating a sense of serenity within me.

While admiring my French pedicure from the Century Plaza Spa in Vancouver, where I had been writing a travel feature on luxury spas in Canada, my focus wandered into the living room. Through the French doors leading to my flower and fauna bedecked sun room, I observed it was a bright April morning and fresh as a newly opened daisy.

Repressing the urge to tug on my jogging clothes and go for a run through High Park, I pulled off my nightgown, made my bed and proceeded to do my six yoga exercises right there on the duvet. It was a routine I'd begun just before my Vancouver trip. A personal trainer had designed a workout for me that could be done anytime/anywhere, taking into account my hypoglycemia so the exercises needed to be smooth and release stress optimally. The hypoglycemia was hereditary and I had gone over the edge too frequently due to my work schedule. It's in my DNA and if one carries that gene, a little extra care and attention to one's diet and exercise might be wise. **

From the age of sixteen to my early thirties I had always been very body conscious, watched what I ate and how much, got proper rest, took vitamins etc. At that time my prudence was mainly due to a career necessity. I modeled my way through university by working my modeling assignments around my classes and sometimes the other way around. It was a career that gave me the opportunity to travel and meet people that otherwise would not have been possible for me.

It was through one of these contacts, a photographer who taught at Ryerson, that I initially came to work for a major media company; first in the Public Relations Department and then in the production area.

That was a fruitful career until the 1980's layoffs, commonly referred to as The Big Freeze, where whole stations were systematically obliterated. It was said to be a 'clearing out of the deadwood process' but so many good, productive people got caught between the cracks during that downsizing. Unfortunately, it turned out to be the predecessor of many more companies doing the same.

At that time most of my working life involved a very stable schedule so it was fairly easy to keep regular hours and eating habits. Après the *Big Freeze*, however, I began freelancing and that entailed a very different lifestyle and schedule. This circumstance ultimately resulted in my blood sugar fluctuating and frequent energy drops when my normally high energy level would just plummet. Practicing yoga however, first thing in the morning and before bedtime, helped keep my blood sugar levels and energy stable all day long.

After the yoga, it was time for a quick shower. The warm spray felt refreshing and the hand milled French soap that was my flavor of the week was a lemon jasmine scent and gave off the aroma of fresh spring blossoms; a scent so delicious one could almost taste it.

I confess to being mad about scents and must own over twenty fragrances; mostly designer perfumes but several natural essential oils as well. The dresser in my bedroom holds a tray of them along with several scented body lotions.

"Crunch". . While I was showering, Fluff was feeding on his low ash dry cat food. He had always had his food bowl full so he did not behave like other cats do in the morning, bothering about your feet until their hunger pangs were placated. I often wondered if they behaved that way because they were really hungry or just out of the instinct of self-preservation - just in case they *might* get hungry!

While swallowing the last of my fruit and yoghurt, the buzzer sounded downstairs.

"Package for Miss Laird" Interrupted a voice through the intercom.

"I'll be right down!"

And so it began.

**I did quite a personal research on blood and DNA at that time and found out that diabetes (and hypoglycemia is considered under that category because it is the stage just prior to full-blown diabetes) is the most prevalent *dis-ease* of the century. Often described as the Prosperity Disease because the escalating type *D (Type II Mellitus) is caused by overeating, especially food rich in fat and sugar and can be contacted by ANYONE. The usual patients are people over forty who have put on extra weight and stopped exercising, i.e. the couch potato syndrome. If it is in the DNA, however, it is possible to bring it on if similar conditions, especially stress, are prevalent. *(D - Type I differs in that it is a childhood onset disease which some researchers believe could be caused by a virus.)

What is NOT well known about diabetes Type II is that it is very manageable and totally controllable, so needles need never be necessary. Proper diet and exercise can even rebalance the body within a year and may in some cases illuminate it. The Asians, particularly the Chinese, have many herbs for treating Type II diabetes. Due to their diet, which is high in starch, it would make sense that their culture would be at high risk. They also have high rates of success in stabilizing blood sugar as well.

Chapter 2– "The Seventh Scent"

11:00 A.M.

A light yet distinct scent of frankincense emitted from the package, even though it was wrapped very thoroughly with twine and several layers of heavy paper. The unwrapping of the package somehow sent my mind into a reverie; peeling away the layers of incidences and events in my life that had caused me to take the directions I had to become who I am.

The olfactory had always played such a large part in my life. My sense of smell was so profound at times that it seemed to overwhelm all the other senses. Perhaps because the nasal area was located so closely to the pineal gland, I could experience intense psychic awareness when certain scents were in the air. This I called the Seventh Scent.

The Seventh Scent related to a level beyond the five senses and even the sixth (that of instinct). It belonged to the realm of the Angels; The Angelica. I could actually *smell* their energy. They brought their presence and their revelations to me through wafts of fragrance in the ethers and filled my cranium with visions of enlightened splendors and visual (and sometimes invisible) wisdom.

It has been said that there are no coincidences; that everything happens for a reason. Even the names we wear, like shields, are ones we, our souls, have 'sensed' or chosen. When I 'sensed' I should have my name pronounced *Angelica*, it became a self fulfilling prophecy. In turn, I became a vessel through which the Angels could channel their messages.

The Light Ones began their visits with me when I was three. Sinister holes had been torn throughout my father's aura, due to a serious illness. As he healed at home, I saw dark images of unexpected horror and evil, trying to shape themselves through the miniscule tears that the pneumonia had begot. The offensive scent that accompanied the expelling of his lung fluid was a stench that belonged more to the beings that were trying to interfere with my fathers energies. I saw and smelled them as they drifted into my room at night, keeping me awake with their frightening imagery and expressions.

Then the Light Ones came! They shone like miniscule light bulbs and upon entering my room became enormous candle flames; luminous and glowing; smelling of fragrant lilacs.

"You cannot have the child!" they resounded. "She is OUR Realm!"

The dark images oozed angry protests and circled my head and body.

"TELL THEM YOUR NAME!" The Light Ones blared out.

"Angelica", I said softly. I could not pronounce the French Angelique and at the age of three the sound formations came out as Angel-ee-ka.

At the sound of the name, the dark images froze and stopped their frenetic circling.

"Say your name louder, child", the Light Ones commanded me, firmly and yet so gently.

"It's   ..." I began quietly and then stronger and louder. "ANGELICA!"

The dark ones seemed to lose their focus as the sound of the word broke apart their energies. Realizing my name carried with it some sort of power, I spoke my name louder and with more confidence.

"ANGELICA!" I finally shouted. To my amazement, the dark ones fled as if invisible spears had pierced them away.

"We dwell within you. *We* are The Angelica", the Light Ones spoke again. Then, after the last dark ones faded into space, the Light Ones sprayed their lightness and luminosity throughout my room and the room turned the color of morning sunshine. Golden flecks of stardust, millions of them, bright as fireflies, covered the walls and circled under the ceiling, spreading mists of sparkling white light everywhere.

Accompanying the light was energy of love and joy such as I had never encountered before or since. The four Pillars of Light (Ones) then merged together to become one great expansive sphere of energized Love and Unity. "We are The Angelica", they announced again and circled over, around and somehow right through me, "and we are within you", they continued.

The JOY LIGHT LOVE parted my molecules like they were specks of dust and filtered through my being, illuminating my body, soul and spirit until I gasped with the ecstasy.

Then, as quickly as they appeared, they vanished and I was once again in the Summerland of sleep.

Chapter 3– "Jacey"

After folding back the last of the three paper wrappings that protected its contents, I was struck by the sheer beauty of the antique contained within; a book covered in exquisite tapestry.

I had collected antiques for some time; mostly silver, jewelry, vintage clothing and quite a few first edition books. From the style of the book and design of the fabric, I guess-timized it to be Russian, probably early 1900's or around the time of the revolution.

Beautiful pink roses, violets, lilacs and lilies of the valley scattered themselves artlessly across a pallet of what was at one time a white silk background but now time faded to an ivory hue. A strip of amethyst toned water stained silk served as a marker, laying itself sleepily over the front cover and tapering to a V two inches longer than the book itself. Attached to the point of the marker was a remarkable and exquisitely carved miniature silver toned egg that was about the size of the top of my thumb from the place of the first joint. At first glance the antique appeared to be a bell and although it committed a little rattle when shook, it did not indeed ring. Upon closer observation, I discovered it was the egg that emitted the aroma of frankincense, which was and still is frequently swayed from brass burning incense pots by orthodox priests during religious services.

A memory came to mind of when I was about eight and out in the country attending a Christmas Eve mass with my entire family, including grandparents, aunts, uncles and cousins. We waited for what seemed an endless time before the priest, the star performer, finally appeared. When he did my eyes flew wide open. It was quite a spectacle! The Russian Orthodox priest seemed solemn and ancient; he was likely about seventy; dressed in white and gold vestments wearing an unusual covering on his head. He carried a smoking brass incense pot and I will never forget the scent of that incense as it permeated the entire church. Frankincense.

"Take the egg from the marker and wear it. It will benefit you greatly."

The woman's voice was there again, speaking clearly and expressively. I scanned about me but of course saw no one. Who was that woman?

"Wear the amulet. Anya…" she said again.

I found a tiny slip ring that joined the silvery toned egg (probably white gold) onto the silk marker. With a pair of jewelers pliers, purchased while out west to fix the clasp of a jade bracelet that constantly stuck, I spaced open the slip ring and fitted it onto an antique silver chain that was originally from Russia. I had discovered the chain over ten years ago in a charming antique store named Pippins located not far from me in Bloor West Village and fell in love with it.

The manner in which the egg balanced the chain made it seem absolutely divined for it. I had not worn the chain in years as nothing seemed to 'work' with it. It was either too ornate for most simple pendants or too odd a length to be worn on its own. With the silvery egg it was perfect and the pendant sat just below my collarbone.

While admiring the pendant's ancient beauty in my mirror, the telephone rang. Twisting round to retrieve the receiver from my night table, the 'bell' rattled again and the scent of frankincense wafted up to my nostrils from the egg. I assessed that the incense was one of the amber pebble type sold in religious stores, which meant the egg must open somehow. That would have to be explored later.

"Hello there, Angel girl!" came the voice on the other end of the telephone.

"Jacey! I had about given up on you!"

Jacey was a beloved old friend from television production days who had also been laid off during The Big Freeze and was now CEO of a publishing company that included a Conde Naste type of travel publication. He now divided living between New York and Paris.

"Never mind about all that, dear girl. I am about to make it all up to you. How long will it take you to pack for Paris?"

Jason Christopher was every woman's ideal of a man. As well as being tall with blond hair that streaked heavenly platinum in the sun, he was handsome and from a well established Ontario family with a pedigree that dated back to the time of King Arthur. Jason was a true gentleman of the highest order and the perfect date. That meant of course that Jason was gay. It hadn't always been so, however.

I met Jacey in the late seventies when we were both attending Ryerson in Toronto. Jacey was a nickname that was derived from his already established nickname of "J.C.", after his initials, but also after the very popular Jesus Christ Superstar film and his quite extraordinary physical similarity to the popular idea of Jesus' appearance. During our sojourn together at RyHi, Jacey wore his abundant locks to below shoulder length accompanied by a mustache and trimmed beard. Tall and slender of build, he cast a romantic and poetic figure in those days.

Although Jacey possessed the type of eyes that were large and slightly turned down on the sides, there was absolutely nothing depressed or pathetic about him! As a matter of fact, he possesses the wickedest of wits I have come into contact with thus far. Jacey was ever humorous and fun loving but never vicious; quite the opposite actually, constantly rendering himself to random humanitarian acts of kindness and forever helping others out. One might say, and many who were envious did, that it was all very easy for him to be so generous, wasn't it, what with all that family money. And yes, it may be easier to give when you had more of it to give, but Jacey gave of his time and understanding as well as his money. Let's face it, he didn't have to. Most of his upper class old boy schoolmates didn't. He did. That fact alone marked him as special.

In those days everyone wore jeans to classes, especially if you were enrolled in the arts as we were. We both wore our hair long and parted in the middle, falling down our shoulders to mid back. More than once comments were made that we looked like brother and sister - "And from behind, the two of you look like sisters!" Well, my auburn hair did take on golden highlights in the sunlight and Jacey did have those slender hips and long legs.

Jacey was the first artist to really photograph me. Part of his curriculum was to photograph a nude human form but the way he moved and positioned my body however, he was careful that no private parts were exposed and not cause me embarrassment. The way he turned my head, so that my long full hair swept over my face, it was also impossible to tell who the photo was of.

I was not totally nude in that photograph, or any others for that matter, just the illusion was there. That particular shot had me stretched out over his white studio floor covering wearing a length of ivory silk draped over my body like a long Grecian robe. It hung over one shoulder and was loosely belted at the waist with a gold drapery cord found in the back room. Laying outstretched, my right arm straight out on the floor appearing to point to a far off destiny and my right leg bent at the knee and hugging the floor, Jacey brushed my then almost waist length hair over my face and laid it out in a sunburst pattern over the floor in front of me. Then, for a reason incomprehensible at the time, he got up, went to the sink in his darkroom, came back with a watering can and proceeded to sprinkle water on me as if I were a flowerbed! Later, upon viewing the finished product, I realized the reason behind his seeming madness. By attaching a particular type of glycerin lens onto his camera, he was able to make the 'gown' appear to take on a 'life'. In the light the wet gown glistened iridescently and the water drops gave the appearance of myriads of fireflies (or stars) dancing across its canvass. He then superimposed two backgrounds onto the photo: One of an ocean tide ebbing in and the other of a misty cloud formation. The effect was pure Aphrodite and he actually titled the finished photograph "Truth: The Birth of Venus". When Jacey featured that photograph in his private showing several months later, he made a fortune in prints of a limited edition, which he graciously and generously shared with me.

Until that Photography we were very good close friends. Our relationship changed at the end of that photo session, however.

After taking the last photograph of me, Jacey put down his camera, crossed the floor and sat down beside me, looking at me in a way he had never done before.

"You have a certain look about you, Angel. It's like a cross between Bridget Bardot and Joan of Arc. There's something of the virtuous sacred warrior about you that I find fascinating and irresistible. Did you know you have a light that encircles you? You don't need artificial light", he said as got up and pushed the lighting apparatus away. He moved forward and knelt before me.

Gently taking me by the shoulders, he stared into my eyes with his own ocean depths, which were lit by a fire unknown to me until that moment. Laughing, with a kind of self conscious astonishment, he said "You possess a power that can only be likened to an undiscovered radiant planetary star. For me this experience has been like finding a beautiful yet uncut stone, brushing it up and finding pure diamond. You light up any area and everything that is in it with the intensity of a comet that has suddenly and exquisitely landed on terra."

With that Jacey so gently yet so passionately kissed my lips and drew me back onto the cloth flooring. We made love as if we were under a hypnotic spell, cast by the night taking over the day and the sky and the sun and the moon and the earth in between. Jacey's lovemaking was fluid and breathtaking. I have not felt such intensity of oneness with any human being since then.

I was a virgin until that night. So, as I found out later, was Jacey. The two of us found Truth that night for through our union we felt we had touched the face of God and the mystery of the universe was revealed to us in all of its glory and splendor. Afterward, when we gazed into one another's eyes, we realized what we had encountered and the revelations that were understood. I knew then that I would never again feel as intimate with another human being as at that moment in time. I was in love with Jacey and he with me. From that moment, we shared a love so deep and so profound that our souls spilled out spectrums of lifetime after lifetime spent together in love and in grace with the universe. Our light had touched far beyond the stars and the sky.

But where could we go from there?

"Angel?" Jacey continued as if this invitation was so common place that it required no explanation. "I'd like you to leave today if at all possible. My client is a top drawer publication". (Meaning all expenses paid with five star accommodations for a high priced glossy travel magazine as opposed to a newspaper travel feature which usually paid scale). "They want to do a feature on Lourdes. You know, where the

'Song of Bernadette' originated with the miracle of the healing waters and the visions of the Virgin Mary".

"Yes, I know of the story very well. It was one of my favorite books in high school".

"Really? Well", he continued, "I want you to do a preamble to the Pope's visit to the area. There seems to be quite a resurgence and interest in all things religious and spiritual. People are looking toward hope and miracles in the times coming what with all the Nostradamus predictions of the coming times at the approach of the millennium - especially anything that has to do with religious fervor and visions of Mary and Jesus. And of course, of angel intervention. So I naturally thought of you. You're the perfect person to cover the story."

"What story?" I queried.

"You know…"As Jacey spoke, I could see him holding up his hands and imitating parentheses in the air as he added, "'The phenomena of the Holy Mother and her messages to the world, speaking though the voices of innocent peasant children'. This could actually make for a feature series and I sense you could handle that beautifully for us. So are you interested? You land in Paris for a two day briefing and a bit of shopping - and then off to Lourdes and the holy site."

Obviously Jacey had already made up his mind that I was going and admittedly I couldn't think of any reservations.

"What about tickets?" I asked, speaking of reservations.

"They'll be waiting for you at the airport at 3:00 P.M. this afternoon. Your flight leaves at 4:30 so I'll let you get on with it. I trust your passport is timely?"

"Of course", I said matter of factly.

"Of course" he mimicked me. "I expected no less. There will be an advance cheque for you included with the tickets along with some French currency for travel expenses like taxis and tips. As for the rest, do as the world does, pay by plastic!" With the exception of Fluff there were no responsibilities to be tied down to and he could easily be taken care of by my neighbor Rose who loved to feed and play with my feline when I travelled.

"Paris it is, then!"

While placing the telephone receiver back in its place on my night table, my eyes glanced over to my Austrian crystal clock.

"Holy, Fluff! It's past noon! I have to pack, call Rose and ask her to take care of you, eat lunch so my blood sugar stays intact and be at the airport by 3:00 PM! No pressure!"

"Jason Christopher, much as I love you - and I always will - your capacity for spontaneity sometimes just surpasses the pale! Lord love a duck, how am I to accomplish all that's needed in less than two hours without benefit of wings and a halo!"

Well, fly I did! Starting with first things first, I grabbed a tangerine from the fruit bowl on my dining table, brought it to the kitchen and hauled a bowl from the fridge that was filled with fresh garden salad and heaped some onto a leaf shaped salad plate. Opening a small tin of salmon, I flaked it overtop of the salad, then peeled and sectioned the tangerine and spread it artlessly across the arrangement of vegetables. A bit of yoghurt for dressing, a toasted twelve grain bagel and lunch was taken care of.

Sliding open the doors of my walk-in closet in the front hallway of my condo, I pulled out my traveler-on-wheels and first off systematically packed all necessary toiletries in the matching tote bag. For the makeup bag I selected earth toned eye shadow and cheek contour. I never wore blush - never needed that! A rosewood lipstick would work with everything, a peachy gold lip gloss for highlights, plus a vitamin C lip balm for the sun. I threw in a pretty lilac lip gloss - because of Paris - and my nude makeup base in a tube, gratis Estee Lauder. Her products for both skincare and makeup are some of the best on the market. I wore her White Linen perfume for years. It became my signature scent at the television station.

"You were just in the newsroom, weren't you?" they'd tease. "Ahh! Eau de Hawaii!" It was all in fun but I did try to be conscious that a little goes a long way. I didn't want the little snide jokes and comments, like the ones that were made about one of the more flamboyant female producers, that were not always in good fun or good taste but, I suspected, spoken more out of envy than anything else.

A vision immediately came to mind of the time she was standing in the outer office talking to the production manager whilst awaiting her contract meeting with the then single and fresh faced twenty-six year old program executive. The *wunderkind*, as he was known, was brilliant as well as being boyishly attractive to women and this producer was not immune to his charms.

In the midst of her conversation with the production manager, she reached into her Gucci tote bag and brought forth a small spray bottle of Joy (one of my personal favorites) and proceeded to spray perfume down her blouse.

The production manager stifled a smile behind his beard but the young executive assistant blinked in naive disbelief as she commented in all innocence, "I've never seen a producer perfume themselves before going into a contract meeting!"

The production manager drew himself up to his full six foot four and a wide grin spread across his face, accompanied by a belly laugh that resounded down the hall. This aroused the attention of the production secretary who poked her curious nose into the outer office, known as the 'little Kremlin'. The production manager then turned on his heel, went into his office, retrieved a copy of the "Undress For Success" booklet and boyishly teased and plagued this producer for weeks by first taking it into the program directors office, relayed to him her perfumery episode and then photocopied the booklet for the benefit of the entire station! It was all quite funny, really. What I got out of it was that the producer had very good taste in perfume. Joy, as I said, is one of my personal favorites. I guess it all just went over my head. (P.S.: This producer apparently negotiated very well because she and the program executive were married less than two years later.)

"Well, toiletries, makeup, shampoo, conditioner, passport ... in the tote!" I placed each item in the custom designed compartments that I had installed in my carry-on bag which made it more efficient for travel.

My 'travel wheelie', was then hauled up onto my bed and I immediately threw in a short black slip with spaghetti straps as it always came in handy for sleeping in case of humid weather. Deciding to treat myself and buy some lingerie whilst in Paris, I bypassed packing those.

From my bedroom closet, I pulled my sleeveless black silk linen blend go anywhere dress and decided to team it with an ivory or lavender pashmina shawl. Both? Sure. The strappy gold Italian sandals and classic black patent leather sling back pumps and my Nikes of course, would suffice for a shoe wardrobe. Then, my fisherman's vest with all those great zipper compartments for holding film rolls, lens and notebooks went it the bag. Many times it was more expedient to have these items close at hand instead of in the camera case. The Nikon was faster on the draw as well as being top drawer in the camera world but I favored the Pentax for its durability and it was especially good for rough or unexpected terrain. Something said "take it" so take it I did. I also threw in a little pocket Minolta and a few drugstore instamatics; an indoor flash and an outdoor exposure. I have found them to come in handy at those moments when the film runs out in your 'real' camera just as the shot you've waited for all day comes up. You just never know. Most professional photographers abhor them, but I was caught 'sans film' once too often and almost missed the shot of a lifetime - the one I had featured in Life - but for the grace of a tourist who lent me his 'instant' so I could catch the two pandas kissing in a sweet embrace prior to the first ever zoo mating of the pandas in captivity.

"Throw in the tan Gap pants, the ones with the big leg pockets - again for carrying 'gear', the dove gray Armani pantsuit, slip on my black non-crease linen blend pantsuit and I'm set!"

Rose was at her office and as usual she was tickled to take care of Fluff. The taxi would be in my driveway at exactly 2:00 P.M. I had just enough time - it was 1:20 - to take a quick shower to freshen up.

I brushed my below the shoulder length hair (it grew like a healthy weed) into a French twist and left a few tendrils loose at the sides and front to frame my high forehead. The makeup is best left simple for air flights: A dot of ivory base on forehead and cheeks and blended well with fingertips, taupe brown eye shadow applied on the arch of the upper lid then blended down onto the outer edge and smudged onto the lower outer lid for definition. A light flick of natural black mascara on the upper lashes only as it avoids messy smudging and I would be on the aircraft for almost 8 hours. In my opinion the little earth pots of bronzing powder that you can dip a brush into and dust all over for a sunless tan and glow work wonderfully on lids, cheeks and lips for an allover healthy appearance but works especially well on cheeks which is where it was placed. The final touch was a yummy clear peach lip gloss so the look was not too make-uppy; just a nicely finished face.

"Buzz." The intercom sounded, announcing that the limousine was downstairs. I made one last trip to the refrigerator for my Lifesaver; a small lunch tote containing a bagel and cheese slice in a Ziploc bag, along with an orange and a mini chocolate bar. It was a snack I always carried when traveling in case I 'crashed' – a term for blood sugar falling quickly and without warning. I plunked it into my tote bag beside my Gucci handbag and pulled on my black trench coat, leaving it open..

"Come give mummy a kiss, Fluffy." I cooed as I lifted Fluff up in one arm, Fluffy wagged his squirrel tail and tilted his furry head up to my face. He was used to the drill. Gently placing him down upon the sofa, I gathered my camera case, tote and 'wheelie' and headed out the door.

I instructed the driver to take the South Kingsway through the array of west end mansions onto the Lakeshore to the Lester B. Pearson Airport. It was a prettier drive with far less traffic than the 401.

The sky was overcast and the air close, leaving ones clothing feeling stuck to the skin. It was typical Toronto weather. I was glad to be out of it for a while. Paris could be much the same during the summer but was normally quite fresh at this time of year. The south of France in the Lourdes area would be a bit cooler but still dry and comfortable.

I arrived at the airline ticket counter to find the flight would be delayed by an hour. The ticket agent handed me my airline ticket over the counter after returning my passport, which assured her that I truly was this person with the incredibly long name.

"... And this package was delivered here for you, Ms. Laird." The blond agent smiled pertly as she handed me a thick brown eight and a half by eleven envelope.

"By the way Ms. Laird, your business class ticket offers you the privilege of complimentary service in our executive lounge while you wait for your flight." The agent, whose jacket pin indicated was named Suzy, leaned closer and advised in sincere tones. "You may want to take advantage of the service in case of any further delays. We can advise you immediately in there."

After thanking Suzy, I proceeded over to the duty free shop. Spying the elegant pewter mosaic face of an Anne Klein watch, I picked it up along with a bottle of Cartier's 'Oh So Pretty' (because it is oh so pretty) and handed the sales clerk my credit card.

Settling into a comfortable armchair in the executive lounge, I allowed myself a sip of lemon herb tea before undoing the tab of the brown envelope.

At the bottom of the envelope was a small box wrapped in simple gold paper. That was so Jacey; simple but elegant. I carefully opened the exquisite wrapping, which reminded me of gold leaf. It was a purse size bottle of Joy perfume.

Chapter 4– "The Christophers"

Jacey had introduced me to my very first bottle of Joy years ago when we were in university.

He had invited me to his parent's home in Forest Hill for Christmas. I had never seen such a mansion before, never mind been entertained in one. Jacey's parents were terribly old guard and therefore extremely unpretentious and had that wonderful knack, as did Jacey, of being able to put everyone at ease. His sister Penny, Penelope Elizabeth this is, was fabulous and we got on tremendously well right from the start.

Penny toured me through her wing – that's right, her wing! Later, I sat in while she did her daily dance exercises. Penny had been attending the National Ballet School for six years. She pirouetted on tip toe round and round her ballet room. Her tall (she was nearly six feet) elegant arrow thin body and long straight brilliant flaxen hair that fell to her waist, moved in total and complete unison together as one piece of motion. Her energy was pure Persephone, so lovely, so natural in her grace; like a dancing poem.

Penny's sapphire eyes were like Jacey's, large and heaven dealt. I thought only Angels could have eyes such as that but there she was, flesh and blood and beautifully human.

After changing into her Christmas dress, Penny confided "Mummy and daddy are so ticked that I want to be a model after all the years of ballet they put me through. Yes, of course, I wanted to become a ballerina", she breathed as she spun around one last time and followed her long blue velvet Camelot dress into a wingback chair. ".. But I was a little girl when I chose that. Then it became mummy's dream. The truth is I would simply be too tall for it! Whoever could they partner me with? Anyway, I do want to go on and do something meaningful with my life, but for a year or two I just want to travel and *see* life."

After having her photograph featured in Harper's Bazaar while attending an international fund raising event in New York with her parents, the most elite modeling agency in New York City had fallen all over Penny to join them. They told her they would have her travelling all over Europe. She would be the next Supermodel - and Canada's first! All of this impressed Penny not in the slightest but viewing the world from a very different angle did. Penny was innocent due to youth and inexperience but she was not naïve. She was sheltered yet sophisticated; an old yet beautiful soul.

"Angelee ..." she began, using her pet name for me, "Let me call the agency and courier a photo or two of you to New York. I'll bet they'll snap you up in a second." Her sapphire eyes were afire as if stars had been placed behind them. Her eyes were enormous even with those pale eyelashes; now they were half of her face!

"Then we could travel together!" Penny was on the chair seat jumping up and down in sheer youthful exuberance by now. "I love it. I just love it!"

"You love what, P.E.?" Jason's impish tease proceeded his lanky stride across the floor, followed by a catlike perch on the arm of her chair.

"Being nosey again are you, brother sleuth?" Penny drew out her words regally as she looked down upon him from heightened advantage on the chair before effortlessly folding herself in half to assume a sitting position with her knees tucked under her chin. Her long expressive arms waved in the air like a set of blue velvet wings as she expanded on her plans.

At the end of her posturing, Jason turned and looked right at me and said "I think it's a great idea. It would be great exposure - AND you could keep an eye on my crazy little sister too", he teased.

"Do I have anything to say about this?" I queried already sensing open defeat.

"No!!" They both echoed.

"First of all", I interjected, ignoring them, "I have no photos, no experience and no agent!"

"That's easy", began Penny. "I have the contacts and will set it all up - and Jacey will take some photos before dinner!"

"In what? I only brought what I have on and some jeans."

I was wearing a vintage 1950's cashmere sweater set in dove gray in mint condition that I had found in an antique clothing store on Queen Street in Toronto and teamed it with a full mid-length black velvet skirt. I loved shopping on Queen, partly because it was trendy but also because I was not from the moneyed background Jacey and Penny were. I added a pair of ivory cotton lace tights and black ballet slippers. A strand of my grandmother's pearls graced around my throat was all the jewelry that accompanied the outfit and that was it! I tended then and now toward a classic wardrobe. I loved my outfit but knew it would never do for a fashion shoot.

Well, to make a long story shorter, Jacey had me put on one of Penny's leotards and posed me in a yoga asana. For the next set of shots, he took a beautiful antique Belgian lace table cover and placed it on the inside of my tartan shawl, folding the scalloped lace edge over the outside of the head covering and draped (and tied) the fringed ends over my shoulder. He then loosened my hair so it fell in wisps and waves down the front of the shawl.

It was an inspired shoot. The backdrops he used were the family's huge stone fireplace in the not so common room and beside their elegant cedar Christmas tree in the dining room. He left my makeup alone, saying it would only ruin perfection. So I had only a flick of mascara, a bit of clear gloss to moisten my lips and the flush on my cheeks from the fireplace between me and Jacey's camera lens.

The entire production took less than an hour to accomplish. Then I completely forgot all about it.

Even though Jacey's home itself was rather intimidating, his family members were anything but. Both of Jacey's parents were tall and slender with blazing sapphire eyes, like Jacey and Penny, and both had similar coloring. His fathers' hair however was slightly darker than his mother who had natural platinum hair like Penny. Jacey had revealed earlier that his parents were distant or second cousins, explaining their similarity in appearance.

"Inbreeding, you know", I remember Jacey teasing whenever he made a mistake or did some frivolous act of stupidity.

I found both sets of grandparents to be particularly enchanting. His maternal grandmother Kate was the soul of Penny. A natural beauty, she wore her hair pinned straight back off her face in a French twist. Her violet eyes coordinated beautifully with her simple knee length silk shirtwaist dress, which also set off her ballerina legs to perfection. At sixty-two she could have been her daughter's sister. She reminded me of Margot Fonteyn.

Jacey's grandfather Jack was Kate's husband. He and Jacey's paternal grandfather Tom were cousins and so similar in appearance one could hardly tell them apart. Both of Jacey and Penny's parents and both of their grandfathers were "sown from the same seed" as the saying goes and the family resemblance was to say the least extraordinary.

Tom's wife Madeleine was the family matriarch. Petite and lithe as a whippet, Maddy, as she was called, was as vibrant and energetic as Kate was regal and serene. The two got on exceptionally well. Maddy's pale green eyes and short titian curls made her look every bit the Celtic lass she was. With the temperament to match, no one had to ask why Grandpa Tom donned her "My firebird".

"So good to have another redhead around", Tom said as he extended his hand to me and with his eyes twinkling added, "It really is time Maddy had some competition you know. They say it takes one to handle one. I've been trying for years", he added, rolling his eyes to the ceiling.

"That's enough of that out of you Thomas Christopher!" Maddy retorted in the Celtic accent that betrayed her whenever she was excited. "You'll have the poor girl thinkin' we're a fair lot of savages!"

Maddy turned her fascinating eyes upon me and continued. "Some of our people do admit to being highlanders mind, but that doesn't quite make us savages".

"I would never have thought anything of the sort", I assured her and smiling slyly added. "Half of my family heralds from the highlands of Scotland as well".

"Ah, brought home another then have you Jason", joked his father, handing me a crystal glass of Dubonnet with a twist of lemon that he himself had fixed for me. "I thought you might enjoy this", he smiled kindly.

I savored the delicious flavor and its sweet yet piquant aroma.

"Thank you. It's delicious".

"A sweet drink for a sweet girl", Jacey winked.

"Gir-ell, Jacey!" jeered Penny. "GIR-ELL!"

"Oh Lord, I've done it now", winced Jacey as he rolled his eyes upward, just like grandfather Tom, and slunk into the high back wing chair that was almost as green as his shame.

"Lady then", he appeased.

"Lord, Jason. That's worse than girl. First you call her a servant and then you give her a title!", further tormented Penny.

Instead of shrinking deeper into his chair, Jacey straightened upright and protested "And think you her not worthy of a title!"

"Of course Angelee is WORTHY of a title ... any title actually" Penny offered sweetly "but as to whether she'd actually want one or not is another matter. Not even royalty is much for that these days. I've heard a rumor that Ann doesn't want the title of Princess before her name anymore. She apparently thinks just Ann is sufficient and she can stand on her own, thank you very much."

"She's quite right, of course. Her ability as a horsewoman alone speaks volumes for her. She has an excellent seat", dignified Kate.

"Oh ... Hadn't thought you'd noticed, darling" teased Jack to the glee of all.

Everyone in Jacey's family was a superb rider, some near to Olympic quality and well knew of what they spoke. Although it was never mentioned, I had the distinct impression the bit of knowledge about Princess Ann came first hand. All of the Christophers spoke of royal personages by their first names only, in a personal yet deferred manner. It was an 'inside thing' I was later to acknowledge.

The Gift Opening was done after dinner so that all of the other relatives, cousins and close friends would be in attendance and presumably stay for champagne, coffee and Maddy's famous Noel Baked Alaska, prepared by their cook Josephine. The superb dessert could have been a Martha Stewart dream. A collaboration of the most tasty of Christmas fruit cake ingredients, Josephine's specialty was a concoction of dried exotic fruits such as papaya, pineapple and mango with Brazil, pecan and whole English walnuts. The one time Josephine had asked for Christmas off, Harrods fruitcake had been flown in from London but it just wasn't the same. As well, Josephine's homemade ice cream could have been sold in any specialty store in any country. For Christmas it was traditionally a creamy delight, with rum trickled through it in a ripple pattern with finely chopped slivers of candied ginger.

Josephine's presentation was to center an enormous round fruit cake on a huge silver platter and then place four rectangular fruit cakes so as to form a large Celtic cross. The frozen ice cream was arranged over the cake after having been slightly softened and then sliced into the exact dimensions of the cake. A frothy mixture of egg white, sugar and cream of tartar was quickly spread lavishly across the top and sides of the entire cake. The procedure was a tricky one and had to be handled in a timely manner so the ice cream did not melt before the topping could be lathered on. (Otherwise the dessert would be ruined as the meringue would fall away from the entire cake).

After the 'icing', the platter with cake would be placed in a very hot 500 degree oven for five minutes or until the peaks of the meringue became toasted. The cake was then immediately taken out of the oven and ceremoniously brought directly to the dining table which had been cleared of all remnants of the magnificent turkey dinner. The 'stage' would then be set. The lights would be extinguished and the candelabra directly over the dining table would be set aglow by the flames of the freshly lit silver candlesticks.

A piper was donned in the dress tartan and kilt of the Royal Stewart pattern. (I recognized it because it was the same one my father's family had on their scroll. I never questioned its authority in our home or at the Christophers'. I had always assumed it was due to it being the official tartan of the royal family and thereby showing respect out of tradition.)

The Scottish piper, decked in his full dress regalia, wailed his bagpipes to the tune of the traditional Christmas carol "Noel" through the entranceway of the dining room and piped out his tune all the way around the table. The cake followed suit, wheeled out on an ornately carved tea trolley. The Noel Baked Alaska had been adorned with a crown of tall drip less white candles, lit and set in the circle of the cake, each candle representing a hundred years in Christ's life. It was a magnificent birthday cake for Jesus! A Cherries Jubilee sauce in a silver terrine with accompanying ladle was carried in by Kate who always did the honors and drizzled the luscious burgundy sauce in an artistic circle formation in the centre of each of the crystal dessert plates. Jacey's grandfather Tom, the patriarch of the family, being two years Jack's senior, traditionally rolled in the cake trolley and cut each piece of cake, placing the section in the centre of the cherry sauce halo.

The dessert would be accompanied by tall crystal flute glasses of Dom Parignon, usually 1955.

The Gift Opening was done around the tree in the great room (where the photographs had been done). Everyone took their champagne, coffee or drinks into that area. It had the space to accompany a chamber orchestra (and sometimes did) but was surprisingly warm and cozy despite the stone floors and fireplace.

The gifts the Christophers presented to their relatives and friends were always tasteful and personal, showing care and consideration had been put into the exercise. Jacey's parents gave me a lovely hand crocheted French lace tablecloth as they knew from Jacey that I was partial to antiques. It was so huge I later used it as my bedspread.

Jacey gave me an exquisite Victorian amethyst ring in a white gold filigree setting. He also presented me with my first bottle of Joy perfume.

Joy has as its essence the oil from the Bulgarian rose, which is very rare and of exceptional quality. I had never before beheld such an exquisite scent. From the moment the diminutive crystal bottle was opened and held to my nostrils, I felt the essence of the cosmos overtake me.

It has always been that way with me and that fragrance but it was totally unexpected how it overtook me that first time in the great room and pulled my own spirit essence right out of the wingback chair in which I was sitting right up to the full height of the chandeliered ceiling. My spirit literally collided with the crystal 'earrings' on the magnificent antique and one could hear it 'sing' at the spiritual collision. The rest of the evening I viewed from that vantage point. I truly was having a wonderful time and could see how my eyes glowed, as must have Jacey, when he put my ring on my finger. The golden light from the fireplace brought out all the best light and tones in my skin and hair. My unpainted canvas was luminous in the light and I remember thinking that it seemed as if a star was placed directly behind me and lit me up from within and a light akin to a halo threw out luminous color about my head and shoulders for about five feet. The natural waves of my hair were brushed off my face and pulled up at the sides and held by a black velvet ribbon at the crown allowing the back and sides to spray themselves across my shoulders like delicate trickles of cognac sea foam. My eyes took on an amber hue from the light and seemed to have bits of stardust aglow inside them. The dark lashes stood out on my ivory face and made my eyes appear even larger by contrast to my paleness.

My naked, and as yet unkissed lips, looked like delicate rose petals set in place by an ethereal artist. I always appeared younger than my years and although almost nineteen at the time I would have seemed no older than fifteen or sixteen to the beholder. Looking back now I can understand why Jacey and Penny had no hesitation about pushing me into a modeling career. The Angels threw their light all around me then and created an aura very warming and enveloping. It was the same aura they threw around young Diana when we first saw her and it drew us in. It was love energy in its sweetest and purest form. It made you feel you were part of the Angelic realm when you beheld *It*.

At the time however I was oblivious to *It* and could only think that I wasn't blond and blue eyed like all the cover girls of the time and I wasn't six feet tall and angular like Penny, whom I regarded as the epitome of true classic beauty.

You could have knocked me over with a snowflake when the call came in three days later from Penny's modeling agency in New York from the president herself wanting to know who this long legged Celtic Princess was!

I was still at the Christopher's home, having been invited to stay on over the holidays and go with them to their ski chalet on the weekend.

Penny took the call on her private telephone as we were sorting out our ski gear for the trip. I had skied in the Rockies but had left my equipment out west, not expecting to be using it in Toronto. Penny wore a size 9 AAAA shoe so that wasn't going to work for me, as I wore an 8

1/2 AA. Penny's mother however wore exactly my shoe and dress size so I was installed with her equipment; all in sky blue with a coordinating blue ski suit. Penny was packing her own Cherry Red ski outfit when Eileen phoned.

"Eileen wants us to fly down to New York tomorrow to sign you up so we can take over a swimwear and holiday wear assignment in the Bahamas. We'll leave Friday". Penny floated from her bed to her closet, hanging up her ski clothes as she spoke, ever so nonchalantly, as if this was just an everyday occurrence.

"Christy and Cybil were booked for the shoot but they both came down with the same flu - it's a horrible thing ... going all over New York ... and Eileen needs replacements. She absolutely loves your photos. So... after she checks you out in the flesh to see if she likes you - and she will", admonished Penny positively, still putting ski equipment back in its place, "She'll sign you and we'll head off for a holiday in the sun for a few days of tanning prior to the shoot days."

"Well"... I began, never being one to fight destiny even then, "I guess that means we pack bathing suits instead of ski boots. So much for the chalet!"

"Oh, by the way", continued Penny as she disappeared into her bathroom for her cosmetic and skincare bags, "How do you feel about being the next Angel Face girl?"

That was how it began. The next thing I knew I was in Eileen's office and via telephone she was telling the Sea Queen executive about her new "find" to replace his original choice.

"I think you'll like this girl as much as Cybil - not that anyone could replace Cybil", went on Eileen very diplomatically, "but Angelique is just as stunning and has just as much presence. - Yes! Very charismatic! Hair? Fabulous mane! Down to the middle of her back and falls in silken waves... You want straight hair? Well... it could be blown dry to straighten it, but it's perfect just the way it... Blond? No, Angelique has rich auburn Maureen O'Hara-like tresses".

Then I saw Eileen go in for the kill. "Combine that with amber green eyes, classic nose a la Elizabeth Taylor and a pout of a rosebud mouth... Body? Trim but shapely. An athletic body with legs Cyd Charisse would envy", she said, giving my bust, hips and thighs a steady glance as I sat adhered to the leather armchair across from her desk. My feet were planted together in front of me and my hands folded over one another in my lap. I stared at her non-blinking for an unseemly amount of time as her words filtered through my ears.

Was this *me* she was talking about? It sort of reminded me of the way they sold horses out in Alberta. How are the teeth? Does she have a good mane? What about strong legs? Eileen would be wonderful selling livestock, I mused, imagining her on an auctioneer's platform.

"How much am I bid for this little red filly? This young roan has no markings on her and is fit as a fiddle and never been ridden!"

I started to giggle at this illustration and received a sidewise glace from Eileen.

"How tall are you?" she whispered, her hand covering the phone.

"Five hands ... uh, I mean five feet eight something: About five feet eight and a half".

"That's fine for photography honey, but for ramp work put down five nine and always wear heels to an interview", Eileen advised, motheringly.

She had been put on hold whilst the executive took another call. I didn't realize until much later how difficult a sell this was for Eileen. The executive of one of her major companies had been promised a top super model for his new line and was being sold a brand new and totally inexperienced novice because all the top models were either booked on other assignments or down with the dreaded flu. She was putting her reputation on the line with me but as I later noted about Eileen, she had a sixth sense about people and she never failed to be right in all the time I knew and worked for her.

When the executive came back on the line, Eileen was ready for him.

"Let's put it this way. Angelique looks like a cross between Rita Hayworth and Bridget Bardot. And I haven't seen a body like that since Marilyn posed for Playboy."

Well, that nailed it. I was on my way to the Bahamas!

As I walked out of Eileen's office, I had to stare at myself in the wall mirror to see if what looked back at me was still really me or had I magically transformed into this ethereal creation.

"Celtic Princess meets girl next door" was how the agency later sold me to Angel Face Cosmetics. Although I didn't realize it at the time, I was being given the gift of an education in marketing through my modeling days that proved to be invaluable to me in my ensuing media career.

Penny and I had arranged to meet at the Plaza Hotel for afternoon tea after the meeting. I layered my camel coat over my navy turtleneck sweater and gray wool kilt, tucking the Hermes scarf Penny had lent me under my lapels and headed out into the fresh air. New Yorkers were experiencing a brown Christmas that year, one totally devoid of snow. It was like a pleasant autumn day with just a hint of a nip of frost in the air. Tripping down the snowless sidewalk in my leather loafers, my feet had never before felt as light at that time of year.

My first visit to New York was a wonder of new sensations, visually and audibly. New York has what the residents (or locals) call a 'buzz'. In many ways New York is akin to Paris in that there is certain energy to the city that is particular to that area and that area only. Where Paris is a city of light and strong relationship energy, New York is a city of almost electric connections. People move and think faster there than any other place in North America, perhaps the world. Its energy is kinetic and charismatic. "If you want peace and quiet, go to the Hamptons!" was a phrase Penny used to describe New York and she was very accurate.

Penny was sitting at her favorite table in the Plaza Hotel lobby restaurant reading the latest issue of Vogue. She was resplendent in an Yves St. Laurent Cherry Red (her color of the season) pant suit which had a tie belt jacket and contrasting black silk turtleneck. On the chair beside her was positioned a Gucci shopping satchel already filled to overflowing with purchases from Tiffany, Neiman Marcus and Bergdorf's.

"So have I missed anything?" I queried as I sat down across from Penny.

"Jackie Onassis with her kids and Ted Kennedy were just having lunch at that table across the room but they left twenty minutes ago." Penny leaned across to me and whispered, "Don't look too hard but Michael Douglas is sitting two tables behind you. He's in the company of a stunning auburn haired woman who could pass for your double. Actually, I think it's his fiancé. She's quite gorgeous, really".

It amused me to realize that Penny could be just as inquisitive about film personalities and celebrities as anyone else.

Penny had just had her hair cut and styled at Sassoon. Her platinum curtain was now parted down the middle and fell to her chin where the cut angled down and around her back, falling perfectly straight to about four inches past her shoulders.

"Your hair is stunning!" I beamed.

"Sassoon is great. You must let him do your hair. He's in town from London for a few weeks. He'd love to get his hands on you, I'm sure. Let the agency set it up for you. I assume you're in?"

"Amazingly, yes!" I answered.

"Great! Then let's have tea. I'm starving!"

Penny, being blessed with a naturally thin structure, proceeded to order a selection of three desserts. This was on top of the six tea sandwiches she helped herself to from a silver tray, elegantly presented by a tuxedoed waiter. I, on the other hand, still too hyped from the interview to be hungry, chose Earl Gray tea with lemon and two small tea sandwiches. Eileen told me I would be modeling the majority of the bathing suits as Penny's cleavage was a bit too sparse so she would be modeling most of the sundresses. I assessed it was just as well to keep my tummy nice and flat. That seemed to be my 'weak' area, as Eileen termed it.

"Have to watch that", she pointed out, "Especially for bathing suit assignments. Otherwise your figure is great. I wish all my girls were that nicely toned; slim but not skinny."

"I always thought models had to be thin."

"Like Penny?" Eileen smiled.

"Well, yes."

"Bodies like Penny will always be in vogue but you have a much more versatile look and your figure type is really in style. The Christie Brinkley and Cheryl Tiegs types are getting all the work right now. Penny is a classic beauty but her repertoire will mostly be high fashion. Your look, on the other hand, is classic but 'All American' as well. 'The well-bred girl next door', as the sponsors call it and they love it. Have you ever seen Michael Douglas's fiancé, by the way?"

"No", I answered.

"Hmm. You look a lot like her. I'd love to sign *her*. Well... I have you, don't I?" she smiled. A bit victoriously, I thought.

"The Season of Summer White" was how Harpers picked it up. The photographers had a brilliant plan to use our Canadian fairness to fashion advantage.

When we first arrived at the Grand Bahamas Island Hotel, the photographers fell all over the 'light' that came from our complexions. "You look like two Angels! We want to photograph you just as you are. Get a tan later if you like but we want to do the shoot with you pale."

As we were sipping iced tea on the outdoor terrace of the hotel - the shaded area, of course - an idea came to me. Turning to the photographers, I said "More and more information is coming out about the dangers of sun tanning. You'll be hearing and reading all about the receding ozone layers soon. Scientists are about to bring this information out in a BIG way. It could be a real scoop to include some of those details into the story with the fashion layout."

They loved the 'twist' and asked me to write up a story idea with facts and the modern young woman's perspective on this new information. It turned out to be not only my first fashion layout but my first published article as well. And the rest, as they say, is history: My personal history, that is.

"Please fasten your seatbelts" filtered the voice of the flight attendant through my reverie. "We will be starting to descend momentarily."

Peering out the window, I could see the mist parting, giving me visual snapshots of venues on the ground of my City of Light. It was typical Paris weather which is much like that of London. Many tourists are surprised not to find warmth and sunshine in this city. (That's in the south of France; Nice and the Cote d'Azur.) Paris can be quite drizzly but it was spring so it should also be fresh and alive with new blossoms on the trees and soon newborn flowers in the window boxes. The song *"April in Paris"* is not an exaggeration. Having only been in Paris over the summer months, I was excitedly anticipating this 'first spring' visit in one of the world's most extraordinary destinations.

Threading my way through the tapestry of the Charles De Gaulle Airport, something of the scents in the air and the texture of the language and culture sent my psyche back to another time and a similar airport in Montreal. It was my last meeting with Jacey as lovers. I staggered to a table at one of the cafes and eased myself onto a chair. This wasn't going to be an easy one. I opened my bag and took out an orange. My blood sugar was plummeting. The stress of the unexpected flight delay and the in-coming memory were causing a reaction. I felt my mind go inward and was helpless to stop it.

"All right then", I breathed, bracing my elbows on the cafe table and holding my forehead in my hands.

"Let's just get it over with!"

Chapter 5 – "End of Love"

"Do you think that we could remain friends if ... if something were to happen?" Jacey voiced tentatively. For the first time since I'd met him, Jacey sounded unsure of himself.

We had spent the last two days filming a documentary in Old Montreal and turned it into a long weekend for 'us'. It was the early 1980's and love was in the air and in us and all around us. After completing our filming on Friday night, we spent Saturday perusing Old Montreal, taking a carriage ride by the St. Lawrence and spending a romantic evening in Bistro Forget. Jacey had surprised me with a ring we had seen in an antique store a few rues away. The ring consisted of a gigantic natural pearl in a baroque setting of white gold, framed by small fine diamonds set almost like a constellation around the milky pearl. It resembled the moon at its full cycle. It was a very classic antique but somehow very contemporary as well. Jacey said he felt like he could sense what outer space would be like as he observed it discerningly.

I have always loved pearls, far more than diamonds certainly. The ring however was tres expensive so I passed on it and purchased a darling Herkimer diamond (a high form of crystal) ring with an antique silver setting that I liked almost as much. Jacey obviously made an arrangement with the owner whilst I was unaware.

"What do you mean", I queried. "What could happen?"

Jacey didn't answer my query, which was very odd for Jacey as he always answered questions. Something ominous filtered in the air as we sat there in silence and I sensed even then that our relationship would somehow never be the same.

"I'm staying in Montreal a few more days, Angel, so I won't be flying back today. There's some last minute ..." Jacey floundered.

"You're lying, Jacey!" I blurted out. I couldn't help it; I just shot it out. "You've *never* lied to me before. Why aren't you flying back with me now?"

Jacey's face crimsoned in shame. He didn't even look into my eyes as he resumed. "I can't go into it now, Angel. Some other business has come up."

"What other business? This isn't like you to be so mysterious. We share everything, especially when we're working on mutual projects. Darling, what is it?" I implored.

"Angelica", he began, looking into my very soul with dew clouded eyes as he reached out and held my hands between his own two long slender ones.

"I love you more than I will ever be able to express to you, my Angel, and I always, always will. Remember that, regardless. No matter what."

Jacey kissed my hands then slid out of his chair and walked quickly past me out of the airport. And out of my life.

I pulled my hands away from my face and began to breathe slowly in and slowly out. I peeled and ate the small orange from my bag and waited a few minutes for my blood sugar to balance out and return to normal.

After sitting back and allowing my memories to release themselves, I recalled not seeing Jacey for years after that. He had finished up the documentary in Montreal, phoning in to reception only briefly for messages. A month later he had flown to England.

The newspaper and television footage of his marriage to London socialite Davina Regina Sinclair Louis, one of the Spencer cousins, came as a gunshot through my heart. I watched Jacey and his elegant tall blond wife exiting Westminster Cathedral, Jacey helping Davina gather up the folds of her gossamer wedding gown as they entered the golden carriage that would take them away to the honeymoon that I imagined we would have had one day.

We didn't correspond after he moved to England. Life goes on. I had my life to lead as did he and what was done was done.

Jacey lived in London for almost ten years until a horrible auto accident took the lives of both Davina and their nine year old son. Again it was via the media, a television newscast, that I'd heard of his family tragedy and sent him a sympathy card. To my utter surprise, he responded immediately upon receiving it, saying he would be in touch when he settled the estate.

Jacey moved to New York after that. Too many painful memories in England, he related to me after settling into his new position in the states.

We hadn't seen one another since he moved back to the North American continent but he had kept in touch by telephone and emails and been wonderful with assignments for me. I was a single working girl in a highly competitive field and the work was very much appreciated. He said he felt it was the least he could do under the circumstances. I was always gracious enough never to have brought up those 'circumstances' and Jacey respected me for that. A lot could have been said but I felt the death of a wife and a son was punishment enough for anyone to have to bear.

Feeling the strength return to my body, I re-entered my coat, put my bag over my shoulder and stood up to go claim my luggage. Turning to leave the table, I felt a familiar breeze of enveloping warmth and knew before I could see. It was Jacey.

"Hello Angel girl", Jacey smiled his greeting and bent to kiss me. "I see you're as slim and lovely as ever", he commented as he perused me approvingly.

I could have kissed him just for that. I'd been trying to take off five pounds for weeks.

"Well, don't just stand there with your mouth open", he teased. "Let's get your luggage and a taxi and take you to your hotel." He took my tote bag from me and started walking to the baggage claim. No one has or ever will surprise me the way Jacey does. I just shook my head and followed after him.

Jacey took care of the porter at the hotel and had my bags sent to my room at the Hotel George V.

"Have a good rest and I'll meet you for lunch here at the hotel. Don't forget, there's a time change. It's 6:30 AM here."

My room was in a quiet section; a corner and high up relates to a better quality room in the travel business. The room was well appointed with a queen size bed, small sofa, a breakfast table with two chairs and a desk; all in French provincial decor in hues of rose, apple green and gold. The true Provencal colors are blue and yellow but the citified French use pink and gold quite a bit as well.

I thought of Jacey and marveled at seeing him again after so many years. He looked good with the years. Still tall and slim, he seemed to have grown into his height more. He looked like a man now but the boyish smile and twinkling eyes yet remained. Jacey was blond and with the years just got blonder. His face remained fairly unlined but for the smile creases on either side of his upturned mouth. Only his eyes betrayed a haze of sadness. No, more like regret.

Jacey wore a tan Armani leather jacket over an aqua toned light wool turtleneck with Polo jeans when he picked me up at the airport.

"Jacey at nearly fifty and still looking like a Greek god in blue jeans!" I mused while drifting off into a light dream state after slipping into my hotel bed.

Later that morning, my eyes awoke to a blaze of glorious brilliant sunbeams sparkling through and past the window drapes, having neglected to close them before retiring.

The clock radio on the night table read 11:00 AM, so I sat up smartly and moved with quick execution to the salle de bain. Jacey hadn't specified the exact time for our meeting but 'lunch' in North America generally indicates 12:00 Noon.

My face is always thoroughly cleansed at bedtime and doesn't need more than a splash of water in the morning. However, even though I bathe in the evening, my morning shower is always a daily ritual.

In ten minutes I was in my robe and sitting on the chaise stool opposite the mirrored counter applying my makeup and trying to decide how to wear my hair that wouldn't require too much fuss. And what to wear for a luncheon with a man I had once loved and adored and had not seen for over seventeen years!

We had said surprisingly little in the taxi to the hotel. Mostly I just enjoyed the comfortableness I still felt in Jacey's presence. We had enveloped the quiet indigo of a still Paris early morning and the hypnotic spell cast by the street lamps marking the aisles of the streets. Paris was still bathed in magic and we simply let it slip its ethereal energy into our beings. Our light bodies felt the night magic and came together in a joyous crescendo that was more ecstatic than sexual. We felt a tantric union as we surrendered ourselves to our souls uniting. Jacey and I had always possessed powerful energy together. This had not changed.

There were so many things left unsaid about a soul mate connection, more than simply a love relationship, which had lasted over ten years and then ended abruptly without a word of an explanation.

Eventually I decided on wearing the soft gray crepe pantsuit over a black Anne Klein bodysuit. It was a neat and polished look as well as being quick to assemble. A stylish pair of slip on black walking shoes, my black Gucci handbag and a set of pearl earrings finished off the ensemble.

The clock read 11:50 AM. A light touch of my new perfume "Oh So Pretty" on the inside of both wrists and behind the ears and I was off. "Like a herd of turtles!" I expressed to myself, perusing my reflection in the full length mirror, appropriately positioned near the door, and appraised my appearance as simple, elegant but chic. My hair was pulled back into a low ponytail with a black velvet scrunchie, except for a few tendrils that were allowed to loosen themselves around my face. It was a humid day and the side hairs would eventually turn that way anyway. At least this way they could be controlled with a bit of gel and good old fashioned spit. "Work with what you have" being the models famous motto.

While sipping my cafe au lait awaiting Jacey, the waiter slid a note onto my table.

Angel:
Je regret beaucoup. I am unable to make lunch.
I will send a car for you at 8:00 P.M. for dinner.
Enjoy the day.
Jacey

Ah, yet another surprise a la Jacey. 'Sa va!', I thought and proceeded to order a lunch of garden salad with smoked salmon and french bread with strawberries and whipped cream for dessert. My blood sugar required regular meals and I had missed breakfast due to the time change. When I asked for the check, the waiter informed me that it was 'taken care of'.

"Sa va bien!" I decided this turn of events would give me convenient time for shopping and headed for the Champs Ellyses. A wonderful perfumery was located close by that was a frequent venue of mine whilst a summer student at the Sorbonne too many years ago. This would be a wonderful opportunity to engage in a research expedition for my lost Parisian haunts, via taxi.

Alors! The perfumery boutique was still in existence and the taxi let me off at its entrance. The daughter and son now ran the boutique. Inquiring if they kept their old records, the response was a positive!

"Oui madam", Corinne responded quickly. "As far back as 1952!" Sure enough, they had kept my file and personal 'recipe' of a floral scent I loved.

"Muguet, lilas, rose et jasmine", read Corinne.

"Parfait." Smiling my reply, I ordered two eight ounce bottles and a purse size cut crystal bottle of the 'pur parfum'. The personalized scent of course cost the earth but from past experience I knew it would last forever. Besides, who knew when my next trip to Paris would be?

The air outside was damp and chilly and I was without a topcoat. In the window of a boutique directly across from the perfumery was a stunning yet simple black pashmina shawl; so it would be warm as well as being light. I bought it right off the manikin, threw it on over my suit and proceeded on down l'avenue.

Les couleurs de Paris have always seemed so incredible to me. Loving the Parisian sense of balance and composition, I also admired the style in the designs of their clothing for their pure simplicity.

This day turned out to be a feast for my eyes. My purchases were, I felt, quite reasonable in consideration of the vast resources at my disposal. My second find was a tres chic light weight wool combination day and evening dress that was mid calf length and displayed a foot long side slit from the hemline to above the knee along with a deep cowl collar. It was very Chanel and would naturally 'go everywhere'.

In a tiny boutique that was literally located in an alley, I happened upon a meter long strand of antique faux pearls that looked fabulous knotted and hung loose in front. - You know me and pearls! So, naturally, my third purchase was the necklace and a lovely pair of faux baroque pearl earrings to match. "They would have gone well with that pearl ring from Montreal", my memory whispered to me.

There wasn't much chance of that happening since the ring was shipped back to Jacey in Montreal when he hadn't returned after a month. "Was he back to dance all over my heart again?" I wondered fleetingly. "It's best not to dwell on old memories. Just let the mystery unravel and reveal itself as it will", counteracted my higher 'adept' self.

A stop at my old favorite cafe bar at the end of the Champs Ellyses was a must as was fortification of a cafe au lait et croissant avec fromage. "Pas de vin!" I protested at the offer of a gratuitous glass of red wine from the owner who remarkably still recognized me from a hundred thousand years ago!

My blood sugar situation only allowed a glass of wine a day and if I was dining with Jacey that night that would be it. Still, the memories of my university days and studying at this table were alive and well. Sa va bien! Life was still good.

I checked over my afternoon haul and admired a pair of classy little pointed toe pois de soie pumps (in black of course), that had been discovered almost hidden under a low shelf in that same tiny boutique on the rue down the way. It was here that I also found a matching black cloche hat with faux gray Persian lamb trim and gloves to match, two sets of coordinating silk briefs, bras and chemises (in black and gray respectively), and an elegant silk negligee in dove gray consisting of a simple slip of a nightgown that was slit to the knee in front with a kimono style robe. Tiny seed pearls adorned the wrap belt that could also be worn adobe style.

A feeling of completeness filled me. Then one glance at my hands changed all that. Travel always seemed to wreak havoc with my nails. "Right then, where is a good manicurist?" I inquired of the woman at the next table over who I recognized as the sales clerk at one of the boutiques just frequented.

A french manicure would fit the bill, as it always looked so professional and classic. The salon was in the Latin Quarter area of the city and also housed several hairdressers, one of whom recommended a more modern hair style.

"For such luxurious hair as this, perhaps a bit shorter and a more contemporary, youthful look, madam", suggested the artistic looking young male stylist. He proudly displayed several awards on a shelf over his mirror and he appeared to know his stuff so I decided to go for it.

My arrival time back at my hotel was just after 7:00 PM. "There is just barely enough time to shower and dress for dinner!" I exclaimed aloud, sliding out of my pantsuit and bodysuit and into the glass encased shower stall.

I opted to wear the *outre* piece de resistance that was uncovered in another little boutique off the rue de Bernadans, where my old pension still existed and thrived, I was happy to discover.

The dress was a lavender gray fitted empire gown in crepe de chine with a square cut neckline and cap sleeves. The bodice was sprayed with gray seed pearls and silver tube beads in an arrangement that looked like a constellation of shooting stars and comets. The dress was knee length in front and curved to ankle length in back. It came with a four tier seed pearl choker and a sheer chiffon shawl in a matching tone with seed pearls and lavender beads ornamenting the edges, which gave the shawl some weight.

I wore the shawl so that it covered my head and fell over my shoulders in back. It behaved better that way. Although loving my new cut and style, I knew my hair would look better with the dress if it was up. Pulling the sides of my hair up to make a high ponytail, it was combed so that it fell loose and soft in back. The dress was fancy enough. I didn't want to overdo it with a full upsweep. I could have worn the black Chanel with the faux pearls or even my Toronto sheath but I felt like wearing my latest acquisition for some reason so despite whatever Jacey had in mind for dinner, I was wearing my new Paris gown and that was that!

"You look like a true Russian Princess", were the first words out of Jacey's mouth as he greeted me when I entered La Gavroche. The limousine had arrived smartly at 8:00 PM and the driver was waiting in the lobby for me. After stepping out into the night air, I was so happy to have acquired the pashmina shawl as warmth was needed for the brisk Paris spring evening.

Jacey gently removed my shawl himself and handed it to the coat check.

La Gavroche always was and still remains one of Paris' finest restaurants. In an age seemingly devoid of charm and elegance, La Gavroche truly renews ones belief in the power of the undaunted spirit to create a corner of beauty and serenity in a turbulent and unstable era. La Gavroche had its origins during Napoleonic times and had seen ruin and renovation through several generations and several wars. After World War II, Jean Pierre St. Germaine III, descendant of the original owner Jean Pierre St. Germaine (whose ancestor was apparently a highly respected if mystical character in France's history), totally rebuilt the ruins of the inn and completely remodeled the building, turning the boarding rooms into private dining rooms for separate functions. It was lush and gilded and very French provincial. When 'J.P.' renovated the restaurant again in the 1980's, it was simplified, bringing in more of a neo-classic design. He kept the warmth and charm by retaining the original stone floors but enlarged the restaurant by tearing out the walls that divided the lobby from the main eating area and bared the stone structure beneath the main walls at the sides of the restaurant, adding a trickling waterfall ending in a manmade brook with rock garden on the feature wall. That was the view one beheld upon entering the establishment: Beautiful fung shui.

Our maitre de's name was Max and our waiter was Serge. Max, as I found out later, was from a very aristocratic French family and held a degree in l'histoire from the Sorbonne. He resembled a dignified Armand Asante. Serge had been a head waiter at La Gavroche for thirty years and not a thing missed his eye. Jacey told me over dinner that Serge was one of the restaurants treasures and every establishment in Paris would pay him any price for his employment.

Max had seated us in a private corner in front of a large stone hearth. Serge was at our table immediately with a bottle of Perrier Jouet Epoch which had always been my favorite champagne because the bottle has painted lilies on it. I assumed Jacey had given previous instructions on this but not so.

As Serge poured the bubbly liquid perfectly into my crystal glass, he peered at me with his gentle eyes over his bifocals and said "May I suggest the framboise flambé for dessert. But wait for an hour after dinner to have it so it will not affect la plasma - blood. It is a beautiful piece de resistance consisting of fresh raspberries et crème glace in a crepe to which a framboise liqueur is added and then ignited. The flame burns off most of the alcohol as well as the sucre."

Raspberries and Framboise, the liqueur derived from it, are two of my most favored indulgences. A coincidence I supposed, but why would he mention sans sucre (without sugar)? And an hour is the least time required for a diabetic to wait between feedings.

At Max's suggestion, I allowed Serge to order for me. It was as if the man had telephoned my mother! He started us both off with Scottish smoked salmon but brought Jacey his portion on a platter with french bread, onions and capers. My salmon was served atop a colorful leafy salad of various greens accompanied by cucumber, celery and artichokes.

"Madame should eat a lot of greens for the minerals, oui?" offered Serge discretely.

Next, our waiter who I was convinced was clairvoyant, bought me a vichyssoise topped with three prawns and three basil leaves. Jacey received a covered bowl of their famous onion soup topped with Swiss cheese and a sprig of parsley.

My main course was a beautiful salmon filet, flavored with lemon olive oil and topped with fresh dill, grilled on cedar planks and served over an enormous green salad. Accompanying this was a side dish of wild rice and wild mushrooms cooked in cream. To my knowledge, this recipe was never seen anywhere but in North American native kitchens. My eyes opened wide as Serge set it down and I gazed at him in astonishment.

"I had this prepared specially for madam". Serge smiled sweetly as he placed it neatly beside my salmon. "This is one of madam's favorite dishes, n'est pas?"

At the end of this extraordinary meal Serge indicated, "Madame, a decaffeinated sugarless cafe latte and a large glass of ice water au citron. Then we digest before la dessert, oui?" he winked.

I simply blinked and shook my head at his adeptness. For a few brief moments I considered marrying this waiter.

The reprise from eating finally gave Jacey and me a chance to talk. Jacey perused my gown and winked.

"I love the dress, Red. You always were the chiquest chick in school - or anywhere else for that matter." Jacey eyed the room, which contained some of Paris' most stylish and elegant women and I knew precisely what he was thinking. Of all of these women bedecked in classic black evening frocks and traditional and appropriate gems only I would 'disobey' and wear a vintage find (even though he knew I would have a 'classic black with pearls' on hand) and get away with it. "You may even start a trend", he smiled.

Curiously enough, several well heeled young women were looking over at our table and at my gown particularly.

"Wonder where she got it?" I overheard an American woman say to her friend as they passed our table.

"It's very Givenchy, isn't it?" said her friend. "And gorgeous color on her."

Well, I guess I still did possess a certain style about me after all these years.

"Well, it's time I told you why I've brought you all this way, isn't it?" Jacey began, leaning forward with his arms on the table, looking down pensively.

I leaned back in the wingback chair, feeling its support cuddle my spine and very happy Jacey had chosen this part of the restaurant. It was warm and cozy by the fireplace, which Serge lit especially for me.

"Madame is not fond of the cold, n'est pas?" Serge ascertained as he eased his wiry body behind our table and organized the fire. As he rolled up his sleeve slightly to reach into the hearth and light the fire with the long fireplace matches, I noticed a set of numbers emblazoned on his forearm. Serge looked quite youthful to have been in a concentration camp but it was obvious he had been.

In my mind appeared a flash of German soldiers in their long grey coats, marching... and then of a young boy of no more than eight being scooped up in his mothers arms just before one of the soldiers drew a pistol and shot a handcuffed dark haired man in the head. The woman with the little boy, whom I sensed to be Serge, screamed and began to cry. She was young, not much more than a child herself, very petite, dark and French.

"It's his own fault, being part of the resistance" shouted the same soldier in German. "Shut up or the same will happen to you."

Another soldier pushed the woman, still holding the young boy, toward a truck already filled with doomed French partisans. The man lying dead on the ground was Serge's father.

"Andre!" cried Serge's mother as the truck drove off to the German made hell known as Auswitz.

With a start, I 'came back' and felt a tremendous emotion of sympathy thrill through my being for this brave little boy and what he must have endured before he grew into the man standing before me.

"Oui, madam. Tres difficile, those times." he addressed me softly, fully realizing what I had just envisioned. He bowed his head slightly and departed with a quiet dignity.

Jacey seemed oblivious to my communication with Serge. I detached myself from the scene and spoke to Jacey.

"Well, what are the details of this assignment?" I inquired.

"Assignment ... Oh yes", he spoke as if he was caught off guard.

"Sorry, Angel but I was caught up in a bit of reverie for a moment, just pondering our fates if we had remained together."

I had wondered the same thing so many times, especially after the confusing months that followed Jacey's hasty departure in Montreal and then his sudden move to England.

"You never married, did you Angel?"

"No, I never did…" I said hesitatingly, not knowing just how much detail to give forth at this moment.

"Well ..." Jacey shuffled a bit in his chair before proceeding. "Naturally, when you sent back my ring, I assumed you had found someone else ..."

A cold shock that felt like Alaskan ice travelled down my spine while I listened motionless as a deer caught in highway headlights to Jacey's words. How was it possible that this could be the secret to the mystery that had separated us so many years ago?

"After receiving your ring back with no message or note, I couldn't bear returning to Toronto to the humiliating jibes and stares from our co-workers, so when offered the opportunity to take over an office in London, I thought it the best way to bow out of your life gracefully. I want you to know it was a move I regretted the rest of my life."

Jacey turned his intense sapphire gaze directly at me. I was utterly speechless, probably for the first time in my life.

"I should have stayed and fought for you if it took that." Jacey's voice expressed a sincerity that was beyond doubt. Jacey then reached into his jacket pocket and retrieved a small familiar velvet case.

"I've kept this all these years, hoping I'd have an opportunity to return it to you. Honestly, Angel, I've tried so many times over the years since Davina and Christian were gone, but I could never... our schedules I guess... arrange a meeting. Somehow, it just happened with this assignment. I think it was meant to be our time at last."

Jacey took my hand in his and looked at me apprehensively. "Unless, of course, you're involved ... or something ..."

I fell into Jacey's eyes at that moment and finally found a voice.

"Jacey ... I don't know what to say to you."

"Just tell me if I still have a chance. Are you seeing anyone?" he implored.

"No, Jacey, I'm not seeing anyone. I ..."

"Then that's all I need to know. Nothing else matters." He breathed securely now and opened the miniature case and lifted out the baroque pearl ring I had returned to him over fifteen years ago.

"Ohh ... Jacey!" I exclaimed. Jacey held my left hand and slid the ring onto my ring finger.

"It's back where it belongs now", he affirmed and pressed his fingers over mine as if to somehow affix the ring there permanently.

"Jacey, I don't know if you'll want to give me that ring when I tell you ..." Leaning forward into the embrace of his eyes and energy, my words travelled straight to his heart.

"I sent the ring back because I thought *you* had left *me*! When you didn't return to Toronto after a month and only telephoned the office to pick up messages, it felt like it was over between us. The way you left the airport in Montreal, I just sensed you had gone out of my life for some reason. You didn't call me during that entire month and I just couldn't imagine why ... Unless you'd changed your mind about us. The last words you'd said at the Montreal airport kept running through my thoughts... 'If anything should happen, could we still be friends'."

Jacey blinked as he understood my words. "That was just a phrase, Angel. I didn't realize you would take it so seriously. "He looked at me in disbelief for several seconds before going on.

"I was tied up in an editing room without a phone that month. There was no point calling you at home during the day as you were at work. Those were the days before you got an answering service, remember? I tried calling you at your office when I could break out for meals but kept getting a fax number... That I now realize obviously wasn't yours!" Jacey rolled his eyes as the truth hit him.

"There was a change in management just at the time we were in Montreal. Don't you remember the memo? My extension had changed when the new Program Director came in and rearranged all our offices. And no one at the Montreal office had a number for you at all. I kept being told you were editing and unreachable. There was no home number either, so you obviously weren't staying at a hotel."

"No. I was at a private residence. It was like a retreat, a kind of monastery really, where I was enrolled in some spiritual teachings similar to the seminars you, Penny and I used to attend, only much more intense. There were no telephones. No cell phones then either."

We sat and stared at one another for several moments, not speaking.

"And would madam like her Framboise Flambé, maintenant?" inquired Serge, who had returned to our table with perfect timing. Serge presented the silver dish a sizzle with the delicious and aromatic indulgence of crepes, raspberries, liqueur and crème glace hidden like a welcome thief beneath the lacey blanket.

"Eating anything is impossible right now", I apologized frankly.

Jacey looked at the flaming dessert and offered a wink to Serge who de-flamed the crepe expertly.

"Sure you can, Angel. I'll help you". He smiled and released a dessert fork into the crepe, spouting the ice cream across the table, just missing my beaded gray handbag, which was instantly retrieved by Serge. Then, I picked up my dessert fork and proceeded to do precisely the same thing! It was too funny!

"Those desserts are dangerous!" Jacey exclaimed, laughing uproariously.

"Oui, monsieur", admonished Serge. "We could have found a use for them in the resistance." Serge smiled dryly, then asked, "More champagne, monsieur?"

The remaining part of the evening I can remember only in segments.

I was on what could only be defined as a 'sugar high', due to the dessert and the extra glass of champagne. We opted to walk back to Jacey's pied a tier, which was located just around the corner, as Jacey said he had the rest of my itinerary there for me.

We took the stairs up to the second floor of a lovely stone building. The flat belonged to a family friend, Jacey informed me. The stroll helped bring my blood sugar down somewhat but I was still reeling a bit.

Jacey made us coffee in the tiny closet of a kitchen in the flat. Although beautifully decorated in lush velvets and antique water stained silks of green and gold, the apartment was quite small. This was customary in Paris as in most large cities in Europe where space was at an optimum.

"Kitchens are made so small here", I remarked while peering in at Jacey as he poured the brew into two mugs.

"That is because, my darling", he retorted, kissing my forehead as he handed me a steaming turquoise and yellow pottery mug and continued, "... The Europeans in general don't cook much in the city." He seated us on the jade velvet settee and produced gilt edged coasters from a drawer carved into the circular coffee table before us.

"That is why they have numerous bakeries and butchers, etc?" I offered.

"Precisely so!" Jacey sounded very pleased at my reasoning.

"Because of the long hours people would work, they hadn't time to cook or bake; at least not in the larger cities," he said as he sipped his brew and waited for me to do the same. "And that was what made it possible for those in the food trade to have a good living, so it was beneficial to all."

"It sounds very win-win", I commented. "Very egalitarian" I mused aloud.

Jacey went to retrieve the docket with my assignment information from the office located beside the bedroom. He smiled as he placed it on the coffee table and replied softly, "Very." Jacey then leaned over and kissed me tenderly.

I remember getting rather emotional and felt tears flow down my cheeks.

"Oh, Jacey ... I can't believe what we've done. How stupid. Stupid! We could have been together all this time ..." I was crying right out by now. Jacey moved over and put his arms around me, pulling me to him. I blended into his arms as we embraced with a kiss that drew us into a union of the soul.

Here is where recollection gets somewhat blurry.

Jacey scooped me up from the sofa and carried me into the bedroom where he laid me across the bed and tenderly removed my clothes. I was unable to move and my mind kept drifting in and out of consciousness. We made love... That is to say Jacey made love to me. Over and over, it seemed, as I drifted in and out of dreamland.

I dreamed I was carried into a large ritually appointed room lit only by large white candles, similar to monastery candles. The man carrying me into this room wore some kind of head covering. I couldn't make out his face yet I sensed it was Jacey. He wore a white satin robe which felt smooth and soft against my skin. I too was in a white garment, long and flowing, of fine silk.

Jacey carried me over to another man attired in a robe of pink, which I recognized as Serge! Jacey then made a ceremonial signal to Serge who returned the gesture. The man, who I was sure was Jacey, then brought me over to what appeared to be an alter, which was draped in a white cloth emblazoned with a gold cross at its centre. A gold vase with a single red rose was its only other adornment. Behind the alter stood another man, attired in a purple robe, who had his back to us and was looking up toward a large gold cross on the wall above him. He made a type of benediction sign and then turned toward us. I recognized him from the portrait at the restaurant. It was Jean Pierre St. Germaine, the owner of La Gavroche!

Jacey laid me down across the alter, which was between Jean Pierre and himself. Then, as if watching myself from outside of myself, I saw several other robed 'priests' move toward us.

Beautiful cathedral music and sounds like the voices of Angels surrounded me while this scene went forth. The various priests and priestesses moved about me, extending their arms out to me, seemingly to send me energy through their hands and fingers. The rays of energy appeared as glowing golden rods, full of powerful yet gentle love emanations. I had never felt so loved or so energized in my life.

Then, I was back in bed being loved by Jacey. Then, back in this cathedral once again. Then, back in bed with Jacey and back and forth.

Upon waking, I was indeed in Jacey's flat and in his bed. Jacey was sitting in a green velvet tub chair across from me, smiling and holding a coffee cup in his hand.

"Good afternoon, Sleeping Beauty," he jibed.

"What time is it?" I asked, still half in a fog. Sitting up halfway and then back down again, I grimaced. "I should never drink!"

"Sure you should", Jacey assured. "When you're in safe hands." With that he handed me a delicious smelling cafe au lait.

"Yummy ..." I sniffed. "Hazelnut?"

"Tres bien, madam!" Jacey replied, accompanied by a kiss on the forehead.

"Oh ... I had the strangest dream, Jas."

"Oh?" he queried with a small start of surprise. "Well, do tell."

"We were in some kind of old church. In a ceremony of some kind... and you were there... but I can't explain what it was all about; didn't understand it at all."

"It's alright, Angel", Jacey reassured me. "It was only a dream." He said it so emphatically that his tone typed away any possible doubt of it being anything but.

Jacey propped a sumptuous fine cotton pillow behind me and I sat up, pulling the sheet over my breasts and tucked it firmly under my armpits. It was a bit chilly due to Jacey's habit of sleeping with an open window. I noticed a red rose beside me on the bed; so fresh it still had dew on its petals. Jacey must have gone out and picked it for me that morning. How romantic, I thought.

Meanwhile, Jacey was over at the oak wardrobe, drawing out a gold toned silk cable knit sweater for me to put on and laid it out across the bed. Then he pulled open a drawer in the antique dresser beside the armoire and took out a pair of his jeans for me as well. We had always worn the same size in jeans.

"For my long stemmed lily," he teased as he carried them over to the bed and laid them beside the rose.

I observed Jacey as he moved about the room. Still so handsome, even dressed simply as he was in black sweat pants and top.

"You were quite extraordinary last night!" I half blushed, then sipped the milky brew he had set down for me on the side table.

"Not bad for my age, hmm?" he teased.

"Well, yes and especially considering you're ..." I stopped and bit my lip in embarrassment.

"Especially considering I'm gay?" he finished, giving me a mockingly wicked grin.

"Well ..." I went on, releasing my coffee cup to the side table and reaching for the sweater. The dress was worn sans bra, as it had an empire waist and didn't require one, so I simply pulled the sweater over my head and slipped on my briefs under the sweater. After pulling back the water silk duvet, I sat on the edge of the bed to put on Jacey's jeans.

"Bisexual!" I emphasized, while tugging the jeans up over my hips.

"Not even a bit!" Jacey reinforced in a definite tone.

"But"... I looked down sheepishly. "It was well known that you had turned gay after ... That was the reason for the separation from your wife, wasn't it?"

"Davina and I never exactly separated", Jacey began as he seated himself in the tub chair again. "It was time for me to go forward to the second level of a very devout spiritual study in a mystical order; the same one attended in Montreal where I attained the first level."

"You mean, you were studying to be a priest or a Tibetan Monk kind of thing?" I asked naively.

"In a way," Jacey nodded. "It involved a very serious study of the mystery school teachings going back to ancient Egyptian times that explained the true meaning of life, the real reason for the evolvement of this planet *and* this universe ... And the role humankind is to play in God's movie."

"You mean God has a script?" I offered.

"In a way." he laughed. "But it's a script that WE write, each one of us, individually, for our own lives, interconnected with the other lives we come in contact with. It is based upon the theory of every human being trying their best to make the planet a better place in which to live."

"But not everyone does that, do they Jacey. I mean, consider Hitler."

"Precisely, not everyone does. It's understanding the reason for such monsters and the roles they play in our evolvement that teaches us certain lessons, some of them global, some of them perhaps more personal."

"Wait, let's go back a bit. What would this have to do with you being labeled gay? And couldn't you have simply denied it?"

Jacey uncrossed his legs and leaned forward toward me. His face turned more serious.

"It's a bit of a secret brotherhood, this order and when seen keeping company with some of the brothers members, who indeed were perceived to be of the homosexual persuasion, it was naturally assumed I was amongst their creed and was judged guilty by association. There was no point in bothering to deny it as that would only have added fuel to the fire, in those days especially."

"You didn't wish to dignify it with a response, in other words." I expressed.

"Pretty much," Jacey admitted. "And actually", he continued, "It worked out quite positively. My involvement with the order was kept private so I was able to bring the enlightened learning that I was studying out to the public through my media productions."

"Some of which won very prestigious awards." I offered.

"And more importantly brought out knowledge and cosmic theories that would otherwise not have been addressed and hopefully assisted in enlightening some souls out there to bring them closer toward their higher potential and inner clarity and beauty." Jacey ended.

I retrieved my forgotten cafe au lait, still quite warm, and sipped from the brim. I needed a bit of time for reflection.

"Wow, Jacey. I hadn't any idea you had pursued your spiritual path so seriously. You never gave indications of having those leanings to that degree. You certainly are a dark horse, aren't you?"

"It would appear so", Jacey expressed. His face became serious again and he continued on in a more solemn tone.

"Angelica, I haven't been entirely honest with you about my reasons for bringing you to Paris."

"You mean your intentions weren't entirely honorable?" I smiled knowingly; brushing my hair into a low ponytail and securing it with my beaded scrunchy.

"No, it isn't that," he began as he got up. Jacey took me by the hand and led me into the parlor, seating us on the loveseat. The flat looked so much more alive and youthful in the morning as it was beset with striking rays of Parisian sunlight that danced golden light bulbs throughout the entire apartment.

"The assignment isn't quite what I interpreted it to you to be, darling. It's part of a spiritual quest, actually, and sponsored by my order, which as you may have gathered is rather elite."

"Go on", I encouraged.

"You've probably heard and read a lot about the impending energy shifts predicted for the earth at the beginning of the millennium."

"Yes. The advent of renewed feminine energy has long been awaited, bringing with it a renewed balance and harmony to the planet's ecology, as well as to humanity." I quoted: I had written a few articles on the topic.

"World peace is hoped for as well as a reintegration of the true ideals that the planet was intended to personify: A new Brotherhood of Man and Sisterhood of Woman. That, in essence, is the true code to the secret of the next millennium." Jacey continued.

"There have been a continuous sequence of events, visions and visitations by the Holy Mother over the past century and a half, the most striking being the visitations to a young peasant girl named Bernadette in the village of Lourdes from 1858 to l862.

"*The Lady*, as Bernadette called her, brought many messages for the world to hear. However, a number of these messages, due to political circumstances of the times, were never brought out or expressed so humanity could take heed of them. There were documents written of the messages, and more information about the other visions and experiences Bernadette had, which were kept secret. Also, her true reasons for seeking sequester in a convent were basically for her own protection. There are those souls out there who do not see the light and only wish to pursue their own greed and self gratification, striving to keep the earth in darkness and ignorance. These souls were and still are very powerful, some inhabiting very high ranking positions in government and global businesses. The most dangerous of this lot however are those who are not even aware that what they are pursuing is wrong. They are the 'masses asses' and simply follow like sheep those who propose to bring them prosperity and eternal youth, even immortality! They follow for the wrong reasons; therefore what they reap will not be what they had hoped for.

"The new age of Feminine Wisdom will be able to bring us closer to the true nurturing, caring ideal that humanity was intended for. We were meant to be a race of the Tenth Level of Angels. The celestial hierarchy has nine. We are Angels in Training; Mary being Queen of the Angels.

"France and North America are the two countries most involved in this action. France because she is the forerunner, the revolutionary, of the ideal of equality - the true plan behind Napoleon's conquests, by the way. North America because she was initially formed from the ideal of the Brotherhood of Man, symbolized by the emblem of the eye in the triangle emblazoned on America's currency. This is a powerful symbol of God watching over us and us being Gods in the making. We are here to take care of one another, not compete and fight to achieve precedence over one another. The Age of Technology, which followed after such great forefathers as Benjamin Franklin and Thomas Jefferson, brought in much technological advancement to mechanization but it was unfortunately to be the demise of many more spiritual principles."

"Such as ..?" I interjected, leaning back against one of the tapestry cushions.

"Such as the ideals of love; brotherly love and peace. Only devastation results from wars and conflicts of nations. The higher, loftier ideals suffered so a few industrialists could prosper immensely at the destruction of ancient civilizations.

"Hitler was not behind the second world war. He was merely a pawn that could be used effectively by the banking barons who ran Europe's economy. It is believed *they* were behind World War II. Hitler was nothing more than a union organizer who was voted into power - and went nuts. They used Hitler's insanity as a beard to affect urban renewal."

"But, how?" I asked, incredulous.

"Much of Germany in the 1930's was in sorry need of rebuilding and renovation. This of course was very expensive. However, if a war was in progress and those rundown areas could be bombed and brought down in that manner, it was far less costly. Monies were always available for wars. With some of those banking families also owning munitions factories, guns and machines of war could be sold to both sides, achieving a profit for them no matter who won."

"And how does all this relate to the Lady of Lourdes and my part in this global scenario?" I commented, gradually comprehending Jacey's words.

"Right, then", Jacey sighed. "It has been revealed to our order that the Holy Mother is ready to appear again at the grotto in Lourdes to bring forth her *unheard* messages, as well as other new revelations for the world to hear.

"It was also revealed that She would only reveal herself and communicate with a few special human beings; women with whom she found favor by their soul nature, in other words by their incarnations. And also, by their lineage.

"Davina, my wife, was part of an ancestral lineage connected to the line of Christ. Her soul was also very pure and she was found to be the reincarnation of Jesus' younger sister Leah. Through a special mystical ceremony, Davina was revealed to be acceptable. She was on her way to Lourdes when her car went off the road and she and my son Christian were killed."

"Your son's name was Christian?" I echoed, incredulous at the coincidence.

"Yes. Unfortunately he was in the car with Davina at the time." Jacey blinked back a tear as he continued.

** "Diana, the late Princess of Wales, was also of the same lineage and ancestry as Davina. Her soul was believed by the Order to have been that of St. Ann, Mary's mother. Diana's death also occurred in Paris."

"What are you getting at, Jacey?" I responded.

"What I'm trying to say, Angel, is that this could be a very dangerous 'assignment'. I'm not sure I should have brought you into it. I strongly believe that Davina was killed because of her involvement." Jacey put his head in his hands and rested his elbows on his knees.

"But I didn't know what else to do. There are so few women acceptable. These messages are of such nuclear importance to the future, if there is to be one for this planet, and humanity."

"Why would I be acceptable, though? I'm not a 'blueblood' like Diana or Davina."

"That, my darling, is where you are so wrong. Had I been gifted with that information years ago, our lives would have been entirely different."

"You received a package just before you left for Paris, did you not?" Jacey proceeded.

"Yes", I nodded my head. "It had antiquated writing all over it and contained a book."

"A book ..?" Jacey questioned.

"A book", I reiterated.

"What kind of book?"

"I don't know, Jacey. It was old and had an embroidered silk cover but there was no time to even find out the title because you called directly after my receiving it. There was barely time to pack and make it to the airport on time." I breathed.

"That 'book'", Jacey went on, "was a diary of the late grand duchess Anastasia."

The words seemed to echo out of his mouth and take the form of thousands of tiny Angels evaporating into the air. I blinked and shook my head at the vision.

"It, this 'book', was sent to you because, first, Anastasia - and her brother Alexei as well - did survive the royal massacre of her family and was ushered out of the country. She married and gave birth to a son and was alive until a few years ago. She has a granddaughter who lives alternately in Montreal and the Caribbean. However, Anastasia also had a child out of wedlock previous to her marriage. This child was your mother, who was sent secretly to western Canada and adopted by a religious family in a small, quiet town in Alberta", he finished.

My mind was blown wide open in astonishment for several moments at the incredibly of his words. Yet I sensed in my heart that what he had said was true.

"My mother was adopted", I murmured on. "Why would you not seek out her legitimate granddaughter, then?" I managed to ask.

"For one thing, your mother was the first born and that gives you 'seniority', if you will, but more importantly, you are more spiritually acceptable. You see, your soul is that of St. Mary Magdalene, the bride of Christ and mother of his three children."

My mouth literally fell open. I was beyond stunned by Jacey's message. Incredible as this revelation was however, deep within me I could hear and feel a rejoicing of remembrance. My mind was filled with a vision of a beautiful woman with long thick auburn hair and a tall man with gentle green hued eyes who adored her. They held between them a magical and mystical love and union that was unfortunately not entirely understood by the followers that accompanied them. The followers increased and the crowds that gathered wherever they appeared became larger and larger. They tried to come between this man and woman, even calling her a...

"Wasn't she a fallen woman, though?" I asked, reaching beyond my own astonishment and reverie.

"No. She was maligned by certain popular interpretations of the bible, but not the truthful one. No, Mary Magdalena was a very wealthy woman, the daughter of a high priest and schooled as a priestess herself, much as Mary of Bethlehem was. It was Mary, mother of Jesus, who selected the Magdalena as the bride for her son. These misinterpretations of her reputation were due to several things, one of them being the erroneous translations of the scriptures. Remember, the bible was first taken from scrolls written in Hebrew, translated into Greek, then Latin, then French (as England was French - i.e. Brittany - until the thirteenth century) before finally being written in English. What was interpreted as the word 'whore' was actually another term.

"By the way, Mary - Jesus' mother - wasn't a 'virgin' either. That was another misinterpretation."

"Wow! I'm being hit with a lot of information here, especially before breakfast." I suddenly remembered. "Jacey, get me some food!"

"Croissant and cheese work for you?" he queried as he got up and went into the miniscule kitchen.

"Perfect!" I answered.

"Here, catch!" Jacey laughed as he gently tossed me a small apple from an exquisite Lalique crystal bowl on the table.

I gratefully bit into the crisp flesh of the fruit and allowed it to ooze around my lips. The apple grounded me somehow and I needed that badly at that particular moment.

Nibbling on croissant and brie from a pretty blue vintage Ainsley plate Jacey had placed before me on the coffee table, I sat with my legs outstretched on the sofa. My French manicured toes, looking like tiny white daisies, rested on Jacey's lap.

My mind went back to something Jacey had uttered earlier. "What did you mean, if you had known about the information of my lineage earlier, it would have been so different for us?" I queried.

Jacey's face saddened, as he placed his own croissant back on the same blue plate.

"Alas", he voiced. "My family, as you must know, is one of an old and noble heritage. Some of them probably 'savages'", he laughed, "as grandma says, but nonetheless old and respected and a lot is expected from its descendants.

"My embarking on further mystical studies was part of a long family tradition. It was 'expected' of me at my age at that time to be interred into certain mystical truths. Hence, my hasty retreat at the airport in Montreal. I had received a telephone call just that morning, informing me that the plans were in place and arrangements had been made for my initiation. I had no choice but to leave immediately. It was impeaching on the instructions from the order to have even taken you to the airport, but I couldn't not say goodbye. As it was what I did say came out so badly, it clearly devastated you. And for that I will be forever regretful."

Jacey faced me and continued.

"From the airport I was flown by private airplane to a small island near mainland Quebec and entered into an ancient abbey that is now being used by our order as a training centre for initiates. I was allowed a small room, a few simple belongings and not much more. It was against the rules but I was allowed a weekend dispensation to return to Montreal to complete the editing of the documentary, which I accomplished by pouring my sweat out over the editing machine for days with no sleep and little food. It was believed by the order that it would be a sublime exercise of my discipline. You know; what doesn't kill you makes you strong? This didn't leave me much time to try and contact you, as you can imagine.

"Part of what I was learning had to do with being spiritually trained in the true rites of marriage. Due to my lineage it was preferable to find me a bride of similar ancestry. So, grand Uncle Seamus in England had been contacted to set up introductions to some proper young ladies so we could produce ..."

"Some proper young heirs", I almost sneered.

"Quite ... Anyway, Davina was of the 'right stock' but I can't say I was madly in love with her. That I openly reserved for you. But she was sweet and a really great girl so I agreed to meet her."

I believed Davina truly was special. She strongly resembled Earl Spencer's eldest daughter Sarah; tall, thin and sweet faced but Davina was a very light blond with shortish fine curls that whipped about her face like a platinum halo as she moved. The newsreels of her were, I recalled, very flattering as Davina photographed well. She was probably a model wife and mother too.

As if reading my thoughts, Jacey responded.

"Davina was a truly exceptional woman. I do wish I could have been in love with her. I know I tried", he sighed." Maybe it was because it was an arranged marriage by two families who wanted similar backgrounds for their future descendants. I don't know."

Suddenly a thought sent that Alaskan ice through my veins again.

"Wait a minute, Jacey", I interspersed as reason slowly eased into me. "If, as you said, you had to marry someone of your similar background ... and you hadn't knowledge of my true bloodline at that time ... then you couldn't have married me at all, could you!" Narrowing my eyes while speaking the newly understood truth that explained it all, I continued. "And worse, you *knew* that you would never be able to marry me - ever! Yet you dated me, tied up my time for ten years and even bought me a ring!" I shouted, pulling the offending baroque pearl off my finger, "before you finally signed me off without a word of an explanation!"

The truth finally struck me and I was livid. Needing to expend the energy that accompanied my anger, I stood up and walked around the room. Finally, pointing the ring in my extended hand out to him, I cried, "You and that fine refined family of yours just played me for a fool for ten years!" before turning away from him, seething.

"How you all must have laughed at me for being so naive as to think you would actually marry a woman you really loved! And you did really love me that much I *do* know - even though you didn't know I was one of your bluebloods!"

"I wish you would refrain from using that term", Jacey winced.

"Why? I'm one of you, aren't I! And because you've somehow ascertained my royal bloodline, you can actually seriously consider marrying me - *now*! But for ten years you just strung me along. That's cruel, Jacey! You and your damned 'class' can go take a flying leap. I want no part of you!"

After stomping into the bedroom, I grabbed my elegant gown, draped carefully over a chair, threw it into a lonely shopping bag near the closet and drew on my cape. Storming through the flat in search of my shoes and finding them by the doorway, I slipped on the pewter pumps and dramatically flung open the oak wood front door.

Before exiting, I turned to Jacey's silent form standing by the window. Feeling the pearl ring still in my hand, I threw it across the room at him.

"I won't need this anymore", I jeered and tore down the stairs as quickly as my high heels allowed me.

Once outside, the message that the pewter evening shoes were not the cleverest mode of transportation through the Paris streets was sent to my feet. Fortunately, a taxi was parked a short distance away. While stepping over to the car, I caught my reflection in a nearby mirrored glass doorway. Oh well, I did look rather like Princess Di, out for a shop!

"That's macabre, now isn't it?" I unwittingly spoke out loud to myself. Then looking nervously around hoping no one heard me, I whisked into the backseat of the taxi and yelled, "George Cinq! Vite!"

**Diana

There are times when our soul takes us on a journey within our dreams. I recalled the time, about a week or so after Diana, Princess of Wales, passed through, when I dreamt of being 'sent' to where she now dwelt to return to her some personal photographs. I do not recall even looking at the photographs, having not being given 'instructions' for that. All I knew was that it was imperative that the princess have those photographs returned to her, personally.

Walking through clouds, I finally came to a kind of gate. Prince Charles came forth and asked me my reason for being there. Relating to him my 'mission'; which was to give Diana some personal photographs; he did not question me at all and allowed me to pass through.

Diana was sitting on the grass beside a pond within a lovely meadow. Wearing a simple white cotton blouse and a dirndl skirt patterned with small blue flowers, she looked just as she did when we first saw her at nineteen; very natural, no makeup, no blonde highlighted hair; just sweet and simple, innocent and lovely. Carefully approaching her, I handed her the white envelope and said, "I thought you might want these." She sweetly and gently accepted the envelope in her hand. Looking up at me with her large doe like eyes, that were naturally fringed with elegant long lashes, she humbly and graciously said, "Thank you."

I did not linger but left her to look through the photographs in private, surrounded by a glorious summer land of idyllic English country beauty. It was such a lovely and pleasant place to be. Knowing that it was not meant for me to tarry, I soon approached the gate to leave.

Charles was there again and asked me what I had given her. Telling him it was some personal photographs, "Here is a copy of them", I handed him a second set of prints that I was unaware I possessed until that moment. As he perused the second set of prints, the most extraordinary circumstance occurred. The images on the photos began to fade and then disappeared altogether, leaving only a white background where the images had once been. It was as if the photos were not meant for him to see. He was a bit perplexed by this occurrence but allowed me to pass through the gate and return to my own world.

Diana had created a serene 'otherworld' for herself where she could be what she really was, not defined as the 'career princess' she had become in her mortal existence. I felt she was at peace at last and was happy for her, having felt her spirit so many times after her death where she had been anything but at peace.

The night of her passing I felt her spirit energy protesting that she did not want to leave. "Not now! What will happen to my boys!" was the impassioned outcry. Hers was a disturbed soul for several days until finally I felt her accept that it was her time to pass through. During those few days I swear I had never seen such a sky! The Angels were taking their own back. *"To a world that does not appreciate what we have sent; we will keep her here no longer!"* I sensed their cry as their fragrance engulfed the earth with the scent of lilies and roses, for purity and love.

The Angelica does not anger, but I knew they were disturbed. The passing of Diana was an unspoken omen to the world. *"Did you not recognize who she was? Were you unknowing of what she came here to do? Do you take into your mortal hands what is not yours to do? Then, let your actions be an answer unto them!"*

The news of Diana's death sent a scent of fear developed to the degree of awe floating through the newsroom.

"The queen has really off'd her!" The silent exclamations from the choirs of lineup editors, script assistants, news reporters and even news anchors whispered in the ethers throughout the newsroom. It was not only our newsroom that bee-hived all week. All over the world, the news people were in a state of near frenetic shock.

"She actually did it! She off'd Diana! No one thought she'd dare. Not with the way people felt about Diana. But she did - and they're trying to blame it on us!"

The media was of course held to blame for the circumstance, as Diana and her Dodi were fleeing from the paparazzi when the accident occurred. Celebrities, that included Cher and Madonna, band-wagoned together to blast the media to take responsibility for Diana's demise. They had all felt the crush of their privacy to great degrees, although not as great as Diana's. What a perfect time to protest media invasion.

I cannot pass any judgment either way, having not been a celebrity. I have been part of the media however and most of the people I worked with and knew personally were very honest, decent individuals with a high degree of integrity. There will always be those who are not, as in any profession. High profile figures, especially if they are as greatly loved as Diana was, can run the risk of becoming victims to the unsavory of the media lot. I always felt Diana 'gave as good as she got' and handled it all very well most of the time.

Personally, I do not believe the queen had Diana killed. I also do not believe that her death was an 'accident'. On the highest cosmic level, it was her destiny fulfilling itself. There may well be a system at a very high level that establishes the world order and decides what best serves the world and truly believe their actions are righteous. Whether we agree with their actions or not, they do what they do (they believe) for the best. Who they are for most of us will be an unanswered question. The way I was inspired to see it, these actions won't really affect our individual soul evolvement unless it is our destiny for it to be so. We will live our individual lives, learn our earthly lessons, and hopefully understand what we really are and were meant to do here on earth before we pass through to the next level. I for one would not want the responsibility of running the world. To those who do, it is probably their destinies. I know it is not mine.

(My Seventh Sense does tell me though that the royal family was likely unsettled with Diana for her favor, her grace. "How can she be so loved? *We* didn't grant her that". No, but obviously God did.)

****

Chapter 6– "The Mystery Is Revealed"

The sun settled happily on the entrance of the George V Hotel. The day was a beauty, with sparkles of sunlight spilling everywhere, as only it does in Paris. Yet all I could think of was getting away just as soon as my airline reservations could be changed. Fortunately, my ticket was an open one.

The telephone was pleading to be answered as my key opened the door. The only person who knew my whereabouts in Paris was Jacey, who I decidedly did not wish to speak to now or ever again. On the fourth ring my intuition finally begged me to answer the telephone before it went onto the message service. "Hello?"

"Angelica?" breathed an agitated and slightly frightened sounding voice of familiarity.

"It's Rose", she continued quickly. "Angie, I've been trying and trying to call you. When I went in to feed Fluff, I discovered your condo was broken into! Someone really went through it too. Books and drawers were tossed everywhere. And ... I can't say this ..." she expressed sorrowfully. "Fluff is missing. I've looked all over the building. He must have got scared when the burglars came in and ran out. I just hope he wasn't kidnapped!"

My body sank down onto the sofa. After all that had been encountered in the last twenty-four hours there hadn't even been a consideration of a go-wrong at my home, my haven. I was speechless.

"There didn't appear to be any valuables missing and the break in was reported it to the police, of course. They need you to file a something or other and they were of course informed that you were away and the exact date of your return was unknown. I'm so sorry to have to tell you all this, Ang.

"When Don and I were together we had a break in too. I just felt so violated! And you're out of the country and there's nothing you can do. And poor Fluff… He may have been taken in by one of the neighbors, though." Rose added brightly.

"Its okay, Rose", I finally managed. "You did well under the circumstances. All that could be expected of you and more. I'm concerned about Fluff, of course, but other than that whatever might be missing I can live without. Keep me posted on Fluff. I may be back as early as tomorrow evening, Rose." I added.

"That soon ..? Did everything go alright?" asked Rose discreetly.

"Well, a lot has happened. Let's just say things haven't gone as planned." I suddenly felt very fatigued. Saying goodbye to Rose, I laid down on the bed for a little rest before calling the airline and repacking.

The telephone rang again, awakening me.

"Rose?" I responded into the receiver.

"Angel, its Jacey. Don't hang up!" he commanded.

I sighed into the telephone and sat up against the bed pillow.

"Listen carefully. You're safe where you are for now, but I'm sending a car for you. Pack as quickly as you can ..."

"Jacey, my condo was broken into yesterday and my cat is gone! I don't know what's going on but it's important for me to return to Toronto." I interrupted.

"No, Angel!" Jacey implored emphatically. "That is one thing you cannot do. Fluff will be alright. They weren't after him. I know about the break in. I just heard about it from ..."

"The order, right?" I punctured. "Just what doesn't this organization of yours know about, Jacey? Why was my home violated?" I asked, angrily.

"They were after the diary, Angel."

"Well ..." I managed, with a mental image filtering through my mind of tossing the diary into my tote bag, "They wouldn't have found it then."

"Did you hide it?" Jacey inquired with anticipation.

"No. I brought it with me." The words fell out before they could be stopped. Suddenly, I wondered just how much Jacey should be trusted now. Still, I had no one else here and things didn't look good.

"You're incredible!" Jacey laughed into the telephone. He soon regained his composure however.

"Put your things together as soon as you can and bring the diary with you. There is no time to explain now, Angel. Hurry please." Jacey implored.

I operated on instinct at this point. Some unknown force moved my body over to my tote and removed the diary from the zippered section. It dropped on the floor and fell open to a page with the words Maria something and a once red rose pressed on the page. Quickly, I picked up both and looked about for a container in which to hold the diary. My focus fell on the dresser and the blue velvet case that held the faux pearls. After opening the case and removing the pearls, I inserted the diary. It was a fit! There wasn't much time, so I speedily rode the lift down to the front desk.

While packing up, a feeling of fatigue overcame me. My body was stressed and I hadn't eaten for hours. The telephone rang again.

"Angel, its Jacey. Don't worry about packing everything and don't check out. It will look too suspicious. Just take what you'll need." Click.

My head felt foggy as I retrieved my toiletries from the bathroom. Thank God my period was over several weeks ago so at least there wasn't that to fuss about. I stuffed my tote bag with the items that I figured would be needed and included a camera, film and a mini tape recorder out of force of habit.

The telephone rang again. "Your car is here, madam". It was the voice of the concierge.

"I'll be down directly", I instructed.

Slipping into a reasonable pair of walking shoes, I threw on my shawl, grabbed my tote and headed for the lobby. Exiting the George

V, I observed Serge standing by the door of a gray Volvo and then promptly fainted.

It wasn't exactly a faint; just pushed my energy level too far, I reasoned.

"It was not that, madam." I heard Serge's voice administer. "Your blood sugar is fine", he whispered. "It was shock ... of the entire day's revelations."

"Your health issue is actually very miniscule now", Serge said further, after he had assisted me into the gray Volvo. He peered at me from the front view mirror. Serge had seated me in the back, so I could be more comfortable and lay down if need be.

"If madam does not take offense", Serge went on humbly but not gratuitously. "Madam is a beautiful lady and a good size, slim yet not thin. However", he went on. "I believe you would find your blood sugar would balance out totally were you to weigh ten pounds less."

"No offense taken. But why would that make any difference?" I inquired while arranging myself in the back of the Volvo.

"You will likely have noticed that madam's health has been more ... vulnerable when she has put on a little weight, oui?"

Thinking back, during my early teens I had what my parents termed 'baby fat' and for those few years had been plagued with colds and flues. Then, in my early twenties while taking a hiatus from modeling to complete my education, I put on twelve pounds due to sitting and studying in class all day and much of the evening with not much exercise. It was true; that was a time of headaches and sinus trouble. After graduating I got active again, the weight came off and my health was fine.

Mind you, 'normal' weight then for me was 115 pounds, which at my height was really too little - except for a model, of course.

"Remember, madam is also quite ... uh ... petite structurally ... small boned", Serge finally figured out.

It was true. I was on the tall side but my height was mostly in my legs.

"But madam has those long legs." Serge completed my thought.

There was one other time my blood sugar had to be considered as well; then and also upon entering my forties. Accepting this as part of a pre-menopausal symptom, I had put on weight at that time and still carried it, weighing between 125 and 132 pounds yet was still considered slim. I hadn't really been concerned about my weight, figuring that at my age it was a bit better to have something on my bones. "If you get ill, it gives you something to fight with!" my friend Nurse Betty, would say. Bets was always concerned about me being too thin. She would actually telephone me every two weeks from Alberta to make sure I was eating enough!

"You carry a certain genetic code, madam", Serge proceeded. "And, when one has that particular gene, it is important to keep the body quite thin. Otherwise a disharmony can be created. When weight fluctuates, as with puberty, pregnancy, menopause; the normal phases of a woman's life, it can upset a normal balance in the blood, which is a very sacred and spiritually connected facet of our anatomy.

"When one is a highly spiritual and sensitive individual, this balance can be even more important. A person who is very psychically attuned for example will, in all likelihood, be subject to sensitive blood sugar levels. It makes sense, oui? That is one way it is possible to recognize a true clairvoyant, medium or medical intuitive."

"You mean, the more intuitive or spiritually inclined one is, the more sensitive their body is?" I expanded.

"Exactly" Serge smiled. "You should be very careful of what you put into your body, as yours is a particularly sacred temple. Your condition is particular to your bloodline, madam."

I remembered reading of the little Alexei, the only son of the last Tsar of Russia, and his affliction with a blood condition. It was believed it was this condition - hemophilia - that brought down the royal Russian empire, via Rasputin. The peasant monk was the only being who was able to, through a type of meditation process, stop Alexei from bleeding and because of it became a close confidante of the beautiful yet highly religious Tsarina. Intrigue and innuendo whispered through the court and all of Russia like a mistral about a more 'personal' liaison between the Tsarina and the monk. This caused the mistrust of the Russian people and discredited the royal family, thus setting the stage for the revolution.

"Hypoglycemia, hyperglycemia, diabetes, hemophilia are all part of the same theme; conditions or sensitivities of the blood. There are ways however that they can be controlled and even cured. We do that." engendered Serge.

"We ..? Oh, you mean your order?" I queried. This was becoming more and more interesting.

"Precisely. Our order is one of healers. Healing is the highest ideal that we aspire to. And we do it gratis, without any financial compensation. We gain our support from other private resources."

"Is this healing medical?" I questioned naively.

"It is a more spiritual healing that we ascribe too, believing that any disharmony of the body is also one of the mind, possibly through what the mind accepts."

"As a man thinketh", I quoted.

"Ah, oui, c'est tres important to keep the mind 'pure'; clear thinking evolves from this. That is why, when we proceed toward the higher levels of our order, our initiate is sequestered to a retreat which holds an atmosphere of silence and sacredness. It is imperative so that the mental body, soul body and spirit body can attune to the higher frequency levels of the cosmos... God." he offered.

Jacey's explanation of his spiritual internment and confinement began to make more sense now.

"Of course, disharmony can also be the result of genetic coding ... ancestral inheritance ..." he smiled, "And sometimes referred to as a 'family curse'." He continued, "Oui, we deal with such things as well." At this point Serge handed me a small basket. Under a blue checkered cloth napkin was fruit, a large French baguette, several small rounds of camembert and a small container of fruit yoghurt.

"Eat ... now!" Serge ordered softly but firmly. I selected an orange from the willow basket and peeled it slowly.

"I don't know if you are at liberty to disclose any of this information to me, but ... how would you handle something such as a family curse?"

"No ... I cannot disclose our means to you at this point madam. But I can tell you that when the, shall we say 'issue' rather than the other word, is removed from one family member, then the issue no longer remains for any other family members; past, present or future .. Ancestors or descendants", he affirmed.

"It is removed from them all?"

"It is vanquished from the genetic code", Serge affirmed again.

"This is all rather like a new language to me right now", I replied, breaking off a piece of the baguette and offering Serge a section. He extended his arm and took it. I offered the camembert. "Fromage?" and handed a round to him.

"Merci", he accepted. "You mean ... like you say ... it is like Greek to you?" Serge uttered between bites of crust and brie.

I laughed. My mouth was full and I nearly choked.

"Aqua in the bottom", Serge motioned to the basket again. I lifted out one of several small bottles of water and took a long drink from one. I needed that water more than I knew.

"Ah, oui", Serge responded. "Lots of water is good for you. It will clear the body. Water is also sacred. It works well with the blood. Did you know that when the spirit leaves the body, the blood and water separate?"

"When they pulled the spear from the body of Christ, it was said it poured out blood and water. That was how they knew he was dead ..." I revealed to myself.

"Ah, but ... you know when you add vinegar to milk that it curdles and separates? When Christ was given vinegar on the cross ..."

".. It separated his blood and water! So perhaps he really wasn't dead after all!" That theory had been one of the main objections and discrepancies to the Qumrum theory when the Dead Sea scrolls were published.

"So, now you understand", Serge shrugged as he nodded his head from side to side in typical French fashion.

We drove in silence for several hours. Yes, I was beginning to understand events and circumstances of history on a totally different level. Up until today I hadn't any idea of having any relationship to historical past events of government, royalty or religion. I was now faced with a reality of my life that was alien to me. That my heritage was related to members of families that had created the world's history was akin to a monumental and Olympic tidal wave sweeping over me at that moment. Suddenly exhausted, I allowed sleep to overcome me.

Serge peeked at me again in the rearview mirror and let silence rest with my thoughts. Finally we turned onto a long dirt road. I don't remember how long I had slept. I opened my eyes at the sound of my name.

"Where are we going?" I finally thought to ask.

"We are going where it is safe; the countryside."

The narrow graveled road led up to a grove of tall cypress trees fashioned so closely together it was impossible to see beyond them. Suddenly and sharply there was an opening of about six feet wide and Serge swerved the vehicle smartly through the cypress arched driveway and up to a charming stone farmhouse. The house was balanced on either side of the front door by lilac bushes. By the front path, a garden of lavender and rosemary decorated and scented the tranquil air. A tiny older woman stood by the front door which was painted the color of evergreen.

"You will stay avec ma mere, madame", Serge announced.

Serge introduced his mother as Madam Lavallee then spoke a few words of Russian to her that I could not understand.

His mother eyed me keenly, yet sympathetically as I climbed out of the Volvo.

"Simone", she smiled as she extended her hand to me, cupping my own long fingers in her petite yet strong ones.

"Tu est ..." she began en francaise but recovered quickly and switched to English. "Ah... you must be tired. Entree ..." She motioned to the half open green door. Simone's accent was quite strong but her English was understandable.

I was led through a cozy front room garlanded throughout with ivy that threaded its way across the ceiling beams and right over to the doorway of the kitchen.

The kitchen held an old fashioned exposed stone fireplace to the left, a large cast iron stove to the right and a spacious wood hewn table with six chairs in the centre.

Simone had laid out the table with several plate settings that were patterned with a blue and yellow floral design. It was a color scheme very popular en Provence (the south of France). The tablecloth was antique white linen, very old and very beautiful with its original hand embroidered Battenberg lace edging.

Simone wore a classic navy blue cardigan over a crisp white linen blouse and plain slim blue skirt. She moved adeptly through her domain as she prepared the famous French cafe au lait for us in a pot on the stove. The aroma of freshly baked croissants and brioche meandered to my nostrils as Simone arranged a floral platter of the treats on the table for us.

"Mangez!" Simone enthused.

You didn't have to ask me twice. I picked up a piping hot croissant with my fingertips and gingerly tore its layers open upon my pretty plate. Freshly baked bread of any kind is ambrosia to me, although in a limited amount.

Farm pickles, fresh cream, cheese and strawberries appeared one by one, sur la table. I could enjoy staying here, I reasoned. If one need be in hiding, this place would do fine.

After allowing myself to relax into a blue cushioned spindle back chair that was surprisingly comfortable, this realization finally swept over me. Yes, I was in hiding and for what reason still unsure. There was something about the diary that was particularly significant and important to Jacey and some mystical 'order'; one that apparently was bent on saving – and healing – the world of its negativity so that our humankind could fulfill its earthly purpose. That much I surmised. This 'purpose' seemed to involve showing us how to purify ourselves so that we could ascend to a grander and more spiritually enlightened 'next level' of development.

"We are a tenth level of Angels in the making." Jacey's words echoed back to me.

The information gained over the past few days was still incredulous to me. To be part of such a global, no, cosmic mission was quite beyond my comprehension at this point. Yet, here I was in this little farmhouse with a family who had suffered far more than I could ever even imagine and who obviously were trying to stamp out the evil on the planet so that the next generations need never undergo their own personal tragedies. I had lived a blessed life compared to their fare. Perhaps I was placed in this position to help give back to humanity in some way. 'There are no coincidences', has always been a guideline in my life, having always held the belief that we are placed where we are supposed to be for the lessons we are sent to learn in life. I am here at this moment for a certain purpose and must try and assemble just what the lesson could be and try my utmost to accomplish it. This 'purpose' may well be my soul's salvation or, as Serge inferred, my way of eliminating the family 'issue' connected to the Romanovs.

Through my history studies I had deducted that the Romanov dynasty was a particularly bloody and horrific one for the Russian people. Beginning with Ivan the Terrible, then Alexander and of course Catherine the Great, the reign of this Russian lineage was anything but peaceful. Even Nicolas was seen to be quite cruel and high handed in his dealings with the peasant caste of the Russians. He grieved solely for his family situation, his son and heir Alexei, and let the nation 'go to pot'. At least that was how he was assessed by historians. His mind was not upon the affairs of state when it was of the foremost necessity for it to be and he was judged guilty by history and even believed himself to be responsible for the death of millions of Russian people. This was a heavy cross to bear and it was difficult to comprehend the weight of such a burden.

If it were true that I had a connection with this great but tragic family and it was impossible to imagine Jacey inventing such a supposition, then perhaps it would be possible for me to help those doomed Romanov souls to achieve salvation at last.

Horrific images of the bludgeoned royal Russian family sequenced before my mind's eye like an edited format of a newscast. Theirs was a macabre and brutal fate, made all the worse by the fact that they were not allowed proper graves or burials. The Tsarina, Queen Victoria's granddaughter, the Tsar and their entire family were noted for their religious devotion. For a devoted catholic to not be assigned priestly sacraments was... Well, it was the epitome of the worst that could befall them. It meant their souls would be condemned to hell and total damnation forever to follow. Albeit, what Nicolas had sown he henceforth reaped. He was punished for his crimes. The Tsarina, by her influence over him, suffered the severest punishment as well. Yet the young grand duchesses and Alexei were all innocent. A more unfair fate to befall star-crossed youths one could fail to imagine. Surely there must come some redemption for them. Perhaps that time was now.

Was it all in my hands now, I wondered? Was the fate of the souls of the descendants of this illustrious yet doomed family; past, present and future; to be decided by my actions at this place and time? This was a pressure I was prepared to live without.

My room was the garret, a darling affair with a sloped ceiling on both sides.

A window seat in the centre of the far wall was flanked by lace curtains hung to resemble Angel's wings. The wallpaper throughout the room was of pretty pink primroses on an ivory background. A brass bed nestled the left wall and was covered with a white Chenille bedspread. Several antique toss cushions, colored with sprays of pink, yellow and blue flower blossoms, perched nonchalantly atop the bed cover. A small writing desk sat on the right side of the room supporting a Tiffany desk lamp which danced multi-hued light throughout the room. The narrow white painted armoire beside the desk would be sufficient for the few belongings in my tote bag and an antique white dresser with lovely ivory drawer knobs would hold all of my personal articles.

The garret room was accessed solely by a secret stairwell behind a faux wall in the back of a hall linen closet on the second floor. Obviously this was a holdover from the Second World War and employed for use by the French underground. It would be impossible to guess its existence from the outside of the farmhouse. The gabled window faced the back of the house and overlooked the garden while on the front of the house only a vent was visible from outside. The vent did however give a slated view of any oncoming visitors from the inside.

The outside of the gabled window in back was covered by large flowerboxes and their vivid blooms hid the existence of a window altogether. From the inside however it was deceptively easy to view out. It was a well conceived design and likely put to good use during wartime.

Simone had kindly informed me that dinner would be in an hour or whenever I came down for it. She motioned to a floral curtain, draped to one side and held by a cast iron hook which had been painted white. The drape sectioned off a makeshift 'salle de bain' which was fitted into a corner by the front wall and was complete with commode, bidet and washstand and a white ceramic water pitcher with basin for washing. A water tank with a brass spout stood by the washstand so it was possible to obtain hot water without the necessity of wandering downstairs and risking the peril of being discovered. I marveled at the room's efficiency, much as I hoped my necessary duration in it would be short-lived. After advising me of the room's 'operation', Serge left me to my own devises and some privacy.

After Serge had deposited my bag on the bed, I sat down on the inviting azure blue window seat which was large enough for two. Discovering two large stuffed cushions set on the carpet below the window, I lifted one up to act as a pillow, curled up on one side in a fetal position, and rested my head on the gold fringed cushion.

A soft knock on the door pulled me out of a light sleep. Serge entered quietly and voiced knowingly, "Madam must remember she has to eat, oui?" He was right, of course. A crystal table clock on the nearby dresser exposed that it was 7:00 P.M. and well past my feeding time.

"Merci, Serge." I replied, lifting my legs down to the blue painted floor. "I'll be down momentarily."

Serge exited discreetly as I stood to face the French sky, which was now indigo and sparkling with tiny crystal diamonds. The tiffany lamp gave me light to attend to my toilette. After using the commode and obtaining a pitcher of water from the tank, I lightly bathed my face and hands with the sweet smelling farm water and hung the lace edged hand towel back up on its ring by the washstand.

My hair felt the need to be unbound, so I pulled it free of its beaded scrunchy and brushed the waves out a bit. It somehow made me feel safe to stay dressed in Jacey's clothes, so I refrained from changing and simply proceeded to go downstairs to the kitchen.

Discovering the stairwell actually had two exits; one to the second floor linen closet, the other going into the kitchen; I proceeded toward the kitchen exit and opened the cupboard door that allowed entrance into the cooking area. Simone startled a bit when the cupboard opened and I stepped down onto the tiled floor.

"Ah ... mon dieu!" she voiced as she touched her heart. "It has been so long since that porte has been oozed."

"USED, mama", Serge emphasized.

"Ah, bien ... Il fait tres bon we have a visitor. It will help me avec m'anglais", Simone shrugged. "I need to ooze ... uh ... USE ... it more," she whispered.

"Come, ma cherie", Simone beckoned me to the table. Serge pulled out the chair at the head of the table for me. "Dinn-hair", Simone expressed as she spread her prideful arm out toward the set table.

"DINNER, mama", Serge sighed and rolled his eyes upward.

"It's alright, Serge." I laughed. "C'est bon, madam", I countered. "It would be good for me to practice ma francaise as well, oui?"

Simone affirmed with a dignified nod and regal stance that included a sideways glance at Serge.

After years of family get-togethers with Jacey, I soon realized who really ran those households and here was no exception. Mama was boss and I bowed to her authority, having no desire to offend such a gracious hostess.

Simone ladled out delicious French pea soup from a white porcelain terrine into large almost flat bowls. Enormous soup spoons were laid out to direct the thick broth to the mouth. Inch thick slices of freshly baked herb bread were set atop an antique platter placed beside the terrine. A colorful salad dressed with a fragrant tincture of herbs, mustard, olive oil and balsamic vinegar bedecked the table and a small cold ham had been sliced up and set beside the soup terrine. Simone had placed pear preserves in their original glass jar on the counter for our dessert. "We eat simply, but well", Serge voiced proudly.

"Oui. Tres bon!" I agreed.

After dinner Serge nestled a thick log onto the fireplace in the homey front sitting room, while Simone carried in a wooden tray that supported a teapot of brewing fragrant herbal tea and three tall glasses wrapped in lapis blue cloth napkins. As Simone poured our tea, I realized the 'teapot' was actually a Russian samovar. It was of silver and obviously an antique. Simone handed me the first glass of tea Russian style, with the napkin tied around the thin glass.

"The silver holders pour les tasses sont ..." annunciated Simone, explaining their scarcity. "'How you say ... were bartered for sanctuary during the war."

"The tea glass holders and the samovar are very old. Part of a set given to my mother's family", offered Serge. "Unfortunately, only three remain of a set of twelve."

Simone pulled a leather bound photo album down from the shelf over the fireplace and handed it to me. The album itself was of exquisite quality and remarkably well preserved.

I opened the front cover and beheld a large sepia photograph circa 1915 of a very attractive well dressed aristocratic family adorned in exquisite hats and coats, obviously on a family outing. I recognized that it was Tsar Nicolas and his family. Simone pointed to a man, woman and little girl in the background. "Mon pere ... ma mere ... et moi!" she advised. They seemed to be part of the household staff.

"Ahh ..." Simone gestured to me to turn the pages and stopped me at a page with two cameo portraits; one of Nicolas and the other of Alexandra respectively. "Voila!" she exclaimed. "Alix et tu ..." she gestured. "Tres similar."

"Mama is trying to say you and Alix look a great deal alike, madam ... The face. The hair ..."

For the first time I really looked at a photograph of the Tsarina and their speculation was surprisingly accurate. I did resemble her! We even possessed the same hair color.

"The Holy Mother also possessed auburn hair and Mary Magdalene as well." Serge advised.

"I always thought the Virgin Mary had black hair and blue eyes".

"No, madam. Our records go into antiquity and it was recorded Mary of Bethlehem had long auburn hair and eyes that verged on blue, but were probably more like the color of the ocean."

"Extraordinary." It was all I could say.

"Your parents were employed by the Tsars family then, madam?" I queried, settling into the oversized wingback chair by the stone fireplace.

"Oui, they were in their service. The silver et some jewels were gifts from the Tsarina to ma mere et mon pere après their evacuation from the winter palace." Simone enunciated her words slowly.

"Votre anglais est parfait, madam", I declared and then winked at her. "A little more practice and it's the embassy for us!"

Everyone laughed. After all, we all enjoy a good white lie ever so often.

Simone relaxed and was more at ease now. She relayed her childhood growing up amidst such splendor and elegance. It all must have seemed so magical to a small child. She was three at the time.

"They were CRA-ZEE, madam." Simone spoke of the Leninists and Bolsheviks. "They never should have overthrown the Tsar. Un grand faux pas. Terrible." She shuddered and continued. "The Tsarina", she leaned closer to me, "Was a very holy woman. And the Tsar ... Such a good kind man. The grand duchesses, madam, were like angels." Simone expressed as she lifted her hands up eloquently. She reached over and held my hand. "Do not believe l' histoire ... the history books. They are WRONG", she emphasized. "Your great grand mere was a saint." Her eyes carried truth.

"Why do you think they were slaughtered the way they were?" I needed to know. After all, they were my family.

"Ah ..." Simone sighed. "Theirs was a terrible fate, cosmically. The higher plan held for them the supreme service. They were sacrificed for their people... for their country."

"Sacrificial lambs", I echoed quietly.

"Oui, madam. Mais, only the best and most worthy *can* be sacrificed." Simone emphasized. "Quel domage ... Quel, quel domage." Simone's eyes lowered and teared as she shook her head again.

"You have the diary, oui?" Simone looked up directly into my eyes.

"Oui, Simone. Was it you who sent it?"

"Oui. It belonged to the littlest duchess, Anastasia (pronounced Ann-ahz-tash-ya). It contains prayers et messages that were spirited to the Tsarina and the youngest grand duchess... from La Sacre Mere." Simone crossed herself.

"The Tsarina would kneel in rapture. Sometimes she and la petite juene fille would kneel or sit together and the sun would shine all around them. Their faces would be aglow... It was unearthly." Simone beamed as she spoke, in reverie of her remembered childhood. "The Tsarina kept a special diary for her and Anastasia." Simone continued. It was there that they wrote of their experiences but in a kind of code. *'Only she who is pure of heart and sent by the Angels shall be able to reveal the messages to the world. Only she shall be able to translate them'*, the Tsarina said.

"This diary, she gave to me. *'Entrust this (diary) to the sanctity and purity of the young maid'*."

"The grail maiden", I thought out loud.

"Oui madam, but not for me." Simone lowered her eyes humbly. "It was for me to *give* to the grail maid one day. It was to be placed in the hands of the grail princess."

Then Simone and Serge performed an extraordinary gesture. They arose from their seats in unison, stood in front of me and dropped to one knee before me.

"We serve the Bringer of the Grail."

Part II

"The Lady of the Waters: The Lady of Lourdes"

Chapter 1 – "The Lady of the Waters

That evening I lay under a warm handmade quilt in my new sanctuary and peered up at a stargazer's night, reflecting upon the events of the past few short days and particularly on the incidences of the last few hours. The crystal clock recorded 12:00 midnight. Having no recollection of making myself ready for bed, I must have fallen asleep in the parlor and been carried upstairs via the secret cupboard stairwell.

My last memory of the evening was that of Simone and Serge kneeling before me. As their words: "We serve the bringer of the grail" echoed out to me, I remembered them bowing their heads and extending their arms straight out before them directly at me. A gentle yet extraordinarily powerful energy emitted from their hands. It was actually visible. Rays of purest white surrounded by the sun issued toward me and lifted my being into a symphony of ecstasy.

My spirit ascended out of my body and flew higher and higher upward into the night sky, heavenward and closer to the stars. A choir, consisting of myriads of white glowing angels, encircled me. A tall beautiful feminine angel carrying a white lily advanced in my direction. Dressed entirely in silver, the angel had glowing red hair and silver light danced all about her.

Then, from the centre of the circle of angels, a woman appeared. Glowing with the sun all around her, she stood on a crescent moon. It was almost blinding to look at her yet not painful to the eyes. Amazingly, her internal light seemed to heal and refocus my eyes. The lady held her hands at her sides at about a foot from her body. Golden light beams emitted from both palms as she raised them up and out toward me. As these sunrays radiated over me, it felt like I had become a being of purest light. Power of an indescribable enormity was infused into my light body and when I opened my hands and looked at my palms, there appeared to be tiny fireflies dancing in a spiral in the centre of each one.

The lady seemed familiar somehow yet I could not assemble from where. Her eyes were unforgettable; luminous and golden, holding all colors of the spectrum and some not of this world within them. They were like orbs of sparkling jewels with a sapphire hue streaming through them, likened to the colors of a Paris sky at sunset, yet to say they were blue would be a vast understatement. Her face was youthful with glowing lineless skin yet her presence was ageless. The lady represented all women in her nature.

"*Come to my waters*", she spoke, "*And I will heal you. Come to my waters*" she repeated again, "*At the holy time*".

Then, her arms motioned me downward. I fell to my knees before her and felt her energy float me down, down through space.

Sunlight flickered from the window like a flashlight across my face. Aromas of fresh espresso coffee and uncured bacon cooking floated up to me. The crystal clock seemed to sparkle that it was 7:00 AM. I sat up; full of energy and vitality I hadn't felt in years. I was wearing a long white nightgown of fine linen, edged at the neck and hem with Battenberg lace. It appeared to be a vintage item and beautifully made. Simone must have undressed me before putting me to bed.

I stretched my arms up and out to the sun. Then, using my toes, I felt for my slippers at the side of the bed and bent over to ease them onto my feet. Upon further inspection, I noted Simone had unpacked for me and had laid out my belongings with considerable care on the antique dresser. Longing for a shower or bath, I filled the bidet with water and chose the rose scented soap from the dish of hand milled French savons on the washstand. My toiletries were assembled for my use beside the soaps. After my face was given a thorough cleansing and moisturizing, I slipped into the bidet for a good wash. Having not showered since the night of my date with Jacey, which was a day and a half ago, the water felt heavenly on my skin.

After emerging from the curtained off bathroom area, I found the bed had been made and clothing had been laid out for me, complete with a strand of pearls accompanied by matching earbobs and bracelet. These were all placed very deliberately upon the white linen runner atop the dresser. Beside the items of apparel appeared a fine glass bottle etched with the word "Lilas" (lilac) across it. To the right of the bottle was my makeup bag.

Simone had laid out a lavender cashmere pullover and a charcoal colored three-quarter length wrap skirt for me. Along side the clothing was my lilac lace bra and panties and a pair of gray pantyhose that Simone had retrieved from my tote bag. After dressing, I sat down at the dresser and addressed my countenance in the oval mirror. My complexion was glowing and didn't require any foundation so I simply applied a few dabs of mauve-pink lip gloss, to match the sweater, a quick brush of lavender-gray eye shadow and a flick of black mascara to the top lashes only. I brushed my hair and styled it in a loose pageboy, parted to one side.

The pearl set was exquisite and Simone had chosen it especially for me. After gliding the antique bobs through my pierced ears, I unfastened the intricate clasp of the necklace and bracelet and put them on. The pearls picked up the tones of the sweater beautifully and gave me the appearance of a sprig of fresh heather! A few quick squirts from the bulb of the bottle of 'Lilas', into the air around and above me, allowed it to settle into my essence.

"Madam is now ready to descend", I spoke mockingly to myself in the mirror in a snooty nasal English accent. Then stuck my tongue out at myself and giggled at my faux pompousness.

"Bonjour, mes amies!" I smiled, opening the cupboard door and lowering myself into the kitchen. A low step rest had been placed below the cupboard for me to allow descending easier.

"Ah, failed to give you a fright this time, Simone!" I continued, folding my arms around her in an embrace. "Thank you so much for arranging my things for me."

Simone blushed. She smelled of violets.

"It is our honor to be of service madam." Serge bowed his head.

"Thank you for all your kindness as well, Serge." He too received a warm and appreciative hug.

"But you must remember", I continued, "I'm not used to such formality. It's not necessary to bow to me and my name is Angelica."

"Ah ... like the Angels!" Simone expressed in amazement. "And you look like an Angel, aujord hui." Simone gestured at my attire approvingly. She herself was dressed in a simple yet elegant tailored navy linen dress with a pert white cotton lace collar and a single strand of pearls with matching pearl studs.

"We will have une petit dejuener and then we go to the mass a l'eglis", she informed, while gesturing to me to sit at the table. We were going to church.

Surprised at my own ravenous appetite, I helped myself to omelet, bacon, freshly baked herb biscuits and more pear preserves, left over from the night before. If the Lavallees noticed, they were far too polite to acknowledge it.

While enjoying 'ma café', I fingered the exquisite and certainly very valuable pearls on my neck.

"Madam, I don't intend any rudeness or mean to sound ungrateful, but these pearls... I cannot accept them. They are far too valuable a gift."

"They are not a gift, ma cherie." corrected Simone. "They are part of your heritage. They belonged to your great grand mere and had to be left behind when they moved them. Alix, the Tsarina, gave a jewel box to ma mere ..."

"To keep for Anya, when all this is over." There was that voice again, speaking as if she were in the same room; the same voice I heard upon initially opening the parcel containing the diary!

"Who was Anya?" I inquired of Simone.

Simone looked at me in astonishment, but answered. "Anya was the ... oh, how you say, pseudonym..." She gestured helplessly to Serge.

"Nickname", Serge offered as he poured me more cafe au lait.

"Ah, oui ... the *nickname* de la petite grand duchess Anastasia, cherie", Simone smiled incredulously. "But how had you knowledge of this?"

"From a voice I hear sometimes; a woman's voice. I have been hearing it since receiving the diary and sometimes, as a little girl but I'm not sure. The same voice was in my dream last night. In the dream, there first appeared a myriad of white angels ..." Then stopped, not wishing to sound self indulgent.

"Go on, please", Serge insisted.

"Well ... in front of the white angels was an Angel that appeared to be made out of silver, possessing silver wings and covered in silver stars. She had curling red hair and carried a lily."

"Gabrielle!" exclaimed Simone.

"And then ..." urged Serge.

"Yes ... and then", continuing, "A beautiful lady appeared from the circle of angels. It was as if the sun were behind her. The light about her was blazingly bright, yet very healing. My body felt like it was being balanced and brought into harmony in her exquisite presence."

"What did she look like, this lady", inquired Serge.

"Oh ... She had very shiny auburn hair that fell over her shoulders ... And she wore a white dress that shone red gold tied with a blue belt and a long blue cape. But it was her eyes! The most extraordinary I have ever seen. It was like they had hundreds of different precious jewels dancing within them over a sapphire sky."

Simone and Serge stared at me in almost awe.

"Did she, the lady, say anything to you?" asked Serge.

"Yes, she did! She said *'Come to my waters at the holy time and I will heal you.'* She said it twice", I replied.

The rustic rural church was not far from the Lavallee farmhouse and Serge suggested we walk. "For the exercise and fresh air", he smiled, breathing in fully and patting his chest.

It was indeed a fresh and lovely morning. I marveled at the beauty and elegance of the pastoral scenery. The vineyards would be starting up soon and anticipation of new life scented the air with an aroma of abundant expectation.

We were not alone on our country sojourn to church. Many other provincial parishioners had much the same idea of a brisk morning walk to church to do the system good.

"Bonjour Serge", two young schoolgirls tittered, as they rushed into the pews ahead of us.

"Bonjour Simone", sounded a dignified female voice behind us. It belonged to a full bodied self possessed matronly woman, who eyed me sternly. She was accompanied by a doe eyed juene fille of about seventeen.

"Ah, Murielle et Agnes", answered Simone. "Ma niece, Cybele", she motioned to me and then crossed herself quickly. I doubted that Simone was in the habit of lying at all and particularly not on the steps of a church.

Serge ushered us all in quickly to avoid further conversation and introductions, seating us in a private pew inscribed with the family name but which I noticed was spelled La Vallee.

The provincial simplicity of the church exterior was deceptive. Once inside, a tasteful but elegant decor kissed the eyes. The stone walls were painted white and adorned with large ancient paintings, some of Egyptian depictions. Beautiful Belgian lace covered an alter that supported a large antique cross of what appeared to be solid gold.

A beautiful statue of a young holy mother without a veil possessing very long hair with roses scattered at her feet was set against one wall. I also noticed an extraordinary alabaster representation of a young woman of about fifteen wearing a peasant dress under an armor vest and holding a sword by her side.

"Who is the statue of?" I asked.

"La Femme d'Orleans", whispered Simone.

"Saint Jeanne d'Arc", Serge included, "The Maid of Orleans. We honor her in our region. She gave up everything to help her King win his wars and save France from the English. Then, he of course betrayed her", he shrugged.

I was beginning to think Serge was quite a feminist. I was also in admiration of the fantastic physical condition he was in. He had to be over sixty yet could easily be mistaken for ten to fifteen years younger. Simone as well must have been over eighty but was as spry as could be. She appeared to be the age Serge was!

"This church is very old, going back to Napoleonic times and before. It is believed that Bonaparte came here to pray before all of his major battles. Unfortunately, he did not visit here before Waterloo." Serge smiled.

I stifled a giggle, not wishing to appear rude by laughing in church.

"Great blessings are believed to be bestowed from this church upon those who are … deserving", Serge added.

It was a lovely service, executed entirely in French of course but interestingly it was in very old French resembling that of the Canadian Quebecois.

"Your Quebecers speak an antiquated but very respectable French dating back to the fifteenth century. We in France are embarrassed when we do not understand it. Here in our village it is still spoken by those who have had it handed it down to them by their elders."

During the ceremony, the congregation rose to sing a very beautiful hymn. It was in old French so I simply stood in respect. A stained glass window flanked the Lavallees pew from behind us and I could feel the warmth of the sun upon my back and head. It lasted throughout the hymn and for the rest of the service the church retained a beautiful golden light.

As we departed the church, the priest and the other parishioners allowed the Lavallees and me to pass down the aisle in a respectful silence. Even the stern Murielle and her daughter Agnes bowed their heads and stepped aside for us to pass.

As we made our way down the dirt road, Serge leaned over to me and with a sly grin said "Madam is shining."

As we approached the cypress arched entry to the farm, Brie ('the Lavallee hound', as Serge called him) ambled up to greet us. Brie, named after the cheese he so loved to ingest whenever the opportunity presented itself, normally resided in the barn. Brie was dancing in vocal frenzy now. As we turned into the yard, I realized why. There were fresh tire tracks on the grass!

Serge quickly pulled me back behind the cypress hedge near the road. One of the neighbors walked over to Serge, whispering to him in French. Simone pulled my shawl up over my head and pulled me into the centre of a gaggle of approaching parishioners on the road. The tall overbearing Murielle made her imposing size useful by eclipsing me from view of the Lavellee yard. I slouched and pulled the shawl further forward over my face. The group of parishioners continued to converse amongst themselves as if nothing were out of the ordinary and indeed seemed to be oblivious to the situation.

Murielle drew a parasol from the crook of her arm and opened it fully over herself, thereby further blocking any view of me.

"Ah, la soleil!" she exclaimed, fanning herself. "Il fait tres chaud!"

The group laughed and moved along the circular path so that we all walked back to the church and entered through a side door. Simone and I rushed down to the basement and through a secret passageway hidden in the paneling.

"It was used during the resistance. A tunnel underground exits to a field, if we need it." Simone advised.

"Is all this really necessary?" I asked as we squeezed through the narrow opening.

"Oui, madam, it is", assured Simone in a serious tone. "These people are worse than the Bolsheviks. You will need sanctuary, madam", Simone insisted.

We walked through a dark narrow passageway, our only light source coming from a beeswax candle that Simone had taken from the entrance and lit with a long match from the alter.

"What you will see may be familiar to you," Simone advised.

Single file, we approached an open door. As the light of the candle engulfed the opening, I gasped. It was the same room in the dream from the night recently spent with Jacey!

I turned and stared at Simone in the dimly illumined doorway.

"Simone, how did you know I would recognize this room?"

"Ah ... you were here, cherie", Simone said, matter of factly.

Serge burst into the hall abruptly. He had remained at the farmhouse and checked it out for any danger before joining us in the church.

"The house is clear" he breathed. He had run all the way and was breaking a sweat on his brow. Simone and I breathed deeply. "But the hiding room has been discovered. The cabinet door was open and your room was searched. They were looking for the diary. Was it in the room, madam?"

"No. It wasn't in the room."

"Bon! Do you have it with you?" Serge questioned.

"No."

"Where, then ..?" Serge eyes denoted concern. "We must have it before we affect the ceremony. It is tres important, madam." Serge emphasized.

"It's ... in the hotel safe in Paris. I wasn't sure what to do with it and just felt a strong instinct not to take it." I admitted.

"No. It is good that you did not. It would have been found by now. They will not return to the room, so you are safe there tonight. We will have Monsieur Christopher pick up the diary and meet us at the farmhouse. It is better this way." Serge said half to himself.

Once back in the farmhouse, Serge telephoned Jacey in Paris.

"Allo? Monsieur Christopher? Oui, the house has been searched mais l'objet is in the hotel safe a Paris. Oui, madam is quite well... oui ..." Serge handed me the telephone. "He wishes to speak to you, madam."

"Jacey!" I breathed.

"Angel, are you alright?"

The Lavallees left the sitting room so we could talk privately.

"Yes, I'm fine. Confused, unbelieving, but fine." I answered, sitting down on the loveseat and slipping off my walking shoes.

"Listen to me Angel. You're completely out of this now. I don't want you put in any further danger."

"It's alright, Jacey. I want to go through with this. Whatever has to be done must be extremely important."

"You have no idea", Jacey confessed.

"I think that I am beginning to." My intuition was pulling me strongly to trust and have faith. "My feeling is to trust you in this."

"Hopefully, that trust is a personal one as well." Jacey said softly. "Although you have every reason not to, as I must have seemed like such a cad to you in Montreal. But it wasn't the way you thought.

"I was rushed off to that retreat - monastery really - near Montreal. What with the studies there and sleep deprivation because of the editing sessions, I probably wasn't thinking right. It was a time-out-of-mind kind of thing. Not being able to contact you because of our time schedules didn't help. Then you sent your ring back and I thought it was all over with us. When seen to be free and single again, I was shipped off to England and pressured into making a decision. Please don't think these are just excuses, Angel. It just all happened so fast. I was a married man before realizing what all was happening."

"Jacey, I think we're better talking about this at another time. Obviously there were situations being put in place that were beyond our control at that time. Cosmic forces, possibly. And it was all so long ago." I tucked my feet up under me on the sofa. "We've been brought back together again for a purpose, it seems. It's best to allow the divine plan to reveal itself. This is obviously about more than just you and me."

"You're right ... but please believe we're being given a second chance here. It's something necessary for *me* to believe, at any rate."

"I'm still taking all this in right now and although the confusion and haze are beginning to clear, my senses tell me we're better off allowing life to play itself out with us ... and see what happens." Accepting the cup of hot herbal tea Simone quietly handed to me, I mimed "Merci" to her.

"I'll fly down to you in a private plane just as soon as I retrieve the diary from the hotel." Jacey offered.

"Are you sure they'll give it to you. I left strict instructions ..."

"The hotel will give it to me. The owner of the hotel is ..."

"..Connected to your order?" I completed.

"In a way", was all Jacey offered. "I'll be at the farmhouse by tonight."

The telephone was then handed over to Serge who listened to Jacey's brief instructions and hung up. Brie accompanied Serge into the sitting room and sat on the floor in front of me, placing her long Alsatian nose in my lap.

"Ah, she has taken to you." Serge smiled.

Animals and I have always had a good rapport. Stroking her head and ears, I cooed to her, "Good dog". She eyed me with her ancient wisdom and whined.

"She loves her ears being scratched." Serge winked. I acquiesced.

Simone beckoned us to the kitchen for a light lunch of brie, French baguette and apples. It was sufficient after the generous breakfast. Brie was accorded her favorite treat by Serge, under the table. Simone eyed him silently over her bifocals as he slipped the buttery cheese into Brie's watering jowls.

"La chienne ... ne mange pas dans la maison", she muttered under her breath, but was otherwise obviously grateful for the dog's earlier warning.

While brushing a few crumbs of my baguette from the lavender cashmere sweater, I noticed for the first time the front of the sweater was embroidered with tiny seed pearls all across the bodice area.

The sweater and skirt was a lovely ensemble but I couldn't help wondering who they had belonged to. They were perfectly preserved vintage early 1900 designs but they couldn't have been Simone's. Even if she had been bigger in her youth it was doubtful she would have been able to wear my size. I wore a 34C bra for one thing and was about a head taller than Simone.

"They are your grand mere," Simone answered my thoughts. As she sipped her tea, her eyes lowered, not looking at me. "She was your size but not so tall ... And the skirt was longer on her ... to the ankle."

"But ... these clothes are from about 1918 ..." I protested.

"Oui, cherie." Simone agreed.

"Ma mere et mon pere aided the young Tsarinavich and Tsarovich out of Yekaterinburg after their wounds were attended too", Simone continued in a solemn voice. "Mes parents escorted the young Tsarinavich to France where she stayed avec ma famille in exile before going to England. They told everyone she was my older sister, Anya.'

"Anya ..." I repeated.

"But what happened to the Tsarovich ... To Alexei ..?" I questioned.

"He was taken in another direction. It was believed to be safer... to separate them." Simone informed.

"How awful for them, being so young ... Were they badly hurt?" I asked softly.

"Well ... not so bad, but the left arm of the Tsarinavich was scarred from the bullets and not so strong after. Tendon damage." Simone advised, patting her left arm. "And her left knee would ache in the dampness, but that could have been hereditary as the Tsarina had weak legs."

"My left knee stiffens in the damp", I confessed.

"Ah, so you see", Simone continued, shrugging like Serge.

"How was it possible to get them out, then? That last photograph of the royal family just before they were executed had them all together."

"Oui. The Tsarina and her daughters had sewn their jewels into their corsets and Alexei's vest. The Tsar refused it. He would be strong and die for his iniquities, but Alexei did not deserve to."

I could see images like a movie of the Tsarina and her children going through their last moments together as Simone spoke.

"They were told they were going to travel but first they would have their photograph taken. So, when the Tsarina sewed the jewelry into their corsets, she sewed more in the two youngest ones because she must have thought they would have a better chance of escape in the travel - or they would be less likely to have the search. C'est va. Who knows?" Simone shrugged. "It was destiny, perhaps. It was the jewels that protected them from the bullets."

"The historical records and documents attest that ALL of the Romanovs were thrown onto the truck, driven to that horrible place and buried."

"Oui mais ... there were others in the party ... et it had rained ... It was messy et confusing ... It was not so difficile to remove the two petit enfants."

As Simone spoke, my mind showed me a movie of the monstrous ride of the Romanovs to their burial place. Sympathizers of the crown however were posted outside the holding area and were privy to every move of the Bolsheviks.

"They followed in secret behind the truck et when the soldiers stopped to rest at night, the sympathizers took the young ones away." Simone advised.

There was indeed a lot of chaos. Incredible as it seemed, the two bodies were carried off without detection.

Or ... Perhaps it was divine intervention.

"Votre mere was conceived en France but Anya was in England before she discovered she was with child. At that time in Europe it was still not so safe for Romanov descendants so votre grand mere was sent to England to stay avec close friends of the Tsarina's family, where she had her baby. Then, a twist of fate happened. The decision was made to send votre mere to Canada with a couple who were loyal to the Romanovs and Anya would follow shortly. Votre mere's protectors (who had specified on their passport documents that votre mere was their child) were killed in an automobile accident just after they arrivee au Canada. Votre mere was sent to a hospital where she was adopted by an older couple from a small town in western Canada. It is unknown if they had knowledge of votre mere's ancestry. It is very doubtful that they would... mais ..?" she shrugged.

"Well ... if they had, they never told her. Or, at least my mother never said anything to me about it. That's not really the kind of thing you keep secret."

"Unless to protect you", Serge spoke at last.

"Protect me from what ... whom?" I wanted to know. "From whom am I hiding? Just who exactly is it who wants the diary - and why? And what could they do with it if they did confiscate it? I mean, without the appropriate person to interpret (or channel) the messages of the Holy Mother, what good is it to them? Knowledge of my ancestry doesn't seem to be known to them or I would have been done away with... Like Davina." I shuddered.

"It is true. At present they have no information about your heritage. Files of a sensitive nature are very carefully cloistered in our order. Mssr. Christopher had no knowledge of your lineage until a year ago after he had accessed his highest level of attunement. It is not likely these people have this information. They know only that the diary was sent to you so you would bring it to France unnoticed. An innocent messenger, which is, of course, exactly what you are" Serge explained.

"Well ... If all this is as you say, then the diary would be useless to them, would it not?" I queried.

"No it wouldn't be", spoke a familiar voice from behind me. "They have Penny."

I turned around quickly and viewed Jacey standing in the kitchen archway and gasped. "Penny!"

Penny and I had not seen one another in over five years since she had moved to Lyons after her divorce. Penny had travelled extensively with her modeling career and for a time became a high fashion icon of the 'beautiful set'. She settled in Rome where she met and married an Italian aristocrat. Although his father was Italian, his mother was English and, like his father before him, he possessed a passion for tall fair haired Anglo-Saxon beauties. It was a good match for quite a while. Penny's no nonsense but well-bred style of feminine feminism handled the macho leanings of Giorgio de Seville exceptionally well. She was strong enough for him and he for her. They had two lovely boys; Emmanuel, twenty-five and Jacobi, twenty-three. Their main home was in Rome but they possessed a dozen others across Europe as well as an enormous estate in Australia where Geordie (as she called him) had vast land holdings and numerous other investments. After they parted, Penny got the home by the ocean in Sydney, the ranch in California, a townhouse in London, a house in Lyons and - of course - the apartment in Paris! It belonged to Penny, I suddenly realized!

"She's been missing from her home in Lyons for three days", Jacey advised sadly. I could tell he was angry but it was not an emotional energy emitting from him. There was a power pouring from his being that had not been there before.

"With Penny to decipher the coded messages and the diary itself, a fait de complete could be possible that would bring untold catastrophes to humankind. In the wrong hands, this knowledge could be turned around to destroy", Jacey advised.

"Destroy?" I questioned.

"Destroy our earth as we know it." Jacey turned to me with such a solemn expression that it caused me to become quite anxious.

"What can we do? What can we do to help Penny?" I asked.

"Whatever we do we must do it quickly", Serge, our voice of reason, ascertained.

"You're right, Serge", Jacey acquiesced. Reminding me of a stealth tiger readying into motion, he laid out a plan.

He would place a telephone call from his cell phone to Paris (as he knew the call would be traced by our pursuers) and pretend to arrange to have the diary picked up by a rouse that would drive out of the city and throw them off track.

"I have a better idea ... and safer", interjected Serge. He explained his coup. "First, call our connection at the Hotel George V and tell them to have a package prepared to be couriered to an address where it is possible for it to be intercepted, yet harm will come to no one. We can take care of that.

"Next, we must fly to the Pyrenees where we will meet up with Celine ... My wife" Serge explained to me. "The ceremony must be done tonight. It is of the essence because of the timing."

I understood this to mean that the occasion of Easter made this a fortuitous time... And because of the Lady's message in my dream. *"Come to my waters at the holy time"*. Sunday was Easter Sunday.

"Arrangements have already been made in Lourdes for our conclave. It is not for nothing it is unfolding as it is. We must follow the path that is being given to us... And trust. Have faith, mes amies." Serge patted Jacey's shoulder.

Serge's last words as we left the farmhouse were "Be of good faith and be cautious." He kissed us both but held me back for a moment.

"You have been very blessed, madam. You are carrying a child."

Serge's words echoed through me as the three of us lifted off in the little Cessna Jacey had flown in from Paris. I knew the instant he voiced the words "You are carrying a child" that Jacey and I had conceived during our union. Having been so overwhelmed by all of the recent happenings, I had uncharacteristically not been in touch with my body enough to have diagnosed it for myself. Yet my inner sensing told me Serge was right. The glossiness of my hair, the luminosity of my skin, the glow about me like 'a halo', as Serge had observed in church earlier. They were all familiar signs. I was going to have a child.

Serge had faxed his wife Celine to meet us at a certain location. It was important for Celine to accompany us due to her role in the ceremony that was about to take place. She would also drive us undetected through the Pyrenees Mountains to our ultimate location.

But what about Penny? How would she fare?

Serge had gone on to relay the rest of his coup while Simone helped me put my things together upstairs in the farmhouse.

Whilst the bogus diary was en route to its destination, the official report would be that an 'accident' had occurred: The car would be run off the road and an ensuing fire destroying all the contents. Once news was received of the diary's destruction, the holding of Penny would be futile and she would simply and quietly be returned to her home. It was the diary's existence that posed a threat. I could not see Penny ever agreeing to go along with a diabolical plan such as this, but if these people were capable of anything, as apparently they were, they would likely threaten the lives of her children should she refuse to cooperate with their plans.

While repacking my faithful tote bag, Jacey relayed to me that Penny's bloodline was 'appropriate' and connected to the same lineage as Davina's. More important, her past life soul DNA was connected as well: Penny was the soul incarnation of Jesus' second wife, about whom little was known other than that her name was also Miriam.

"You're still sure you want to engage in our ceremony, then?" Jacey asked, as he piloted the Cessna into the clouds.

"Yes", I reinforced emphatically. "In all conscience, it would be impossible to refuse to comply with a purpose that would be so essential to the future of our world. Besides", I went on with a smile and an attempt to lighten the situation, "Your order is paying me very well for my 'travel story'." Then more seriously, "Who are these people who want to work for the dark?"

"Many are the soul embodiments of certain members of the Sanhedrin, the wealthy priest faction who were responsible for the crucifixion of Christ. They have incarnated into the souls of some of the wealthiest and most prominent industrial leaders in our nations. Fortunately, some of the most enlightened soul beings have also incarnated at this time into some of the most prominent families and leading executives on our earth. The Spencer family is one of such families. Diana was a great loss to the world. And so was Davina."

"What will save us?" I postured. "What, if anything, will save humankind?"

Jacey paused and then very gently but emphatically said "We are all, each one of us souls, engendered with our own set of pure and holy Angels."

"Even the Sanhedrim", interposed Serge from the backseat.

"So it is possible if we get in touch with, that is, become aligned with our higher beings, that each one of us can overcome our earthly soul natures, if they be impure?" I offered.

"Oui. This is possible, madam. With the influence of the Holy Mother so close to us in these times, it is indeed possible that even these tarnished souls can be saved", Serge countered.

"I truly believe that there is no such thing as a 'bad' person. Genetics all aside, the true soul within each of us has to be very pure because we are all, in essence, a part, a cell, of God. Perhaps the nature of a being may be programmed by a thousand soul incarnations and the issues ensued therein, but the essence in all of us is very pure and it is to this part of ourselves - and especially of these dark beings - that we must appeal."

"Their issues need to be cleared so that their Angels can be heard by them." came a message from within me; a channeling from outside of my being but from inside of me as well.

"Madam's angels are speaking, out." mused Serge, "And madam's halo is glowing."

The Cessna, named *Bebe*, was approaching the coastal area near the Pyrenees Mountains which border France and Spain. This mountain range was a sacred one going back to times of biblical antiquity. The lore of many religious pilgrimages was set within these ranges.

"The fog is high", Serge interupted in a concerned voice, as the small plane suddenly plunged into a dense mist. The mist billowing up from the high rocky masses obstructed vision. It became increasingly clear to us that this was not going to be an easy place on which to land at this time.

I could feel confusion overcome Jacey as he worked the knobs and gears of the aircraft. He had become disoriented for a moment and was pushing down instead of pulling up. He reoriented himself just in time to avoid connecting with a mountain relief. I could hear the wing of the plane brush the side of the mountain as it regained altitude.

The designated landing location came into view as soon as the mist cleared. Jacey had barely enough time to prepare for landing. The descent was abrupt and the plane came in for a jarring landing that bounced me hard in my seat before we came to a full stop. My stomach lurched forward into my seatbelt which made me feel like vomiting, so I breathed deeply to regain my composure.

My door opened and a slender woman's frame dressed in a brown leather coat appeared in the doorway. A spray of curls the color of dark honey circled a face full of light. The light spoke, "Are you alright? That was quite a bump you took." The face of light put its hand out to me and golden white sunlight sprayed across my torso. "There. You will be fine now', the light said.

"Madam has hemorrhaged", the voice uttered as I opened my eyes to a blur of surreal images. Blinking helped my eyes regain their focus.

Serge's face was looking down upon me as I strained to sit up on a gurney in the hospital admitting room. My stomach was very tender and there was blood on my skirt. The doctor in attendance in the small emergency room had completed his examination and turned to make his report. The hemorrhaging was minor and the nurse had fitted me with an appropriate undergarment. The doctor released me but advised Serge to have me remain quiet for a few days.

"Madam would like to change", Serge stated and handed me my tote bag.

I alighted gingerly to the cold tile floor and moved carefully to a curtained area to remove my skirt. The nurse had fitted me with an absorbent pad but the bleeding wasn't heavy. I opened my tote and unfolded a pair of black trousers and a black merino wool pullover. There was no pain.

Celine was standing in the small waiting area of the rustic hospital where I could smell the wounds of a thousand soldiers that had passed through the ancient building. The presence of Napoleon himself had left his essence in the air. He smelled of a lemon tinged cologne - and brandy, of course.

Celine introduced herself, although it was unnecessary as I recognized her from the airplane. She must have been in her late fifties, yet Celine possessed the body of a young girl. Under her classic but chic leather coat, she looked lithe and slender as an arrow. Her coat was worn open and revealed her chocolate sweater and matching stirrup pants. The brown tones matched her peach complexion and short hazelnut curls perfectly. She was clever to wear it, I observed, as black would have been too harsh for her. Celine wore no makeup but a sheer lip stain and only a light whiff of the gentlest white flowers surrounded her, smelling like lilies in water.

Celine easily flung my tote over her shoulder as we walked to her car.

"There has been a change of plans", she informed me in almost flawless English as she opened the door of the mini van for me.

"Serge and Monsieur Christopher are working out some details ... Of an alternate plan."

"Where have they gone?" I asked sensing something was amiss.

"We received word about an hour ago that the courier carrying the package containing the diary was intercepted en route to its destination."

"Wasn't the courier to experience an 'accident' of some kind, to throw these monsters off the trail?" I postured, drawing my cape around my shoulders.

Eyeing me, Celine noted "It gets a bit chilly in the mountains", and turned the heat on.

"Yes", she answered my question. "Unfortunately, these 'monsters' were a bit too eager to grab their find and managed to swerve the courier off the road just outside of Paris before there was time for our people to create an accident. They then searched the car and found the package that was picked up at the hotel. However, when they opened it, they of course found it empty", Celine finished.

"Is the driver alright?"

Celine turned to me, "I appreciate your sympathy, cherie. They left him for dead but he is with our people and is fine now."

Their 'people' were of course healers.

"You stopped my bleeding, didn't you?"

Celine smiled. I started to express my gratitude but she responded. "There is no need for thanks. It is what we do."

It can honestly be said that I had never been in contact with anyone whose energy was as powerful yet as gentle as Celine's. The strength of her energy seemed to vibrate and permeate the vehicle. I could not resist staring at her and noticed that her apricot skin glowed like alabaster.

"What is the alternate plan?" I questioned after we had driven on a bit.

"Monsieur Christopher and Serge have made contact with our people in Paris who have advised them that their pursuers know the diary was not with the courier and must therefore be with ..."

"Jacey", I interspersed.

"Yes. Monsieur Christopher and Serge have worked out another plan of divergence."

Serge's participation with the resistance was obviously coming in handy. Jacey would place a bogus call to Serge on his cell phone (so that it would be intercepted) advising him to take the land rover and deliver the diary to an appointed destination. Serge would then arrange a car accident that would completely demolish the vehicle. In the mountains it would be much easier. Jacey would fly back over the Pyrenees and join us.

"And then Penny will be safe?" I inquired anxiously.

"We trust so", Celine sighed and patted my arm gently. "I think you have quite enough to be concerned about", she spoke softly.

Touching my tummy and feeling energy there, I breathed a deep sigh of relief.

"Where are we going?" I asked Celine.

"The diary is not with us so we will be unable to perform the ceremony the Lady requested at midnight. Arrangements have been made for us to stay at the chateau of the imperator of our order."

I was speechless but finally managed, "I am much honored."

Standing under the gilded head of the shower, allowing the pure mountain water to cleanse and refresh my entire being, I shampooed my hair with the fragrant liquid from the French hand labeled bottle by the antique bathtub and lathered my body with the lavender scented soap in the shower stand.

My guestroom was an exquisite blend of French Provencal charm and elegant bourgeois decadence. Pale yellow water stained silk wallpaper patterned the walls of the unit. I would spend the night in a gold tasseled four poster bed that could have slept an entire family. White Marie Antoinette furniture dotted the expansive room in perfect placement. I was simply happy to bathe.

Frederique, the butler, had greeted Celine and me earlier in the spectacular entranceway of the chateau. Featuring stunning Egyptian blue walls with coordinating carpet, the foyer was home to lovely white oak woodwork and a beautifully carved oak staircase that faced the doorway. He immediately guided us up the stairs along the continuing sky hued carpet to the second floor. It seemed we walked forever down a hallway of blue walls, more blue carpet and curved azure ceilings. As we were stepping through this maze of sky, it felt more and more like we were entering heaven.

A knock on the door and Frederique's voice announced dinner would be served in half an hour, which still allowed me time to blow dry my hair, dress and fix my face.

After folding myself into the butterfly yellow silk kimono that had been laid out for me, I placed my feet into the matching silk slippers, which were embroidered with tiny mauve butterflies and seated myself at the ivory vanity. There was no flushing, no blurred vision and my blood sugar was surprisingly harmonious.

I opted for wearing my hair up at the sides and long and flowing in the back. My complexion was still aglow so after moisturizing, a sparse application of sheer powder with a large soft sable brush sufficed. My eyes received a few flicks of the brush from the earth pot and my lips were glazed with a bit of sienna gloss. The upper and lower eyelashes were brushed with an almost dry black mascara to separate and add definition. The classic perfume Chanel No. 5 in its familiar crystal bottle sat on the dresser and my wrists received a gentle tab of its cheeky elegance.

After slipping on my new French lingerie; affixing a sanitary napkin just in case; I stepped into my new three-quarter length black dress and Paris pumps. I hadn't brought much jewelry, just the Russian pearl ensemble. The earbobs were fine with the dress but the strand of pearls needed something. My eyes were carried up to a gilt framed portrait by the mirror. The painting was of a lovely Queen Josephine, formally dressed in a ball gown, wearing a triple strand pearl neck choker ornamented with a teardrop pearl attached to it by a tiny black velvet bow.

Pulling my velvet jewelry bag from its compartment in my tote, I retrieved the tiny filigree egg. Detaching it from its chain and slipping it over the clasp of the pearls, I then wrapped the opera length pearls around my neck twice, closed the clasp and let the filigree egg hang down in front. A piece of very narrow black silk ribbon was in the jewelry bag, enough to snip off and tie a tiny bow above the egg, making it look more like a pendant. Another bit of brilliance struck me and I snipped off a few more bits of ribbon and tied teeny bows just above the pearls on the hanging ear bobs. Josephine would have been proud.

I hadn't been within such opulent walls since my days of the Christopher family visits. However, if memory served me well, one usually proceeded to the drawing room for cocktails prior to a dinner.

My lavender pashmina shawl worked perfectly to warm my shoulders. These big old manors were characteristically chilly: 'Iced for the gentry or frosted for the frosty' as Jacey and I would joke during our youthful explorations of his family estate.

The drawing room had stone flooring but despite the temperature there was nothing cold about its atmosphere and the stone fireplace was lit and inviting as one drew near it. The room was formal but very warmly so, decorated in rich tones of apricot, gold and yellow. There was nothing at all somber about this room and I had never sensed such a welcoming ambiance.

Celine was already seated in a wingback chair by the fireplace, sipping a glass of red wine, looking elegant in a long coffee colored wool skirt and matching cashmere sweater. An antique gold bracelet and gold neck chain were the only embellishments to her attire.

Frederique poured me a glass of wine and directed me toward the fireplace.

An elderly man sitting in a wingback chair, that flanked the opposite side of the hearth, rose and lithely strode toward me.

"Madam", he smiled charmingly and, in perfect English, introduced himself. "I am Jean Pierre St. Germaine."

"You are the owner of La Gavroche!" I smiled in return and extended my hand automatically.

"Oui", he acknowledged and kissed my hand courteously. "And I am also your grandfather."

"Please, sit down", Monsieur St. Germaine spoke softly and offered me his chair. Feeling like I was floating down into it in slow motion, the arms of the chair steadied and helped me regain composure. He was my grandfather!

"Is madam alright?" asked Frederique in a concerned tone.

"I think I just need to eat something."

"Shock and long hours between meals unbalances madam's blood sugar", advised Celine.

"Ah", spoke Monsieur St. Germaine, understanding perfectly. "So it goes with the bloodline."

Silently, Celine raised her right arm and extended it out in front of her in my direction, her palm facing me. Slowly, a golden ray of pure iridescent white light effused out toward me and spread throughout my being. She held her arm thus for several minutes, at the end of which my body was brought back into total harmony.

"Goodness, Celine", I spoke, "Is that magic that you do?"

"No, cherie", she smiled. "It is a healing technique we use, similar to reiki."

"Healing technique?"

"Oui. It is a method of healing through the hands, allowing the energy of the universe, or God, to pass through you and out to wherever healing is required. It is believed to be the method Christ learned in Tibet and then practiced when he performed his miracle healings. We in our order know this to be true from our records."

"We would be happy to instruct you in this method. It was once only for the select elite, but now anyone can be taught this powerful technique", offered Monsieur St. Germaine.

"That process could come in very handy, monsieur. I gratefully accept your gracious offer", I replied.

"This would be very good for you to know", smiled Celine. "Frederique, une tasse du l'eau, s'il vous plais - avec citron ..."

Celine turned to face me; her eyes were the color of aqua crystal and sparkling with luminescence.

"I am going to initiate you into the rites and then show you some exercises to practice."

Celine took the glass of water and lemon and walked around behind me. "Lay down on the sofa and lose your eyes", she requested. Celine then performed a few initiation procedures on me, following them up with a demonstration of hand positions on locations of the body where the energy lines connected. Demonstrating on me, she placed both hands first on the crown of my head, then the back of the skull, on either side of the neck, then to support both of the shoulders. Placing her hands across the eyes, along the sides of the face, the top of the chest, down along the abdomen, then down each leg (one at a time); first, the thigh, the calf, the ankle and the foot. Then down the other side, front and back.

She then lay down upon the sofa and asked me to imitate the same positions of the hands upon her that she had just shown me.

"What about the healing you did on me, where you sent energy out through your hands?" I asked as I proceeded to lay my hands on her as instructed.

"The long distance technique does not require the receiver to be in close proximity. They could in effect, be a thousand miles away." She held her hand out and made a special signage which she had me copy and then advised, "Hold your arms out and your palms outstretched until you feel the procedure has taken. The length of time is not important. A few minutes will suffice. Also, do not be concerned about the exact location to direct the healing energy. The energy goes where it is needed. Now, focus your mind on sending the energy out to someone. It could also be sent to an animal, if you wish."

I immediately focused on Fluff.

While processing, I felt a burst of pure white light flash into my mind and caught a vision of Fluff sitting on Rose's sofa, purring softly. He felt my energy. He knew I was communicating with him and he winked at me! One eyelid dropped over an azure orb in a sign of recognition. Good. He'd been returned and was safe.

"Another point, cherie", interjected Celine.

"Please, it's Angele", I said using the French pronunciation.

"Oui, Angele … It is not necessary to actually touch the client at all, even if they are in close proximity. As a matter of fact, there are those practitioners who advocate not to. Some of the masters of this healing technique object to the direct hands on approach as it may be invasive to a client who is already apprehensive or if there is certain sensitivity within the body itself. Also, this applies if the practitioner is inexperienced or simply has exceptional sensitivity themselves."

"Incredible. Thank you so much." This practice opened a new and expansive window for me. I would now, with a bit of practice, be able to balance my blood sugar and bring my body back into harmony when it went wonky.

"What a wonderful method for everyone to know. It could circumvent the need for hospitals and put people in charge of their own health." I commented thoughtfully.

"Exactly", expressed J.P. "That is precisely why this method is affordable and available now. At one time, things were very different. It was offered only to a select elite group of people and very expensive: Ten thousand dollars for the master's level. This was to ensure the students were serious in their undertaking. With the millennium so near and the necessity of humanity to achieve higher enlightenment, the decision was made on the cosmic level to send the information out there for all who were interested. It would not be such a lonely trek for the pilgrim anymore." Our host then bowed, smiled and said "Now, shall we dine?"

J. P. (as I now secretly called him) escorted Celine and me into the connecting dining room. Although a simpler affair than other areas of the chateau, the circular shaped room had one spectacular feature; it was bestowed with an extraordinary domed glass ceiling that extended over its entire area. The room was darkened and lit only by candlelight, allowing Space and all of her constellations to be exposed. While sitting beneath the diamonds of the universe, it was difficult not to gasp at the utterly breathtaking view of heaven at night.

"I am showing off for you a bit, Mesdames. It is not every evening I have the opportunity to dine with two such beautiful women. And at my age, it is not likely to occur frequently in the future!" J.P. announced, his eyes sparkling at his own wit.

He had to have been over ninety, but J.P. could have passed for a youthful seventy. His smooth unlined skin, lightly tanned by the provencal sun, glowed of good health and physical fitness. This became very evident as he entertained Celine and me with a discourse on his climbing and skiing expeditions.

J.P. still possessed a full head of striking white hair and it was quite evident from the proportions of his features that he was once a strikingly handsome young man. Now he was a debonair older one.

Frederique served our dinner himself, beginning with plates of freshly sliced mixed fruits; pineapple, orange, mango, melon and grapes, "Fruit to cleanse the palette." I remember Jacey's father teaching me.

Next, a clear bouillon, lightly flavored with brandy. Following this, the entree consisted of a framboise fricassee (chicken roasted in a puree of fresh raspberries), accompanied by a fresh garden salad and jasmine rice.

Throughout dinner, I couldn't help thinking about Jacey and Serge and how their undertaking could become potentially dangerous for them.

"Serge will meet us here as soon as he disposes of his vehicle and arrangements have already been set into motion for his return. We have not yet received word from Monsieur Christopher", explained Celine, as though listening to my mind.

A loud chime from the doorbell interrupted our discourse, just as Frederique was pouring our café.

His facial features appearing quite distraught, Serge strode directly to the dining table. He was likely starving as well.

Serge exchanged an embrace with Celine and sat down next to her at the table. Frederique offered him a glass of wine before returning to the kitchen to attend to his meal.

"My news is not entirely good", Serge began. He sipped his wine, his eyes focused on the table before him. He was still slightly out of breath as he reported the details to us. "I arranged for the destruction of my vehicle. It was designed to appear as if it went out of control and over a cliff. It burned unrecognizably. Any item within it would have perished."

"Parfait", complimented J.P. "As for ..."

"I have had no word from Monsieur Christopher", Serge continued.

"Then shall we ..." spoke J.P., although it was really more of an order.

Having been asked to be a participant, I awaited J.P.'s instructions along with Celine and Serge. After observing the others and copying them, I sat straight backed in my chair with my feet a few inches apart and my hands upon my knees.

"Breathe lightly in and out with no breaks in your inhaling or exhaling", instructed J.P. As we did this for a few moments, J.P.'s voice filtered through my mind like a soothing mist. He went on. "Feel yourself rising out of your body, up and out of this room, this house and up higher and higher into the hemisphere until you reach a certain location within yourself that you and the universe share. It is called your inner sanctum. Here you will be able to find complete beauty and peace. It will be your true home in the cosmic universe; your souls' delight, where you will be able to achieve your own perfect heaven as you desire it and design it to be. You will also find within it your soul's retreat; a place of solace where you may go or bring anyone when in need of healing, at any time."

As J.P. spoke I felt my spirit body rise up and out of my physical body and fly up to the glass ceiling. With another leap 'I' soared upward toward the stars. 'I' was free!

Higher and higher I went for seemingly endless miles and passed myriads of stars and planets, sailing by glowing beings with large white wings; some of the angels flying low. Airplanes flew below me and there were manmade 'stars' in the form of posts or satellites. Occupying space as well were other vehicles, which I sensed were not of this planet, that piloted the atmosphere and passed by me. Suddenly an enveloping cloud scooped me into its center and I fell into a stream of sparkling, vibrant warm water. Allowing myself to enjoy being afloat upon this stream of total happiness, I finally opened my eyes and realized my body was drifting along a beautiful creek of fluid starlight, not water at all! The light was astonishingly bright but also embracing. Silently, a beautiful temple glowed before me and the knowledge came that when I walked through its entrance, the answers to all of my questions would be explained and I would find God.

Just before entering the temple doorway, however, I felt a presence to my right and turned. It was Jacey! He reached out to me and held me close. "We must be fast." Jacey quickly put his hand over my eyes.

A thousand light bulbs flashed in my mind, and then, suddenly, J.P.'s voice was there again.

"Open your eyes!" he ordered.

I slowly pulled my eyelids away from one another and opened them to face Jacey sitting directly in front of me on the table!

"Where were you?" I asked.

"We haven't much time", Jacey began in earnest. "You must make the meeting at the grotto tonight as the Holy Mother instructed. It is most imperative for all of you to be there. I have already made contact with those others necessary to participate. There is a reason the Holy Mother has chosen this night for Her connection. It is of course Easter weekend and a sacred time because of Christ's crucifixion, but it is also important as it is precisely at midnight that the planets align to form, what is called by the Great White Brotherhood, Mary's Crown.

"It is only every thousand years that the planets are in a certain configuration for this circumstance to occur and it is exactly this alignment that can attune the universe and all beings on earth - and elsewhere.

"This means peace, love, beauty, freedom; all the dreams of our sixties generation; can become a reality. If you look skyward, you can see a particular curve of stars formed on each side of the North Star, also known as Venus. This formation will be at its pinnacle tonight at midnight when the ceremony MUST be performed. I may or may not be able to be there. If not, do it without me."

"Without the diary, which you have monsieur, it is not possible", protested Serge.

"It is possible. You have what you need. You have Angelica." With that Jacey's image visibly disintegrated before our eyes.

"I don't understand", I offered.

"Nor do I", stated Celine. "But nonetheless, we must do as he says. It is the wish of the Holy Mother and must be obeyed."

"Without the star of the crown, it will be impossible," advised Serge. "And that the diary holds."

"We must proceed and trust." spoke J.P. emphatically. "As Jason alluded, perhaps it is Angelique who is the true Star of the Crown."

It was almost 10:00 P.M. and Serge advised it was an hour's drive to the grotto at Lourdes. The evening was clear and surprisingly warm for the season. The lavender pashmina shawl would probably be sufficient but I fitted my black cashmere cape into my bag just in case and changed into my black walking loafers before proceeding with the others toward J.P's limousine. Serge sat in the front seat by Emile the chauffeur, while Celine, J.P. and I fitted ourselves into the back seat of the rich leather upholstered vehicle, with J.P. in the centre seat.

"Ah! I am a thorn between two roses!" J.P. expressed humbly.

"I'm not so sure of that, monsieur." I patted J.P. arm, having become very fond of this lovely man. The fact that he was my grandfather was a story yet to be explored but a connection that was ancestral as well as spiritual was something I was neither surprised by nor felt objection toward. I could well understand how a grandmother of mine would be attracted to a man of such personal as well as spiritual charisma.

"My grand mere", I began, trying not to sound too eager. "How did you meet?"

J.P. sat perfectly still in his silence. When he spoke of my grandmother, his warm vocal tones evoked a hundred libraries of his sentiments toward her.

"We were in love a million centuries ago, it seemed. Truly, our souls had connected and been together for many, many lifetimes. This one was a complication of birth, timing, ancestry and also political intrigue. In other words, cherie, we did not stand a chance. Our fates, our destinies, were not designed to last; in the spiritual infinity, yes but in the physical 'real world' alas, no."

J.P. took my hand and spoke softly to me. "I came to know Anya; my 'personal' name for her; when Serge's maternal family, the Fournier's, first brought her to France.

"Anya looked about fourteen and was gamine beautiful, very fairy like. I was enchanted with her from the moment I first saw her. She possessed the beauty and coloring of her mother, as do you, only she was not as tall as you.

"Anya had suffered greatly from the wounds she received at Yekaterinburg and many times would awake from her sleep, screaming in the night. She was badly wounded in her left hip, thigh and knee, which brought her great discomfort in her elder years. Also, her left arm and collarbone were a bit disfigured with scarring. However, Anya was young and had tremendous vitality so she overcame any mobility difficulties as she recovered.

"The Fournier's were taken care of financially for 'adopting' the young royal so the family lived simply but well in Paris, where they had a spacious apartment. Also, in the small Provencal village where I grew up, they had a small farm. Anya's identity was known by the villagers but France had great sympathy for the tragic circumstance of the Tsar's family, so her whereabouts was quite safe. The villagers were always very respectful and charged her nothing when she shopped at the market. Anya was always humbly grateful for their kindness. Surprising for a royal, Anya was very special and a true libertine, believing in the freedom of all people. She was kind and honest, fair yet strong. In truth, she would have made a very good ruler!" He laughed.

"Anya was willful yet sweet: A child-woman who could steal your heart and then give it back to you with a thousand blessings. Yes, I was very much in love with her."

"My family actually owned the farm where the Fourniers resided; the same house Madam Lavallee inhabits now where you stayed. We were not so poor, so the Fourniers occupied the farm house in return for running the activities of the farm, which they achieved very well. So much so that the farm became theirs as a recompense for the revenue they produced from it.

"Alas, Anya was not really a farm girl. She much more enjoyed the excitement and activity of Paris, but she grew strong and healthy again at 'De la Breyeres Jolie'. Literally translated as 'Of The Pretty Heather', this was the original name of the farm on the estate owned by my family. My family occupied the larger manor house at the further end of the property. You may have seen it?"

I had noticed a larger building covered in ivy and surrounded by heather that appeared to have been allowed to grow wild all over the front grounds. It was a beautiful display of majestic color and quite a striking view. J.P. smiled whimsically as he continued. "The spelling of the family name, from which the estate name was derived, was changed from the original *de la Bruyere* to *de la Breyeres* when one of our ancestors was into too much wine from his own vineyard. By chance, it was on the very day he inscribed the family name onto the vintage bottle label. Apparently he was too drunk to spell his own name! Once the name was on the bottled wine it was too late to change it, so both the family name and the estate name has been spelled so since then. He thought it was a great joke and laughed to himself whenever he opened a bottle of the de la Breyeres vintage wine. As you may know, ours is a very respectable wine which has the benefit of traveling well and is therefore enjoyed worldwide."

"Anya spent much of her time at Mason de la Breyeres Jolie (manor house) and was accorded her own room there as well. While she was in France, she appeared to have lived very well. When she left for England, it seemed her circumstances were a bit up and down for a while."

"Like her mama and like you as well", J.P. went on, focusing on my lavender shawl, "Anya was very fond of violet and heather colors. Her rooms in both houses reflected that. The lavender outside of the farmhouse was originally planted by her hands."

"And her room ..."

"Was the one you had occupied during your stay with the Lavallees ... And the room in which your mother was conceived", he added with a small wink.

"What happened that caused you to part?" I asked.

J.P. sighed. "Anya loved her Paris and she was in Paris when the news came. Certain factions that our order continues to fight to this day were heading up a movement to obliterate any relations of the Tsars' family. It was not totally clear if they had knowledge of Anya's existence at Mason de la Breyeres Jolie but it was simply no longer safe for her to be in Europe. She was herded off to England before she had time to be in touch with me. By the time she knew of her pregnancy, Anya was in hiding in England and it was impossible to communicate with her.

"Shortly after your mother was born, she was taken out of the country for her own safety. It was believed the best place for the two of them was Canada. Anya was to follow on her own, several weeks later, in order to avoid any connection between a mother and child. That way it would be impossible to prove any heirs. It was very dangerous for any descendants of your family at that time.

"You may already know the rest of the story. The couple, who posed as your mother's parents, was tragically killed in an automobile accident shortly after arriving in Canada. There were no known relatives or next of kin listed on their documents so your mother was placed in a hospital and put up for adoption. I myself knew nothing of her existence until much later. Your grandmother believed that your mother was killed in that accident. She never knew your mother was still alive and lived in Canada. Quel damage!" J.P. put his hands to his eyes to brush away his tears. I felt great compassion for this honorable man; my own true grandfather.

"I am here now, grand pere," I said softly, holding his sun weathered hand. "And we will always have each other now."

The limousine approached an underpass in a mountainside which had a sentry in attendance. Emile spoke a few words to him that I did not understand; I believe they were in Latin; and we were allowed entry. The limousine drove a fair distance through a dark tunnel and then stopped sharply. Ahead of us, the cave like entrance bore a red doorway flanked on either side by lighted torches.

The red door opened to reveal a dimly lit stone staircase at the bottom of which was a passageway. Shivering, I pulled my shawl closer around me. It was not the cold but the unknown that chilled me. As Celine and Serge advanced our group down the passageway, I assessed there must be a river near by from the sound of rushing water through the stone walls. At the end of the passageway, a large monastery door opened to an ante-room and within the room were several more ancient wooden doors.

Celine directed me to enter one of the chambers, where I noticed a gown of white linen hung on a rung on the left wall by the entrance. After instructing me to undress and put on the gown, Celine silently exited the chamber. I removed my clothing but sensed my jewelry should be kept on. Beside the gown was a thin muslin slip, which I put on before donning the overdress.

Just before leaving the chamber, something glowing on the stone wall facing me attracted my attention. There, a tiny grotto, which had been carved into the ancient stone, held a small exquisite statue of the Holy Mother. While kneeling before the statue, I noticed a narrow fountain pool about four feet long protruded out from the stone wall and from a copper spout, located directly beneath the Madonna, water poured forth into a pool.

Taking several deep breaths to quiet my thoughts, I prayed. "Holy Mother. Protect my dear friends here with me, guide us well in our endeavors to bring peace and love to your universe and please bring Jacey home safely."

Keeping my eyes closed, I bowed my head and breathed in and out in the meditative manner that J.P. had showed me. Suddenly my essence was being drawn into the misty cloud again and an energy of great power could be felt to my left. A woman's voice told me to open my eyes. I obeyed but instead of Celine, who was expected, a vision of a woman with long auburn hair and exquisite features stood before me. There was a luminosity about Her that made me think a light had somehow been turned on behind Her but as She moved closer, I realized it was a light that She somehow carried *within* Her.

From one slender hand, She held a rosary of blue stones out to me. As I reached out and took the rosary, a mild electrical energy flowed through my body that both stimulated and awoke my chakras. Motioning to me to hold the crucifix, She spoke the first rites of the rosary, then directed me toward the first bead, eliciting the words for me to recite. I spoke the familiar words.

"Glory be to the Father and to the Son and to the Holy Spirit, as it was in the beginning, is now and ever shall be. World without end. Amen."

I then recited the Hails Mary: "Hail Mary, full of grace, the Lord is with thee. Blessed art thou among women and blessed is the fruit of thy womb, Jesus. Hail Mary, mother of God. Pray for us now and at the hour of our death. Amen."

With a depth and sacredness I did not know I possessed, I prayed the entire rosary with the Lady.

"Now, remove your gown but keep on the undergarment and bathe in my spring water." She directed and pointed to the pool beneath the Madonna.

Obeying Her instructions, I drew off the overdress and stepped down into the fresh mountain water. It was brisk but felt energizing.

The Lady further instructed *"Now bathe in the spring water and drink of my fountain."*

Laying down as flat as possible in the narrow pool; resting my head on the stone edge; I allowed the fountain to wash the water over me. Then, sitting up in the pool, I leaned my head over to the fountainhead and drank from the spout.

"Dress and know that your prayers are answered."

I removed my head from under the fountain and turned to thank Her, but the Lady had left the chamber.

After stepping carefully out of the pool to prevent water from going everywhere, I removed the damp slip and placed it back on the rung. A circle of warm air wafted though the chamber and silently wrapped itself around me, evaporating the tiny droplets of water from my body. There must have been an invisible vent somewhere as none was in sight.

Feeling freshly air-dried, I drew the white linen gown on over my head again, just as a knock on the door broke the silence. It was Celine.

"Come", she motioned.

Following Celine into the ante-room, I observed she had changed into a long satin robe. As she handed me a pair of white slippers for my feet, her attention was drawn to a few remaining droplets of water on the tendrils of my hair.

"You are wet, Angele!" she voiced, touching my hair. "But, how ..?"

"The bath", I replied, bending to slip on the satin footwear.

Celine stared at me curiously. "Bath?"

"The lady who came into the chamber instructed me to remove the gown but not the slip - the undergarment she called it - and bathe in the spring water."

Celine stepped back. "Did she tell you anything else?"

"And drink of my fountain." I completed.

"*My* fountain?" repeated Celine. Her eyes opened wide.

"Yes." I stood up. "And then she said, 'Dress and know that your prayers are answered.' She also did the rosary with me, before the bath."

Celine looked down and drew a deep breath. She linked her arm in mine and spoke softly. "Come. It is time."

With Celine ahead of me, we walked single file down another passageway. The end of the passage led up more steps and then to a doorway which opened to the night. We proceeded down a short hill and turned left where a small procession of candles lit both sides of the path down to the grotto. We seemed to have come from somewhere beneath the church and were on the trail to the grotto of Lourdes.

Tall white candles resting on black cast iron stands lined the downward pathway to the little grotto. The same large gold cross, which I recalled from my dream, was placed at the entry to the grotto.

More candles on cast iron stands were lit all around the area surrounding the little spring where Bernadette first saw her Lady of Lourdes. A group of about a dozen or so people lined the tiny grotto path and as I passed by and viewed them, I could see that all of them were dressed in satin robes of various colors. To my amazement, Jacey's parents were in attendance as were his grandparents. One by one I passed Tom, Maddie, Jack and Kate.

J.P. stood at the centre of the grotto area with his son Emile on one side and Serge on the other.

The evening was still as a deer and the night air encircling the grotto area was cuddled in warmth by the light of the candles.

I felt utterly safe and insulated by an energy of intense power yet also of the most gentle love and compassion.

After making a certain signage before the tall cross, J.P. motioned everyone to be seated. Two wooden benches had been placed to face one another on either side of the spring about ten feet apart. J.P. first read a beautiful scriptural piece in French, then, in English, he advised, "We will wait on the visitation." With that he took us into the meditative breaths.

I flew rapidly to my sanctum this time. Waters that echoed of healing energy spoke over the rocks and stones in the running brook beside me but in my mystical kingdom, I stood atop a mossy bank, soft yet buoyant beneath my white slippers.

Across the brook stood the woman I had seen in the chamber. Again, as before, She wore a simple floor length white dress under a long blue cape. Her azure eyes extended rays of pure sapphire light out to me. As She crossed the brook and came toward me, Her small feet barely touched the guide stones in the water. She stood at the edge of the brook and smiled saying, in Her eloquent melodious voice, *"You have come."*

I felt a presence to my right and turned to see Jacey walking toward me. He wore a long robe of royal blue satin. He came to me and took my hand in his as we faced the Lady by the water.

"Open your eyes", the Lady said simply.

After acquiescing, I found myself once again amongst the group gathered at the grotto. J.P., however, had been joined by another presence beside him.

"Jacey!" I cried out loud. Without speaking, Jacey stepped over to the cross and made the signage that J.P. had made earlier.

A familiar woman's voice spoke my name and, turning to the direction of the grotto, I saw the Lady from the chamber step down from the glass window that covered the little spring.

"You have brought me the star of my crown." She spoke in a very definite tone.

I simply stood and stared at Her. Surprise had fixed me to my spot but instinct dropped me to my knees and bowed my head before Her magnificent glory. Then, She placed Her hand upon my crown and the energy of the cosmos poured through my being like a waterfall.

"Raise your eyes", the Lady beckoned.

Raising my head, my eyes looked up at Her countenance.

"I have come, my Lady, but I know nothing about your star", I said regretfully.

The Lady smiled again, saying, *"You wear the star of my crown … And you carry yet another star for humankind."*

She focused on my stomach as she spoke. *"You have brought both of these to me and both I must take for now. It is necessary. The star will bring balance to your universe and then harmony will come to Earth. It is so sorely out of balance at this time, but I will speak further of this at another time. For now, I will tell you this: I appear before you now, to retrieve the star that once was in the possession of a ruler who was not right for this challenge."*

"The Tsar?" I interjected.

"He was unable to fulfill his destiny. By not doing so, he has left all of humankind in mortal and spiritual danger; an abyss into which once fallen,

would never again regain soul connection with the Most High. Therefore, it must be returned in order to rebalance the world for the next term: What you call 'the millennium'."

With that, the Lady bent over toward me. Placing Her hand to my throat, She easily snapped open the clasp of my pearl neck choker and released the tiny silver egg. Holding the egg in one hand, She lightly twisted it open with the other. As She parted the two halves, a light of indescribable brilliance broke out and rays of hues unseen on this earth kaleidoscoped forth.

The Lady lifted the tiny gemstone, which made up the stars composition, and held it before Her. The tiny gemstone seemed to unfold and grow in Her hand. Radiant wings turned out as a glorious Angel of light raised herself up and stood before us.

The Lady held the gemstone high above Her head and as She did so, it was as if the main light bulb from a set of Christmas tree lights had been screwed in place. Suddenly, twelve stars glowed about Her like a magnificent crown of Angels; Gemstone Angels.

I realized the Lady had now regained Her crown and the Gemstone Angel, which She now held, was its seventh star. Her power to affect earth and humanity would now be restored and Her power, which was Her incredible Love, would now save us.

The Lady bent toward me again and refastened the clasp and egg about my neck.

"There is something else I regret I must also take ... For a time", spoke the Lady in a tone tinged with sorrow. *"But this Light of the World will be returned to you at a later time: At the time of the millennium."*

"You already have a great Light in your life." She smiled. Then, the tone of the Lady's voice changed as She leaned forward and whispered to me. *"You must tell him of your secret, Angelique. To not do so will put him in great danger. His mortality – and immortality – depends upon it. And so does yours."*

In a voice both majestic and compassionate, She continued. *"Let your world's leaders know I will appear and meet them here tomorrow at 7:00 in the evening, for then I will give a message to all people of all nations for all to hear. There are many whose souls are at great risk at this time. These messages are for them as well.*

"Inform the woman know as 'O' in America that I have a special message for her. Tell her my exact words. She will know what to do."

With those words, the Lady drew the sign of the cross on my forehead and stepped back onto the glass covering over the spring. Her energy then slowly faded from the grotto. I turned to Jacey but he had already disappeared.

The luminescent light within the grotto had dimmed with the departure of the Lady, except for a round ball of beautiful golden light glowing in my lower abdomen, which suddenly but painlessly extracted itself from my centre and floated effortlessly up and over to where the Lady had stood. Then, it disappeared as well.

Unexplainably, I felt moisture flow down my thighs. Feeling all earthly energy drain from my body, I weakened and collapsed into my own pool of blood.

"Tell the woman known as 'O'. She will know what to do." The words echoed out through my unconsciousness.

A mist began to form beside me and from its centre came a voice I recognized. It was Jacey. When I spoke his name, the mist cleared and we were once again at the brook where the Lady had gathered us.

"Angele, I came to say goodbye to you, for now; at least, in this lifetime." Jacey smiled as his words floated out to me, although neither his mouth nor countenance made any movement.

"No! Jacey, you can't!" I implored him.

"It's the only way, Angel. The diary must be destroyed. Otherwise the entire planet is in mortal danger and it's Penny's only chance. What could have been for us is gone now too."

He was referring to our child that the Lady, true to Her word, had retrieved from me.

"The child was my purpose for being with you; so I could raise the next Light of the world with you. Now, the dynamics have changed. My existence is not essential any longer. Don't you understand, Angel? There is no one to train."

I stared blankly at his solemn face for a moment before speaking. The Lady was right. He had to know.

Taking Jacey's hand gently in mine, I spoke softly. "Yes, there is."

A quizzical look appeared in Jacey's compasssionate eyes as he tried to comprehend what I was trying to tell him.

I began to speak words to Jacey I thought would never be said, but they poured out of my soul and spirit into his like water from a newly burst dam.

"We have a daughter together." I began. "Her name is Christina. I became pregnant on that last weekend in Montréal but didn't know for sure until it was too late … and you were gone. Then, you married so quickly. …" Tears flowed down my cheeks but I continued.

"That was the reason for my move out west and keeping a location there. Christina was born in Alberta. I stayed there with her until she was five and then enrolled her in a private school to enable me to travel and work to support her.

"You are the only man I have ever been involved with, Jacey." I went on. "You were, and still are, the only man I have ever known and loved and never will I love another man as I have loved you."

Through the sheer will and the power of my spirit, I released to him all of the intensity of feeling held for him all those years and still kept within me, allowing him to feel and see the beauty and the joy of his daughter as she grew from childhood to young woman.

Closing my eyes, I spiritually sent him an image of his daughter with her honey amber colored hair moving and waving like shaped toffee as she glided, for Christina did not just simply walk.

Christina had loved horses as a baby and could ride like an equestrian by the time she was ten years old; an inherited trait. Christina was tall and held no weight on her yet she was a glowing jewel of health. I sent Jacey a moving picture of her sun streaked spine length mane, all one length, which she artlessly brushed off her face and let fall over her shoulders. I showed him the pearl essence of her skin, the permanent blush of health on her high cheekbones and the blaze of her smile from lips that were the color of tender pink rosebuds. Then I let him see those large luminous eyes. Framed with lashes so dense they would never require mascara, their color was a combination of sapphires and emeralds. The world had never seen such eyes and Jacey gasped slightly at their exception.

Then, for the first time, he understood what I had experienced during the time I raised her. He saw my devotion to her and also everything that had to be sacrificed in order to raise her and protect her. Life wasn't easy for me throughout those years. Layoffs and downsizing were the trend at that time and since my major work required me having a residence in Toronto as well, my expenses were high.

The choice to raise Christina on my own had required an extraordinary organization of time and money. I had to work constantly to support my daughter and keep her in a private school at a geographically remote location, which was expensive. On weekends, when I was travelling or working, she boarded at a private riding school so she could pursue her passion. I loved and adored my child and my only regret was not being able to spend more time with her.

In Christina's early years, I faced challenging financial circumstances and work was not always available to me in my field. My reputation was sterling but that was part of the challenge. Due to my experience and the quality of my work, employers knew they would have to pay me adequately. These were the years when all the dollar stores started up and controlled the mass mentality. Basically, the financial scenarios came down to stockholders wanting to see more profit for their shares and the easiest way to show this was by the layoff of employees. Also, youth employment was being pushed as a mandate of the government and employers were allowed certain breaks for hiring students just out of school. The advantage of hiring them was, for the employer, a financial boon in another way: They didn't have to pay them as much. The youth of the country needed jobs. I understood that and had no problem with it. However, I had to demand a certain salary because of my responsibilities with my daughter, but I also could not reveal her existence, sensing that to do so would somehow put her in a vulnerable position. I would protect Christina no matter what I had to do.

So, when times were slow, I typed scripts long into the evenings, took temp jobs in offices doing computer entry, made and sold crafts; including designing and putting together jewelry and selling it at exhibitions and trade fairs. I also designed an ensemble consisting of a simple evening gown, shawl and bag that were quick to put together and flattering for all women.

I wrote a book at this time as well and sold it at whole life trade fairs, offering a personal consultation for a price that included the book and managed to survive, keep Christina boarded in a private school, buy a condo in Toronto and keep an on-going residence in Alberta. When I started publishing my newsletter on the internet and my travel articles brought me some notice, more lucrative contracts came in to write travel articles with a spiritual slant to them. I was the mystic traveler and the time was right for it!

I felt Jacey's heart entwined in mine as his soul silently expressed regret.

"No, Jacey, no regrets, no guilt, no recriminations! I made that decision and took the responsibility for it to protect Christina. It was the Lady who insisted I must tell you. *"To not do so will put him in great danger. His mortality – and immortality – depends upon it. And so does yours."* Her words were repeated to him.

The particles in Jacey's image began to crackle and they would soon break up and begin to dissolve but I knew he had heard and listened to the Lady's words and took heed of them.

"I must go now, Angel", he spoke.

"Jacey! Stay!" I cried and reached out to grab him and hold him to life but I pulled only mist and air into my hands.

While laying on one of the benches by the grotto, my eyes opened again with the words of the Lady filtering over my head and into my brain. *"Tell the woman known as 'O'. She will know what to do."*

Celine bent over me. "Do you wish to go to a hospital?" she asked.

"No. Do you feel I should?" I actually felt surprisingly strong and rested.

"I am a trained naturopathic doctor and have examined you. During your ecstasy you suffered a miscarriage, which you probably know, but everything is surprisingly clean and perfectly intact. It is just like you have started a normal period as there are no traces of pregnancy at all", Celine surmised. "What did you see, Angele?" she inquired.

Sitting up on the bench and pushing aside the blanket that had been put over me, I asked, incredulous." Did you not see *Her*?"

"We saw no *one*, but we did see your neckpiece float in the air and an extraordinarily luminous ball of light fly upward. Look at the sky, Angele. It sits there now!" Celine reported, pointing to the heavens.

Sure enough, high above us, in the constellation we had observed in J.P.'s dining room, a new bright star, glowing with the intensity of a thousand times the wattage of any other star, had taken its place and achieved its complement of twelve. It was indeed for all to see the Star in the Crown.

Remembering the words of the Lady, I relayed the events and messages She had given me and of Her next visit.

"The Lady has told me I must contact the woman in America known as 'O'. She said she, 'O', would know what to do."

Away from the crowd, Serge was preoccupied on a cell phone call. Abruptly, he shut the flap down on the cell phone and ran over to the grotto.

"Monsieur Christopher's airplane has crashed in the Pyrenees. The Cessna collided into the side of a mountain. There is so far no news of any survivors", Serge offered sadly.

Had Jacey decided to become the kamikaze pilot of his own destiny after all?

"I believe he was trying to save his sister", Serge injected, reading my thoughts. Surprisingly, I desired neither to scream nor to cry. 'If it was over, it was over.' The thought came and quieted me.

"Hopefully then, Penny will be released. Let me know when you receive word on this," I replied calmly. Breathing in the fresh mountain air, I continued.

"We must get to work immediately. It would be Jacey's wish and, as he advised, there isn't much time." Engaging into action, I stood up and began giving instructions. "J.P., you must call the president of France and the United States, and of course the Queen of England, and inform them of the Lady's message."

"That is no problem", J.P. affirmed, bowing his head.

"Right. I will require a cell phone and a laptop, maintenant!"After gingerly rising off the stone bench, I began to walk back up the hill from where I had descended. "First, I must change, and then we must all attend to organizing the arrangements for tomorrow's visit - *immediately*."

Mindlessly listening to the footsteps of the group following me, halfway up the hill, J.P.'s voice articulated behind me.

"She is indeed made of the right stuff."

"Hello?" I spoke into the sleepy ear on the other line. It was almost 10:00 P.M. U.S. and the woman known as 'O' normally awoke at 4:00 A.M. for her morning program. I knew this because a 'fan' of mine had sent her a copy of my book a few years ago and she had done a brief interview with me on her show. She told me she had enjoyed my book, "Ordinary Angels", and 'O' was getting into the spring of the Angel well that was occurring at the time.

We had got on well. (Who doesn't like 'O'?) She asked me to keep in touch and mentioned she would like to have me on the show again when I wrote another book. That was about it. Except that a few months later, she had called me in the middle of the night from her home to ask me a question on how to interpret an Angelic dream message. She got my answering service and left a message with her private telephone number. Fortunately I have a bit of a photographic memory for telephone numbers.

"It's Angelica Laird. Sorry for calling at this hour but I have just witnessed some extraordinary events and was instructed by a very high personage to call you." Taking a deep breath, I plunged into the instructions the Lady had given me.

"I have just come from the grotto in Lourdes where Bernadette had her visions of the Holy Mother. The Lady of Lourdes showed Herself to me and told me She would appear there again, for everyone to see, at 7:00 P.M. Easter Monday. She asked for all the world leaders to be informed. Then she said, *"Tell the woman known as 'O'. She will know what to do."*

A silence fell on the other end of the line for several seconds before her reply.

"It was because of a celestial message that I received that gave me the inspiration for a most beloved project of mine. The Lady told you *She* would appear at the grotto in Lourdes at 7:00 P.M. Easter Monday? Appear to everyone?"

"That's right", I affirmed.

"She wants the world to hear *Her* message?" Her voice held a sense of awe yet I sensed this request was not unexpected. Then, as if a light had been switched on, 'O' snapped into action and it was literally All Systems Go!

"I'll get on the telephone right away and arrange for a television crew to set up there a.s.a.p. The best way to do this is to patch feeds to different networks globally. I'll get there as soon as I can. By private jet if I have to. This is one mother's visit I don't want to miss!"

I would ask 'O' at another time why she had agreed so readily to help in this request. All I knew was that absolutely nothing could surprise me at that moment!

"They have found the airplane of Monsieur Christopher in the Pyrenees Mountains madam." Serge spoke from the doorway.

"The Cessna was totally destroyed by the explosion when it hit the mountainside and the ensuing fire burnt everything ... upholstery ... et al... Nothing is recognizable. It's believed the body was consumed by the flames. Only scarred scraps of his boots and belt remain out of the ashes. The rescuers had to put out the fire to get into the airplane, so much of Monsieur Christopher's... uh... remains were washed away, madam."

"I know you're trying to be delicate Serge", I replied. "Thank you for that, but it's alright. I understand perfectly. There's not much left of him, is there? Does his family know? His parents ..?"

"They have been told and are on their way", spoke J.P.

"Weren't they there at the grotto?" I questioned.

"They were. Their true spirit selves were very much there, as you saw", replied J.P.

"I see", I said, comprehending that the souls who made up the upper body of this order were indeed very advanced adepts and could manifest their physical bodies, or at least the essence of them, at will to wherever in the world, and possibly elsewhere in the cosmos, that they desired. I supposed that the ideal of the preserving and the saving of humanity would be inspiration enough in itself to warrant divine support and intervention. Their intentions, to say the least, were of the very highest order.

The situation with Penny was a concern to me. Would she be allowed to return to her normal circumstances now that it was obvious that the diary containing the prophetic messages was totally destroyed?

Then it all became crystalline clear to me. Of course! The Lady knew the diary had to be eliminated as it seemed pre-eminent that it could fall into the wrong hands. The life of another innocent would needlessly be taken; Penny, or perhaps her entire family. So the Lady knew the only way that her messages would not be misused for world domination was to give them Herself, and to give them out to the entire world! That way the domination seekers would hear but so would all the decent and peace loving beings that made up humanity. Expressing Her messages to everyone would certainly nullify the dominators attempts.

The Lady would not be stopped this time. She had likely already been in spiritual communication with the world leaders, so it would be perfectly acceptable to them to receive this invitation. As for 'O'; the Lady had obviously been intending such a media event for her to organize because no one could do it better. More so, no one deserved the honor more to acknowledge to the world that the Feminine Power and Energy had been restored to our planet.

It was true. There truly was a difference in the energy emitting from the ethers of the earth since the constellation of Mary's Crown had been restored. It could literally be felt in the air!

Suddenly, it all made sense to me. Since the beginning of the Twentieth century, the main star had been absent. The era, interestingly enough, begat the beginning of the Industrial Revolution during which time many revolutionary inventions were produced but, one must ask, at what cost?

"Yes, it makes sense, cherie." J.P. advanced toward me, obviously hearing my thoughts. "More so than you can imagine", he continued. "You see, the Crown of Mary represents the symbols of all of the twelve astrological components. In our studies we learn of the true significance of each. For the purpose regarding the Star of the Crown, let me say it represents the sign of Leo."

"The sign of the king or ruler, of course", I interspersed.

"Yes, that is true. However, it is actually the sign of the Sacred Feminine. It of course makes perfect sense that this would be the star entrusted to a great king or leader." J.P. continued. "It is also the sign of the greatest of all gifts of the cosmos. It is the sign of the energy of love and there is no greater energy in all of the universes. With its elimination from the constellation, from the Holy Crown of Mary, which is what this constellation symbolizes, then the feminine energy which includes nurturing, caring, consideration and a myriad of other high ideals, was diminished and seen as less important. In the past this forced the female principle and those representing it, women, to endure unjust subjugation.

"The lack of appreciation that has befallen the feminine gender was meant to have been reestablished at the turn of the Twentieth century. The Romanov family of Nicolas and Alexandra was chosen for this mission because of their piety and devotion to the Holy Spirit. The Empress Alexandra was entrusted as the bearer or holder of the star as she was the feminine principle in the monarchy. That and due to her blood lineage from that of Christ.

"As history relates, their son carried the gene of the Holy Blood from his mother and unfortunately in his case the gene was mutant and hemophiliac. This circumstance left the door open to the pirate priest Rasputin.

"The emperor and empress were beyond reproach. However, the world dominators knew their energy could take over Rasputin. While connected to the royal family, he did nothing but help the little Tsarovich handle his health issue. In his personal life it was a different story.

"He was a womanizer, a drunk, ill mannered and because of his association with the Romanovs, destroyed their reputation, honor and sacredness in the minds and hearts of the highly religious Russian people. Had his connection with the Romanovs not sullied and tarnished their pure essence, the barberry that befell them would not have taken place. Remember, this was Holy Mother Russia.

"The fault of that must fall to the Tsar himself. The Tsarina was blameless of any infamy. The Tsar did not defend her in the proper manner and in so doing allowed her reputation to be sullied and the lives of the entire family to be put in mortal danger. His mind was on war when his attention at home was needed and by the same account on his personal family tragedy when he was required at the front. He was a good and decent man, there was absolutely no denying that, but he was by his own admission not suitable to rule a country; certainly not one of the complexity and enormity of Russia."

"But, in all fairness to Nicolas, the man's intentions were never to harm anyone." I interjected. "He simply wasn't a leader - or much of a soldier either I understand. So what could he have done? He was stuck wasn't he? I mean, having been born to rule and all."

"Well, he had a younger brother, Michael, who was a fit and fine solder. Given a chance, he may have exhibited more of the qualities of an emperor than Nicolas did." J.P. insinuated.

"You mean Nicolas should have abdicated sooner than he did and let the country be ruled by a better man for the job?" I replied. (History records that Michael did rule the country for a very short time before he too was killed.)

"It would have been one solution. That, or correct the frailties within him."

"But if it was not in his nature to be that kind of person how could that have been accomplished?" I questioned.

"Nicolas could have accomplished this by accessing a higher and stronger connection with the cosmos. God, cherie. His wife could do it yet he could not. She could do it with a religion that was not even her own, one she adopted when she married Nicolas. Yet it was she who became the devout one, the one who had the faith and the trust strong enough to pray and save her son. It was HER faith that did that, not Rasputin as people believed."

"Alix berated Nicolas for his weaknesses though, did she not? Perhaps she needed to work with him more." I accessed.

"Ah ... Perhaps. Yet as it turned out, the two of them ruled and the two of them were held responsible. They were punished severely and the very severity of their punishment cleansed their immortal souls."

"So they are purified now? -- Can they help us?" I blazed the question into J.P.'s eyes.

"You mean, can they assist us from their spirit forms? Absolutely!" J.P. countered.

"Then how can we contact them?"

My words came forth with such a force because I had a sense that this family could at last have soul redemption if they could assist in a deed high enough and worthy enough to warrant it. In other words, my sense of inner understanding, which knew far more than 'I' did, sensed that their family 'curse' could be nullified and reversed. This could thereby improve the soul enlightenment of not only their descendants but possibly their entire family connections as well; including the royal family of England.

"It will require some instruction for you first, but I believe that you can do it", affirmed J.P. seriously.

"Then, monsieur", I accepted. "Let the games begin."

Word had not yet come about Penny. I somehow sensed that a spiritual connection with the Tsar and Tsarina was what was required to ensure her safety. An inner understanding informed me that the world dominators, who captured and cut short and circumvented the fate of the last Tsar and his family, were also connected to past, present and possibly future atrocities on earth if they were not stopped.

"We have within our inner libraries exact knowledge of who the principle players of this drama are, cherie", commented Celine.

"Accessing the spirits of the Tsar and Tsarina would enable us to better understand the mind set of these dominators", I attempted to explain to her. "Their spirit motivation: In other words, anticipating their moves before they make them."

"Ah ..." J.P. understood. "You truly are your grandmother's granddaughter." He chuckled. "She too had a very adept mind for tactical maneuvers ... *war games*", he chuckled.

"Yes, I guess it is a war", I agreed. "A spiritual war; one that the Holy Mother, the Lady of Lourdes, is going to do everything within Her power to help us to win." I spoke what I sensed.

It was a feeling like a warrior putting on her armor as I layered on mentally, one by one, what needed to be done and the processes required. Knowing there was wonderful support behind me helped immensely. 'O' would handle the media orchestration beautifully, there was no doubt. J.P. and his connections in incredibly high places would ensure that the second wish of the Lady would be fulfilled.

I felt a responsibility for Penny's safety now that Jacey was gone. How would she handle the reality of his fate, finding it incredulous to acknowledge it myself? First, to be reunited with Jacey after all that time, second to heal our misunderstandings, third for him to hear for the first time about our daughter and finally to lose him forever. I could barely comprehend it and knew putting energy and real thought into it would drive me mad. Fortunately, I was too busy arranging the Lady's telecast and special appearance to allow those thoughts and emotions to travel with me. I would miss Jacey so much. Now, gone forever.

"Forever would be a very long time", I heard myself speak out loud while hanging up the white linen dress in the closet of the guestroom that had been provided for me in the small inn near the holy site.

"Not forever", came a voice, a male voice, from behind me. I turned sharply but found nothing but a simple twin bed and a wall with a print of violet flowers scattered across its wallpaper.

"Jacey?" I queried. There was no response. I waited for several moments, shrugged, then proceeded toward my reflection in the oval mirror above the green painted Provencal dresser. Touching my hand to my face, I observed my freshly washed skin appearing so fair yet not pale, against the background of my black dress. There was the appearance of a glow not unlike the luster of fine pearls. I shone! Illumined golden pink light circled all around me. "The Lady's residue surrounds me like an armor", I thought to myself "Protective and impenetrable; yet sacred."

"You will be given your sword." The voice spoke again.

"What sword?" I asked back directly.

"The sword of the Maid d'Orleans", was the answer.

I gasped at the mirrored reflection behind me. On the wall was a full length print of a young woman wearing a breastplate. Above her head, her arms held a beautifully carved sword that was encircled in unearthly golden light. The portrait was that of Joan of Arc.

"You will soon face mortal danger, Angelica, but you will be covered in the Light and you will not fail."

I stood transfixed and unable to move.

"You will receive the great sword once more. This time, you will be victorious", the voice repeated again. "The Maid is one of your soul incarnations at an earlier time. You have been brought here to complete your divine mission."

The voice did not speak again.

I slept for several hours and awoke at 8:00 A.M. to the sound of the telephone wake up call that had been prearranged.

An inner energy sat me upright in the bed I occupied and seemed to lift my feet to the floor. "It is time." I breathed.

I admired the quality of the white cotton Victorian nightgown provided for me before returning it to hook on the inside door of the salle de bain. Standing under the shower spout, allowing the fresh mountain water to spill over me, I closed my eyes and let myself be caressed by the spirit of fine petals of fragrant wildflowers. The essence of the French milled soap engulfed the molecules of the condensation of the water and lilac and primrose steam enveloped me. I felt covered by protective clouds of heavenly fragrance; their energies and strength permeating my cells and invigorating me for my mission. The Angels seemed to coagulate within me.

Wrapped in the white terrycloth robe, provided by the inn for guests, I walked barefoot back into the compact guest room. My vision was again drawn to the portrait of Saint Joan on the wall by the bed.

The face of the young maid was beautiful beyond description in her radiance and rapture, yet she was unadorned. "Simple but not plain" I assessed. She had beautiful color and lines, like one sculpted out of peach alabaster or some refined opalescent gemstone; pale rose quartz, perhaps.

The longer I surveyed her image, the more fascinating she became. Her eyes were soft and Angelic yet full of purpose, spirit and vision. Her soul light shone pure and brilliant through them as it does with all true saints. Their color was a soft gray but her light shield engendered them with an amber hue. "Similar to mine", I thought. Her hair was straight and though sheered short about the top and sides of her head, was left long in the back. From the front, her head appeared to be encircled by a halo of golden gossamer. Her face was full of light and of a rose gold hue: The color of the Lady.

Peering closer at the portrait, I observed that a chalice was engraved on the handle of the sword she held. The artist was trying to depict a connection of Joan of Arc to the Holy Grail.

A glance at the clock on the bedside table brought my reverie back to my earthly space continuum and a realization that I was required to move smartly! A tray containing a continental breakfast had been placed on the dresser and a shopping bag had been left on the bed while I was in the shower. The note was from Celine and informed me that the bag contained some personal items she felt might be required. An Estee Lauder cosmetic bag held some travel size containers of face moisturizer, cleansing cream, lilac lip gloss, mascara, eye shadow, nail varnish, a small bottle of Mugeot (Lily of the Valley) eau de parfum, deodorant and a small compact. Articles Celine had transported from my tote.

Laid out on the bed was a light weight wool knit turtleneck sweater in navy and matching wool knit culottes. The pants were full legged and must have been ankle length on Celine. They would be mid-calf on me but would give, as Celine knew, the appearance of a three-quarter length skirt. A fresh set of matching navy cotton bra and briefs sat atop the sweater in a pristine white bag lined in white tissue. The bag also contained a fresh pair of navy tights and a silk scarf patterned with lilac blossoms on an ivory background with a navy border. The hues of the scarf would pull the navy outfit together and add some color as would the narrow lilac belt I found beside the scarf. Celine obviously wished me to be coordinated, possibly for the press, but warm as well and she also envisioned the necessity for a polished appearance. Since I was a little girl, it was drilled in to me that first impressions were so important and considering I might be focused upon at any given moment, Celine wanted to ensure my reputation remained intact.

"Well, navy is always very fresh. I can live with this." I thought. She selected my best accent colors as well, I observed as I went through the eye and lip cosmetics and noticed they were in the lilac and lavender tones; very French colors.

"Okay, face!" I addressed myself in the mirror. "It's show time!"

My hair remained in its shower time ponytail as I set about applying the eye cream and moisturizer, then the ivory makeup foundation (always with a damp facial brush for a more polished and longer lasting appearance). Blush for me was never required so none was supplied but the pretty amethyst eye shadow tones would work wonders with the navy suit. A good coat of waterproof mascara on top and bottom lashes (to open up the eyes for the camera) A heather lip liner topped with a lilac lip gloss would finish the face. Celine was right; I needed the color. It felt better too as purple is a highly spiritual color and protective as well.

I dressed myself in the clothing provided and brushed my hair, styling it with a side part, so it would fall loose on my shoulders. The pearl ensemble would add a touch of refinement, so I left the necklace long and put the filagree egg pendant in place but removed the bows from both pendant and earrings. My French nails were still intact but a quick brush of clear polish would preserve them. After repacking my black shoulder bag and including an orange and banana from the fruit bowl on the dresser, I opened one of the foil wrapped cheese packages and spread it upon a croissant for breakfast. The grapes on the vine were delicious as was the fragrant and still hot cafe au lait, which I poured from the insulated pot into a large bowl. (The French prefer a bowl to a cup for their café au lait for some reason.) Well, with all the food groups taken care of; protein, carbohydrates, fat, dairy, fruit, came the feeling of fortification. It felt good to be full but not too full. The North Americans love their huge breakfasts but the Europeans were different that way. Well, I have seldom seen an overweight European in Europe, so this may be a reason for it.

Just as I completed repair work on my lip gloss, a soft knocking on the door interrupted my mind meanderings. It was Serge.

"Madam ... If we go quickly, a helicopter is flying to the site where Monsieur Christopher's plane went down. If you wish, we could ..."

"Oh, yes!" I blurted instantly. "Let's go now!" Somehow I felt that going to the site would enable me to say goodbye to Jacey, which my soul knew was something that had to be done. My only wish was to be able to handle it and not fall apart. If that happened, however, I must be open to that as well.

The grieving process is a very sacred one and emotionally trying but still very necessary to human growth. It also makes for completion. I knew this from my father's death.

I had held up unbelievably well and didn't cry but a few tears after getting the long distance call from my sister about my father's passing. Even during the funeral service I was stalwart. However, when the casket containing my father's remains was born out of the funeral parlor by his brothers and lifted into the hearse for his final ride on earth, I knew it was an episode of my life that would forever be remembered as a poignant vignette of my true reality. One part of my life that had agreed to give me life had returned to its spiritual essence and would never again exist on earth in its same material form. I was in awe of the sacredness of that moment and how it touched my heart and soul.

I realized then of the love bond that had existed between my father and me. He was not a man proficient at expressing his emotions yet at that time and place I fully understood the love and devotion he had felt for me. I was his first born. He had given up his freedom for me.

His inability to express his love until the latter years of his life had twisted him emotionally and he had hurt himself more than anyone by not being able to receive love because he was unable to speak it.

"I love you, daddy!" I cried outside the funeral parlor and collapsed into the arms of my youngest brother as my earthly father's soul readied him for his final spirit walk and returned him to the stars from whence he had come.

The Cessna had collapsed onto a high plateau in the Pyrenees Mountains after its crash. Serge was right about the water mess. It was necessary of course to extinguish the flames, but it washed over and sprayed the ashes in moist clumps in all directions inside the plane, or what remained of it.

The helicopter was able to set down about fifty feet from the accident site and a short climb up a rocky slide led us right to it. Thankfully I had worn my black walking shoes as the stones were sharp and slippery on the ascent to the plateau.

Serge spotted one of Jacey's boots about twenty feet from the airplane and carried it over to me. "It must have blown off in the explosion." Serge offered. It was one of Jacey's prized Tony Lama alligator skin boots, which I had always referred to as his Jewel of the Nile boots after the movie "Raiders of the Lost Ark" was released. How he loved those boots. It was hard to believe he still had them. Come to think of it, he must have changed into them while in the airplane because when he left he was wearing Kodiak hiking boots. It was so like Jacey to change into and want to go down in his 'lucky boots', as he always referred to them.

The steel ribbing was all that remained of his backpack where the diary would have been carried. Bits of molten blue plastic clung to the metal structure of the pack. Only fragments of his brown leather toiletry case and his Remington steel straight razor (he always preferred it for a closer shave) were left intact under the wet ashes and debris. I realized a lot of that dusty ash and debris consisted of Jacey's earthly matter; his personal terra monde. Some bones and a skull had been found by the earlier investigation crew and been carried out for the family.

"Well, that was that", I said to myself while climbing up the mountain to a higher plateau to peruse the scene. This was Jacey's last voyage on earth.

"Funny, though", I said to Serge as he climbed up beside me on the narrow plateau. "I came to say goodbye to Jacey, yet I don't feel him here."

Serge looked past me into the side of the next mountain and spoke softly. "Oh ... he has gone, madam."

Aerial buzzing overhead interrupted our silent prayer for Jacey. Another helicopter was flying in and could be observed heading toward the mountain range.

"The press." informed Serge and quickly steered me back down the hill to our helicopter.

"Vite!" he called to the pilot. Serge spoke something to him in very rapid French and our pilot instructed the other two crew members that they would be picked up at a later time. We ran to the awaiting vehicle. "Keep out of sight, madam", he urged as he assisted me into the backseat of our helicopter.

We accelerated very quickly. The other helicopter was just coming into view. It would be able to see us but not identify us. I slunk back into the corner behind Serge and drew my shawl over my head. Sometimes being a redhead has its drawbacks. We can be a bit too visible at times.

The shiny black helicopter descended and set itself down by the Cessna as our helicopter headed north. It had a strangely ominous energy to it. It must be the paparazzi, I thought and was glad to be flying away.

"Goodbye Jacey", I whispered, looking out of the window. "You are and always will be my one true love."

"We are flying back to the chateau de Monsieur St. Germaine", yelled Serge once the helicopter was high over the mountains and away from the crash site. "Monsieur St. Germaine will be preparing you madam. You may want to meditate or rest and settle your energies as we should be arriving there shortly."

A cloudless azure sky was the backdrop of our morning flight to the chateau of my new found grandfather. I was glad in my heart to again have the opportunity to spend time with this enlightened man. There was so much he could teach me and I was an open and eager pupil. Serge had said he would be 'preparing' me. While stressing about how to prepare myself for his endowment of knowledge upon me, my inner voice suddenly but quietly relayed to me, "Just be."

"Just be?" I queried. "Yes, just be in his presence. What you will need to know you will know, for you already have this knowledge within you, and more. Only open your mind and listen with your heart. Your greatest journey is just beginning. Your new true path begins NOW."

As my eyes focused on the pale sapphire clearness of the horizon, my mind flew back to a remembrance of a similar sky on a flight several years ago after embarking on my new career as an author. The flight to Vancouver was to attend a Whole Life Expo to promote my book. It was January and the start of Chinese New Year and symbolically, a new start for me, having just being confirmed pregnant.

The weather of Vancouver can turn faster than a blink and by the time the aircraft had crossed the Rocky Mountain divide that hems Vancouver, British Columbia, the mist from the ocean had melded with the fog and the rain and it was not unlike entering a heightened state of meditation - or the steam room at my health club.

I've questioned my decision in choosing Toronto as my base over Vancouver so many times. Toronto proved to be a good, if hard training ground, but many times there was the feeling of having stayed too long at the fair. Yet, something still kept me there; part-time at least. Alberta is really where my heart is, mainly for personal reasons. My own family is there and one special family member in particular who is very close to my heart; my beautiful daughter Christina.

It was while attending a cathedral named after Saint Ann (the mother of Mary) that I had my first realization of being with child. In the entrance of the church stand two statues; one of Jesus the Christ and one of Saint Ann and an inscription over each statue (which stand side by side) that reads, "Christi - Anna". While gazing at the gothic style lettering and the two statues, I felt a rush of energy in my stomach and a voice spoke to me saying, "She shall be called Sacred".

Immediately came the knowledge that I would give birth to a girl and decided to call her Christiana, but as I was naming her at her christening, I realized in a retrospective moment that the voice of the Messenger meant exactly what she had said. "She shall be called Sacred". So my beautiful daughter's full name is Christiana Sacre Laird. The meaning is holy or blessed daughter of Christ.

So, in a way, Christina has always lived a double life. At her convent school in Alberta, she is known as Christiana Sacre. When with me, she is Christina Laird.

Christina's brilliant eyes were mentioned earlier but not fully expanded upon. They are sapphire and emerald. One of each; her right eye emerald fire and her left eye a sapphire ocean. But what makes them so extraordinary is that both orbs appear to be lit from behind by an incandescent light and catch you like a bear trap when she focuses on you. Startling yet beautiful beyond description, they are undisputedly the eyes of an angel.

At school, Christina dressed modestly, plain bordering on severe, with no jewelry except for a small gold cross. When not in her school uniform, which she wore most of the time, she was attired in plain wool pullovers or cardigans with jeans and riding boots or plain dress pants, straight styled skirts and 'sensible' shoes of high quality. Her hair was always worn long and she tied it in a low ponytail at the nape of her neck, like I do mine so often. She refused makeup, as did I at her age, and admitted to only a peach lip moisturizer and a small bottle of Diorissimo cologne for her special occasions. Christina wore no nail polish and had never heard of hairspray. Her horses wouldn't care for any of that, would be her reply.

And how Christina could ride! Sitting tall and straight in the saddle, Christina was as at home in a cattle drive on the western range as she was on a show jumper in her equestrian attire. She was so like Jacey in that way. They both possessed that true class, comfortable no matter where they were or with whom and always made everyone around them feel comfortable. My father was like that too.

One of my father's favorite mottos was: "Do unto others as you would have them do unto you". Christina and my father both contained humanitarian souls. Dad was always so generous and helpful to his fellow man. It was such a shame he was taken advantage of due to it. It really wasn't right. He had a family to support, yet a lot of people only saw what they could get from him for themselves. In all fairness though, dad was born to give. He had too. So, perhaps people were placed in his path so that he could. I truly hope he is able to do and be what makes him happy now. I see so much of him in my daughter that it feels like he guides her, perhaps toward a path that he would have liked to have travelled... and may make easier for her somehow.

Yes, this sky was so like the one on that Vancouver flight after being confirmed of being with child. I knew then of being on the brink of a new beginning; a new path in my life was opening and it would never be the same again. I felt the same sensations thrill through me while sitting in the helicopter, suspended over a mountain range, turning its direction and mine toward a new destiny.

Christina remained on my mind as the helicopter executed its way over the leafy treetops surrounding J.P.'s estate. I would have to tell him he had a great granddaughter to carry on the family tradition.

The word 'tradition' carried with it an entirely new message for me now. It was beginning to dawn on me that the genetic and cellular message that my ancestors, descendants and I carried was not merely one of a royal code but also one of a profound and highly enlightened spiritual energy.

"Votre grand mere et votre grand pere son tres formidable, madam", filtered Serge's voice over the helicopter noise. As usual, Serge could pierce through my thought forms as if lifting a blind on a window. I wondered if his talent was a natural or a developed one.

"Both, madam", Serge turned around in his front seat and smiled, looking directly into my eyes. His soulful dark orbs floated in his large eye sockets like two ships on a dark yet moonlit ocean.

I merely blinked slowly back to him and smiled a thought note that read "It's understood". Words were unnecessary. In truth, I did understand *completely*. So many times in my childhood and again in my adulthood as well, my mind would pick up sentences and thought forms around me. It was believed to be such a gift that a media P.R. department hired me due to it. It was called ESP in those days and the executives in the 'Kremlin' just thought it was the greatest thing to have someone in their employment that could look at them and tell them everything from where they were born to the success of the latest pilot program that was in production. Particularly the latter, I'm sure.

After tying my lilac scarf Grace Kelly style to prevent my hair from whipping about maniacally as it had when entering the carriage of the helicopter, I folded up my lavender pashmina and placed it in my shoulder bag. It was a beautiful warm morning and the shawl wouldn't be required.

As Serge helped me alight from the aircraft, I noticed J.P. approaching in our direction. He was dressed casually but elegantly in a navy turtleneck sweater and gray flannel trousers. He was not alone. Celine strode lightly at his side, her petite angular body seeming to float over the paved landing pad.

Celine smiled as she observed my attire, or should I say *her* attire on me.

"Tres chic, ma cherie!" Celine chimed delightfully. As she held out her arms for an embrace, I felt her delicate yet powerful energy flow through me with her welcoming hug.

Celine looked charming and comfortable in an apricot cashmere pullover and chocolate brown dress pants. Her complexion came alive with that color scheme. She wore only simple gold earrings and barely there apricot lip gloss to accessorize. I had yet to see Celine appear anything less than perfect and probably never would. Very understated and very French: That's Celine.

"Everything fits", I smiled, returning the hug.

"Only on you; longer!" Celine laughed, looking up at me.

"I think perhaps shorter!" I chided her, looking down at the trousers which were culottes on me.

"Ah, oui, perhaps ..." Celine acquiesced as we strode over to the house.

J.P. and Serge hovered by the helicopter and exchanged serious conversation. I couldn't hear their words but felt it had something to do with the other helicopter that had landed at Jacey's sacrifice. - Sacrifice! - I heard myself think. Yes. It was a sacrifice. And the press arriving in the other aircraft were likely vultures come to feed on the remains. Well, they would have none this time. Not a morsel for scandal would they be fed. I would not allow it!

"Vite!" J.P. shouted and signaled to the helicopter pilot to depart immediately.

"So as not to be seen here in case the ... uh ... paparazzi... decide to follow us", explained Serge as he ran toward Celine and me.

J.P. caught up to us. "Come. Frederique has prepared cafe for us on the backyard patio."

Chapter 2 - "The Secret Garden"

I supped hungrily on the freshly baked croissant and huge whole strawberries that Frederique had set out. The brioche and apple cake looked succulent but bypassed them both and helped myself to more cafe au lait instead. I was absolutely in love with the manner in which the French prepared their coffee and confess to not being able to get enough of it. Somehow cafe au lait never tasted the same anywhere else as it did in France. Perhaps, like many of their delicious table wines, it did not 'travel well'.

Frederique poured me a glass of iced lemon water from a decorative porcelain pitcher that appeared to be an antique, as did the Battenberg lace tablecloth that covered the white cast iron patio table.

"The lemon water is to refresh the senses and also to counteract the affects of the caffeine." Frederique explained. "It acts as a clearing device", he continued as he and J.P. exchanged a glance.

While gratefully accepting the refreshing drink, I imagined this fresh mountain water was what the taste of morning dew would be akin to.

"Would you allow me the honor of showing you my garden?" J.P. smiled and held out his hand to me.

"The honor would be entirely mine." I accepted and reached out to retrieve my water glass from the table.

"You may take this with you. It is a warm day." J.P. signaled to Frederique to refill my glass.

J.P. placed his hand under my elbow as we departed the table. It was a courtly gesture from a more gentile time but it was also a practical one as he used this courtesy to also steer me toward the stone path leading to what I was later to realize was J.P.' s Secret Garden.

"I apologize that it is too early in the year for the garden to show her full majesty. Yet, you will still be able to see examples of what I can only describe as un-earthly earthly beauty."

"You need not apologize, grand pere", I said softly. "That would be to apologize for the season ... for which there is no apology necessary."

"You are so right, ma cherie", smiled J.P. "Spring, or au printemps as we French call her, has a beauty that is indescribably magical ... As you will soon experience", J.P. added with a soft wink.

"Oh, there are fairies at the bottom of my garden", I sang jokingly.

"Ah, possible!" J.P. counteracted.

Tall, majestic cedar trees lined both sides of the path and extended their boughs out to touch us as familiarly as a handshake, as we tread the sun streaked stones down a tunnel of cedar arms.

We walked a lengthy path until we came to what appeared to be a cedar wall. We seemed to be enclosed but J.P., hand still under my elbow, steered me to turn to the right. As we turned in that direction, I realized the wall of cedar was an optical illusion. A path bore off to the right but was not observable until you were actually at the turn off. We continued strolling in silence another fifty feet toward another cedar wall. This time I was prepared and watched for the break which occurred as a turn to the left this time.

"Are we travelling through a maze, grand pere?" I asked.

"Always, cherie", he smiled. "Life is a maze. Many times as we come to what we believe to be an end of one road is actually only the beginning of another."

"Or a new direction upon the same path", I offered.

"Oui, cherie. You make observations quickly yet thoughtfully." J.P. spoke softly to himself.

"It is important to understand that it is our decisions that make the new directions on our pathways. The turnoffs, or new directions, on our path do not really exist until we consciously - or unconsciously - make the decision to change. Then they just appear before us as if by magic.

Yet, it is not magical. It is the magic of our own making. We create our new paths. We create them by what we desire to have in our lives. It is our desire that creates the manifestation of our dreams. The stronger our dreams, the greater their reality becomes in our lives.

"The secret of our life, Angelique, is that our life is but a dream. And we can create in our dream any kind of life that we desire."

"I understand what you are saying, grand pere. Yet it is difficult to understand why so many people would chose to live the lives they do. I mean, the poverty and the hostility that exists in so many lives cannot be a conscious choice, can it?"

"I did not say it was always a conscious choice." J.P. executed knowingly.

"So (theirs) is an unconscious or subconscious choice, then?"

"Oui. Because so many people, cherie, are not truly awake, they live in a dream of unfulfilled reality that they have the power to change at any time yet do not know it."

"How can we awaken, then?" I asked, fascinated by what I was hearing.

"Simply; by making the decision to awaken!" J.P. expounded.

"Then", I pondered, deeply in thought. "In making the decision to awaken, we make the choice to take a different path."

Suddenly, I had realization of silence surrounding me and perceived that, while into my own reverie, I had walked ahead of J.P.

"Grand pere …?" My voice called out. Silence herself enveloped me, making me became somewhat nervous. The crackling of the brittle dry cedars on the forest floor echoed my uneasiness. I turned to the left and then the right, to behind me and before me. In all directions there appeared to be cedar walls and I seemed to be blocked in and surrounded by immoveable objects.

After looking behind me once more, I realized there was no point in turning back. Ahead of me, the way of the future, was not clear and not open to me as yet but I sensed that a path could be taken that would lead me in the direction I needed to go and take me around the block that I could not see through; yet was right in front of me, although not perceivable.

I knew that what was needed for me to do at this time was to go *around* the issue not yet fully understood. However, I also wanted to awaken and understand how to create in my life and live the dreams desired.

My eyes could not see any clearing or open path whatever direction I looked. Although turning round and round a half dozen times, it was futile. I was not yet 'awake' to it.

Past images of thoughts and unrealized dreams and ambitions started to filter across my mind like an uncut film of disjointed scenes that although separate, still formed a whole movie.

Lowering myself softly to the cedar carpet, I folded my knees under me and sat on my calves. Then, a sharp ache entered my solar plexus as though a swift knife was tearing through my flesh and I knew that my life had been a series of unfulfilled dreams. The dreams were strong and real yet would come to a certain point and then something would occur so that they couldn't quite happen. It was a pattern. Everything would seem to be going well and then something unexpected would get in the way and my dreams would dissipate.

Scenes of my life ran before my mind. There was Jacey and me, so happy in Montreal and then, as I watched the 'movie', a grayish mist seemed to appear over us and when it was gone, so was Jacey and I was left sitting alone in the airport cafe.

Another scenario appeared: I was negotiating with a producer at the television station where I was employed, presenting a proposal for a musical variety series. The mist moved in and covered us. When it dissolved, I was alone in my apartment, sitting in front of my television set watching in numb horror and amazement as 'my' program premiered before my eyes, only with that producer's name on the credits.

Again, a management job I had been contracted to do for the government - and done successfully for two years - was finally posted. This same gray mist moved in and surrounded me and I saw myself open the letter at my desk that read that not only was I *not* the successful candidate for the position but that my contract would be terminated at the end of the month.

Then the worst blow of all: Jacey and me at La Gavroche, in love and together again after so long. The mist of fate entered again and I saw myself walking around the site of his airplane crash.

Finally, the movie stopped and as my eyes opened, I felt the tears of regret and frustrated yesterdays flowing down my face.

"No!" My voice echoed out. "No more!" I sobbed out loud in a primordial utterance. "This ... barrier ... to my happiness and dreams has to stop. I can't take anymore disappointments!!" Crying out loudly to the forest wall, I sobbed uncontrollably for several minutes.

When the tears ended, I found myself lying face down on the cedar leaves that blanketed the path. Sitting up and leaning upon my hands, I strained my eyes to view the sunlight that streamed from the top of the cedars in front of me. The golden glow drew me in and enveloped my being. Sitting in its warmth and letting its energy course through me, I closed my eyes and with all the desire I possessed, spoke out to the forest.

"Give me a new life." My words came out slowly and distinctly. "I want a new life of realized dreams and fulfillment and I want it ... NOW!!"

Silence continued to envelop me as I sat on the cedar boughs, looking up at the golden light. Feeling a sensation like warm oil being poured over me, my disharmony suddenly vanished, leaving me balanced and calm. After a few moments, something behind the cedars began pulling my attention to my right. Still bathed in the golden light, I stood up and walked toward the direction I was drawn.

I entered a quiet circular clearing that was infused with a crystalline glow. Realizing I was alone and without any idea of where the path was going without J.P.'s guidance, I also somehow possessed the knowledge that this was something I had to do alone. After all it was my path; my chosen direction. But what had I really chosen?

"You asked for a new life, didn't you?" his voice said. Unsure at first if this was my inner voice or one that was actually addressing me, I peered deeper into the light infused clearing and perceived a male figure in white, just faintly visible against the misty backdrop.

"Yes, I did ask for a new life." My eyes squinted in order to visualize my new acquaintance better. "But I have no idea how to go about achieving it."

"First of all, before we can go about achieving or receiving what we want, we must establish just what 'it' is", the figure responded.

What he was saying was true and it was not a new concept for me, yet until that moment the realization had not occurred to me that what 'it' was had not been truly established in a concise and viable manner in my mind. I now understood that this was the lesson and here was the test.

"I want a life of fulfilled dreams", I spoke out into the misty clearing.

"Then we must first create your dreams", came the answer from within the misty veil.

"How do ... we ... do that?" I questioned.

"Begin with this", the figure replied and his arm produced a glowing silver sword which he held it in front of him.

"This is the Sword of Truth" he announced. "It is from this place, in the presence of the Spirit of Truth where your dreams, your future realities, must first be established in order for them to take form."

I studied the Sword of Truth in the light. It was an unadorned sword, plain by most standards, but beautiful in its sheer brilliance and elegant simplicity.

"Visualize the sword and take it within you", the voice pronounced.

At first I thought that the phrasing was odd. Or off. Didn't he really mean 'with me'?

I focused my gaze upon the shimmering object that the figure held out before him. His strong fingers clasped the sword by the blade just under the handle and he produced it outstretched, like a cross, before him.

Standing in the open clearing, I memorized the appearance of the sword and held its vision in my mind until it was emblazoned there like a crest. Closing my eyes to affix the vision even more, energy of what could only described as unearthly, encompassed my being. Upon opening my eyes, the Sword of Truth had enlarged itself and projected itself all around me, like a hologram, with me at its center. I stood within its seven foot form and, as if by instinct, spread my arms out at exactly the point where the body of the sword crossed the handle.

As a circle of light of the purest white enveloped the sword and me at its midst, I stood in a rapture with my head upturned to the source of the Light.

Once again I found myself back in my body, lying on the soft cedar floor, blinking at the sunlight shredding its way through the high bough into my gaze. After first rolling to one side and resting on one elbow, lifting my body into a sitting position, I felt light but not lightheaded; full of light more than anything.

I focused my memory to return to its last conscious recollection and, as if viewing myself at a distance, my mind showed me a vision of this great Sword of Truth holding me encased within it and, rather than silver or steel, the sword appeared to be comprised entirely of crystal. I witnessed my own rapture and saw myself stare unblinking into the great Light surrounding me, knowing that I was looking into the face of God.

Suddenly, the crystal sword appeared to shatter and decompose. As its form fragmented, it became smaller and smaller and dissolved like diamond dust into my solar plexus. The impact felled me backward onto the ground.

Then the Sword of Truth rose out of the dust it had become and once again took form over my heart. I viewed, in stunned amazement, as the sword, which had returned to its original crystalline form, hovered over my chest and slowly pierced through my breast, then plunged itself into my heart .. Forever.

Had the sword killed me? Was I dead?

I stood up and looked around me. Warm sunlight filled the clearing like a mist. The tall cedar trees enclosing the clearing held a light within their leafy boughs that resembled emeralds and diamonds as they shot the rays of the sun out into the space surrounding me. This place held a certain light that was like a mist or dense fog and encircled me like a warm milk bath. Was this heaven?

"Not exactly… You are in a place out of mind: A time space continuum. You are not to be afraid as you are here for a reason." This voice was a feminine one, comforting, reassuring and familiar.

Staring deeper into the light mist, I ascertained another figure. She wore a white gown with a blue cape. It was the Lady!

She held something in her hands at the position of Her heart. Then, She did a curious gesture. The Lady lifted the object to her lips and kissed it lightly. Holding Her arms outstretched before Her and still carrying the vessel in Her hands, She bade me come closer.

I stepped through the light infused mist, my feet feeling the tender moss beneath me, stopped at approximately five feet in front of Her and perceived the object. It was a silver chalice, quite large and beautifully carved with lovely swirled handles on either side.

"This is the Chalice of Life. You must carry this within you in order to manifest your dreams and give them strength and life."

Looking into the Lady's soft familiar eyes, I knew that she spoke the truth.

"You now hold the Sword of Truth within you. This will allow you the clarity to create your dreams from the fabric of what is good and pure and righteous for your world. The Chalice holds the elixir of Life. Drink from it."

Without hesitation, I extended forth my arms and lifted the silver cup out of the Lady's hands. Holding the Chalice of Life reverently before me and feeling its sacredness flow through my fingers like the lightest of electric currents, I did not need to look at the liquid to know it was golden.

Upon lifting the Chalice to my lips and drinking from it, the aroma startled my senses with its fragrant emissions. It was like drinking Spring, Summer, then Autumn and Winter, all at the same time.

The Lady bade me *"Drink it all."*

I supped back the scent of flowers and sun, herbs and nuts; maple syrup and honey, snowflakes, pine and cedar: An infusion of nature was beneath my nose and flowing down my throat! It was a flavor sensation I had not even imagined existed and knew I would quest for the taste of this nectar again. This was the Ambrosia of Life!

"Take the Chalice within you as well", the Lady spoke again.

Still feeling the tingling sensation in my hands of the electric current from the cup, I allowed it to have command of me and gave the Chalice permission to become part of me.

Immediately after doing this, the Chalice magnified itself until it enveloped me and I felt a part of its sacred content.

While looking into the Lady's eyes; tender and healing as a mystic ocean; I heard a sharp crack, like a gun firing off, accompanied by a sensation of something exploding in my heart.

My eyes opened to the bright sunlight, directly overhead in the middle of the sky. Lying on the soft moss, although feeling no pain, my last conscious thought was that I had been shot. I continued to lie on the soft ground and meditated for a few moments on my last spiritual recollection: Standing before the luminous Lady, I was enclosed within a vast crystal goblet. Unexpectedly, a great ray of light beamed itself at the crystal centre with such a force that the Chalice shattered with a sharp crack. The ray of light was focused directly at my heart and as the cup shattered it exploded itself into my heart chakra. The feeling of its strength of purpose, its Life passion, still remains within my heart.

"It's almost time for you to go", spoke a gentle male voice.

I sat up and turned around to see a tall, slim male figure with shoulder length reddish brown hair, wearing a long ivory toned woven robe, fitted with a sash at the waist. He stood where the Lady had been, which I could now make out was in front of a lovely cedar grove. He was about twenty feet away and as he walked toward me, I observed that he was barefoot.

He stood before me, smiling broadly through his reddish beard. He bent and kneeled on one knee, reached out tenderly with his right hand and freed a small cedar palm from my hair.

The sun was directly behind him and he was flooded with golden light all about him, so much so that it was almost blinding to look at the backdrop. Yet, while looking up into his face I felt nothing but softness and calm caressing my eyes.

The man (or whatever he was) kneeling before me had one of those striking faces, almost startling really. It wasn't because he was handsome; although he certainly was; it was because the features of his countenance projected energy of such kindness and mercy it took me quite by surprise.

When he settled his eyes on my face, I was unable to move from my spot, so empathetic was his gaze. The color of his eyes was unusual; not green and not gray but somewhere in between. They were large eyes with full lids and long lashes. "Beautiful eyes overflowing with love", I thought to myself.

"It is you who embodies love, Angelique. Your name means 'angelic one' for that is what you are. You came to earth to be one of Gods sacred messengers. That is your destiny and always has been, throughout all of your incarnations."

"But", I protested, "I do not know what messages I am to bring!"

"The messages you are to bring are what humanity needs to hear most at this time and in the time soon coming."

He became very serious at this point and sat down beside me. Taking my hand in his, he continued to speak more intensely.

"After the millennium occurs, it will not be an easy time. Havoc and uncertainty will occur across this planet. Technology will have advanced past the point where the human mind will be able to comprehend it all. Your electronic media systems will begin to become confused and malfunction with misinformation ensuing on a global level. This will cause panic and mistrust. Also, the environment will be overwhelmed with emissions it cannot handle and nature will take on a mission to clear and cleanse the earth of the toxins that ail her."

"You are right", I agreed. "Something does have to be done, but all this sounds so frightening."

"Yes, it will be frightening and horrific for many but you must understand and try to make others understand that what is to happen will be a positive action for the planet; a purging of her demons, mostly manmade ones. When it is done and the environmental catastrophes have settled, it will be a new and better world for the future."

"Will there be a Noah's Ark for the survivors?" I asked, hesitatingly.

The gentle man was silent and pensive before he spoke again.

"Those soul individuals who are strong in faith and are not shaken when these supernatural and beyond reason events occur will survive and carry on a new vibration and energy on earth. That is how the intention has been programmed."

"Has God selected who is to go?"

"Those who will not listen will not survive."

"Is there anything that can be done?" I asked.

"Angelique", he began, his extraordinary eyes engulfing and transfixing me. "There are those on your earth who are souls that have chosen to betray and manipulate their own species for reasons of power and greed. They were there when I walked the earth and even long before then. I cannot relay a full explanation to you at this time, but these soul creatures are not of the earth's evolution."

"Aliens, you mean?"

"They are a highly evolved species of life on many levels and originally propagated with the humanoid species of this planet as an experiment of sorts to serve their own needs."

"We were designed to be... sort of... like slaves, then..." I perceived.

"Yes, sort of, like slaves. Then, when the circumstance humans were designed for was over, they left the planet. But not without leaving descendants behind to be left in control of their dynasty, should they choose to return."

"And... Will they return here?" I asked somewhat terrified.

"They will. However, you are not to be afraid Angelique, nor are the rest of the earthlings. For when they return, so will I."

He stood up as he continued. "My Father, who is many times more powerful than these alien nations and has at his disposal mightier armies than could ever be imagined, has promised to send me back when the time arrives. Only this time it will not be the lamb that will be slaughtered."

He spoke with strength and conviction but not with vengeance or malice in his tone. His words felt firm, just and reassuring. The tall, gentle man then put his right hand into his sash and pulled out something to hand to me.

"My mother asked me to give you this", he spoke sweetly. "She said you would know what it meant. You are to carry this as a symbol within your heart. It is *this* energy that you must utilize to express understanding through your messages to the world. It will protect you."

As he cupped my hands over his gift to me, then covered my hands with his, I felt a blessing of extraordinary grace flow through my being and closed my eyes in rapture.

Upon opening my eyes, I saw the gentle man walking away from me and disappear back into the misty grove. The object he had left me lay in my lap. It was a rose. While picking up the beautiful stem, the vision of his extraordinary hands returned to me; long fingers on porcelain skin, each one with an oval scar on the wrist where it connected to the palm.

Chapter 3 – "Break The Arrow"

"Angelique!" A male voice called out.

"Oh, ma cherie, I do apologize." J.P. appeared from behind the cedar wall and trotted over to me, concern gracing his face. He was so agile for a man of his age, lean but muscular and very fit.

"I had thought you were behind me when I turned at the cedar wall." He bent down to help me stand up, his hands clasping gently but firmly under my armpits from the front. He proceeded to lift me up onto my feet like one would a little girl.

"Did you fall, cherie? Were you hurt?" he asked as he surveyed me for bruises and pulled the cedar leaves from my clothes and hair as the tall man had done.

"I'm fine. I must drifted off to sleep for a time... and dreamt the most extraordinary events, grand pere." I admitted while brushing the remaining cedar particles from my clothing.

J.P. peered at me pensively. "Oui. Understood, cherie. People have been known to have 'extraordinary' dreams in this garden."

He took my arm to steer me toward the cedar wall opening when he stopped sharply and bent down to retrieve something on the ground.

"I wonder where this came from", J.P. said half to himself as he held the rose between his fingers.

"There are no roses in this part of the garden." He looked at the exquisite bloom quizzically, then shrugged his shoulders in the typical French manner, bowed and offered the rose to me. He then led me past the cedar wall and back onto the garden path.

As we wandered along the path, which was shaded and cooled by the tall cedars, I pondered just how much of my visionary adventure to relate to him. Intuition told me to keep my own counsel but there were answers required in order for me to fully understand my experiences.

"What you need to know will be revealed to you in time", J.P. responded.

J.P.'s voice continued, almost in a whisper. "You have been through a great deal in your life, cherie", J.P. expressed further. "In many ways, not so different from your grand mere's, as the two of you are cut from the same cloth." J.P. patted my hand sympathetically.

"Your relationship with your father was a trifle… remote?" He enquired.

It was true. I hadn't known my father very well; a fact that troubled me tremendously after his death a few years ago. I had wanted to be closer to him but he was a man of his generation; stoic, holding his emotions inward, unless he was drinking and then he became embarrassingly sentimental both to himself and others. He took good care of his family but he was rather remote to us and found it more comfortable to express himself to his brother and sisters.

He was particularly strict with me, not allowing me to play with many of the neighborhood children or even leave the sanctuary of our huge yard. When school was out, he would take me to my grandparents or my uncle's farm. I would have preferred to have spent holidays with my friends and actually in later years felt this lack of time for making friends halted my social development. It did help to make me very independent however and fortunately Jacey and his family became like my surrogate family when I moved out east to Toronto to attend university.

"He was simply trying to protect you, Angele", J.P. whispered so softly, as if speaking to the child within me.

My eyes began to overflow with the tears of a sensitive young girl who only wanted the warmth of parental love.

Visions of past memories flooded into my consciousness of being awoken on different occasions in the middle of the night and dressed in the cold and dark to drive out to my uncle's farm. Arriving at just past dawn we were always offered an early breakfast of fresh eggs, uncured bacon, newly baked egg bread and steaming hot coffee that was the best in the world. Brewed from newly drawn well water, it was so sweet to the taste that even as a child of ten I could drink that coffee black.

Actually, I loved those impromptu 'long weekends' in the country, sleeping upstairs in the soft down filled quilts, three children to a bed. (My aunt and uncle had five children of their own.) Now, recalling those visits, I began to wonder if my father didn't have an emergency agenda in making them. Did he know of my mother's heritage? Was there imminent danger to my welfare, being the eldest? And then, there was his drinking and the secret whispering of the aunts, his sisters, when they didn't know I could hear. The bedrooms upstairs were like a sound tunnel to the kitchen below.

"It's (the drinking) because of Marian. He can't handle the pressure", Aunt Amelia would say.

"It's just Marian's upbringing. She was the youngest (child) and didn't have the training in raising a family. Her mother was older when she was adopted and it was their housekeeper who mostly brought up Marian. So she just needed a little help early on in the marriage. The poor girl wasn't even taught how to cook let alone bake and keep a proper house", engendered Aunt Nancy who was always supportive of my mother.

"It's the other circumstance that he's concerned about", Aunt Marie added darkly. "Especially for Angelica."

Now the words began to make sense and take on a whole new meaning. Did everyone in the family know of this heritage except for us children? I looked up into J.P.'s eyes, which were the color of my Christina's, and felt the words that went unspoken: Apparently so.

Observing J.P.'s eyes reminded me of another with a similar green cast to them. As we continued walking, I commented to J.P.

"It's interesting that, according to the records of your order (J.P. had given me carte blanche access to his library), Mary, Jesus' mother, had auburn hair and blue eyes ..."

"Oui ... Ah ... Rather a greenish blue, similar to turquoise."

"Um hm", I responded, and continued. "Yet, through all the previous reading I have ever done, the Jews were always described as a dark race of people."

"Oui ... They are", offered J.P.

"And in any of the research or scriptures I've ever read, Jesus resembled his mother. Looked exactly like her", I continued.

"Oui. Very much", agreed J.P. reverently.

"Well..." I expressed in exasperation. "If the Jewish people are a dark featured race... How is it that Jesus was light haired and had fair eyes?"

A voice from behind us summoned our attention. It was Serge.

"Oh, that is very simple, madam. Jesus was not a Jew."

That revelation of the Christ so astounded me that I did not even remember my manners to greet Serge and only blurted out a response. "What?"

"Ah, indeed he was blasphemous to the Jewish faith, but it was because he was not Jewish by nationality that he was crucified by them." Serge walked briskly up the path until he was beside me, on my left.

"Not Jewish - by nationality... Meaning...?" I postured.

"Meaning, madam, that although his family was of a different extraction, as were many people that populated the areas of Israel at the time, he was brought up with and did practice the Jewish traditions and religious customs of the day. To not do so would have caused his family considerable hardships. Many other cultures in that land area adopted the Jewish traditions to fit in and assimilate as well. In our records it relates he was actually of an Indo-European heritage."

Given some thought, it actually made perfect sense as the Sanhedrin and Herod himself seemed to have had few or no reservations in crucifying Jesus. It would stand to reason that this was so if he was not one of their own!

The atmosphere grew quiet in the serene garden as we continued. The birds became silent and the soft breeze from the mountains seemed to still before us as if gods were in their presence.

"It will soon be time for another test of your faith, Angelique", spoke J.P.

Then, as if in slow motion, J.P. on my right took his arm from under mine and moved quickly away; just as Serge on my left jumped and moved further in that direction. At once confused and terrified, I looked from my right to my left, then directly in front of me. A silver tipped arrow shot out from across the lake and was aimed right toward me!

"Break the arrow!" shouted Serge.

"Break the arrow!" I thought. "Are you mad? With what?"

"Break the arrow with your shield", issued the voice of J.P. on my right.

"What shield?" I had no shield!

"The one you carry *within* you. And have always carried within you", reassured J.P.

Seconds seemed to turn into surreal minutes in surreal time. An unbelievably long space of time seemed to hang in that garden as I collected myself and concentrated hard on where my shield would be.

Reflecting upon the love that was at the core of my centre, I took a deep breath and collected all the love energy from the embodiment of all the lives my soul had ever experienced and shifted it toward my heart chakra.

The arrow's direction was headed toward my neck area. In an instant that felt like an hour, I breathed in deeply and meditated to shift my shield up higher to protect my throat. From somewhere came the knowledge that time was not important and I had plenty of it and could quicken or hasten it as needed.

My last recollected sound was like that of a bird about to take flight. Then, as my body fell to the ground, my spirit self rose up and out of me and I saw a vision of the beautiful shining silver sphere emerge suspended in the air before me by a pair of wings made of golden gossamer light.

Patterned on the shield was the magnificent Sword of Truth; its blade pointing downward, which I recognized intuitively as the position of Peace. Sitting in the centre of the sword's handle was the lovely Chalice of Love with twelve beautifully brilliant gemstones encircling it.

Where had the shield come from? Why, from within me, of course! Although I had *felt* the shield many times in my life, this was the first time I had ever actually *seen* it. When it did appear before me, there was instant recognition.

"Claim it, Angelique!" The words were from J.P.

"Claim it?"

"Claim it for your own. And remember it. Your very life in the future may depend upon it." J.P. responded emphatically.

The arrow connected with the shield at my throat chakra. As it did so, I could hear a springing noise - and that is exactly what it sounded like; a bedspring that had been pulled and resounded.

It is believed that the chakras are like spirals. At the moment the arrow hit my throat chakra, it struck a point that sent a reverberation into motion and an explosion of turquoise light emitted from my throat into the air around me. The impact sent me tumbling backward and although I felt a slight sting, there was no pain as the arrow stuck me with its silver tip.

It did strike me, I realized, and it should have run me through, yet it did not.

At the exact time of impact, there was a loud cracking noise and the arrow snapped and broke in two in mid air, before falling to the ground amid a starburst display of turquoise, blue and green light.

All of this action occurred in slow motion. My right hand moved a fraction at a time to my throat and I felt a dent where the silver tip had connected. Knocked off my feet, my mouth opened involuntarily and I fell hard on my haunches.

The sound that issued form my mouth as I hit the cedar floor echoed forth again and again until it filled the hemisphere about me with a veritable light show of color.

The 'sound', for there was no other description for it, resonated before me with the symphony of the spheres and danced ballerinas of light into explosions of stardust and patterns of imagery from a cosmic artist of unbelievable thought forms of beauty and magic.

The music corresponding to these thought forms of luxurious etheric light were performed by an orchestra of instruments born of the nature of the universe. I realized then that the rainbow had a voice, that rain could sing, that flowers laughed as they grew and that the stars of our galaxy were cornerstones of light by which we could find our way as we travelled within: For as above so below and as within so without. Listening to them open their voices, I knew they carried in them, as I did within me, the knowledge and the wisdom of the energy we call Life. I sat back and watched the exquisite performance before me, feeling like the magician's apprentice in Disney's "Fantasia".

My being observed a musical ballet of creation and manifestation, as violet light forms of insightful ideas turned to and fro and became emerald with growth and nurturing from the silver and white energy (of abundance and purity) that encircled them. The forms gathered particles from the air and added them to their spheres until they became myriads of color and shapes. At the finale, the forms all climaxed together and imploded into one enormous golden star engulfed in pure white light. This bright and shining star then moved its light into my own consciousness and entered my heart in a crescendo of the music of the cosmos.

It was at that moment that the greatest revelation of my life was revealed to me: It was *my* own thought forms that had been released to connect with the universal force to create and manifest *my* star, *my* dreams, all in one. The music that accompanied it was mine as well.

My throat chakra had been opened; the chakra of communication and expression and had revealed to me (my conscious mind) what could be created and how to create it. These symbols, when imaged, would trigger signal points within me and when opened, enable me to manifest my desires. To make them form I would first have to express them. *"Say the word, claim the word"*, echoed the phrase in my mind.

"Claim it for your own and remember it", J.P.'s words resonated back to me. Then the other more ominous message, "For your very life may depend upon it."

Chapter 4 ~ "The Lady of the Lake"

Two pair of strong arms on either side of me helped me to my feet. I recognized them immediately.

"Well, you two certainly know when to get out of the way", I remarked, only half joking. I could have been in real trouble there if my instincts of self-preservation had not clicked in.

"We had total confidence that madam would rise to the occasion", Serge smiled lightly, his eyes shining with what might be perceived as admiration.

"Ah oui, you have done well", spoke J.P. with soft pride. I was, after all, his granddaughter. "I believe you are receiving a little extra help also", he continued. "We prefer to call it 'divine guidance'."

"Ah, oui", interjected Serge. "The Angels, they are with her." He shrugged matter of factly.

"Yes." I spoke hesitatingly, feeling the indentation at my larynx. "Well, I am truly grateful for whatever got in the way of me and that arrow!"

"Come, cherie", said J.P., taking me by the arm again. "Sit by the lake for a bit. It will soothe your nerves. It is also quite beautiful down there", he smiled as he led me forward to a small bank peppered with friendly waving wildflowers.

An ancient stone bench rested near the skirt of the lake. Sitting upon the warm stone instantly reenergized me. The sun had worked its magical process of light and energy to heat and also to charge the stone bench with strength and power. It was understandable why the Egyptians revered the sun and held this star to be so sacred.

As my spine leaned into the curve of the stone relic, my body relaxed and I began to enjoy the panorama of nature that encompassed me in this garden of light and fauna. The sun pirouetted fairies of light across the surface of Lac de la Breyeres and reflected the violet hue of the heather plants that surrounded the lake; growing so high in some places they appeared to be trees.

After closing my eyes and reveling in the joy of the moment, I could hear J.P.'s soothing tones behind me:

"Breathe in and out slowly with no disturbance in the flow and allow your body to balance and return to harmony."

J.P.'s voice had a hypnotic affect upon me and my mind started to float in accordance with his words and directions.

The light breeze emitting from the nearby mountain range joined the lake's choir in a harmonious symphony and played on for the sheer joy of being the wind and free and able to accompany the lyrics the lake offered up.

"Hear me, and bend with me.
Flow as a stream
As to an ocean joins
And become a link
In the evolution of Time.

I am your mistress
Here to guide you.
Leave aside the earthly plan
And experience the joy of I Am."

A lone female voice then rose over top of the aqua choir in an unforgettable power of intent. It was as if the foam of the ocean was singing an opera for my ears only.

A kind of tickling intuition beckoned me to open my eyes. Directly before me appeared a shell, well over eight feet high, rising up and out of the water. As it slowly opened, the mystical shell revealed a female form at its centre that could have been angel and could have been goddess.

The sun enveloped her face and drew gold through her hair; hair that covered her naked form in cascades of waves that floated down to her knees. What appeared to be a shield of iridescent pearls lay at her feet, or was it just a massive strand coiled perfectly on the bottom half shell? Then I realized with a start that the perfectly formed silver toned mother of pearl shell was actually my own shield! And the woman at its center was someone I recognized in my soul.

Aphrodite... Venus... Isis... Lady of the Lake... Holy Mother... Mary Magdalene. I knew her by many names, yet in truth She was the one and true Goddess, for She was the energy of Love.

She expressed energy of such peace and bliss and sublime lightness that I felt myself spill tears of joy at a rejoining to my spiritual essence.

Then, as quickly as She emerged, the goddess and the shield began to submerge into the waters of the lake.

"I leave you with two things', her voice echoed as though speaking through a conch. *"One is your new name; the name you will have through all your future spiritual communications. You will be known as Amoura."*

"Amoura", I repeated in my mind. It meant Love in Latin or Italian. I couldn't remember which.

The shell was nearly out of sight when another object rose out of the water and the voice spoke to me again.

Straight up through the top of the water rose the Sword of Truth! This time, however, the blade was pointed skyward and the handle was held by a female arm as fair and glowing as mother of pearl.

"You were heretofore handed this sword in the position of Peace. I now hand it to you in the position of Strength to enable you to do battle should the occasion arise. Take it, Amoura!" She extended the sword high and beckoned me near with her tone. *"Take the Sword of Strength and use it well. Remember... Fight only the fight worth fighting and do not abuse the power of the sword."*

Then She warned. *"Take care that the sword does not fall into the hands of any who would misuse its energy. The sword must be returned should those circumstances arise and it must be returned when you no longer have need of it. Take it!"* she cried and threw the magnificent object into the air.

With barely believing eyes, I saw the sword float and spin over twice in slow motion through the air and land directly on the ground in front of me, the blade pointing down in the earth.

I rose from the stone bench and moved toward the sword. Upon closer observation, it could be perceived that the pinnacle of the handle contained a twelve faceted round crystal about two thirds of an inch in diameter. The crystal likely contained a pointed end that would enter and probably activate the magic of the sword; something I was to learn much more about at a later time. There was a familiarity about the crystal stone that was a bit uncanny.

"Take the crystal", spoke J.P. firmly, almost like an order. I obeyed and to my astonishment the crystal stone released itself instantly into my hand. It did indeed have a pointed end and as it sat in my palm, it began to rotate like a top, seeming to possess a life all its own.

"Ouch!" I cried, feeling the gemstone crystal express its point into my palm. As the stone effused its energy into me, my hand was reshaped into a five pointed star! This was a momentary occurrence and my hand soon resumed its regular appearance.

"Look, madam!" cried Serge. Turning, I observed the great sword as the blade and handle began to vibrate and emit a humming sound. Then it slowly began to fade and disappear.

"The sword is disappearing. It has no power without the crystal", Spoke Serge as he knelt closer to better observe the sword.

The Lady … Was it the same Lady who had given me Her stone? Was it the same stone She had taken from me at Lourdes? Was this crystal gemstone the symbol of the Star of Venus? Or was Aphrodite herself returning it to me? If so, were the challenges ahead of me to be so daunting that I would require such a weapon?

"A weapon so potent it and only it can activate the Sword of Truth." My thoughts were spoken out loud.

"Did you say the Sword of Truth, madam?" Serge questioned.

"Yes. That is the name I was given for it", I said, still half in my head with my own thoughts.

Serge averted his eyes from the fading sword and focused them upon me, saying, "The Sword of Truth is Excalibur."

"The sword of King Arthur." inserted J.P.

"The once and future king", ended Serge.

I blinked myself out of my reverie. "Arthur's sword!" I exclaimed. Why would I be gifted with Arthur's sword?

"Why, indeed", smirked J.P.

"Did the Lady of the Lake give you anything else?" J.P. asked.

"Yes", I answered. "She gave me my new name. I am to be called Amoura in all my spiritual communications in the future."

Serge and J.P. locked eyes. J.P. looked down pensively and remarked, "A-mour-a is an Italian word for ..."

"Love. Yes, I know", I replied crisply. "She pronounced the name *A-mour-a*. It means Bringer of Love. Messenger of the mysteries of feminine power and thereby brings the understanding of Love of the God-Goddess (with no separation) to the world. I don't know why I know that, but I know it to be true."

J.P. stared at me for a long while then commented. "Yes."

He seldom used the English word. "Yes", he repeated determinedly. "YOU will bring the energy that the earth requires at this time to understand what we are here to do. YOU will bring that knowledge out for all cultures to understand!" he ended strongly, his jaw set.

"No." I said humbly. "Not me. I am but the messenger of She who is the giver of all life. I will endeavor to bring *Her* truth to the world. And, if necessary", I held the crystal gemstone up in the air above me, "I will speak for Her!"

Chapter 5 - "The Lady Stone and the Garden of Eden"

So much had occurred in the past several hours that I felt the need to recoup and repair my energies for the night ahead. Fortunately, Frederique and Celine had handled the details of the on-location telecast. How the organizing and facilitating all of the necessary arrangements was accomplished in so short a time was unimaginable, but my total confidence in Celine's ability was not misplaced.

When the three of us arrived back at the chateau, Celine moved like a ballerina as she orchestrated the final details in J.P.'s office.

'O' had arrived and would be meeting us at the grotto via helicopter promptly at 5:00 P.M. The TV crew she had arranged for were presently setting up on location. The secrecy of the upcoming event had been maintained to a military degree. Mata Hari would have been proud.

"It had been relatively easy, actually", Celine beamed, looking up at us over her bifocals from behind J.P.'s massive oak desk.

"One of our contacts in the government here in France; an ambassador; had advised that an event of global religious significance would be occurring in Lourdes at the site of St. Bernadette's famous visions in the 1800's. All of the international television networks were informed and of course none of them wanted to be 'one upped' by the other networks, so they are all linking up for a simulcast live broadcast. Those countries whose time zones do not... How you say... Are not compatible, will of course receive the broadcast at a better time for their area. In this way, only one television crew, the crew 'O' is bringing, will need to be at the site", she finished, flourishing her pen in the air.

I was not so secure.

"Celine..." I began diplomatically, not wishing to offend her. "You don't know the press that well. When news of this event leaks out, there will be media personages of all types climbing all over that grotto. It could turn into chaos and may even be dangerous for those curious but innocent individuals who will be there simply to get a glimpse of their beloved Holy Mother. What I mean to say is... Has proper security been put into place?" Exhausted, I plopped down in the leather wingback chair across from her.

J.P. and Serge exchanged glances with one another. J.P. assured me that everything had been attended to in that regard.

"What I'm really trying to address is ... The interference from our adversaries." Finally the real concern came out.

"We understand your concern", J.P. went on. "Perhaps it is the time to impart some information to you." He advised as he sat down in the wingback chair beside me.

"This chateau is in a secluded area of the countryside, as you may know. It is also a bit more protected than may be apparent on the surface.

"You see, we have a natural system in place throughout this location that possesses extraordinary galactic power. Giant crystals from within the mountains that surround the chateau area blight its observance, indeed its very existence, from the air, land or sea. It is like an impenetrable force field, the like of which was used during the times of Atlantis and which our order still makes use of today for its protection of ancient records. Some of them are contained within these walls."

"You have a highly developed security system, then?" I questioned.

"Oui. It is, as I mentioned, very similar to the type devised by ancient Atlantis to keep their city from detection. This area of France is an energy spot. You are aware of ley lines and major vortexes that lay beneath the earth's surface? Oui, well, where the chateau is situated, the land beneath her contains strong energy grid lines and the Pyrenees Mountains themselves are influences of energy."

"So it is not surprising that Lourdes would have such a strong spiritual essence, being so near the mountain range and was therefore the perfect spot for the Holy Mother to appear!" I pondered aloud.

"But tell me, grand pere, why did She appear to Bernadette? She was such a frail little thing", I said tenderly.

"Ah, oui, but Bernadette was very strong in her spirit faith!" J.P. countered.

"So ... it was that then. Her faith was what prompted the visits from the Holy Mother?" I continued, still unconvinced.

"There is a philosophy; a theory that our order postures concerning this ..." J.P. went on hesitatingly. "It was believed by many that Bernadette of Lourdes was of Lemurian-Atlantean descent."

Part III

"Healing Anastasia"

Chapter 1 – "The Lemurians"

"You see, in the early history of our planet, two prominent and enlightened civilizations developed. No doubt you have heard of Lemuria and Atlantis?"

"Yes, of course", I affirmed relaxing into the security of the wingback chair.

"Lemuria was at once an actual physical location and at the same time a state of mind; in other words a place of and existing in perfection. Lemuria would be likened to what Christians call The Garden of Eden. The inhabitants all existed in total harmony and perfect health. No one ever aged, unless they desired to, and immortality was quite common. All needs were taken care of; everyone worked at whatever they desired and lived in perfect agreement with all Life.

"This was an area of highly enlightened souls. It is in our records that this civilization was originally developed with assistance from beings from another universe; which was similar to ours but older and more evolved.

"It was decided by our Divine Creator that Earth would be chosen for a particular development of the soul. Through utilizing the physical form or body, these beings were to learn to manifest their desires. In other word, this was to be the place where man would learn to create his own life around him. Earth would be the planet where mankind would train to become gods."

As J.P. spoke, I was transferred to a place in my mind where I visualized the imagery of Lemuria and its beings. What struck me first were the colors throughout the landscape: Hues never before seen in my idea of the world. They glowed with vibrancy and light, surrounding all life forms. Life energy oozed out of the fauna, the flora and the water masses like a silent power that you know is there even though invisible.

It was not unusual; as a matter of fact it was part of the landscape; to see enormous crystals of varying heights and sizes dotted throughout the pastoral areas as well as within the cities.

The cities themselves seemed to be built like domes, reminiscent of the dome city Arcosante. (Paolo Soleri, an architect who studied under Buckminster Fuller, had begun Arcosante as a project in Arizona in the 1970's. Arcosante has now become a famous structure based on the theory of a city built like man; upright and on levels rather than a flat surface. Paolo's daughter had shared the second storey of a house on Oriole Parkway with me when I first moved to Toronto. It was through her that I first became acquainted with the Arcosante project. A member of the corps de ballet in the National Ballet of Canada, she was also responsible for inspiring me toward dance and it became my love and passion for many years.)

The huge Lemurian structures were designed like multi level malls and had different venues on each level; supermarkets on one 'floor', houses or units like condos on another, parks on a separate level, etc. These edifices were spaced prettily upon the horizon and the architecture of the cities was very appealing to the eye.

Other than that they were extremely tall and their coloring very vivid, the Lemurians occupying the area were remarkably human in appearance. The tones of their skin in some cases possessed a glowing golden tone, or more infrequently, a slight violet shade. (These were rare and possessed raven hair with violet tones and bright violet eyes. I wondered if Elizabeth Taylor could have been a throwback to this culture.) Most Lemurians however simply had more intense tones of normal human coloring.

The Lemurians all wore a similar form of attire. The usual or 'everyday' color was white but also the shades of precious gems such as sapphire, emerald and ruby were in evidence. The garment consisted of a flowing Grecian style robe in various renditions. Some were long with full sleeves; others wore them covering only one shoulder, while others

- usually the younger ones - wore them shorter, above the knee. It was interesting how fit and perfectly proportioned these beings appeared. In effect, the Lemurians as a race were perfect.

Beautiful as the Lemurians were, it was an unearthly beauty. To describe what it was that made them appear different than humans, it was that there was a certain essence about them, as if they were all connected within to an invisible cord to all of life, and more, to the Life essence itself. Luminosity pervaded the space that encompassed them. It was this light they effused that permeated their surroundings and intensified the colors of nature.

There were two significant details about the Lemurians that were fascinating. One was the mutual connectedness both to one another and to a higher energy. It was as if they were all tuned into the same radio broadcast. Indeed, upon closer observation, a light that glowed incandescently could be detected at about mid brain on the inside of the forehead of each Lemurian. Many of the Lemurians wore crystals around their necks and over their heads like a crown, similar to that worn by the Statue of Liberty, but this light came from a crystal that was actually imbedded in their heads! The crystals, far from being foreign, seemed to be a natural part of their physiology. They were born with them, I sensed. Either that or the crystal was what the human pineal gland once resembled in our past.

The other noticeable detail was that they all seemed to be androgynous! I soon realized this while mentally viewing one of their beautiful spas.

Spas were numerous in Lemuria as caring for the body was very high on their priority agenda. The structures were quite similar, built into a side of a mountain whenever possible and having the appearance of a refined crystal cave.

There were chair-like stations carved right into the insides of the cave walls where the Lemurians could relax and absorb the natural energy of the earth.

Each spa usually housed a large pool of water for swimming, with smaller pools situated at the back by the cave walls. These individual pools emitted steam and seemed to be heated from beneath. Upon closer inspection, the water actually flowed in from a natural hot spring within the mountains.

All apparel was removed and neatly hung on pegs in an anteroom as everyone entered the cave spas naked and saw to their own needs. It was here that I noticed a symbiotic similarity of physical form. Like our own, their bodies had breasts and sex organs. I 'understood' that the nature of reproduction was spiritual rather than physical. A soul wishing to be born would communicate this to the being designated by the Creator to learn and assist the new soul's lessons with them. It was a mutual commitment. The Lemurian then impregnated through a spiritual meditative process of creation and manifested a child, who was also androgynous. The process seemed to be similar to the kundalini method of yoga meditation but one where the energy collected actually created a new life. Sex certainly took on an entirely different level with the Lemurians.

The same kundalini type of meditation was frequently practiced as a form of spiritual attunement and, yes, for sex. This was the Lemurian way of gratification. It certainly seemed a highly enlightened manner of getting in touch with the self, physically and spiritually. If you consider that this would dispel rivalry and jealousy - indeed make them nonexistent - the Lemurians certainly possessed a highly effective form of existence.

"So why did they disappear?" I heard myself issue out loud to J.P.

"Why, indeed." J.P. smiled wistfully. "As in all civilizations, regardless of their enlightenment, there comes a time when 'progress' becomes imperative, both for growth and for further spiritual awareness ... To enable the soul to know God on new levels.

"The Divine Creator established that a new civilization be born, one in which the life form would be divided into two energies; the positive and the negative, the warrior and the nurturer, the aggressor and the submitter ..."

"The male and the female ..." I finished. "So, contrary to the historical beliefs that it was the Atlanteans who divided the sexes and brought the ensuing challenges to mankind, it was actually God who decided this was to be done." I continued, "But why?"

"For the soul to experience connection with its divinity via another method?" postured J.P. in a question that contained its own answer.

"You see," he went on; "the Lemurians had no advance knowledge of what would be created or unleashed by this decision. It was issued forth by the Devine Creator throughout the Cosmos, so the beings of some of the other universes agreed to assist the Lemurians in creating a new civilization of species that were separate energies of masculine and feminine: The Atlanteans."

Chapter 2 - "The Atlanteans"

"The land set aside for this new species was to be called Atlantis because of its geographical location. This was prior to the splitting of the North American continent from Europe and the subsequent shift of these two land areas. Some historians have theorized that 'The Split' actually resulted in the sinking of Atlantis - and possibly Lemuria - although it is generally accepted that Lemuria disappeared first.

"Lemuria was believed to be near where Polynesia was located. The role that the alien beings initially played in the new world scenario was to offer transportation to the Lemurians who desired to be a part of the experiment. Remember, it was through free will alone that these beings populated Atlantis. "Well ..." hesitated J.P. "That is, at least in the beginning."

"Initially, it was a fine and noble experiment. For decades Lemurians were transported to the newly established Atlantis."

As J.P. continued, I had visions of small, refined space vehicles transferring the Lemurians to the new land. Yet I also perceived that in the earliest stages of this new evolvement, the transportation was done by a much more highly evolved means: The beings of the higher evolved universes assisted in quickening the advancement of the Lemurian race so they could virtually teleport themselves by first imaging their physical forms onto Atlantis and then physically manifesting themselves there. This ability was lost by the generations to come; as was much more.

The alien species that had the most influence over the new Atlanteans were of a highly technologically advanced nature. That was the way they were, literally by nature; cool, detached, mentally oriented and very scientific. They loved scientific experiments and were particularly interested in the development of two genders, or sexes, out of one soul. It had never been done before.

Observing the laboratory where these initial separations occurred, I realized that although these aliens intended to be neither cruel nor hurtful, the operations of separation were just that, for not only were they tearing apart the physical sexual organs of the Lemurians, they were also pulling and tearing their souls apart! The soul literally had to be severed in order for the separation of the sexes to be complete.

I winced while viewing the physical and spiritual pain the new Atlanteans underwent and wanted to cry out to them to stop, tell them that they would regret for millions of generations what they were doing and that they had no idea what it would take for the future generations to get back to their original soul beings.

"It was horrific, oui?" asked J.P. as his witnessed my visions.

"Oh, yes ... awful!", I cried, pulling my legs up in a fetal position and cuddling into the plush green velvet of the wingback chair for solace and comfort.

"Ah ..." continued J.P., his eyes dancing, "but it was wonderful too. The splitting of the souls in the beginning was not so nice... BUT", he postured, "it was a necessary process in order for the soul to experience on the two levels; the masculine and the feminine. The soul could now feel the totality of the essence of being man and could as well much more fully experience the nature of being woman: The experience of the Devine Masculine AND the Devine Feminine. It was fantastic!

"You see, although the Lemurians had balance and harmony and a 'perfect' society, they were without the feeling we call *passion*. They knew not hate, but they had never felt the intensity of passion on the earthly level that is called Love. They knew Love, of course, but it was like the energy of unity. Passion would be their gift of separation."

"But would it not also be their, and our, undoing", I interjected.

"Alas. It was so", J.P. agreed.

"But it certainly made for an interesting ride, did it not?" posed Serge.

"Oh, all of that!" I agreed. "Resulting in revolutions, wars and brother fighting against brother. Yet this is what God wanted humanity to experience - the *passion*? Why? There must have been a purpose for God to orchestrate all of this. Some reason."

"It was to experience the passion, ma fille, so that humanity on earth could evolve this planet from being one of karmic lessons to one where the beings would learn to be gods. That is what the Creator of all the Universes wants for us all... here on earth. That is why earth is such an important star and must be preserved." J.P. stated.

"I am a trifle confused", I confessed. "How does understanding the experience of passion assist us in becoming gods, as you say?"

Celine rose from J.P.'s chair and knelt in front of me. "Allow me to put it another way", she began. As she spoke, her graceful hands sculpted images in the air.

"First, to manifest, we need to have a wish. This is followed by our desire, or asking for the manifestation. This sets in motion a creative energy but this creation can only become manifest through the intense energy known as passion."

"Unless you truly want something - anything - passionately, it is challenging and nearly impossible to obtain it", Serge offered as he moved over and sat down on the Persian carpet next to Celine. They looked deeply into one another's eyes and smiled softly to each other. In unison, they turned their gaze to me and Celine continued further.

"When we have perfected the ability to manifest all of our wishes, we are able to create our lives for ourselves in the way we want and become self-sufficient."

"Then we can become gods", Serge spoke softly.

"Then, at this time, the planet Earth appears to be a star inhabited by gods in the making!" I added.

"Yes", interjected J.P., "but it is a star that has progressed and advanced its energy and purpose from being one solely concerned with the learning of karmic lessons to one of creating gods out of human souls." J.P. looked up and cupped his tanned hands together in a resonate clap. "It is so very exciting! What a time to be alive on the earth! This is a fairly recent development and it has only really been realized since the mid eighteen hundreds, so with the exception of a few very advanced souls on this planet, we are relatively new at this."

"The eighteen-eighties were a turning point, then?" I asked. Placing my feet on the carpet and leaning over, my eyes implored J.P. for further knowledge.

"Oui, cherie", J.P. smiled. "As we progress toward the millennium, there will occur many changes on our earth. We are being prepared."

As J.P. spoke, the words of the tall gentle man in the garden were reiterated in my mind. He had said after the millennium occurred, it would not be an easy time for some and havoc and uncertainty would prevail 'for those who would not listen'. Listen to the progress of evolvement on the planet perhaps? Yet, he was positive all would eventually be well after earth was 'purged', as he put it. "Let them with eyes to see and ears to hear" a voice whispered to me. The man spoke of the aliens too.

"J.P., you spoke of beings from other universes that assisted Atlantis and probably continue to assist us even now. However ..." I continued, trying not to let fear enter my tone, "What about the beings that are not interested in our welfare. Those who pursue us now and tried to claim Anastasia's diary with the Holy Mother's sacred messages for salvation... And, instead, claimed Jacey's life." Tears spilled down my cheeks involuntarily as I spoke. "They will obviously stop at nothing."

J.P.'s eyes stayed lowered, perhaps in reverence or silent prayer for Jacey.

"No. You are right. They will indeed stop at nothing." He peered up at me, strength pouring out through his eyes. "Yet our cause is a just one and we are even more determined for our mission. Our order's true mission and purpose on earth is to preserve her and ensure that the adversaries to our purpose are foiled in their attempts."

"Remember, Angelique", J.P. darted a look at me. "Remember that our Most High Creator has allowed this circumstance for our growth as well."

"So ... overcoming them and their purpose of destruction is part of our lesson", I reasoned.

"Quite so." J.P., Celine and Serge echoed in unison.

"And Bernadette", I asked finally. "What was her role in all of this?"

Chapter 3 - "Bernadette's Song"

"Bernadette of Lourdes was of an ancient Lemurian and Atlantean soul incarnation. She was descended from what is called the faerie race and another certain species that evolved in Atlantis and resided underground.

"There were certain mutants that existed at this time that came into being through various means. When some of the Atlanteans wished to understand the 'feeling' of what it would be like to be an animal and projected themselves out into these animals, they sometimes created undesirable creatures. The dinosaurs and other predators were examples of their curiosity.

"Still, other mutants developed that were very helpful. They were less evolved beings, appearing semi-human, who lived beneath the surface of the earth and mainly supplied the work labor. However, if in their endeavors they showed sincere and efficient progress above and beyond their abilities, they would be quickened in their evolution by having their pineal crystal transmitters advanced. It was a process done for those deserving mutants by a high council of the faerie.

"The tiny faerie race was a species of another universe even more highly evolved than the Lemurians, who chose to live beneath the planet and assist the earth's energies - and the mutants as well. At times the faerie souls merged bodies (or mated) on Atlantis after the separation and Bernadette's ancestors were a product of this merging. She, therefore, possessed a special DNA that was passed down to her and had the ability to discern the energies around her. She was visited by and was seeing Angels long before her visions at Massabielle. That was why Bernadette was chosen to be visited by the Holy Mother."

I finally understood. Well, sort of. "I read 'The Song of Bernadette' and have studied a copy of the messages given to Bernadette by the Holy Mother, yet found nothing really remarkable in those messages she was given. Yes, she warned us of global catastrophes; that we as a species needed to change our energy to a more loving one, and I agree wholeheartedly. The earth could be destroyed if we don't. Well... environmentalists tell us that." The analytical journalist was coming out in me.

"While trying not to sound sacrilegious by saying this", I implored, looking from J.P. to Serge and finally Celine. "I honestly didn't get anything of a spiritually revolutionary nature from those messages."

The three were silent as they all rested their eyes on me in the sunlit office. Finally J.P. spoke.

"That is because not all of her messages were revealed.

While resting my head on the calm pale yellow pillow in my guest room, the reality of J.P.'s words registered even more clearly than when he spoke them to me in his office downstairs a short while ago.

It was a matter of Truth. "We were not given the truth!" I said aloud to the gilt edged mirror and Marie Antoinette settee. The truth of our true reality was kept from us. Although not knowing how to accomplish it, a strong intuition told me that the illumination concealed in certain messages given to Bernadette needed to be revealed to the earth, indeed the universe. Especially now!

I sighed and attempted to rest before the evening's event but rest would decide to be a stranger at this point. However, within minutes after trying the breathing method J.P. had demonstrated, the energy of lightness and harmony descended upon me.

Chapter 4 - "Anastasia"

"Angelique", the woman's voice spoke in her soft European accent.

I opened my eyes and saw a slim, fine featured woman with long wavy auburn hair and sapphire blue eyes sitting on the foot of my bed.

"You are so beautiful", she smiled. "You look so much like I imagined you would." She touched one slender hand to her throat as she spoke, an action I sensed that was a nervous gesture of hers. Her fingers caressed a gold framed cameo broche pinned onto the high lace collar of her ivory blouse, which was the same color as her youthful complexion.

While staring at her the realization occurred that I recognized that voice, had heard it many times; its rich eloquent tones and light European dialect.

"Your voice ..." I sat up slightly, resting on one arm. "I've heard you, but where?"

"Yes. I have visited you many times, but until now it was not appropriate for you to see me."

"Who are you?" It was impossible for me not to interrupt her and finally get answers to the mysteries.

"My name is Anya, but that is not important now. I have come to tell you some information that will be very necessary for you to know very soon.

"I wrote it down in a diary that I was instructed would, at a future time, be delivered into the hands of the pure heart that would bring its messages to the world when the world would need its messages the

184

most. Those hands were to be yours", Anya spoke. Her elegant voice was choked with emotion as she reached out and closed her hands around my own and held them close to her chest.

"Oh, dear child", she said, holding back a sob, the tears welling over her azure gaze. "I desire so much for your happiness ... and that of your daughters. Your path has been a challenging one and for that I have great empathy. Yet, you are a chosen one. It is to you that the messages must be delivered." Anya regained her regal composure and continued on.

"As a young girl, I myself was given messages from the Holy Mother during prayer time. She instructed me to write them down as they would be important for humanity in the future. She also told me to keep these messages safe and hidden at that time as it was imperative no one see them.

"Some of Her messages seemed rather alarming and obtuse at the time but I was always comforted by Her visits and Her words, especially after mama and papa and all our family had to leave Tsarscoe Sila and travel to that horrible place at Yekaterinburg." Anya's eyes saddened deeply as she spoke and she shuddered at the memory.

Anya looked deeply into my eyes as she spoke to me. "You were right Angelique in sensing the 'truth' in Bernadette's visions was not given to humanity. The truth of your true reality and that of every human being was withheld at that time. It may have helped, yes, but yet many - most - at that time would not, could not, have accepted it. Now, it is different and perhaps even essential that the truth be revealed and accepted."

Anya then reached into a small ivory linen satchel on her lap and withdrew a book with an embroidered silk cover.

"Ah!" I gasped. "It's the diary! But where did ..."

"Do not concern yourself with that circumstance", Anya related warmly but firmly and opened the lovely antique cover to a specific entry.

"First, in order for you to understand your position, you must know of your lineage... and mine." As her melodic voice filled the room, my eyelids succumbed to a sudden heaviness and I floated back onto the silken pillow.

The sensation overcoming me was one of being lifted up, of rising higher and even higher. The experience was so comforting and so blissful that surrendering to it was almost a command. Anya's voice lifted my spirit even higher until it finally stopped at a place of warm light. It was like standing in the centre of the sun. The brightness and the warmth were beyond anything my physical form had ever encountered, yet not uncomfortable, only energizing.

Anya's words continued from a form located about twenty feet away from me, but as the form came closer to me, I realized it was not Anya who was now speaking. The form was that of The Lady.

Chapter 5 - "The Lady Speaks"

The Lady's luminescent eyes enthralled my very being with their essence. Such energy of love and the dearest form of kindness was engendered within Her and extended from Her, that I sensed the cells of my body being altered in order to be able to stand in Her presence.

"Yes, your energies and cellular structure are at this moment being quickened so that you will be able to withstand the higher frequency of vibration that you are experiencing", spoke The Lady. *"Otherwise your physical structure could not bear up to this energy."* She continued.

Then, She ever so gracefully walked toward me until She stood directly in front of me. I noticed her feet were bare of any covering except for a single prefect red rose that sat perfectly positioned upon each forefoot.

The Lady lifted her right hand to me and touched my forehead, making the sign of a cross upon its centre. As She did so I could feel a slight pressure and a distinct implosion occur in my head.

"I have reactivated your own crystal, that which you already possess, to the degree that your body once held it in your past incarnations. It will be helpful to you within the next few hours."

The cross the Lady had etched upon my forehead felt like it had opened my skull; as if a fine surgeon's knife had made a painless incision. My inner mind felt open and exposed yet somehow freer and able to visualize at a greater distance and with a far greater degree of discernment, as I was later to discover. I also felt something enlarge within its core and it began to throb and pulsate.

"That is your pineal crystal. In the ancient land mass known to your culture as Lemuria, this was actually where the pineal gland was situated. It was at that time much larger than it is in the humans of your earth age. I have engorged it for you as it would have been in Lemurian times. This is also the placement of your sixth chakra or energy point and is also called the third eye. I have activated this chakra first because it will be easier for you now to assimilate the information you will be receiving."

The Lady then put Her arm around my back and touched the base of my spine. I instantly felt a sensation of enormous strength, like a wheel had been spun into motion that escalated my energies. All about me was energy of a crimson hue.

"Red is the color of the energy of the base chakra. When it is operating at its optimum, this is the sensation."

She then placed Her hand on the top of my pelvic bone. As She did so I felt one enormous rush of immensely orgasmic energy such as I have not felt since giving birth to Christina, only without the pain. It filled me with light persimmon light.

"This is your regenerative or creative chakra. It is in this area that you create your desires. When it is operating at its full potential, you can create or bring to life, anything that you desire. It is a very important energy. Remember it and use it wisely and for what it was originally intended. Unfortunately, this is the chakra energy that most humans of this earth age misuse. Or abuse." The Lady smiled, bemused. It was appreciative that She possessed such a wry sense of humor. The Lady was quite correct, of course. Most humans did abuse this chakra and many had absolutely no conception (a little pun) of what it was actually meant for.

"We create life with this chakra but we also create our dreams." The Lady further contributed.

She placed Her fingers in the centre of my solar plexus and gently but firmly reached inside my cavity and twisted some spot there until I could feel the energy begin to arouse and pulsate in a glorious lemon color throughout me.

"This area needed a bit more tuning." The Lady explained. *"Here is the chakra of manifestation. It works in connection with the creative chakra to bring your dreams and desires into material existence. When one of the chakras is out of sync, the others have challenges in functioning proficiently. This is a crucial energy chakra. It is from this location that the physical body*

takes its energy from the food ingested; where the glucose is sent to the body through the blood in order to strengthen the life force. Should there be a malfunction here, not only will the body and brain not gain the nutrition and hence energy it needs, it will also make it challenging to process the life purpose that one was designed for. And also hamper in creating the realities you desire."

Hence, the term 'strong blood'. Yes, my blood sugar imbalance likely had contributed to my inability to fulfill my dreams.

"That was a condition that was inherent in your lineage. Anya will relate this to you at a different time and you will, along with her, heal this energy for her family and the future generations."

"For now, allow me to continue." With those words, The Lady touched my heart with Her hand. Her fingers reached right through my ribcage and caressed my heart into a pulsation of warm emerald glow.

"Here your energies flow with no reservation. You have a truly pure heart, my child." The Lady smiled warmly.

Quickly, Her hand spun to my throat and She touched the spot the arrow had dented. A fusion of turquoise energy flooded my senses.

"This is your chakra of communication. It is now re-opened to activate your talent and ability to express to the world."

She bypassed my sixth chakra as that was already well activated and continued upward to the top of my head. She held Her hand slightly above my crown and a swirling energy of violet speed drilled into the top of my skull and in one instant of sheer mystic revelation, I felt the understanding of the cosmos explode itself into my brain! The information received in that one jolt surpassed years of study and reading. It surpassed all words. I was speechless.

"Yes", The Lady empathized. *"It is much to handle at one time. That is why I quickened you. Otherwise your body and mind would have disintegrated.*

"There is a reason I have activated your chakra energies. It is vitally important to have them functioning optimally at all times for the health of the body but also for your protection and to enable you to have Creative Control in your life.

"I want you to practice activating the energy chakras in your body in the future. Begin by focusing first on the base chakra and imagine setting it spinning clockwise by imaging the color red on that area.

"When you feel the energy resurrect in that location, move up to the regenerative organs and image the color orange to spin this chakra wheel.

"The third chakra in the solar plexus is set in motion by seeing the color yellow flow throughout your cavity.

"The heart or emotional chakra (Love), receives a green color to quicken its turning.

"The throat chakra of communication requires a bright piece of turquoise imaged there and the sixth chakra, the third eye, is one of indigo blue light.

"The seventh chakra works best when a violet color spins that wheel. That is your psychic centre.

"The eighth and final chakra is that of the Christ consciousness and it is a pure white hue.

"The energy chakras I speak of, Angelique, are really crystals similar to the one you received from The Lady Of The Lake. They are rounded on the one end and twelve faceted with a point on the other. The twelve facets have to do with the twelve strands of DNA that were present in the body in Lemurian times. The human body holds only two DNA strands at present.

"The rounded sides of these crystals resemble wheels with twelve spokes. This side faces outward while the pointed side faces into the body. This is so that the wheel side can be turned and activated to pinpoint and direct the energy to a particular area. When all the chakras are activated together, they are lit like stars and also resonate like a song to the heavens. Each chakra has a specific note that corresponds to it. When your 'instrument' is alight and resonating, it sends out a message to the universe. We each possess our own special chord. We each have our own song to sing to God. One of your lessons and that of every human being here on earth is to find your own special song to sing and present it to the world, to the glory of our Most High Creator.

"When you realize your own song, you will understand your true purpose for being. This song also puts an impenetrable field about you that is your own true protection. It is also called your 'shield'. You have already claimed it.

"The Archangel Michael is involved when the Just Ones activate their shield. Michael is the sword on the shield and Michael stands at the right *hand of God and his force is indomitable. When you have need of him, call upon him Angelica.*" The Lady voiced this statement strongly.

"*As strong as Michael is, Gabrielle is equal in strength with her Love. She is the feminine energy of Love and Life, representing the chalice in the shield.*

"*Uriel, the Angel of Light, who will enlighten you with his clarity and wisdom, is the arrow you connected with.*

"*The fourth Archangel is Raphael. You will know him when you meet him. He is the energy of healing and also communication.*

"*These forces are there to assist you, as they are for every human being once they awaken to their true existence and therefore how to activate them.*"

The Lady then stepped back a few steps so that I could observe Her more astutely. With her right hand, She touched each portal of Her being, beginning with Her base chakra and moving upward.

As She touched each chakra point, I perceived the appropriate colors light up and pulsate as they spun in a clockwise direction, with a separate note of music accompanying each one. When She touched the final portal at Her crown, I perceived Her body; glowing and lit up like a Christmas tree. Each colored crystal spun and then melded into one another in a glorious resplendent display of ethereal cosmic light and sound. This unearthly display finally culminated in a symphonic light ballet, dispersing multi-hued star like particles that danced about us like fireflies.

Chapter 6 - "The Lady's Story"

"You need to know some history of my being to be able to relate to all that is occurring in your earthly reality when you return to your physical body, Angelica." The Lady began Her story.

"My parents were named Joachim and Anna. They were raised in the adopted tradition of the Essenes in a very strict and traditional manner. Both of my parents were of a high status of our culture which was Indo-European. They were wealthy both materially and spiritually.

"Joseph, my husband, was of noble birth, descended from the royal David line. It is a lesser known fact that my family was also connected to the Davidic lineage but I will speak more of this at a later time.

"Josephs' family was very orthodox and prosperous as well. Contrary to the popular belief amongst your religion, we were not impoverished; quite the contrary. In the Judaic tradition poverty was considered a curse and both Joseph and I and all of our family, including Jesus, were extremely blessed.

"I had eight children in all, James being the second after Jesus and ending with Leah, our youngest daughter.

"The circumstance of Jesus' birth has always been an area of speculation and naturally a mystery. The fact is there was really nothing mysterious about the so called 'virgin birth' at all. As a matter of fact, it was a very natural occurrence in my heritage, although not considered 'normal' at that time on earth or any since then.

"You see, Joseph and I were of Atlantean descent but our ancestors were originally from Lemuria. Both of our ancestral DNA code and our soul

incarnations existed from this area. The continent of Atlantis was created to bring about an experiment of splitting the soul into both masculine and feminine counterparts in order to experience more fully.

"In our initial lifetimes on Atlantis, Joseph and I were originally one being. We were in fact the masculine and feminine of one another, or soul mates. All of this has a great deal of relevancy to the virgin birth theory.

"Yes, I was a true virgin when I gave birth to Jesus. The manner by which this all occurred has to do with Joseph and my soul incarnation from Lemuria. In the Lemurian culture, it was a normal function and practiced quite regularly to balance and harmonize the chakras, as I have shown you.

"While in this harmonious state, the Archangel Gabrielle connected with us to assist us in creating and giving life to our desires – and the desire of the creator for us.

"I was indeed 'visited' by the Archangel Gabrielle and told that I was to give birth to the Christed One. I was at first unbelieving about being so blessed, about being the chosen vehicle for this honor, but Gabrielle was so adamant that I, of course, acquiesced in reverence to the desire of the Highest Creator.

"It was because of my ancient Lemurian heritage that I was able to be the Immaculate Conception, and undoubtedly, why I was chosen.

"The Lemurians, prior to their Atlantean decision to separate their genders, were capable of creating life on their own. They possessed the physical attributes of male and female as well as the corresponding sexual organs. Through a particular form of high meditation that included the tuning and the harmonizing of the body crystals, or chakras, they were able to synchronize their creative (regenerative) and manifesting (solar plexus) chakras to such a degree that they impregnated themselves.

"I had been trained and educated in the very strict and devout Essene tradition since the age of three and was accustomed to the meditative process. At this particular meditation, Gabrielle advised me of my mission on earth: I was to be the mother of the Christ. It was Gabrielle, the Angel of Love and Life, who quickened the process within me to activate the twelve strand DNA to be able to create a child within myself without the normal human interconnection of sexual union.

"Joseph was given a similar creative experience and I was impregnated; for the obvious reason that he did not possess the physical organs to give birth.

Nonetheless, he experienced a creative meditation where his creative and manifesting power was exploded out into the universe at the identical time that I experienced my own imploding experience. The Archangel Gabrielle reminded Joseph of this during another meditation, after he had learned of my pregnancy. Naturally he knew he had not 'known' me in the physical way, so how could the child be his? Gabrielle advised him that the child was indeed conceived via our natural creative powers in accordance with our Lemurian ancestry and genealogy. This was able to occur because we were original soul mates."

My mind comprehended perfectly what The Lady had spoken. This was indeed a revelation.

"Why this knowledge is of such significance now, Angelique, is due to another connection in process. The Lemurian and Atlantean cultures were both guided by a more highly evolved species of life that existed from another galactic location. Indeed, it was due to this inter-galactic relationship that our species on earth was able to process as well as it did, especially in Lemuria and Atlantis. Much of what the human body is capable of lies dormant for most at present.

"Although there existed extremely helpful beings from other worlds to assist us, there was as well in existence a species of a different galactic influence that possessed a sharply contrasting theory about the evolution of mankind. In fact, they did not concur with the idea of the existence of man at all, or at best believed we should exist as a slave labor force and be discarded and abandoned at the soonest opportunity.

"As it turned out, that is precisely what that species of being did: They abandoned their position and their 'developed beings' on earth, but not without leaving descendants of their 'developed' species.

"Perfectly normal in appearance and behavior, many were connected to major family lineages on your planet. They were in effect programmed via this crystal DNA implant to destroy civilizations of the earth at any given time when triggered by this foreign culture. Most of them do not even have knowledge of what they possess.

"This crystal you have once again received from the Sword of Truth has the ability to deactivate the crystals of these implantations and is therefore a very powerful tool in your hands. It also holds the ability to control the crystal chakras of any earthly life form, including human, animal, fowl,

water life, mineral life and all other life on earth. Were it to fall into the possession of the negative alien forces, the repercussions for this planet would be horrific! All freedom of body and mind could be altered. All thoughts could be programmed. It could, in fact, return the inhabitants of the planet into robots, little more than the slave labor this alien force initially designed us for.

"You may indeed wonder why such a mission should be entrusted to you. This you will come to understand more fully at a future time. At this point, what you require to understand is that it is your DNA code that will enable you to function as the vehicle for this high purpose. Your ancestral connection to the Russian royal family of the Tsar and Tsarina is a necessary factor to the successful fulfillment of this mission. It was due to a frailty of reign, an abuse of power that resurrected the re-evolvement of this species and brought about a karmic effect of devastation for themselves, their descendants and indeed for the future of their country as well as mankind. This effect can and must be corrected or the demise of your earth, as you know it, is eminent.

The Lady was silent and simply observed me lovingly with her radiant eyes before She continued.

"The Highest Creator never demands any action of any of His children. You do not have to accept this assignment as you do have free will. When the time arrives for your participation in this circumstance, you will be made aware of it.

"The Crystal of Creation was entrusted to Anastasia with the premise that she would be the next great chalice of hope for Holy Mother Russia. Alas, the circumstances of her life and the lessons she chose were not conducive to manifesting this reality. I will allow Anya to tell you more of this story in her own words."

Chapter 7 - "Travel Through Time: The Russian Revolution"

These were The Lady's final words as She once again drew the sign of the cross on my forehead and stepped back into the light.

I sensed my astral body floating backward and downward through the sunlight and felt myself plop back onto the yellow silk brocade of the bed coverlet. My eyes reopened instantly upon returning to my physical body and I found myself staring into Anya's sapphire gaze.

Anya still remained sitting on the corner of the bed, holding the antique diary in her lap. She smiled the guileless smile of a young girl and indeed she could have been no older than my Christina.

"Yes", she blushed prettily, lowering her eyes. "My spirit self is very young in appearance", Anya agreed. As she raised her eyes again however and gazed out at me, her focus was far more intense and almost businesslike as she asked pointedly. "The Lady spoke to you through me then." It was a statement rather than a question.

"Oh, yes, very much so", I accorded, yet secretly wondering why She had not addressed me Herself as She had done at the grotto and the other locations.

Anya continued gazing at me and in answer to my thought simply said, "It is because that is a lesson for me. Even as spirits and spirit guides, we still continue to work on lessons in order to further perfect our souls in accordance to their nature."

"To their nature ..?" I questioned, not fully comprehending her meaning.

"Umm ... What we, our souls, yet need to learn", she explained. "It is for our individual soul growth. For instance, where one soul may have advanced tremendously in one area, it may have yet other areas that require more attention and discipline", she smiled secretly.

"I understand", I replied discreetly, respecting her privacy.

As though interpreting my thoughts, Anya addressed me, "In the matter of the soul, it is a quite open topic, for our soul lessons are linked to the universe of all souls. So there are no secrets, you see. Although there are at times some issues recurring with the souls that incarnated, for instance, as communists", she giggled.

"I can just imagine!" My inner and outer spirit laughed with her.

We remained silent for several moments after this, simply sensing one another's energies. Finally, I asked her.

"So ... You are my spirit guide, then?"

"I am one of your spirit guides, yes", Anya confirmed.

Sitting up on the bed and hugging my knees to my chest, I confided to her.

"The Lady said that you would tell me about the story of Anastasia and the Russian royal family."

"Yes. It is time for the true story to be told", Anya replied. Straightening her back and firming her jaw, she laid the diary to one side as she continued.

"I will do better than tell you. I will show you!" In a distinctly regal gesture, Anya outstretched her arm toward me and commanded.

"Take my hand, Angelique!"

After placing my hand in her tiny palm, energy similar to that of a mild electric vibration took hold. Initially it was painless and then a startling jolt of surging current flew through me. I cried out in shock as my being was drawn through a cold dark tunnel that felt heavy and sticky and contained a scent like mildew. It was an energy that was totally unique to me.

I landed hard on a cold bottom. It was impossible to see anything as the surroundings were absurdly black and I was hesitant to move for fear of bumping into objects or worse. "What is this place?" I shuddered.

"This is Russia."

Anya's voice held a sad plaintiff quality as she continued.

"This is Holy Mother Russia just prior to the revolution. It is evening. It is freezing and Russia's people are starving here in the Ukraine, where we are standing in the fields, but elsewhere... everywhere else as well."

I could hear Anya start to sob and sensed her tears.

"People, children, animals ... all are starving on this night. And where am I?" She continued with self loathing. "I am at home in a beautiful palace, cuddling warmly by a blazing fireplace, content with a full belly and glowing in the adoration of a loving, attentive and abundant family. Oh, papa!" Anya cried, almost hysterically. "If only we had known! If only we had been more aware of the suffering ..." She sobbed.

"Perhaps it could have been different. Perhaps we could have made a difference. Then our lives would have counted for something good rather than something so morbid. Russia was a nation that possessed a potential of so much to give to the world. But we shamed her, papa. We shamed her and damned her and ourselves for posterity."

As Anya spoke, I felt our bodies lift and soar, as if flying to another location. Anya and I perused the Romanov family in their leisure. It was the Russian Royal Winter palace and the scent of sycamore lingered in the air. Anya attested that it was one of the signature scents of the royal Romanov family from their private collection.

The royal family was casually assembled in a small parlor, gathered about a lit fireplace. The light from the fire set a warm glow throughout the room, showing us the pretty floral wallpaper and the cozy furnishings. Although expensively appointed with the finest of Russian and European elegance, the parlor possessed a surprisingly sparse decor. This room and, I sensed, the rest of the private royal quarters, were not as lavish as might have been expected.

"All of THAT", Anya indicated with a sweep of her hand, "was for display; for visiting dignitaries. We seldom observed it. It was all useless extravagance that could have been sold to feed or house thousands of people." Regret dripped the words from her lips with the emotion of 'too little too late'.

As Russian peasants gathered in oncoming rows outside of the royal palace, the Romanovs were on the inside, digesting a well prepared dinner in the comfort of their private residences. The contradictions were too stark. The facts of the matter were too obvious. Why were the Tsar and Tsarina not more aware of the conditions of their subjects? These were their people. The monarch of a country is there to serve and protect the inhabitants of their territory, not the other way around. How had this situation got so turned?

It made me recall a story I had covered in 1991 when Ovid Mercredi was elected the Grand Chief of All Nations in Canada. He was a valid choice for leadership albeit a controversial one. He was particularly impressive however when he revealed to us a tradition of the chief of the tribe.

"After the hunt, it was tradition for the hunters, the children, the women and the elders to be fed first. The chief always ate last... and only what was left. In this way, the chief would be reminded that he was elected because he was there to serve." Then he laughed and continued, "And it was the den mothers who voted the chief in, so he would always know his place and understand who was really in charge!"

After viewing the footage of the den mother who chastised one of the guerilla warriors at Oka during that rebellion, I could well appreciate how no chief would desire to incur the wrath of any of those powerful women. I was in total respect of the native women of power. They rocked!

How different were the circumstances in this foreign land; how strange the culture but was it really so removed from the one in which we now lived? How had it all happened? How had the nature of ruling got so separated from its original purpose, which was to serve the people? From the earliest beginnings ruling must have originated as a noble and honorable position. When and how did the ruler go from there to living in lavish palaces so far removed from their subjects, they couldn't even relate to their basic necessities?

Yet I knew from history (and from my own intuitions about him) that Nicolas was not a heartless or ignoble man. Far from it, he cared about his people a great deal. So much so that he left his family to go to the front, much against the warnings of the Tsarina and Rasputin not to, whilst little Alexei - his only beloved son - was ill and in a partial coma.

"That was papa's biggest and most fatal mistake", interjected Anya. She held my hand while we walked through the private hallway that led to their bedrooms.

"Mama said Our Friend begged her to influence and convince papa not to join the army on the front. Papa argued that his soldiers needed his leadership. Mama countered that the people of Russia needed their sovereign to be someone they could view as a god, innocent and unaware of the trials of his people. To be seen leading the soldiers would remind them of the fact that he too was mortal and this could put him in great danger. Keizer Ferdinand was assassinated by the very soldiers that he commandeered!" Anya added with a look of terror in her eyes, "And papa's own grandfather by the very peasants he tried to help!"

Anya's eyes were like those of a doe hypnotized by highway headlights. It was evident how witnessing the slaughter of her family had traumatized her.

"Where were your rooms?" I asked in the hopes of averting her attention from a morbid past memory. Sensing that Anya's spirit needed a healing of its own from that horrifying night so long ago, I began to wonder if my reason for being here was to assist her gentle spirit in some way in crossing over from this tortured place in her mind and regrettably also in her soul … and, very possibly, in mine as well.

Anya blinked and her eyes became normal again.

"They are over here", she pointed to the right and up ahead. "We are nearly there", she smiled sweetly in anticipation, and I felt, of seeing her life again as it was in her happier youth.

"I shared my room with my sister Marie." Anya spoke as she tenderly stretched her slender hand over the antique polished brass door handle. The door made a clicking sound as she pressed the curved handle down.

As the door opened silently, it revealed a medium sized room containing two single beds, which were actually army cots with blue ticking. Observing my surprise at this, Anya smiled slightly and said, "All of the royal princesses from my father's maternal lineage slept on cots before they were married. It was tradition and my grand mama kept it in place. Not until marriage were they allowed to sleep in a comfortable bed. Mama tried to reason with her on this but grand mama was very stern and often not kind to my mother. Mama suffered from migraine and often took to her bed and grand mama was not sympathetic", Anya confided.

With the exception of the royal Romanov insignia embroidered in lapis blue on the hand towels draped across the back of a small water stand that held a pitcher and basin for washing, it could have been the bedroom of any children of that era.

The girls' bedroom was decorated with pretty pink floral wallpaper; the small tender blossoms dancing across its surface with a refined Victorian grace. White linen dressed the beds and heavy white cotton crochet edged the coverlets. Matching doilies set atop the two night tables and down filled quilts were folded in half across each bed. Although the room held a small fireplace, the quilts would undoubtedly be needed for warmth in the frigid Russian winters.

"My sister Tatiana, who was a wonderful dancer, would show Marie and I the latest dances in this room." Anya stepped with a light ballerina grace in accordance with her petite frame into the centre of the bedroom. She smiled and executed a perfect pirouette on the well used carpet, then stopped and laughed out loud.

"Tania – Tatiana's nickname – and I would practice our dance steps in our nightgowns here in the evenings long after we should have been in bed. We would day dream of the balls we would attend and the handsome soldiers we would dance and flirt with and the men we would marry and the children we would ha ..." Anya suddenly stopped abruptly. I could feel her pain, her tortured memories wrenching through her young mind.

The young girl before me could have been any adolescent robbed of their youth by the savage realities of war. Her royal birth did not deny her any of the sufferings that were a part of the process of progress through war and revolution. Yet this was not Anya's revolution, it was not her doing. Why therefore should it be her destiny? No, Anya did not die physically during the Romanov slaughter in Yekaterinburg, yet part of her mind and surely a part of her soul went missing, evaporating into a misty portal of unreality where it rested until the end of her days. No one could rescue her from it.

Dear Anastasia. There was a certain part of her mind that was never the same after the trauma of that evil night when the very demons of the cosmos seemed to infest the soldiers to their actions. May God preserve their souls. Truly, they knew not what they did!

It came to me in a rush - they were programmed! The men involved in that slaughter were incited to their actions by the masters of their fate... and Russia's.

The Lady was right. A blurred vision showed me it was the crystal. It had mysteriously been confiscated from the royal palace. Rasputin had counseled the Tsarina to keep it safe yet somehow it was discovered and it fell into the wrong hands. Thus begat the Russian revolution of 1917 and the horrors that followed for the monarchy. How could King George have turned away his own kinfolk, blood royalty like himself? Yet he did the unthinkable. The shooting of the royal family was so senseless. Now it all became vibrantly clear.

Somehow the Crystal of Creation was later retrieved and entrusted to Anastasia, the youngest daughter, for the youngest two children were to be rescued by the kind peasant folk of the area.

"It would not be right. Children should not be sacrificed." It was the peasant women who demanded the rescue and safety of Anastasia and Alexei.

The crystal could only be activated by one of royal blood and due to Alexei's condition, it was decided Anastasia would be a better trustee and guardian. Who then, I wondered, had taken it from the Tsarina and activated it to their demise? I was not to wonder long.

"It was because of Alexei." Anya finally spoke, answering my thoughts. Her eyes lowered in a humble pose and with her voice echoing compassion and regret, she continued to relate her story.

Chapter 8 - "Rasputin"

"It was believed throughout history that Our Friend was a devil and the cause of our trouble. In truth, it was due to Our Friend that my brother remained alive and was able to live a fairly normal life."

As Anya continued, I visualized her very words and was at the scene of these occurrences.

"Mama met Our Friend through Countess Elizabeth Alexandrina, who brought him to her home on numerous occasions. She spoke very highly of him to mama.

"He is a 'starets', a prophet, Alix and reputed to have amazing healing abilities. Let me send him to you. He could do wonders for little Alexei." The countess spoke to the Tsarina in a whisper, leaving the Tsarina bristling a bit in her chair.

"Let me first explain some background about Alexei" continued Anya. "It was not open knowledge about his illness, at least not the full extent of it, even to our circle of friends. Only close relatives and very trusted friends of our family were fully aware of the suffering Alexei endured. It was for the protection of the monarchy, mama told us. We were not to speak of Alexei's bleeding to anyone outside of our family; just to be sure it was not discovered or leaked to the general public. So to our country people and to the world at large, the Tsar's family was seen as the picture of health and happiness. The gallant handsome soldier Tsar and the beautiful Tsarina with the four graceful, pure, faunlike daughters and of course, the young Tsarovich, heir to the throne.

"It was all a lie, naturally. Papa was a noble, gentle and gallant man but he was a quiet soul, preferring to spend his time with his family, going for long walks or reading and writing poetry... Oh yes, papa wrote beautifully. He had little interest in being the emperor of a country; at least, not one with the volatile history and complications of Russia. He loved his country, make no mistake, calling her Holy Mother Russia, or just Mother when amongst his family.

"Mama was the one who was born to rule and it was often voiced, many times unkindly, that the crown rested more easily on the head of Alix than on Nicolas. It was known that papa kept her counsel and asked her advice, but whether asked or not, mama often gave it, not considering how it might make papa feel or appear to the palace. Mama could be loving and compassionate but she was also very strong minded and stricter than papa. We could appeal to papa easier than to mama, but ..." Anya sighed, "That is how it is with most parents: One has to be the disciplinarian when the other is too gentle. If papa had a fault, that was it. He was too gentle a man to rule an empire. Perhaps he loved his family a bit too much.

"Alexei, on the other hand, may have had a physical condition, but he certainly did not lack spunk. He was always hurting himself, trying to do the things other boys did. I believe he had *inside* what it took to be a ruler. It later broke his heart when papa abdicated for him. Such was his fate. Later, years after the revolution, Alexei and I met up and spoke briefly about it. He told me then of his disappointment in papa's lack of trust in him.

"I tried to explain to Alexei that papa was only trying to protect him, speculating that he would be killed or worse.

"They killed us, or tried too, anyway Anouch (his pet name for me). At least I could have tried! I honestly felt that if I had been made Tsar in place of Uncle Michael, I could have saved Russia."

"Alexei, you were a child!" I retorted, amazed at his gall.

"Exactly!" Alexei returned smartly. "Exactly, Anouch! From the mouths of babes comes great wisdom. The Russian masses may have seen it as a return to innocence of the monarchy and 'forgiven' the Romanovs. Certainly they would not have executed a child the way those monsters tried to do in the dark. I could have been her redeemer. I KNOW it!" Alexei blew at me.

"In truth, I somehow believed him. Alexei was small but great in spirit. His mind was very strong and he possessed extra intelligence; our tutor said so. Alexei also had a kind of second sense about him. He was quite psychically aware and could intuit things, telling you of events before they occurred. We believed this sensitivity was in his blood, another characteristic of his disease. Alexei might have made a difference and changed the course of history. Yet it was not to be his fate. I believed he felt his destiny was taken out of his hands and it took him a very long time to come to terms with his anguish. Maybe he never did. I hope he did.

"For quite a few years after that, we exchanged cards and letters on special occasions such as Christmas and birthdays. We always wrote in a kind of a code that we had devised as children so if the messages were intercepted in any way, they would hold little meaning for the discoverer. There was nothing of rebellion in our notes at any rate. Alexei had no desire to try and regain his throne.

"It is too late", he wrote to me on the occasion of what would have been our parents' anniversary. "What was done cannot be undone at this time. Russia must bear her trials as best she can for now. It is not yet her time to rise."

"Alexei was very prolific in his philosophy and a bit of a prophet. Perhaps he foresaw the future for Russia. The angels tell me however her future is still in the writing.

"The very first time I beheld Our Friend was the night Alexei almost died. Mama was frantic from worry and had been keeping hourly vigils with Alexei but to no avail. The doctors could give her no reassurance. Finally, she sent for Our Friend, begging him to come at once.

"When I peeked into Alexei's room to see how he was, there was an angel standing beside mama in the dim golden light from Alexei's bed lamp. My eyes opened wide at what I beheld. Opening the door only a crack so as not to be detected, I watched, mesmerized, as this tall figure dressed in black moved about the room as if he was floating. His energy seemed as light as his dress was dark. The Dark Angel, as I would refer to him afterwards, spoke softly and reassuringly to mama. He eased her mind instantly and brought her peace. He had that affect upon people.

"He was gentle, like papa, as he smiled warmly at Alexei and stroked his hair. He said soothing words to Alexei and my brother's pallor appeared to return to normal almost immediately.

"Alexei will be fine by tomorrow, little mother", he cooed to mama. "You too must rest now." He added as he patted her hand tenderly.

"He spoke loving respect to mama then and always. There was never to be a question of his loyalty to us in our minds. We knew he was sent to us by God. It was his eyes. They blazed at you. They engulfed you with his supernatural energy and you could not move. He hypnotized you with them, but always for the good. And he was a very good man. He was always doing favors for people to help them. He gave them money, wrote notes to shop owners or banks (he held immense influence) and gave them to anyone who needed help. He refused no one.

"Let me tell you that although there was much talk of his 'impure behavior' and lurid stories were told about him, to us he was a savior and always showed the utmost respect and honor to my mother. I cannot speak for his actions in his private social life, but I will guarantee he and my mother shared only a sacred devotion to the healing of Alexei - and to God. I think Rasputin worshipped my mother as though she were the Holy Mother herself. To him, perhaps she was."

Chapter 9 – "The Gemstone Angel"

"It was Rasputin who brought mama the crystal. He said it was called The Gemstone Angel. Mama said he told her when you looked into the center of the crystal; you could see a beautiful bright angel."

I had to think about this new revelation Anya had brought to me. Could it be that this mistral of a man, who resembled a wild wind in his manner and his appearance, had the capacity to receive celestial gifts?

'God chooses his vehicles non-judgmentally' was the message that came to my mind.

Yes, of course. Rasputin would be the perfect vehicle to transport the holy crystal gemstone to the Tsar; the Gemstone Angel, as he named it. The Tsarina would believe it came from the Divine if he said it did.

"Mama was with him when he received it." Anya stated emphatically as her sapphire gaze riveted itself toward me. Anastasia had inherited her father's eyes; they had an uncanny ability to focus right on you and bore into your third eye, like a wolf enchanting its prey. Surprisingly, it was not an uncomfortable sensation but one that you were very aware of when you were in her presence. As she focused upon me, I received a vision of the scene of the acquisition.

The empress and the monk knelt in the small chapel at Tsarscoe Sela; once the home of Catherine the Great and then the Romanov country residence. The Tsarina wore a somber black dress adorned only by a rosary with a silver Russian crucifix. Someone had just died or was dying and the Tsarina appeared to be in deep mourning.

The candles burned peacefully on the ornate orthodox alter, blending their golden light with the light that sprayed through the stained glass windows on the other side of the alter. Alexandra kneeled reverently on the lip of the alter, with the monk known as Rasputin by her side.

"To receive from God, one must give something in return. Your God requires devotion to His causes. What can you promise God you will do, little mother, in return for Alexei's life?" Rasputin phrased the sentence simply and humbly like a servant delivering a message, which indeed it seemed he was.

"Promise?" responded the Tsarina. As if half in a trance her oval face turned to him, beseechingly. She was weary to the bone and it betrayed itself in her eyes with the shadows beneath almost as dark as her ebony gown. She had not slept in days.

The gaze of the empress moved from the monk upward to her divinity. Alexandra had eyes like those of St. Ann; the mother of the Virgin Mary; lovely but sad. Eyes that experienced grief and pain daily, not of her own but of those around her and, unspeakably, of those she loved dearest.

Alexei, as history later related, was a hemophiliac; in modern terminology, a bleeder. The tiniest bruise could cause him the severest agony for days due to the internal bleeding that could occur. Alexandra would have to endure the suffering of her youngest child and heir in inner turmoil, realizing in her truth that it was due to her own bloodline that Alexei was doomed to live a life of precaution at best. She was the carrier of the gene. The DNA of her bloodline ensured that she and none of her daughters would inherit the malady as it was passed on only to the males of the ancestral genealogy to which she belonged; the lineage of Queen Victoria. The women only carried the gene like a little demon cell in their blood whilst the men were torn apart and bled inside as if the demons held tiny razors and cut them open at the slightest pressure from the outside world. What a fate to own.

I wondered incredulously if this was a hereditary characteristic passed down through the Christ bloodline. It was quoted several times throughout biblical and religious texts that Mary Magdalene was a woman who possessed seven 'devils'. It was further speculated that she was an epileptic and that this malady was one of the 'demons' that Jesus healed her of, or 'cast out' as it is written in the scriptures.

It was a belief during their time in history that any type of illness was thought of as 'demon' or a 'devil' that the individual had allowed to enter them by being impure somehow. Women were even considered to be untouchable and impure during their menstrual time and were sent to a special tent or enclosure that was literally called 'The Red Tent', until the end of their period. Afterward they immersed themselves in a special bath and then returned to their homes and families, cleansed and 'pure' again.

My researcher journalistic intuition was activated and assembled some interesting coincidences in my ever fervent mind:

If Mary Magdalene, who was believed to be the wife of Jesus, according to the information that emerged from the newly released dead sea scrolls, had been in the possession of seven devils, could these 'devils' have realistically existed as several diseases which resulted from a characteristic of the blood?

It has been researched and ascertained that diabetes can be the host cause of numerous other ailments of the body. If gone undetected and/or untreated (and it seemed reasonable this would be the case at this point in history) it can be the forerunner of high blood pressure, angina, blindness, heart disease, lameness, mental confusion, epilepsy and (possibly) hemophilia. Seven devils or seven diseases; caused by the malfunction in the genes of a bloodline?

Jesus 'cast out' the demons from his wife, but she could still have remained a carrier of any and all of these ailments; all connected to the plasma or blood inherited from that lineage. Mary Magdalene had great faith and possessed the devotion and fortitude to release the 'devils' or illnesses that 'possessed' her. Were her offspring or descendants also with the same reserve, or was this holy blood in time diluted by inferior characteristics of other bloodlines that would meld and blend with it? It would be reasonable to expect so.

Perhaps that explains why the aristocracy, particularly royalty, has been so fussy about the mating of the elitist class lines. Diana Spencer, having once referred to herself as a 'brood mare', may not have been far off course. If the royal family knew their lineage possessed this 'characteristic' of the blood (line) that could manifest as diabetes, epilepsy or as in Alexei's' case hemophilia, one cannot blame them for being cautious. After all, as history related and Anya confirmed, it was the fault or weakness in the blood of the young Tsarovich that was the backdrop for the Russian revolution.

I suddenly considered myself to be very lucky simply having to avoid sugar and eat several times during the day to keep healthy. My daughter was in good health, thankfully, and seemed to have bypassed any genetic conditions. As a female she would not be inflicted with hemophilia, but had she been born a boy...

Suddenly a switch flicked on in my head and the realization was brought to me of why The Lady had taken the child Jacey and I had conceived together: It was to have been a boy... And possibly – probably - would have been inflicted with the disease from my bloodline.

"Not at this time", the Lady had said ever so sadly. *"Not at this time…"*

So, was I here now in this place and vision to somehow put it all to right? That would mean correcting or healing the fault in the bloodline... but how? And even if I could do that, Jacey was gone now. There would be no chance for us again. My mind, racing, came to a stop as I noticed a blazing light above the alter where the Tsarina and Rasputin knelt.

"I would make any sacrifice for the life of my child". The poignant words of the beautiful empress were weighted by guilt and scented with agony. My heart flew to her and tore apart as she wept.

"Then pray, little mother, pray deeply to God to bequeath what He will of you ... So that Thy will be done ..", The monk issued the words forth with such depth of emotion that an energy appeared to explode around him. The energy shot out all about the chapel, hitting and infusing the Empress with its potency.

The Tsarina spasmed slightly as the energy bolt hit her. Her arms spread themselves out like graceful wings and her face was infused with the sun whilst she knelt entranced in her ecstasy.

The blazing light above the alter began to enlarge and lower itself in front of the Tsarina. The light was so bright that I had to blink to make out a shape.

The light drew itself into a form and a fair bright angel appeared before the Tsarina. It was a feminine form with long flowing silver hair and seemed to be enclosed in a silvery white filament. Her light and energy enlivened and vibrated life to any and all in her midst.

"I am an angel of the Lord", she said simply.

Then, behind the angel, appeared a form out of nowhere, or had I simply not noticed Her. It was The Lady.

As the Tsarina remained in her ecstasy at the alter, the angel began to implode upon itself and become smaller and smaller until it was the size of a small sapphire ball, glowing iridescently as it sat in the open hands of The Lady, who was now fully visible in the chapel.

"Ahhh...".The monk gasped with a throaty resonance. His eyes began to tear as he beheld Her and he bowed in reverence to Her.

"Matroushka ..." was all he could utter. "Holy Mother, You have come ..."

"Yes, I have come." She spoke. *"I have been touched by the tears of your daughter. There is something she must do. The mother country is afflicted with an evil and must be cleansed and healed for the world depends upon her. The boy suffers as a symptom, a symbol of the ailment of the country. The child must be healed for the land to be healed, or... he will be a sacrificial lamb."*

"What must the little mother do, Matroushka?" the monk asked in sacred tones.

"Your daughter is to take the Gemstone Angel and keep it sacred. It is the source of power for her kingdom and for her country. It has the ability to crystallize and bring into manifestation any created desire. Advise her to use this tool wisely brother, for it can be used to create... and also to destroy."

With that The Lady bade the monk take the Gemstone Angel from Her hands to give to the Empress of all Russia.

And so it was done.

The vision of the scene in the chapel at Tsarscoe Sela disappeared as quickly as it had appeared to me. I blinked and was once again in the royal bedroom with Anastasia, the youngest daughter of the Tsar, quietly staring at me. It was a penetrating gaze. Then, she blinked and quickly shook her delicate head and seemed to come back to the present, at least as it was.

"Then ... it was the monk Rasputin who brought the Gemstone Angel to your mother?" I finally spoke the incredulous words to Anya.

"Yes", Anya answered lightly, almost seeming to dismiss the occurrence, though she admitted, "Mama was to be the chosen recipient of the precious Gemstone Angel for the duty given to her ... But it was Our Friend who intervened for her.. She needed his power to bring it to her."

"Why?" I asked my journalist mind still intact.

"Because ... Our Friend ... the Angels talked to him ... as did the Queen of the Angels." Anya answered solemnly, her face glowing with pious reverence and her eyes blazing from a light behind them that shot their sapphire hue straight through my third eye.

"He was your Dark Angel." I agreed.

"Yes ... And it was because of us that he died."

What an interesting perception, I thought. Especially since history would later recount this to be the other way around.

"How did it happen?" I approached the inevitable. " .. That the Gemstone Angel came to fall into the wrong hands?"

Anya was silent for a time wrapped in her own reverie.

"Poor Alexei", she said finally, her head bowed and humbled by sadness. Then her head bolted upright and she darted her eyes directly at me as she asked. "But what was mama to do?"

The scene of our encounter shifted again and we were in the private quarters of the Tsar and Tsarina. As the decor of the royal couples' bedroom floated into focus, I could see the lilac wallpaper come into view and feature the backdrop of the rulers of all the Russias engaged in the decision that would seal the future of their lives and their country.

Alexandra Romanov, Empress of Russia, sat regally at her dressing table. Even in her most private hours I was struck by her stunning deportment. So elegant, her spine so erect, her neck so graceful, her long fingers so queenly. She was born for this life, I thought to myself. This role was written for her.

"Yes", echoed Anya. "Mama was very fine." Her words were respectful and her demeanor expressed the honor she felt for her mother. Anya's eyes were lowered and her tiny hands were folded in front of her as if holding a sadness that was too painful to release. I knew she was reliving internally the circumstances of her mother's demise.

"Don't do that, Anya", I spoke to her and reached out to hold her as one would a hurting child, realizing as soon as I touched and comforted her that her dam could break and I would be left to deal with emotions I might not be prepared to handle. Still, I reasoned while watching the tears spill from Anya's eyes, was this not what I was called here for? Was the healing of Anastasia's grief not part of what The Lady desired of me... and would the recovery of the soul of my grandmother, even one I had never known, be what I would desire and expect of myself?

As I held the young grand duchess close to me, she sobbed softy; her head resting upon my shoulder. My words of comfort to her expressed forth, "It was your mother's choices that selected her fate, Anya. There was nothing you could have done. It was her destiny. There was nothing anyone could have done. What we can do however is to try and make her sacrifice stand for something."

I pulled her away from me and gently wiped her tears from her cheeks with my fingers. "*That*, we can do. That is something I can do." Speaking to her reassuringly in a promising voice, "I am a writer and a journalist and will make sure her truth is told."

Anya raised her eyes and looked into mine. "Yes?" Anya implored.
"Yes." I swore.

Chapter 10 – "Nicolas and Alexandra"

Tsarina Alexandra Romanov sat before her reflection in the carved oval mirror of her dressing table.

"How had it happened?" read the image of her expression in the mirror. "How had I let it happen? What will become of us now?" her haunted eyes broadcast.

A crumpled piece of notepaper lay across the glass tabletop before her. I glanced at the fine script upon the paper, noting that the writing was, remarkably, in English. Focusing intently on the four words on the paper wrenched by Alexandra's grieving despairing hands, it read simply: "Rasputin has been murdered".

The empress stared at her mirrored reflection as if viewing her own future and destiny. Did she foresee her family's less than fair fortune? Did she anticipate the traumas and the evil that would befall them?

Her St. Ann eyes were the saddest I had ever seen them and the haunted quality that had settled there would never leave and would forever be within them. A ghostlike quality appeared to come over her that would also remain.

Alexandra did become a walking ghost after the death of Rasputin, her dear friend and spiritual adviser. "It was entirely my fault", the words emitted from the Empress' mouth. "I should never have given the Gemstone Angel to Nicky."

As Alexandra remained seated before her dressing table, the scenario of time and space quickened and focused on an earlier morning several months prior.

The Tsarina was attired in her ivory silk dressing gown, her hair still waving down her back from her sleep. Her eyes were large and full of love as she watched her husband, Tsar Nicolas, adjust his official uniform as head of state of the national army of his country. It was a uniform that was dark and elegant, resplendent with the sash that draped from shoulder to waist answering to his gallant sword. (The Sword of Truth, I wondered?)

This was the Tsar's dress uniform, worn for official occasions. He would wear it for the pomp and ceremony of his announcement of his decision to join and lead his troops on the front. When he boarded the imperial train to join his army however, he would be wearing the same regimental uniform of his men.

Alexandra admired the fine form and handsome face of her beloved Nicky. He was not born of the 'stuff' of her rigid Victorian relatives, but Nicolas was a kind and loving man and a welcome change from her cold to the bone Anglo Teutonic ancestors. Alexandra never regretted marrying him and this morning she sat still basking in the glow of their lovemaking of the previous evening and early morning: Nicolas was a man of ardent passion, yet gentle and sensitive with it.

Alexandra often blushed when she caught herself thinking of her ardent 'lover' when she was about her duties at the palace. During much of their marriage she could barely wait for evening to arrive so she and Nicolas could retire for the night to their bed chambers and light up one another with passion's fire. The fact that Alexandra bore four daughters first was all the more reason to 'prepare' an heir and still remain a pious catholic. The throne of Russia required an heir, did it not?

It was only after the discovery of the young Tsarovich's health condition that the couples' nightly routine altered. The Tsarina was forever the mindful mother with all her children, but she knew she must be particularly watchful of Alexei. He was her namesake and she was always to wonder if she did not curse him in this naming. As he had inherited her name, had he also in so doing inherited the bloodline gene of hemophilia? She had seldom reprieve from her guilt. This was another reason for her gratefulness in having married Nicky. He never hung the cross of inheritance of the bloodline about her neck. She was grateful for that blessing for she fastened that same cross to her own breast until it pierced her heart and bled.

"I will not see you again until my return from the front", Nicolas spoke as he finished fastening his belt. "I will leave directly after the announcement and will not be returning to the palace, Sunny." (Sunny was her grandmother's personal nickname for Alix and the name that those closest to her called her in private.)

Alexandra felt fear grip her; fear that her beloved Nicolas would not return from the warring front. Panic ran through her veins like an electric shock that she might get notice of Nicky's demise as he led his men into battle. Her only thought was how to prevent that reality, how to protect him.

Her gaze fell upon the gold Faberge egg that sat in a miniature carriage upon her dressing table. She grasped the egg, which looked like an oval cage set atop the wheels and harness. It opened easily with a tiny latch to reveal a second gold egg. After flipping open the second egg, she removed the final third perfect golden oval filigree from its encasement. On its top rested a tiny gold ring with a miniature cross anointing it.

In a flash of inspiration, the Tsarina opened her ribbon box, took out a black velvet cord of about thirty inches in length, strung it through the top ring and tied the ribbon ends together in a slip knot. Quickly, she unlocked her top dresser drawer and brought out a folded piece of beautifully embroidered white alter cloth. The centre of the cloth bulked and seemed to shine from a strange and radiant light within it.

Alexandra unfolded the linen cloth carefully and transferred the blazing crystal stone into the gold filigree egg. At first glance it appeared the gemstone would never fit inside the tiny egg but the crystal was deceptive. It gave the appearance of being three times its actual size due to its radiance.

The Tsarina closed the egg and brought it over to her husband, slipped it around his neck and tucked it inside his jacket.

"Nicky, take this and wear it always. Never take it off for a moment. It will protect you. It will protect us all."

So that was how it was done. The Tsarina released the sacred stone to protect her husband and bring him safely home to her. She could never have imagined the repercussions that this act would inspire.

My mind assumed that the Gemstone Angel had somehow fallen into the wrong hands but I still could not comprehend how this circumstance could have been the cause of such tragic results. Then, I was allowed the vision.

Father Gregory was charming and full of life, socializing and into his cups with some of his friends. Rasputin was not always a discerning man regarding his companions and he could fall prey to openly discussing that which was better left unspoken. It was under such a circumstance that the Black Monk, as he was also referred to, spoke the unmentionable.

I saw a vignette of a past scene of a party in a less comely section of the city of Moscow. The dancers had danced their colorful movements well into the night and the musicians had flayed their balalaikas and flung their voices into the smoke filled air of the monk's home.

The opium steamed inside the Turkish water pipe and several dozen partygoers were draped over the furniture and onto the dingy carpet on the floor.

"So Rasputin!.." brayed one of the dancers, an aging gypsy woman who covered her face with too much garish makeup to hide the ravages of time and only succeeded in making it worse. Maya was her name. In a vulgar gesture, she threw up her skirt from where she lay on the carpet and flung her leg over Rasputin, demanding brassily, "... Tell us how you ride that Empress of yours." Maya positioned herself on all fours and barked, "Does she like it normal ... or does she like it like a dog, up the ..." With that Maya stuck her buttocks in Rasputin's' face and bumped it up and down, laughing wildly.

"Come here and I'll show you what I'll do with YOU!" Rasputin grabbed Maya by the waist and pulled her over him so she sat straddling him, her underwear resting atop his erection.

"Ahh ... "Maya's eyes widened as she moved back and forth over him.

"Talking of the little German whore gets you full of fire, you old bastard, you. Pretending to be a priest, all the while knocking around with the Tsarina and her little daughter whores ..."

Rasputin pushed the gypsy off of him in disgust. "You jealous cow!" he scowled. "You don't know what you're talking about."

"She's only repeating what every Russian from here to the Urals is saying", blared a drunken voice from one of the sailors who was sprawled across the sofa opposite the monk.

"They are crazy. I never touch her", Rasputin leered.

"Well ..." Maya interjected from the floor, her petticoats splayed all about her, "What do you do with her and those four girls, then?" Maya stuck out her tongue and wiggled it obscenely.

The monk made a face and turned away.

"You are revolting. Do you want to know what I do with the Tsarina and the Grand Duchesses? I'll tell you what I do... I PRAY with them, comrades! Yes! It's true. We PRAY!!"

"I'll pray to God that you're a liar, Rasputin!" scowled the sailor.

"By God, I'm not a liar!" bellowed the monk. His voice softened and he spoke in reverent tones. "No ... it is true. I pray with the little matroushka. I pray with her and with the Holy Mother."

The partygoers were silent.

Drunkenness turned to reverence as Rasputin spoke, "I prayed with the little mother ... and the Holy Mother came. Right there in the chapel in the palace. She appeared... and she put an angel in a crystal stone. She said it was the Stone of Creation and the little mother should keep it with her always: That it would protect the royal family... and Russia as well."

"What is this, some sort of stone of good and evil?" scoffed the sailor.

"Perhaps ..." the monk continued seriously. "She said not to let it fall into the wrong hands as it could destroy as well as create."

"So, whoever has this stone could bring down the royal family?" came another voice from the back of the room.

"Yes ..." answered Rasputin, weaving off into a drugged sleep. "And probably control a lot more ... Control the world ..."

"Let's see this angel stone of yours!" demanded the disheveled Maya, moving to a seated position on one of the cushions on the floor. "I'd like to do a little creating myself", she spoke as she brushed off adhering cigar ashes from the carpet that had mixed with the wine and spittle on her bodice.

"Yes ... Where is this mysterious crystal?" came the dark voice from the dark part of the room.

"I do not have it, comrades. It was given to the little mother", Rasputin spoke, or rather mumbled, his eyelids closing. "She is a saint. She will keep the Gemstone Angel sacred to her... And it will save us all. It will save Russia ... This Angel of the Tsar". The monk snoozed off.

"How is the Gemstone Angel to save Russia ... when it is not even in Russia?" This voice came from behind the sprawling dinner table across the room.

"Hmm ... impossible", sniffed Rasputin. "I gave the Angel to the Tsarina myself."

"Yes ..." agreed the strong youthful voice of the young man who was now standing and leaning over the discarded dinner remnants. "And your Tsarina gave it to her husband to wear to the front."

The young man poured himself a glass of wine, that he did not need, from a garnet toned floral decanter and continued.

"I am one of the palace guards, remember?" The tall blond figure raised his glass and downed the wine in one gulp. He was already intoxicated, now he began wavering on his feet.

"I was with the Tsar when he changed from his formal uniform into his uniform of the regiment. He was wearing one of those Faberge eggs the Romanovs love so much on a black velvet ribbon around his neck. The Tsar himself held it in his hand and showed it to us. When his brother Michael commented on his wearing jewelry into battle, the Tsar said, 'It is from my wife. She said it would protect me and bring me home to her. It has some kind of special holy stone inside of it. Sunny was very insistent that I should wear it.' The Tsar shrugged, like he wore it to please his wife." The soldier belched and returned to his chair.

"That's right, Sergei", laughed the sailor. "You sit down before you fall down!"

Rasputin rolled over and his eyes began to widen as the realization of what had been said registered to him.

"The Tsarina gave the Gemstone Angel to the Tsar ...?" the monk whispered.

"Yes, Brother!" blurted the blond soldier "To wear into battle!"

Rasputin sat up in stunned silence. "It can't be true ..." he muttered.

"Oh, it is true brother! I saw the amulet myself", confirmed Sergei, jutting out his bottom lip.

"Then, we are doomed comrades ..." echoed Rasputin's' voice throughout the room ... And later throughout all of Russia.

Then I saw the vision of how Russia, the once great mother country of all Europe, went into ruin. Once called the breadbasket of Europe, she descended into a land that could not even feed her own. And it got worse. The vision showed the aristocrats in Moscow and elsewhere across the European continent, whispering amongst themselves with voices of treachery and savagery against the Tsar and his family. Later, as history discloses, the Romanov family was even denied sanctuary in England, the homeland of Queen Victoria, Alix's grand mother.

Rasputin's prediction proved accurate. Russia would be no more and the fate of the Romanovs was sealed horrifically by a stone that, as the monk foretold, could both create and destroy.

"But ... where did the Gemstone Angel go after it went with the Tsar?" I pondered.

Shot back to the scene of Rasputin's apartment again, I saw the strange dark figure move toward the front door and silently slip out unnoticed. Once outside, he did not waste time in running through the Moscow streets to disclose his secret information to his allies. Within a matter of hours, a dark plot was instigated and put into operation.

As if in flashback, I saw a covert messenger bring a letter to the Tsar with a forged signature of the Tsarina asking 'Nicky' to immediately send the amulet back to her with the messenger, stating she needed it for Alexei. The shaken Tsar removed the amulet at once and gave it to the messenger who he recognized as one of his palace guards. It was Sergei!

Yet it was not Sergei who was the traitor. After departing the Tsar's quarters and returning via the train back to Moscow, his throat was slit while he slept in his berth. The same dark man slipped off the train into the Russian night.

"Do you want to know why Brother Gregory was really murdered?" queried Anya, her voice bringing me out of my vision.

"Yes!" I answered immediately. "It was because of the Gemstone Angel, wasn't it?"

"Yes. Brother Gregory rescued it for mama, but then he was killed before he could return it to her", Anya replied, sadly.

I closed my eyes and tried to return to my vision. The dark man (the man of dark energy) slithered through the Moscow streets and climbed the backstairs to his equally dark rooms in a building located in a secluded area of the city.

He was home. He was safe with his prize which he would utilize as soon as possible. He slipped into the building, down the dank hallway and unlocked his apartment door. He found the lamp, turned on the light, turned around and came face to face with ... Rasputin.

The monk's huge hand barely touched the thief but his energy sent him nearly through the wall, where he then floated unconscious to the floor.

The monk walked down the icy streets to his own apartment several city blocks away. He was glad of the fresh air after breathing the dark energy of the dark man. It was only a few more feet until he reached his building and climbed the stairs. Brother Gregory turned the key in his door, walked over to the tiffany lamp; a gift from the Tsarina; on the table beside his couch and lit it. The clock on the mantle sounded 4:00 A.M. He would sleep soundly tonight, what was left of it, and return the precious gemstone to the Tsarina the next day. He pulled the shimmering egg out of his pocket and hung it around his neck for safe keeping.

The tall monk, moving lithely for his build, sauntered to his bed and pulled off his boots. He then fell back onto his pillows into a heavy and immediate sleep.

Two days later, after accepting a dinner invitation at the home of the Tsar's cousins, the two princes, Rasputin was discovered and pulled from the river Volga. He was dead, with several pistol and dagger wounds found in his body. But what force had it taken to kill him! Rasputin survived knifing, then bullets and was also found to have poison in his system. What kind of man was this who would not - or could not - die! Until the Gemstone Angel was removed from him.

I saw the vision of Rasputin running on that night. He ran... and ran... and he almost got away. He knew he would live if he got away, as long as he had the gemstone. When it was taken from his body, he was gone too. Such was its power.

"And so went the fate of Holy Mother Russia ... and also the future of the earth." I heard Anya's' voice in my mind while shifting back into consciousness and back to the pretty yellow bedroom at the chateau.

Anya sat still as a deer on the edge of my bed. "He died for nothing and he could have saved us and Russia if he would have lived." Anya lowered her eyes and allowed silent tears to flow down her cheeks. Thank God she is releasing her pain. It was a first step.

Anya may have been a survivor of the horrific massacre at Yekaterinburg but it was she who carried the anguish, the grief, that was to hold and bind her family for generations. My consciousness was sure of it now. My mission was here to heal Anastasia. Healing Anastasia would be crucial for the future of 'my' family... and possibly also for the future of the world.

I watched Anya as she sat motionless before me on the yellow silk coverlet. Suddenly a buzzing sound seemed to encircle me and I looked around the softly lit bedroom to see if a bee had somehow found its hapless way in through some opening. Alas, the 'bee' was in my head! My mid forehead was tingling. It felt like a tiny drill had been switched on inside my brain.

"Your third eye has been opened, Angelique", came the voice of The Lady. *"You are feeling the lapis crystal spinning and tuning into the etheric and invisible energies around you."*

"Think back, Angelique." The Lady continued. *"Think back to a long time ago when I came to you in your sleep, as I did so many times in your younger life, to guide and teach you. Remember when I opened you to see auras and light around people and all other matter of life?"*

I closed my eyes and leaned back into the fine silk embroidered pillows and let my consciousness drift back in time. The Lady had indeed been with me in my youth and also in my early adulthood. She had been with me many, many times! Why had I not remembered Her?

"You were not meant to remember my guidance at that time as I was there to assist you in your spiritual enlightenment." Before she continued further, the Lady's voice rested momentarily. *"Remember how I showed you the different light bodies within and around the human body (or one's life form)?*

"Yes ... I remember." I could see in my minds' eye The Lady 'teaching' me or rather my soul body as my physical body, slept. I was a teenager and lay asleep under my lilac quilted bed cover in my lilac painted bedroom. The Lady appeared in my room, standing upon my lilac carpet, Her form outlined by my white window drapes that covered the entire wall. *I* sat up in bed and walked over and stood in front of Her. *I* turned to see my physical form still in my bed, my hair in long tendrils on the lilac pillowcase. Yet, the circumstance seemed not unusual. *I* turned to my right and viewed my (that is my soul or light body) reflection in the mirror of the dresser. My soul form shone as though an enormous light bulb had been placed behind where *I*, my soul, stood.

The Lady showed me my aura, my etheric body and the other layers of energy bodies, the mental and the emotional and how they were connected with one another.

"*When one layer is out of balance, it will affect the entire being of the life form.*" The words she spoke existed through my lips.

"*Yes.*" The Lady agreed. "*Now, open your eyes and fix them upon Anastasia.*"

Chapter 11 ~ "Healing Anastasia"

"It is odd ..." I spoke in reflection, "that I should be an instrument in the healing of my grandmother."

"How so, little one...?" The voice asked, compassionately.

"Well ... because besides being my grandmother, she is also me, isn't she?" I queried.

"Cherie ..." The voice spoke softly and upon opening my eyes I realized it was Celine who was beside me, not The Lady.

Celine approached the bed and sat on the opposite side of where Anya had been.

"Cherie", she began again. "You were not Anastasia in a past life. Anastasia lived to be a very old lady. She died in 1980. You, m'enfant, were Alexandra."

My eyes fixed upon Celine for what seemed like an eternity. "I was Alexandra ... Anastasia's mother!" The realization finally absorbed into my consciousness.

"Oh ..." I gasped. "Of course! I understand now... finally. Anya was my child... my youngest daughter. It was because of my actions that she underwent such a tragic ordeal... And lived such a scarred emotional life after ..."

As if caught up in a circling wheel, my mind was lifted into another dimension where a movie was played for me of the life Anya led after she and Alexei were spirited away from Yekaterinburg.

Anastasia's broken and bloody body was pulled out of the truck by the hands of the peasant women of the area; mothers themselves with children at home that although starving and uneducated were nonetheless still alive and had a future to look forward to.

"What does this poor lamb have to look forward to? To live for?" shouted one of the peasant women. "What kind of life will she have, all broken and emotionally shattered for life?"

"Shut up!" blared a large peasant woman. With perspiration teeming down her forehead and onto her shawl, she forged toward her horse drawn wagon, carrying Anya in her arms and loaded her onto the wooden cart.

"She is the same age as my Olga and your Natalia…" The woman stood up and leaned her hand behind her to help straighten her back. "If the child is alive and she managed to live through THAT" she said, spreading her free arm over to the slaughtering truck, "then she deserves a chance at life: *Any* life is better than ending that way."

I continued to view the movie of Anya's life as she miraculously lived through her transport in the back of a horse drawn wagon to the barn of the farmer whose wife had gently wrapped Anya in a handmade patchwork quilt.

"Such a pretty little thing", spoke the woman as she stroked Anya's bruised forehead. "And to think, she's a Grand Duchess."

"Yes, tavarich; it just shows you never know how you will end up in life", yelled her husband as he dismounted from the seat of the wagon.

"The girl is badly mangled, but she will survive." The midwife advised as she set a brew of herbal tea prepared by her own skillful hands beside the young Grand Duchess. "How her mind will go is of course another matter. She may be tortured by her dreams all her life, or… she may remember nothing."

"Better for her if she does that", remarked the farmer under his breath.

"Not remember even … who she is", added the mid wife.

The farmer's wife looked at her husband hopefully. "Uri, we could keep her as our own then. No one would know or even care. We live so remote from any village, it would be …"

"No we could not!" blared the farmer known as Uri. "It's too dangerous." Looking down at the pitiful broken girl however, he softened. "Alright, she can stay ... but only until she's healed and then she must be sent off. For her own safety as well as ours, she must leave this country, Anna." He stared at his wife beseechingly. "Surely, you must understand *why*! They are killing all Romanovs!"

"Yes ... I understand ", Anna agreed. But she would keep the girl as long as possible. Her own Olga would be her age if she had lived. Yes. She would hope that the girl didn't heal too quickly, at least not that could be seen.

Unconscious most of the time and when she was conscious mainly delirious, Anastasia stayed hidden in the farmhouse for several months, sleeping and healing in their daughter's bed.

Physically, Anya healed remarkably well under the care of the local midwife, who performed miracles on her torn and broken body. The poultices she applied to her wounds and the herbs she blended for Anya to drink helped her flesh and organs heal with very few lasting scars. Anna cared for her well with tenderness and devotion but Uri kept her to her agreement and when Anya could be moved, the girl was secretly taken to Sweden before arrangements could be make for her to travel safely by train on through to the south of France.

Anya's days at Chateau de la Breyeres were her happiest for many years to come. The nightmares did not haunt her nearly so much during this time of her life nor the pain of her wounds as they later would. Thank God for grand pere, I breathed. Yes, he helped her regain her sense of self again.

It was almost a relief when 'that Anna woman' (as the 'imposter' was called who was believed by some to be the long lost youngest daughter of the Romanovs), became a celebrity in Europe and then the United States. The real aristocracy knew better, of course, but she made a valuable camouflage for the true Anastasia to live in privacy, far from the limelight the world would have focused upon her. Had that happened, it could possibly have unhinged her already delicate and vulnerable emotional well being.

When Anya believed her daughter (my mother) had been killed in the car crash, along with her two guardians, the circumstance sent Anya into shock and a mental and emotional state from which she never truly recovered.

Anya would frequently call out her daughter's name in the middle of the night and often, in her later years when she went through her 'spells', would wander about her Paris apartment calling out "Jeanne ... Jeanne?" asking visitors if they had seen her baby. "I can't find my child. She must be lost... I must find my Jeanne Marianne!"

Anya named my mother after Joan of Arc, the Marianne of France as it was France that gave her sanctuary for most of her life.

Anya's spells began in her mid twenties and were infrequent at first; at times accompanied by fainting and lasting anywhere from a few moments to half an hour. They picked up frequency and length as she aged.

During her years in exile after my mother's birth, Anya lived in the mountain area bordering Switzerland. Although still caring deeply for J.P., Anya with her royal breeding ingrained in her since birth, realized they were not meant to be. She married an Austrian-Italian count, who was also an international businessman, and had a son with him. Her son later moved to Canada where he married a Canadian of European lineage and had a daughter who now resides in Montreal.

Anya's marriage to the count lasted until his death. Although devoted to her in many ways, the count had the coolness of his Austrian aristocratic lineage; so much like the relatives of Anya's mother. He also, however, possessed the passion (albeit the chauvinism) of his Italian heritage. 'He was wonderful - and impossible!', Anya would later relate of him, adding, 'Much like I was, as Karl would often remind me'.

Her Paris apartment became her permanent home when Karl died. She had a steady relationship for many years with a North American banker but was to maintain her position in Paris until her end.

Anya's injuries of mind and body would plague her throughout her life and involve frequent medication and psychiatric counseling. She became one of Carl Jung's hidden yet favorite patients.

"What can I ... must I do, to help heal Anastasia?" I questioned out loud.

"It will be an involved process", Celine answered. "It includes several factors. You see, Queen Victoria's family carried a large amount of responsibility as well. King George refused sanctuary to Alix (the name given by her grandmother Queen Victoria and the one her relatives always called her by) and her family; an act that was to inflict a stain upon England's future royal descendants, as history has proven."

It was true. The tragedy and hapless luck seemed to descend almost immediately with the weakest link that connected to the heritage of the title of Prince of Wales. I pondered that if the chain could be broken perhaps William, Diana's son, could be saved this unfortunate fate.

"Precisely!", Celine responded. "He is to be saved because his mother Diana was a priestess of the Goddess and sent to earth by Aphrodite Herself.

"Diana's death wounded not just the planet and its etheric energy but inflicted a wound to Aphrodite as well. Aphrodite is the Goddess of Love. It is this energy that has been affected here on earth. If it is not healed, the planet cannot survive as we know it.

"These gods and goddesses are like metaphors or symbols of certain energies that prevail throughout the hemisphere of the planet Earth, the universe *and* the cosmos as well. Can you understand that as the strongest and purest and most important energy of all is hurt and lessened, it affects all living creatures throughout eternity?

"The repercussions that resulted from the atrocities of the Russian Revolution had affects in World War I that were never resolved and resulted in World War II. The unleashing of the holocaust, the maiming from the attack at Pearl Harbor, the Viet Nam war and the Middle East conflict can all be connected back to circumstances of the Russian Revolution... and the misuse of the Gemstone Angel."

"How was the stone retrieved?" I asked.

"Our order finally located its whereabouts and returned it to its rightful inherited owner after World War II."

"It was given to Anastasia?" I queried.

"Yes", Celine responded.

"What affect did the Russian Revolution have upon the Viet Nam war?"

"Ah ..." sighed Celine and pulled her feet up under her on the bed and continued. "Yes, there was a time interval when the Gemstone Angel went missing."

"It was stolen?"

"It was mysteriously taken from the Grand Duchess and spirited out of France. It went missing for about a decade and a half."

"The approximate duration of the Viet Nam war", I replied.

"The major part of it, yes", responded Celine. "It was believed to have been stolen by a 'trusted' servant, Anya's maid, who also went missing right after the theft. It was returned to Anastasia in the 1970's and she wore it constantly until her death in 1980."

"Alright, I just received this Gemstone Angel several days ago. My question is, where has the stone been for over eighteen years?"

"It took us a while to find Anastasia's next of kin, after ..."

"After?"

"After Alexei's' death..."

"Alexei...!" I sat bolt upright, knocking the diary from the pillow onto the coverlet. I had not considered Alexei in all this. "Alexei ... my great uncle ... was alive all this time?"

"Yes, cherie, he was alive for quite a long time."

"Where? In France?"

"No. Alexei was in Russia. He stayed in his homeland. It was too dangerous to move him too far because of his hemophilia as it was not certain he would live. He wasn't as strong as his sister. Alexei was adopted by a family with tsarist sympathies, raised as any other soviet citizen and became a regular comrade, working in a factory. He was also kept in Russia as tsarist sympathizers were secretly planning a revolt and a return to 'Romanov Rule' and they wanted Alexei there to take his position as Tsar of Russia. Also, Alexei was too loyal to his Holy Mother Russia to want to leave."

"Did he have children?" I leaned forward, anxious to know if Christina had any cousins.

"He married a woman named Svetlana and had two children, a boy named Uri and a girl named Katya. There was a grand daughter who died very young named Larissa. He nicknamed her Lara, after ..."

"Dr. Zhivago!" I finished.

"Yes." Celine smiled. "It was his favorite novel."

"Mine as well", I confided and lowered my eyes pensively and also in some way as an attempt to honor Alexei's memory. The youngest of the Tsar's family and the least regarded. The fall of Tsarist Russia was always to be partly his blame in history. What must his life have been like, this (from all accounts) brilliant but luckless boy; the carrier of the blood.

"How could he have stayed alive for so long?" I requested of Celine.

"Ah ... yes. How indeed", responded Anastasia.

I turned to her, still sitting poised yet aware on the left side of the bed now.

"It was thanks to Our Friend. Brother Gregory had taught Alexei certain breathing techniques; what you call yoga; that allowed him to control his condition. He taught him meditations and a particular healing technique." Anya held up her arms and looked at her palms. "He used his hands."

"Reiki?" I wondered out loud.

"Yes. I think it was something like that but he called it by another name", Anya responded.

Chapter 12 ~ "Forgiveness"

"Angelique."

I heard The Lady's voice again and upon doing so felt my body relax and recline back against the pillows. My eyelids lowered and closed.

"Take Anastasia back to the point of her pain and anguish." The Lady bade me.

"The point of ..? I don't understand", I answered. I felt The Lady take my hand and linked it with Anya's.

"Take Anya back to Yekaterinburg."

"No!" cried Anya. "Please. I can't go through that horror again!"

"This seems unnecessarily cruel." I offered. "Are you sure this is best?"

"Take her back!" commanded The Lady, softly but firmly and placed Her hand over our hands.

The mists gathered up around us and a startling wind like a mistral encircled us, lifting us off the bed and out through a tunnel of some kind. I wondered if perhaps it was the same time tunnel Jules Verne wrote about.

"That is a fairly accurate analogy", The Lady replied to my thought. *"This is necessary for us all, Angelique."* She continued, *"It may seem cruel, but it is the only way."*

"Bring them downstairs", spoke the Russian soldier to one of the guards. The soldier was of some rank indistinguishable from his uniform. His gray eyes were cold as a hunter trained by a wolf.

Moments later the family of Nicolas and Alexandra Romanov, the Emperor and Empress of all the Russias, appeared on the staircase. They stood regal and still, as if waiting to be beckoned or announced. Neither occurred, so Alexandra and Nicolas turned to one another and descended the stairs elegantly and serenely as if waiting for an answer to their fate.

The Tsar was still handsome in his well cut but somewhat tired clothing. Alexandra, surprisingly beautiful for her years, exuded an air of calm and prideful duty. A lady even in disgrace, I discerned.

The four daughters glided down the creaking staircase like ballerinas from Swan Lake. First ventured Olga; poised and serious, then Tatiana who truly was visually exquisite, reminding me of Botticelli's Venus. She was followed by Marie who looked down pensively at the small bible she carried in her hand as if remembering a place or passage.

Then appeared Anastasia, who possessed a pretty face but one with character as well. She looked like a little sparrow. Although young Anastasia was slightly plump, she was also gamine graceful, reminding me of a tomboy just discovering the feminine details and charms of lace petticoats and cologne. She twitched her nose and stopped momentarily on the second last stair, lifting her left hand to her hair to adjust the ponytail, sighing with the relief loosening it had brought. She was seventeen.

Alexei was carried down the stairs by his father. His face startled me. It was cast with the soul of an ancient warrior king. His eyes alone could have run a nation. Poor Alexei; betrayed by his father out of having any chance to save his country.

"Over there", commanded the soldier dispassionately, pointing to a spot a few feet from the far wall of the drab nondescript room. "You are to have your photograph taken", the soldier continued crisply as he stretched himself behind the camera.

It all occurred so rapidly, I had barely time to accept it.

A flash from the camera, then the clicks of the soldiers' rifles resulting in gunshots resonating in the air like firecrackers. The room was still afloat with the scent of gun powder when the feat was accomplished.

The Tsar's family sloped over one another; blood oozed from their clothing, blood sprayed across the back wall, blood scented the close little room as only the odor of human blood can.

A gasp followed by a moan escaped from the execution scene.

"Papa…!" Anya screamed, gripping my hand to her. "No!!" she screamed again. "Help them … Help me ..," she cried out in pain.

"Now!" declared the Lady. *"This is the point of entry, Angelique. Make the healing symbols and lay your hands upon Anya. Do it NOW!"* The Lady commanded.

The winds of change whistled around us in this tunnel where time could be moved and transformed by thought. Could thought also arrest a condition and place a healing? Would these winds alter circumstances by eliminating and blowing away the old energy, of pain and horror, to be replaced by new energy of renewal, rebirth and new life... even in the etheric? Anya was now in the spirit world. Could she still be healed... there?

I held onto Anya's hand to steady her and with my right hand made the symbols of healing that had been shown me by J.P. and Celine. Then I placed both hands on Anya.

What occurred next is only possible to relate as a 'feeling' for it occurred on an etheric or spirit level.

Anya's soul exploded. Remember, this is a feeling. I felt her soul *ex*-plode, expressing its life force outward to the cosmos, releasing old stagnant energy. Visually, it was like watching rainbows of sorrow blast out of her tiny form, until only a steady mist of silvery white encircled her.

"Is Anya healed?" I asked The Lady.

"Partly", she replied. *"There is another step you must do before the healing can be completed."*

"What is that?" I asked.

"Your soul must return to the empress."

As The Lady spoke these words, She placed Her hand on me in what appeared to me to be slow motion. Upon the point of contact, something inside of me cracked and was ripped out of my body. The next instant 'I' lay enclosed in the body of the late Empress of Russia.

"Oh, Nicky, what will become of us!" The impassioned thoughts cried out from my Empress self. I lifted out and stood next to my

Empress body. Then I felt myself pulled back in. 'I', the Empress, was not yet dead!

There is no pain, yet I know I cannot be alive but somewhere in between. Is this hell? Will we be sent to hell? "Oh, Lord!" I felt a freezing cold wind blow though me. I am so cold yet the chill came from knowledge of the future that could only come from a sixth sense... or the spirit world.

"Oh, God...! Nicky, they are going to dismember and fling our bodies, the children's too, into a mud pit... and just leave us. We will not be given a burial!"

In this body the emotion that ran through me was one of sheer and total horror. It was of course the very worst situation that could befall a pious catholic, which my empress was. "How could they do THIS to us? How could they damn our souls like this?" 'My' thoughts continued.

"They cannot condemn us lest we condemn ourselves", a voice beside 'me' spoke. "Forgive them Alix." The voice came from the Emperor Nicolas, but the sound was familiar of another voice I knew very well. The 'I' that was now me recognized the voice, but whose?

"Remember the words of the Christ, Alix ... 'Forgive them for they know not what they do'."

As Nicolas spoke, a mist gathered about him. I watched as his essence, his spirit, pulled out of his body. In the etheric energy that released from Nicolas's body form, I viewed a myriad of soul lifetimes he had held until the features became those of Nicolas once more. Then, one more switch... And before me stood the form of the body that matched the voice.

"Forgive them", spoke Jacey.

"I cannot!" Alix sobbed. "Not this. I cannot. I will not forgive them for *this*!"

"It is your pride that cannot forgive, Alix", implored Jacey. "It is no holy thing."

"It is not possible!" Alix cried.

As she spoke, the figure of Jacey began to grow dark. Then the form began to lose its shape.

"Little matroushka", spoke a deep and soothing voice from across the blood stained floor. "Your husband is right. It is crucial for you to forgive your oppressors. Much will depend upon it." Rasputin glided toward the bloody scene as he spoke.

"But ... Oh, how can I?" As the Tsarina's words were spoken, the spirit form of Jacey/Nicolas gathered itself up like a small tornado, turning into a darkly smoke. "Then I am doomed", whispered the words from the centre of the smoke as it shrieked, darted quickly out to the sidewall and disappeared.

"You must do it now!" The Lady's voice commanded. *"To redeem Nicolas' soul and your own, you must forgive all that has been done to you and your family."* A fervent blue gray mistral circled and twisted around us all. *"Only when you forgive will you be forgiven."* The words of the Lady rang through 'my' ears. *"You must forgive while you are still alive... before your soul leaves the Tsarina's body."*

Being within the body of the Tsarina was a distinct experience, for I felt 'her'. I *was* her, yet I also felt and possessed my personality and my own individuality, if you will. How could that be? What occurred at that scene was beyond the mystical.

"Remember my love for you all, my child." The gentle voice spoke with light forms accompanying his words. The angry cosmic storm raging about the execution scene was suddenly stilled and as I turned I saw the gentle man from the labyrinth in J.P.'s garden. He wore the same simple white loose garment that covered him to his feet. This time I noticed the pierced marks on each foot as he effortlessly walked toward us.

"My Lord!" Alix cried in rapture at the sight of her savior.

"Remember my words and keep them. Then you shall dwell with me in my kingdom", spoke the man simply and gently.

"If God so gave his only begotten son that the world may live ... then what must you do my child?" The words of the gentle man filled Alix' soul with light and renewal.

"Yes!" Alix cried as she finally understood the truth of his words. "Yes, it is true. It is in our forgiveness that we are forgiven. It can only be that way!"

I realized through the Tsarina's words that, as she spoke her truth, she also declared the truth for all on this planet and within this universe. Only when we release and allow love, through our forgiveness, to express outward can we ourselves be released from our own horrors and fears, which are in truth only our own unloving thought forms. These negative thought forms hurt not only ourselves but can affect and severely harm our planet as well.

Earth absorbs our thought forms as part of her etheric energy. Like a circle, I sensed, the lack of love will only go round and round until it is no more.

"Let Love win out!" I spoke into the mind of the Tsarina. "Love yourself enough to forgive your own frailties and shortcomings, just as God forgives us ours. He does not ask perfection of us. He does not punish us! We only seek to punish ourselves through lack of understanding of His laws... particularly the law of Love. All humanity is a part of us as we are a part of humanity. Divine Love is within us all if we but realize it and extend it out. As you express your love to God, you express it to all of humanity. All you must do is to express Divine Love out to humanity KNOWINGLY. Your love is your forgiveness, Alix and the world is crying for it! Forgiveness is the best revenge!"

The words seemed to enlighten Alix from within. Her inner soul energy flowed and as the words of forgiveness and love fell from her lips in a prayer, once again I felt an explosion of the soul... and then a rip and a tearing within the centre of my being.

Upon opening my eyes, I recognized the vision of Anastasia still sitting on my bed. I refocused my eyes to view her aura. The light about her was radiant! Lovely rings of white, gold and pink energy emitted from her spirit form like a song of love.

"*Yes*", the Lady spoke in agreement. "*She is healed.*"

The Lady's voice drifted off in my mind as I felt my eyelids close and fell into the sleep of the serene. With a certainty that goes beyond reason, I knew that the physical, mental and emotional frailties that had beguiled me for far too long had now exited from me forever as well.

In that hour, it seemed like I slept a lifetime of exhaustion. Yet it was one of release and exhilaration as well. It is difficult to explain but I felt... free.

"As we forgive, we are forgiven ... As we heal, we are also healed."

Chapter 13 - "Healing Aphrodite"

"As we forgive, so are we forgiven ... As we heal, so we heal ourselves."

I opened my spiritual eyes as the essence of these words lifted my consciousness to another level in the cosmos. Through the back drop of space came a glowing white hand, passing like a torch of light through all levels of my being.

As my physical eyes lifted their lids, I saw and felt the hand of white light pull back from my being. As it did so it revealed its owner leaning over me on the yellow embroidered bed coverlet. My amazement and joy were absorbed by the radiant dear smile of his loving presence.

"I am so glad you are here, Jacey." My voice evoked the feeling I still held for him, even though I was physically still between worlds and a bit wobbly.

"You needn't speak. Rest." Jacey's voice soothed as he reached out his hand to hold mine. "I came to extend my thanks and gratitude to you for what you did earlier. Not many would have had your courage. You have helped to change and redirect the course of humanity to a new and more enlightened direction and level. On a personal level... you have been my savior."

"I don't know what you mean ..." I whispered, my body feeling heavy as lead. My eyes could barely stay open.

"You will know later", Jacey responded as he laid my hand on my heart and released it. "Sleep."

"Will I ever see you again?" I formed the thought in my mind and drifted into that dimension our soul retires to during the night.

"Angele." It was Celine. "It is time."

My eyes opened spontaneously; my spirit ready to respond to action as I sat up on the bed and set my feet on the antique carpet.

"Make your toilette tout suite, cherie." Celine implored. "Everything has been arranged for you dans la salle de bain."

Celine extended her arm in the direction of the bathroom, where the sound of a running faucet could be heard.

"I have drawn a bath for you. Hurry, while it is still warm." She smiled as she, noiseless as a fairy, crossed the floor and left the room, leaving me privacy to prepare.

My hand turned off the faucet which was shaped like a pretty golden sparrow and molded out of brass. I rolled up the sleeve of the butterfly yellow silk robe I had changed into. A few droplets of water sprayed across the silk and formed a small watermark.

"Darn", I muttered to the nowhere that our words go to when we talk to ourselves. I leaned forward and grabbed my scrunchie from the ivory marble vanity and pulled my hair up into a ponytail on the crown of my head. After loosening the robe, which fell elegantly upon the chaise longue, I lightly lowered myself into the lemon and lavender scented foam. The warm water was surprisingly refreshing and my mind was clearing and becoming aware of my surroundings again. After using my pineal gland for so long, it was usually necessary to ground myself but within my body I sensed that physically there was calm and balance.

Surrendering to the luxury of the antique bathtub, my nose twinged with another scent other than that of the bath salts.

On a graceful silver tray, on the far end of the vanity, Celine had nestled a small crystal bowl of strawberries, a freshly baked croissant and a generous slice of fresh camembert.

"Umm ... I will miss this place", I spoke out to the nowhere again and relaxed on the chaise longue; a piece of the brie in one hand and a succulent strawberry in the other.

"Life can be so very good." After allowing the fruit to descend down my trachea and nourish my body, I let my mind drift away from all thoughts of any frenzied media preparation and the upcoming global event to simply focus on my senses and allow them priority.

My inner self realized the importance of being in balance and harmony for the hours to follow. Sitting up straight on the chaise and lengthening my spine as much as possible, my feet placed flatly on the floor and my palms laid lightly on my thighs, I began the slow inhalation and exhalation exercises. After completing the full cycle of breathing exercises, I began to focus my attention on my chakra centers.

Starting with the first (base) chakra, I directed my attention to the base of my spine, focused on the color red and imaged my hand turning this ruby crystal wheel in a clockwise direction. I giggled a trifle as a humming sound vibrated at the end of my tailbone. Curious visions of early homo-sapiens traipsing about with elongated extensions attached to their lower extremities flashed before my inner vision. Perhaps at one time, prior to our other worldly visitors, we did have cousins from the animal kingdom. It would not have surprised me. The faces of these interesting animal beings however possessed a more compassionate eye and gentler soul than those of their later descendants.

They were tender, spiritual beings, so sweet to one another. Then I saw them gathered together by their alien masters and whipped into submission until their power was gone. The tails fell off in the process as if speaking of their victimization.

Those that were caught were harnessed and used as slave labor in the fields to mine for the white gold their masters were so fervently intent upon. They were used for other purposes as well. The females were bred (for there was no other term for it) by their masters to raise and train a future race of earth beings to continue to mine for their precious white gold. It was a mineral that seemed essential to their survival.

The females were bred with their alien masters and their female offspring were bred in the same manner and so on and so on until there appeared on earth a 'human' being of the same likeness of the present.

By this time my focus had raised to the centre of my pelvic area and after flipping the tangerine crystal wheel, I felt the creative process of our human nature begin to alter and shift as the genetics changed with each subsequent generation.

The process of the breeding was as individual as the masters themselves. Some masters were kind and humane as they rejuvenated their own dying species by propagating with the earth race. Other masters were ruthless and unfeeling and simply and cruelly used the earthlings for their own carnality and vicious abuse. I watched in horror as many from this early species were beaten and raped, forced to sleep tied up in cages in their own excrement and taken out and untied to work in the mines; the females taken in the night and used for sexual outlets by the more twisted of the masters. No wonder mankind proceeded on as it did. Old habits being hard to break and some things never changed kind of thing.

Then a curious scenario began to reel upon the inner screen of my vision. After spinning the golden crystal within my solar plexus, I viewed the 'cloning' of an assembly line humanoid being manifested by their master creators.

The first thing I noticed was that the alien masters were a rather colorless lot, very bland in their appearance, with the exception of the super beings which will be discussed later.

There was not just one alien race that conquered us. These other masters, as if acting on direction from their superiors, sat around huge stone tables and drew up color schemes - for humans! White, yellow and blue were the predominant hues, but with a variety of different shades, like a rainbow.

A dozen shades of blue were ordered for the eye irises. Skin tones of white ranging from palest ivory to golden peach were chosen. The hair swatches lay organized on a luminescent slab under a light in the highest tech salon I had ever been witness to. Lady Clairol would have sighed in heaven at the levels of blonding being selected.

The colors seemed to have been selected from nature as these master beings were very fond and admiring of the beautiful flora and fauna upon our earth and seas. They particularly loved the color of our oceans and skies and made the decision for the eye hues from there. Hair bright as our sun, eyes as blue as our seas and skies and skin as fair as our snow and sand: This was the chosen color scheme for the main 'model'.

The genetically altered species came out of the slave wombs like assembly line robots. I witnessed a realization as the babies birthed their new programmed truth out into the world. These blond, blue-eyed beings were not engineered to be the master or super race of the neo-

Nazi theory: These beings were architected and drafted and bred - to be slaves! Robot slaves, to be exact!

I noticed something else as well. Beautiful as these beings were, there seemed to be an element missing from their character. It was difficult to put my finger on it but as my focus moved up to my chest, where the crystal of emerald velocity was spun, it was as if they had no heart! They did of course possess a physical organ in their bodies that pumped blood, yet there seemed a lack of caring or emotion connected to it. They didn't *feel*! Their intellects were perfect, yet they felt nothing emotionally. (That was an element that could have travelled down through the decades, I ascertained with a slight smirk: The cool blue-eyed blond demeanor; the Ice Princess syndrome.)

They were designed to be nothing more than pretty little doll robots, I realized. The dolls or robots were also designed to be very slim, I noted. Not too strong or heavy so the poor things couldn't fight too hard if they tried to escape. Well, they certainly held their robot rebellion!

My throat chakra energy burst forth. The turquoise energy spun fervently, as the slave robots found a voice and through their superior intellect created a language so they could communicate with one another. In so doing, they began to organize themselves. The first union, I surmised.

As the sapphire crystal at my mid forehead started to turn and buzz, I saw the cruelty within of the robot race creators begin to rebel as well. (The dark eyed and dark haired beings were initially placed in positions of higher status as they possessed more advanced spiritual attributes and ideals along with aspects of compassion and sensitivity, making them more useful for doctor, teacher and leadership roles.) With their robot rebellion, the 'whiter' race revolted not only against their masters but used their cold conniving natures to overthrow their earthly counterparts and put themselves in the positions of power and leadership to further continue the lineage of abuse and 'inhumanity'.

The final crystal at my crown chakra whirled and tingled (with the hope of the future, I prayed). Yes! It was so! I envisioned the future of our human being-ness and it was beautiful! Mankind turns his intent fully around and realizes his true nature of being. He finally comes to know what he was sent here to become. Love and kindness and service prevail. No one is above anyone else and all levels of beings have value.

Life continues on and every nation's beings help every other nation's beings to attain optimum health, wealth and happiness. All is well on our planet of Love.

Then... we learn to fly!

Hope thrilled my heart as I opened my eyes and stared directly at my reflection in the gold leaf framed mirror opposite me. I blinked and refocused my eyes and looked again. There was no mistake, I could really see them.

I stood and let the robe fall from my shoulders onto the chaise lounge. Seven gems of light were swirling and shining throughout my physical body. At the base of the pubis a brilliant ruby crystal glowed. At the mid stomach, a crystal that appeared like a fireball swirled energetically. At the solar plexus, a huge golden orb sprayed out dazzling light rays that extended several feet from my body. My manifestation chakra was radiant. The heart area beamed luxurious emerald light to the world; its pulsations felt by the objects and life forces all around the room. I could see the primroses and the violets in their ceramic pots lift and embrace the energy of Love emitting from this chakra. The throat station held a more earthly note as it expressed its vibrancy and light about my head. Then the pineal gland throbbed with a sapphire luster, brilliant but refined. I felt its depth. The final spot, the crown chakra, literally exploded to the ceiling with a violet energy. The crystal here had the appearance of a rare lilac diamond, a gem not familiar to our planet as yet but nonetheless a powerful stone. This one I sensed would be a highly prized stone of the future, once humankind raised itself to its frequency.

"Divine Light of the Eternal Cosmic; infuse me with the knowledge, wisdom, strength and clarity to enable me to accomplish the task you have sent me to this night. Amen."

I uttered these words softly and reverently to the Master Within and to the Infinite of the Cosmos, which are one.

Chapter 14 ~ "The Cosmic Robe"

I rewrapped the papillion jeune robe about myself, tying the braided sash lightly and slipped on the matching ballet slippers to avoid a chill. After meditation my body often feels slightly cool albeit refreshed.

On the back door of the closet Celine had hung a garment bag that bulged at its bottom, meaning that she must have included an item of footwear as well as an article of clothing.

Enclosed within the zippered garment bag was a dress composed of a fabric that I was totally unfamiliar with. It felt like cloth but looked more like metal. The color was indescribable as it literally adapted to the hue of whatever was near it. The overdress had the appearance of powdered crystals which had been poured over an under dress (or slip dress) of sapphire blue. The overdress skimmed the body with its princess line and fell to my lower calf. It was probably designed to be floor length but due to my height and length of leg it naturally hit me higher, but not unflatteringly, on the leg. The sleeves, on me, were three quarter length and looked like creamy iridescent silver on my arms. The dress portion that covered the slip however turned to a glorious lapis shade and reminded me of the Paris sky at night, which is probably what it was designed to do. The crystalline fabric over the slip gave the gown the appearance of a constellation of stars on a Gallic evening. The dress was extremely simple and subtle in appearance but very striking when worn. The scoop neck was cowled a bit, so it could hide the amulet quite nicely, if I desired.

I found shoes in the same midnight blue shade and upon examination, realized they had been layered with the same material as the dress. They had Queen Ann heels and squared toes and appeared to be antique yet possessed that intrinsic contemporary quality that would be in fashion in any era. Upon further viewing of the dress, it as well could have been a creation from any decade, so subtle and refined was its composition. I was wearing a masterpiece that was likely priceless.

Carefully hung up in the garment bag was one more article: A long simple robe with a clearly cut hood and simple silver fastener at the neck. While withdrawing it from the covering, I noticed that both hood and cape were lined in the same material as the dress and shoes. The only details on the cloak were two simple invisible slits for arms to go through, if so desired. When worn, it was a statement of simplicity which of course also made it the epitome of elegance. The cloak could have been worn as an overcoat to the bank, to school, to business, for dinner, to a wedding or a funeral, to the shops or to the opera. In short, it fit any and all occasions.

The cape was of the lightest and softest wool and practically weightless when worn. There was an energy to the cape I could not describe but it was like wearing something I 'knew'. The energy was so familiar it felt like it could be held in my hands. If the energy had not been so comfortable, it would have disarmed me.

While crossing over to the vanity to inspect my appearance, I saw a small floral bag atop the glass covered vanity table. A note with Celine's handwriting was attached and read simply, 'For the cameras.'

The bag held little treasures of several cosmetic articles submerged beneath the tissue. First emerging was an eye shadow duo of lapis and lilac hues. Next, a duo eyeliner pencil in sapphire and lavender. Then up came a little pot of shimmering heather face highlighter that looked so fabulous over cheekbones and brow bones. Last but not least; a darling little lip gloss pen in the perfect mauve.

I must keep in contact with Celine if for no other reason than with her taste and sense of color she would be invaluable on a fashion shoot! I'd hire her in an instant!

Carefully sliding onto the vanity settee so as not to disrupt the ensemble, I put my face into action. The result was magical and I could barely believe my reflection. It was as if an unearthly energy had guided my hands while painting my canvas and the objet d'art was the face of a fairy queen. I wondered if there were wings beneath my cape. Then I could have simply flown to the site on my own!

After stepping back from the vanity mirror, I sensed the long dress and long cape required long hair. Bending at the waist I brushed from the nape of the neck forward, flipped my full mane back and gathering it up at the crown and sides with a single tendril, wrapped it around the hair at mid crown, allowing it to cascade in waves down my back and off my face. Then it was secured with a simply hairpin. Perfect.

Upon setting down the ivory hairbrush, my hand upset the lilac patterned mini bag and spilled out a minute blue velvet jewelry case. I opened its clasp to find a set of antique platinum framed sapphire earrings, which I instantly set in my ears. The fish hooks let them dangled decorously yet not obnoxiously.

Only the scent of the purest lilies would do for the occasion and that was exactly the fragrance that was set upon the vanity in a petite apothecary bottle which had only a delicate silver antique label on it stating simply, 'Muguet' (lily of the valley). The scented oil was so powerful in its essence that I felt I was in a country field filled with thousands of tiny lily flowers as a celestial breeze blew their fragrance into my tender nostrils. It was the most healing scent one could ever imagine. I was enchanted. I was also, I realized, finally... ready.

The knock on the door marked my signal to emerge and walk the lapis ceramic hallway and staircase down to the foyer. The lights were dimmed on the stairs and landing and the area was lit only by white candles.

A solemnity pervaded the home that could be felt in the bones of the house. It was not a sad or obtrusive energy but rather an energy that hung in the atmosphere with strength and a sense of the sacred, which was of course the essential purpose of our gathering.

I descended the staircase feeling full of light and enlightenment. J.P.'s man Frederique stood on the landing. He spoke quietly to me, "You are full of the Light. Entree", and gestured me toward the dining room.

The magnificent oak dining room doors opened before me as I stepped forward. Crossing the carpet into the dining room felt like I was leaving the mundane world behind and entering a celestial Egyptian temple.

The air of the 'temple' was filled with the pungent but pleasant aroma of rose incense. At first breath it quite arrested my nostrils but after becoming accustomed to the scent, my consciousness actually pirouetted higher and higher.

Serge and Celine stood directly before me and in front of the oak dining table which had been adorned with a magnificent ornate gold cross holding a rose in full bloom at its center. The scent of the flower overpowered that of the incense, so great was its essence.

Behind the table stood J.P., who wore a twin to the cape in which I was attired. Behind him was another gold cross. This cross was held to the far wall and the flower at its centre was formed out of blown glass and lit from within by a large white candle.

Serge stepped forward and took my arm, guiding me through an intricate set of steps toward the alter table; three steps forward, three to the left and three forward; like military formation. Celine made a symbolic signage with her hand over her heart. Serge nodded for me to respond in like manner, which I did.

"Do you come as the Angel of Light, representing the Gemstone Angel, to embark our great order on a further quest of healing and restoration to this planet to bring Purity, Love, Light, Truth, Honor, Clarity and Healing to our brothers and sisters of Light? Are you this vehicle of the Cosmic Creator? Do you wear the Cape of the Cosmos with honor?" Celine voiced solemnly.

From the depths of my inlaying spirit came the words, for 'I' did not speak.

"*I Am* here for this purpose. My mission is being executed within this body. I will do my duty honorably. *I Am* here to be of service."

With these words I bowed to Celine, who led me in another set of intricate footsteps to the edge of the pedestal where J.P. stood.

Once before J.P., I felt the overcoming urge to bend on one knee and bow. Behind me I felt Celine make a circle with both arms and a light wind swirled up inside the room. The wind whispered, "Here comes an Angel…"

Head lowered, I bowed to J.P.

"Child of the Light", J.P. spoke. "Be blessed in the Light of God's purpose. As a representative of the Angel of Light, be instilled with the Strength, Protection, Power and Love to ascend to your Master Within and fulfill your cosmic purpose on this planet.

"Do you understand and willingly undertake this assignment? Remember that you have freewill to accept or decline."

"I accept this mission. I understand what is being requested of me and I fully agree to undertake whatever is necessary to save and heal humanity on this planet."

J.P. said nothing but I 'understood' that an agreement was being made that I was being taken into something. As this message pervaded my mind, my eyes closed and my spirit being was raised up and out into the cosmic space where my consciousness had the knowledge of the ages alighted into it by a gentle yet persistent energy similar to an electric current. This knowledge went far beyond the words of any language: It was primal and it was powerful.

My being was permeated with sacred and supernatural consciousness possessed only by the gods. I sensed this knowledge would not have a lasting affect but would be there on an intrinsic level when needed. I expressed my wordless thanks and gratitude and came into agreement with the Infinite. Then, in a second of earthly time, I felt my presence float back into the temple room at Chateau de la Breyeres.

Through yet another intricate set of footsteps, Celine led me to a sidewall. She gracefully perfected the same footsteps and placed herself directly opposite me along the other sidewall while Serge was positioned along the wall with the door opposite J.P.

Celine raised a small copper musical triangle which she rang then sang a set of musical sounds like a mantra. In unison, we all sang forth the same chant.

As our voices united in the room that acted as a temple, I felt my spirit rise up and out along with the consciousness of J.P., Celine and Serge. We all met in what could only be described as a pyramid of light and mist, where I recognized us in our spirit bodies. Our energies had shifted and intermingled with the Great Light Energy Body known as God Creator.

This was truly the most extraordinary experience of my life. For the first time in my existence, at least in this lifetime, I realized what 'I' truly was and what the human 'being' was actually about. I understood why the purpose of this planet was so integral for it was here that we developed in the Mind/Body/Soul essence and without this planet there would be no 'training ground' for our soul growth.

In this expanded consciousness 'we' were all able to hear, feel, and know all past, present and future events. I saw how history, now and the future were interlinked and how one single event done differently changed all three presences. I understood how the earth, indeed the universe and the earth within the universe, were intended to run its course as was the original intent and plan of the Master Creator.

The beauty of what we were intended to do and be astounded me. How had we fallen so short of our potential? I saw how we had shifted and changed God's good for us into one of another making. We had almost destroyed our beauty: Almost, yet not quite. There was still time. I saw, in a future vision of being-ness, that we were still intact, meaning that we could still evolve into and become our Higher Selves or our perfect godlike beings, which was the intent and purpose of our process on earth.

In this state that J.P., Celine, Serge and I were now in, all things were possible. We could 'fly' anywhere we wanted, feel and 'be' any being, animal, mineral or human and perfect anything within ourselves; be it body, mind or spirit; or perfect anything outside of ourselves. In the Infinite Energy of Creation, we could heal anything that was not perfect. This thought permeated through our beings and our beings were with the One.

"This is where souls come between lives." spoke the Infinite. "Lifetimes exist on all the planets of the universes with their different lessons or realities. It is important to understand that what we create we have dominion or reign over and what we create evolves our soul on its voyage. By this same effect, as we evolve our souls, so we evolve our planet. What you have seen developed in your planet's history has been a direct result of its human developmental process.

"What has developed is not wrong, for the lesson was to be allowed freewill. The larger part of the lesson, which was not to abuse authority by having freewill, has to a great extent been learned. The earth beings have come along a great and difficult path to this discovery, likened to a child being allowed to eat all the candy it wishes. Sooner or later the wisdom enters that other foods are necessary or the body suffers.

"So your earth beings have understood: Too much is not necessarily better. After a certain amount, the sweetness loses its charm and appeal and the body becomes too saturated, resulting in the malfunction of mind, body and eventually spirit.

"Humanity has been allowed an overabundance of the sweetness of life; or what you would call freedom. Freedom misused is freedom abused and your planet has been rampant with it.

"The choices for good, for evil, for love, for hate, for truth, for falseness, have been allowed but the so-called negative energies were not birthed by the Infinite. They were solely 'being' inventions. I say this because not all the energies pervading your planet were of an earthly origin. There has been 'assistance', both negatively and positively from other universal beings. Yet you have always had the freewill to choose or not to choose.

"The future is set for a beautiful reality for your planet. Only your beings freewill choices could complicate this future. You have seen by history what the choices of greed and power have resulted in. Again, the choice will be yours. Choose wisely, my children of Light and understand that whatever your choice, the Infinite Love of the Universe is always there for you. You are My children, an individual part of Me and I have, and will, love you all always.

"Know who and what you are, my Light Ones. You hold the individualized essence of all Creation. You have the Love, the Light and the Power to do all things. At this point, you are all being quickened in your evolvement for you have proven yourselves ready and deserving. All humanity rests in this potential, for your beings have progressed far and well. Yet, alas, not all are conditioned as well as you for this soul voyage. Remember who you are and what you are sent to this planet for. This will be imperative to you on your present mission and also your future growth lessons.

"You are the beautiful Light Warrior Beings of the Infinite and come under the guidance of the Archangel Mikhail, whose sole direction now is the protection and evolvement of your planet beings. Mikhail brings his great strength and light and clarity to you. Nightly, while

249

your planet sleeps, he and his legions of angelic warrior beings cleanse the energy of the negative thoughts and thought patterns sent out into Earth's atmosphere by the majority of your Earth beings who are still struggling with the habit of ancient thought patterns and behaviors. Were these angels not to be about this great work, your planet would have destroyed itself long ago during your Earth time of World War II. However, because Mikhail has been assigned Earth thought cleansing as his sole enterprise at this time, your planet has been salvaged.

"Gabrielle has joined with Mikhail since the 1960's as she clears the path for feminine nurturing energy to return to your planet. This energy is known on your planet as Venus, Goddess of Love, and the brightest guiding star in the heavens. The reputation of Venus has been misinterpreted by many in your more modern times as the sensual goddess associated with carnal intimacy. However, she has far greater powers and her wings stretch over areas governing brotherly love, or unity, caring family values and humanities, love and devotion for all of mankind.

"She has been neglected as her energies have been seriously misused and abused by your beings. Her wound, caused by the energy of the male ego, is severe and needs attending by your beings. Her symbol on your planet is represented by Woman, the female, the Mother counterpart of the Male Father Infinite Creator. It has been your planet's treatment of Woman or Feminine Power that has resulted in her wounds and if she is not healed, then Love will cease to be a reality within your beings. If this occurs, this lack of love will permeate your planets energy, resulting in the end of fertility of vegetation and animal life. If the plant and animal life dies, so ends humanity. The Feminine Mother Power Infinite Creative Force governs life and the birthing of it. She is your Goddess. You also know her by the name given her by the Greeks: Aphrodite.

"Aphrodite deserves your Earths' honor and she greatly requires your healing. Your agreement to help set this healing into motion may involve some challenges as not all the planetary beings desire to see her Feminine Mother Infinite Creator Energy revived. It is not in the interests of those who have chosen to focus upon the superpower masculine energy to serve their own chosen mandates.

"The Infinite does not judge that their choices are wrong; only that they do not serve the better interests of all of the planetary beings of the universes. In fact, they do not serve the Infinite at all, for they have invented their own god. Their god is not a balanced one (god/goddess). This is why you see such obvious imbalances permeating throughout your planet and it extends to other planets as well.

"How was this done, you ask? Let us say that inharmonious thought projections resulted in negative and inharmonious results. Therefore, when a group of beings desiring inharmonious or unbalanced results (such as greed for money where a few such individuals wish to have ownership over the majority) and enough of them voice their prayers or demands for these results, their constant thought patterns can result in the invention or creation of a mutant type of god or creator that is a false god, for he was built upon the illusion of greed. Although illusory, the god, real or unreal, may still attain a credible degree of power to manifest and, yes, to destroy... and also to create a mutant type of being.

"This was begun within another solar system that has experimented with life on your planet and has succeeded in procreating on your Earth. It has already begun in your world and your beings, for the most part, are without this knowledge. They are innocent. Innocent of the fact that within them are certain chakra crystals, that when activated by a negative source that had knowledge of their function, could initiate actions for their own purposes and succeed in turning your beings into robots. Your beings would not understand their own behavior and insanity would develop on a planetary level.

"Worshipping a different god that is not Infinite is illusory and may result in a false or illusionary race of beings who would be without knowledge that they were illusion, or not real, and as such could be used for all matter of manipulative gains by their creators. These creators desire to control, not just this universe but the entire galaxy and beyond. Such is their quest for power and control.

"Why is there such obsession for such power? It is best explained as a comparison to a lone cell that has gone rampant in order to have the area, entity or body all for itself, only to realize all too late that when it kills off all the other cells that comprise the body, the body itself dies, resulting in the death of the renegade cell itself. So what is truly gained by an obsession of the self? Destruction is the gain which is not gain at all, but loss.

"Understand that none of this is wrong in the Infinite. It is however, one must agree, rather defeating the purpose of life itself, which is to grow and evolve into spiritual truth and reality. Life has to do with creation not destruction. Life is about Love and it is Love that creates. A planet without the energy of Love cannot sustain itself.

"Aphrodite has been your planet's great Goddess of Love, and beloveds, She may die without your help. For 2000 earth years Her energy has been repeatedly eroded. Your planet's great opportunity for growth and renewed feminine power and energy is closely approaching as you head into your next millennium. It is imperative that your goddess energy is revived prior to this time for She must be within Her strength and power at this important date. Why? It is because at this time, the vibratory rate of the planet is being realigned. It will then be time for the Love energy to reemerge and allow your human beings to become what the Infinite Power designed them to be; the actualized physical replica of the Infinite or God/Goddess source.

"You have heard it voiced by your philosophers and new age thinkers that you are gods in the making. They have got it quite right. In your future there will be many more enlightened soul beings processed with great wisdom. You can expect much knowledge to be shared that was once kept sequestered within certain mystery schools. That knowledge will soon become universal knowledge. That is the plan of the Infinite: True knowledge for all who wish to access it. Your planets' technology, in the form of your websites and internet systems, make this possible for nearly every being in the civilized parts of your world. It will be there free of choice; in other words, freewill. That is unless the free flowing natural energy coordinating the new feminine energy is not granted freewill. This could happen through the blockage of this energy to your planet by the masculine energy creators imposing their will instead of 'Thy Will ' (be done) of the Infinite. Be aware, they will try.

"Be blessed on your journey, Angel Warriors and know that the great magnificent Archangel beings travel with you."

The symphony of the cosmos, which radiated a sound identical to Celine's' mantra musical notes, rang out abound and within our unified beings. Our voices joined in the song and soon we felt ourselves back in our bodies again within the chateau.

Following the same intricate set of steps, we all existed the sancted temple of Chateau de la Breyeres; Serge in the lead, followed by Celine, me and last J.P.

"The helicopter is ready", announced Frederique. "It is also known as the Sky Train!" Frederique's humor helped to ground us and bring us back to earth.

"The robe becomes you", smiled J.P., adjusting his own identical one. "But your clasp has come undone. Allow me", J.P. whispered softly as his slender fingers closed the silver fagot at my throat.

"Parfait", J.P. smiled with his eyes emanating the greatest love toward me.

"I feel so protected under this cloak, grand pere. It's hard to explain... It's", I floundered, not knowing quite how to express myself. "It's as if I know the cape! It feels like a person ... and I know that person well."

"You do", spoke J.P. softly. "The cape belonged to Jacey."

"It is time", interrupted Frederique as he stepped aside to open the front door for Celine, J.P., Serge and me.

"Alors ..." Serge gestured as he directed our group to the right side of the chateau where the helicopter pad was positioned. The Sky Train's engine was being started by Emile, J.P.'s pilot.

Our party stepped lightly over the clover blanketed lawn en route to our vehicle. I felt immersed in the dusky light enveloping our forms in the early evening light and sensed again the presence of the cape surrounding me, its essence bleeding into mine.

"Jacey!" I whispered to myself. "It's you!" Within the protective fabric of the cloak was Jacey's life force and he was alive within it. My mind was so absorbed in this revelation that I nearly slipped on the dewy grass beneath my feet. Serge leant his stronger than expected arm to assist me and lifted me into the helicopter.

J.P. was seated by Emile in the front of the helicopter, while Serge and Celine were positioned on either side of me in the back. We strapped ourselves in, ready for takeoff.

"There is a protective force field that surrounds Chateau de la Breyeres", J.P. related to us as Emile made preparation for our takeoff.

J.P. turned and rotated his seat one hundred and eighty degrees to face us as he spoke. His voice was postured with an air of deadly earnest.

"Within this force field we are safe. The crystalline energy sets up a shield that prevents any detection from land, air and any other means. We are quite invisible, ma cherie". J.P. was speaking directly to me at this point.

"However", he gestured, holding up his first finger for emphasis. "When we leave this concave area, we will no longer have that advantage. On our flight to the Lourdes site, we may encounter some danger. Try not to be alarmed if this occurs. Be calm and as still as possible", J.P. emphasized again. "We will not be harmed. Indeed, we will not even be seen."

"How so...?" I asked, reclosing the clasp of the cape again.

"Ah ... the cape is too large for you, so the clasp does not fasten properly", commented Celine. "Just be aware of it and hold the cape close to you", she finished.

J.P. continued. "Oui, how so... These capes are lined with a crystalline substance that appears to be a fabric. It is substantially more than that. It is comprised of the same composition as that of the energy force field around us here. The same crystal substance is woven together to seem like a cloth. You also have it over your gown", he gestured to my overdress. "And it is on your feet as well." He pointed to my starlit sapphire slippers and smiled.

"The color of the cape covering is of great importance. The sapphire blue is the color of the celestial heavens. It therefore carries a very high vibration and operates with the chakra crystal of the pineal gland; the third eye", J.P. gestured, touching his mid forehead with the first two digits of his left hand. "It can be activated in just this manner," He demonstrated the gesture again using his left hand. "When you need to be invisible, the cape with this gesture will make you so.

"In our Order, we have learned to make ourselves unseen by a number of different means which you may learn at another time. It is not simply for invisibility that the cape is used. The crystal lining includes an impenetrable force field of protection. It will also react to your thought energy and is activated by your crown chakra crystal which is your Christ consciousness or your Higher Self. It will be activated by what and how you think. Let your thoughts be positive and empowering, for with them so, nothing in your world is impossible, cherie!" J.P. shouted in a whisper. "Nothing!" His voice sent a chill clear through me.

I observed Celine and Serge and spoke to J.P. "Our capes are blue but Celine and Serge have brown capes. What is the difference?"

"You have asked a clever question, cherie. The blue capes are adept for land, sea and sky. The brown capes are designed more for land areas, but they have some other unique abilities as well. And"... J.P. continued as he rotated his seat back to its frontal position and gestured to Emile to engage the lever for lift off, "Remember that within the capes are contained our sword and our shield, should we have need of them."

Emile set the vehicle into motion and the propeller cut through the skyline like an enormous swirling blade, reminding me of a wild handless machete.

My stomach lurched slightly as the helicopter lifted and tilted into the night. The sky still contained a fair bit of light and the air was cool but clear. We rode our stead skyward in silence over the low mountain range of the Pyrenees.

I focused on the purple and gray lights settling over the mountains and the ancient sense of peace that sighed within them. I wondered how many crystal caves might exist inside those lazy sloping edifices and in my mind imagined an entire race of inhabitants living solely within the confines of those rocks, in a world of their own, unknown and never seen by our beings. Perhaps they were indeed Bernadette's ancestors; a dark faerie race of people, small and slight, maneuvering over the inner mountain terrain like surefooted mountain goats, with their tiny bare claw like feet grasping the rocky paths to the inner caves.

My reverie was interrupted by a mysterious scent accompanied by a bizarre mist that had begun threading its way through the open area of the helicopter. At first glance it appeared that a fog had approached but the odd color of the mist dismissed that speculation.

"Grand pere?" I queried, as apprehension gave way to fear.

"Remember ... be still and remain calm", answered J.P. "And activate the pineal chakra. Vite!"

I applied the appropriate hand gesture to my mid forehead as J.P., Celine and Serge accorded the same signal. I immediately felt a light imploding just above my eyes, rather like a camera bulb flashing and I was almost sightless for a few seconds. "Ahh ..."

"The sensation will pass shortly." spoke Celine and patted my hand.

It did. I was confused however. "Grand pere ... I thought we were to become invisible", I expressed looking around me. "But I still see you and Celine and Serge."

"Yes, cherie. We will see one another as our pineal crystals were quickened earlier in the temple. Others however, will not. Emile?" J.P. turned to his pilot. "Are you able to see any of us?"

"Non, monsieur", Emile answered after he turned his head toward J.P. and craned his neck to look in the back seats. Emile himself, I noticed, was dressed simply in sweater and pants.

"Will Emile be seen?" I asked with concern.

"He will, yes, but he is the pilot. It would seem very unusual not to see a pilot, oui? It will simply look like he is making a routine flight, solo", responded J.P.

Suddenly, through the mist, a black helicopter appeared before us, startling me. I uttered a scream at what I saw and lunged forward in fright to hold onto J.P. In doing so, the clasp of Jacey's cape was inadvertently loosened and the wind that was blowing in and about the helicopter whisked it off my head and shoulders, exposing my face and upper body. Emile quickly spirited the helicopter up and away from the imposing vehicle, but it was too late. I realized from the expression on the faces, of what I could only describe as creatures within that black helicopter, that they had seen me.

Celine's hands worked quickly to retrieve my cape as it fluttered like a tortured butterfly in the sulfurous winding mist invading our helicopter.

"What were those ... things?" I shrieked, recalling the faces in the Black Mariah helicopter. "They ... their faces ... looked like snakes! Their heads were those of snakes!" Reason and logic had totally deserted me. What was seen was unfathomable and I was eerily afraid.

The freakish mist that encircled our helicopter now seemed to organize itself and form a type of lasso. Then, like a whip with an invisible wrist, the mist cracked and toppled our helicopter upside down in midair.

I screamed but my cry was cut short by the seat belt pushing against my chest and stomach as the helicopter turned over. Then an incredulous occurrence happened. My cape fell out of the vehicle. As if possessing a life of its own, it drifted down and flew directly at the opposing helicopter, entirely covering the surface, making any vision from within impossible. Caught by surprise, the black helicopter wobbled in the air and attempted an emergency landing.

The mist lasso released its hold immediately and exited The Sky Train with a loud 'whoosh' sound. Emile instantly retrieved control of the vehicle, returned it to its normal upright position and immediately increased velocity and sped the helicopter off toward our destination.

My body hung in fear and silence on the seat, my mind grappling to accept what had just occurred. I had not anticipated this type of danger - and certainly not from beings unrecognizable as human!

I remained in a dazed state for the duration of the journey. Then my mind cleared and a renewed clarity kicked in when I observed a brightly lit albeit small area in the distance below.

"Is that Lourdes?" I queried, leaning forward to J.P.

"We should be at the site of the spring of Bernadette very shortly", affirmed Emile.

My relief occurred too quickly for seconds after Emile's words were uttered, I smelled the sulfuric essence return. Immediately, the engine of the helicopter stalled and Emile could not start it up.

"We must land, tout suite" Emile's eyes implored as he turned to face J.P., who immediately nodded in acquiescence. We noiselessly floated downward to a grass knoll between two small mountains. We were so close to Lourdes, I speculated.

"Do not be afraid, cherie", gently spoke J.P. "What must be done will be done", he finished solemnly.

Our helicopter landed in a small valley between the mountains. Serge immediately disembarked the vehicle and ran around and over to Emile. Serge observed what I had not during the scare; Emile was bleeding from a slight head wound that likely happened when the helicopter overturned. Emile self-assessed that he would be fine and waved Serge away.

I leaned forward to open the first aid kit that sat between Emile and J.P. but Celine stilled my arm and simply put her hand over Emile's forehead. The wound and blood disappeared momentarily, leaving only a thin red line that I knew would not remain.

Celine's' serene expression rapidly changed to alarm as she jerked me back into my seat, hard!

I had not even seen the blast of light shot at me which instead hit the side of the mountain. Thanks to Celine's' quick instincts, its destination was missed. Its destination was me! I felt a sharp stinging sensation on the right side of my collarbone however, which stopped short at the cowl neckline of my overdress. My burnt flesh scented the glass bubble of the Sky Train. I felt no pain but it was tender to the touch and had left a thin black graze of about two inches in length on my skin.

J.P.'s eyes were filled with pain and horror as he rotated his seat to face me.

"Non, ma cherie", he expressed softly, putting his arms out to embrace me. Tears filled his eyes as he continued. "No, cherie ... this is not your war to fight. It is MINE!"

In a swift and defiant gesture, J.P. unclasped his silver collar fastener and protectively flung his cape over me.

"Grand pere, no!" I cried out. "You mustn't!"

J.P. closed the cape about me, hard. He looked at me with a kind of fierceness I would never have expected from him. It was a look that froze me in my seat.

"This is not your battle, Angelique. There is what you would call in your culture, 'unfinished business'. It is a circumstance that was inevitable and it is a part of MY destiny.

"You were quite right, ma petite. The face you saw was not human." J.P. voiced emphatically as his eyes blazed clear through mine, sending alarming messages into my pineal crystal. Visions of beings on another planet in a far-off galaxy where the inhabitants could change their forms at will and warriors fought in other guises as the inhabitants of this galaxy turned on one another in power battles for control of more and more spatial territories. What I envisioned in the movie playing in my mind finally made me want to scream out to make it stop.

"It cannot stop or end until I end it." J.P. reinforced.

"But, grand pere", I implored, tears flowing onto my scarlet cheeks. "That ... thing ... isn't human ..."

"No", J.P. interrupted. "That ... thing ... is not human, cherie." J.P. paused. He inhaled deeply and allowed his breath to exit through his nostrils.

I stared in silence as J.P.'s breath turned to a grayish smoke that gradually turned to a scarlet flame color. His eyes blazed a sapphire fire as his face sculpted itself into a reptilian countenance.

"He is not human", he reaffirmed. "But he is my brother."

Chapter 15 - "The Pendragon"

My last conscious recollection of that scene was of J.P.'s head enlarging as its reptilian features became more definite. He reared himself back with a hissing sound of battle that I knew was intended for an opponent and not for me. I fell back into the seat and lost consciousness. Not however before witnessing, in slow motion, his descent from the helicopter, landing on the green with his large lizard legs.

"Angele ..." I heard Celine's' voice as if from a distance. "Angele ... you must activate your pineal crystal", Celine insisted when she saw my eyes open and acknowledge her presence. "Now!"

After making the signage I felt my mid-brain implode again and saw the flash between my eyes, leaving me blinking frantically for sight. It returned momentarily as before. A sound like the roar of a charging dinosaur shook the helicopter with its intensity. I sat up and turned to view how close that assessment truly was.

I gazed in amazed disbelief at the sight before me. At a distance of approximately forty feet, two reptilian forms of extraordinarily large proportions faced one another with about twenty feet between them. They crouched like samurai warriors and eyed one another with vindication. I recognized the snake faced being from the black helicopter. In this place he had taken on his full form and he was enormous, nearly twenty feet high. He had the appearance of a cross between a Brontosaurus dinosaur and a lizard but with a python head. His color was a darkly olive shade and he had scales of an ugly grayish black covering his body. The tail was pointed and slithery, like a rat.

The scent emitting from him was foul, like the smell that had infused our vehicle earlier. He released a bellow again and slunk back in a sly temptation. "Come and get me", he seemed to imply.

J.P. responded with a sound that was between a hiss and a deadly sneer. There was evidently no love lost between these brothers.

It was J.P.'s transformation that truly transfixed me. As the grayish dust settled from the landing activity, I leaned forward to obtain a more clear view from the open door.

My grandfather was magnificent. Whatever he now was, he was a spectacular specimen of it. I was breathless at the very sight of him. J.P.'s new form was even larger in proportion than that of his 'brother'. Where the appearance of the other reptilian dinosaur was ugly and distasteful with its actions and movements vulgar and slithering, J.P.'s form was noble in its carriage and demeanor and expressed an air of dignity. At about thirty feet tall, it was also quite beautiful, possessing emerald colored scales that flashed a silvery crystalline essence throughout the mist that had fallen from the mountains and now surrounded them. Looking closer, it became evident that J.P.'s form had one sapphire eye and one emerald colored eye. "Just like Christina!" The words flashed in my mind.

Where the rivaling beast more resembled a creature one could imagine rolling about in the dust and crevices of foul water ports, J.P.'s creation seemed more belonging to an ethereal and celestial essence and indeed, upon closer inspection even possessed a form of wings on his back. He reminded me of something yet I couldn't remember what it was.

Unexpectedly the foreign creature blared a deafening raucous call and spewed forth a noxious green fluid from its mouth as its fangs lunged for J.P.'s underbelly. The venomous fluid would have poisoned J.P. had it connected. Instead it left a putrid stench resting in the mist. When J.P. jumped back, or rather flew back with his now visible and quite remarkable wings outstretched, I realized what he was. Positioned regally in mid air, while the fiendish creature flayed his tail fatally back and forth in an angry dance of inferiority, I knew what J.P. resembled.

"All he needs is a castle." I spoke aloud.

"He is very regal", agreed Celine, eyeing me curiously.

"He is more than that", I responded, fascinated as the crest of the great warrior banner held high videoed through my mind. Finally, I was able to utter: "He is The Pendragon."

"Ah, then you know", breathed Celine.

"No Celine!" I shouted to her in exasperation. "I don't KNOW! I can SEE what he is but I don't know who he is!" I looked into her eyes beseechingly. "WHO is he? Is he Uther? Or is he an alien mystical beast who was also Uther's dragon? Was he what Uther slayed? Or was he what Uther *was*?"

"He is both", Celine replied quietly. "Symbolically he is Uther and he is Uther's dragon. The two are one: Uther slayed his dragon. Now your grandfather must slay his."

"By becoming the dragon", I completed.

"Yes; by becoming the dragon outwardly, to defeat the inner dragon. We carry within our souls a duality, Angele. One essence is of our highest good and when fully expressed is our Higher Self or our personal, also named, Guardian Angel. When you are fully in your place of goodness, you are your higher self and can become attuned to your personal Angel and bring that greatest part of your soul essence to you. In other words, you become your Angel. However, before that can happen, it is necessary to rid the soul of another essence. We call it unawareness."

"You mean evil?" I asked simplistically.

"Well, it is only when we are unaware that we are evil ... or *in*-human." She smiled. "You could also call it our lower nature or ... our ego."

"And, as you can see", Celine said motioning to the scene before us, "the ego does not like to let go."

I followed Celine's' gaze out the door and saw the open competition for power in front of us.

"J.P. is fighting his own demon, his ego", I postured. "Yet, he is such an enlightened being. If a man such as he has such a huge demon, what hope is there for the rest of us? "I stared at her wide-eyed at the very premise of it all.

"You have already answered your own question, cherie. J.P. is qualifiedly an enlightened being. He is also a man. As a man, he is open to the same temptations as any mortal human and as a point of fact, considering his position; he is tempted all the more. The higher the level of spiritual attainment, the more one's soul will be tested. This is a very serious and possibly fatal test of your grand pere's attunement to the Most High."

"Should he fail?" I queried, perspiration seeping from my brow at the possibility of it.

"Should he fail to defeat his dragon, he will perish." Celine spoke softly and with finality.

"He'll die!" I asked, incredulous at this possibility.

"He would leave this dimension, yes." she answered.

"Oh, no! No!" I exclaimed, turning my frantic gaze to the window. "He can't. He can't die. Not after I've just found him. I won't let that happen!"

"You have little power over that, ma petite", came Celine's' healing tones.

At that point I am want to describe what possessed my action, save what can only be called a vast rush of passion of the immediate scenario.

"We'll see about that", I touted. To Celine's' utter horror, I wrenched open the door nearest me and jumped downward, out of the helicopter. As I was achieving this disembarkment, J.P.'s cape, still clasped securely under my chin, floated up and exposed my alighted form. It was only for a brief instant but it was enough time for the fiendish beast to catch sight of me and lunge its fierce python head in my direction. I startled at the sight of its immense ugly head so close to mine and broadcast a scream that could have been heard throughout the Pyrenees. The strength of my windpipes startled the demented dragon and he immediately leapt back.

"Coward", I thought. "Afraid of someone a tenth your size..."

My cloak had fallen closed after my descent from the vehicle and I was aware the beast could no longer see me. I was also aware of the situation of the battle raging. J.P. had executed an array of concise cuts to the beasts' neck and shoulders. The wounds were oozing a disgusting smelling slime. Cunning stood instead of intelligence and strength, yet I sensed its power emerged from a source of a primal evil ready to execute its threat upon its enemy of goodness at any given opportunity, which I was unfortunate enough to give it.

"Angelique!" It was Serge's voice coming from behind a large boulder hid from view by a thick bush about twenty feet to my right. Serge exposed his left arm and beckoned me to move behind the boulder. In abeyance, I began running over to the rock barrier. However, while doing so I neglected to close J.P.'s cape and the speed of my action resulted in the protective cape being blown open and again displaying my form.

The speed with which the beast could react was alarmingly fast. His attention raced to the boulder and with a twist of his feral body, he spun his long python neck in my direction. He lost no time. His attack was instant. In a time span as brief as a sparrow's heartbeat, the beast lifted and raised his rat like tail that was fashioned with scales of razor like disks, and swung it toward my body in a swipe that echoed in my ears like an ocean tidal wave. Had it connected with me, I would not be telling this tale. What occurred next was a scene that I will relive in my memory until leaving this dimension.

J.P. had also caught sight of my torso in flight toward safety and had fathomed the demonic dragon's next move. To keep the dragon's tail from severing me in half, J.P.'s dragon embodiment had lifted himself up by his wings and flung his body in front of me. The rat like razor tail struck the great dragon king a devastating blow in the chest and sliced open his scales. Blood colored with a hue of the deepest blue seeped down his chest area. J.P. expressed a primal cry of the vital life force itself as he held his balance upright as long as he was able before falling to the earth like a graceful and noble tree.

The beast dragon flicked his rat tail around and snickered with glee, laughing a roar into the oncoming night. His python eyes glinted wickedly as he leapt to the top of the boulder beside Serge and licked his lurid lips.

"No!" I shrieked at the evil slayer.

J.P.'s dragon king lay heaped upon the ground and was helpless in front of his pursuer. The dragon beast poised himself for his fatal attack on his brother. With what I realized could be a final play of wits, I threw back the hood on my cloak to expose my head to the attacker.

"Over here!" I yelled to the reptile, to divert him from the wounded dragon king.

The beast startled and jerked his head back with a hiss.

"Not afraid of something you can't see, are you?" I taunted, hoping to give J.P. time to compose himself. I turned to see him remaining on the ground, still and motionless. The beast sneered and turned his evil attention upon J.P. once more. Grabbing my cape, I quickly flung it open to brazenly display my presence to the beast. Fear possessed no part of me now as I moved into full view of the aggressor and hollered up to him. "I'm over here, you coward! Or do you prefer to fight helpless old men!"

The beast reared up and back in the biggest hissy fit ever and stood poised to strike. Instantly I pulled my cloak shut with one hand and my hood down with the other and noiselessly slid over behind the boulder beside Serge and in back of the enemy. I felt the wind of his tail as he swiped the space momentarily left behind.

"That was a bit too close", Serge voiced in a barely audible whisper.

"What do we do?" I implored Serge. "We can't just leave him here!"

The beast swung around upon hearing my voice and peered with unseeing eyes into the face of the bush in front of us.

"It is what YOU must now do", voiced Serge, looking directly into my eyes as if delivering a prophecy.

"Me?" I questioned in a whisper.

The dragon king blared out a cry, shifted and tried to lift his broken form up in an attempt to renew the battle. Yet he could not. The regal Pendragon uttered a sigh and lay his head down on the clover.

"Grand pere!" I cried out, hoping to revive him. Instead it merely succeeded in alerting the evil one who returned his attention to my direction. In a surprise move, the beast swiped his right arm into the space where I stood and this time it did connect. I was thrown forward off my balance and landed face down on the ground. My cape was lifted and I lay open and displayed like a fruit to be taken. The beast moved toward me to crush me like an insect when Serge's' voice cried out.

"Protect yourself. Use your shield."

What do you mean, I thought? I had no shield.

"The shield you received in the garden" J.P.'s voice filtered the air. Instantly, I recalled the scene near J.P's labyrinth.

The Lady of the Lake, who had appeared before me on Lac de la Breyeres, was again clothed in her mother of pearl iridescence.

The Lady had handed me the Sword of Truth.

I remembered her words.

"You were heretofore handed this sword in the position of peace. I now hand it to you in the position of strength to enable you to do battle, should the occasion arise."

Also recalled was her warning to me about the use of the sword.

"Fight only the fight worth fighting". Then also, *"It is not to fall into the hands of those who would misuse its energy."*

"Angelique; the shield! Quickly!" shouted Serge, concern patterning his face.

The shield! Remembering in a panic - I had not taken the shield! The shell was my shield; this was made known during the encounter but I had not received the shield even though I knew it to be mine. What was I to do? The reptile beast was quickening himself for an advance.

I looked over at J.P.'s dragon king who lay expired on the ground. In what appeared to be slow motion, his huge eyelids fluttered open and he gazed his soul out to me through his gemlike eyes. He expressed not a sound, he didn't have to. His eyes spoke.

"Image the shield of Purity and Justice. See it in your mind."

Closing my eyes, I visualized hard on the shell that had ascended from the Lady of the lake. The silver toned mother of pearl shimmered in the light and possessed the aroma of the sea. It's back was marked with the hues of the ocean bottom, colors of peach and sand, and winged circles formed by eons of ocean waves washing up upon it. While focusing and meditating on the shield, I noticed the coil of beautiful natural pearls at the feet of the goddess and realized they were attached to the bottom of the shield as a sort of chain with which to hang the shield over ones shoulder. When feeling the image of the shield to be clear enough and the focus of the intent to be strong enough, I pulled the image to me and held it over my body, and not a second too soon.

The monster's python fangs plunged into the conch side of the shield, the impact and pressure of which sank my body two inches into the ground. The alien creature leapt back with a shrill hiss.

"Broke your little tooth, did you?" I taunted, desperately seeking to keep its attention away from J.P. The thing lunged for me again, its fangs bared and bloody, arched for a target.

I held the shield over me again and let the beast connect with the strength of the cosmic conch. The reptile responded with a hysterical shriek that echoed out into the printemps night.

Wasting little time, I scooped up the flyaway cape, quickly wrapped it around myself and rolled sideways over to where Serge was positioned behind the boulder.

"Are you alright?" Serge beseeched me, pulling me further behind the rock barricade.

"Did you see the other guy?" I responded gallantly.

"Do you always answer a question with a question?" Serge retaliated.

"Tougher than I look, hey?" I quipped, winking at him.

"You will do", he affirmed, adding, "Where did you learn to do that little rolling motion?"

I gazed at Serge matter of factly and responded straight faced, "I grew up in Alberta, Serge: The wild wild west."

"You truly are a force to be reckoned with", Serge replied with new respect in his eyes.

"Yes. I'm just beginning to realize that", I answered to myself humbly but with what I understood was a new sense of self realization. I really WAS becoming a force to be reckoned with.

"J.P. has trained me well", I acquiesced.

"Oui, mais madam, the metal must be there before the form can take shape."

"You mean, like the right stuff?" I smiled.

"Exactement."

It was then that I realized what was necessary for me to do. There was no other way. From the crystal in the sword that was handed to me by the Lady of the Lake, I focused intently and imaged and materialized the great Sword of Truth before me. It returned to me pointed upward for battle, passing from the Lady's hand to my own hand. Grasping the sword boldly, it sent strength surging through my body.

"Madam ... "Serge gasped as he sensed what I was about to do. "No ... please. It is too dangerous!"

"Keep out of this Serge", I spoke sternly. "This is a family matter."

Part IV

"The Light Of The Goddess"

Chapter 1 - "A Family Matter"

Serge riveted his gaze from me to J.P.'s Pendragon as if receiving a silent coded message. Serge then lowered his eyes and gave a slight bow of acquiescence toward me.

From the peripheral vision of my left eye, I noticed Celine's' petite brown shoes tripping lightly over the foliage toward the Pendragon. To avert the attention away from Celine's' rescue mission of J.P.'s alter reptilian embodiment, I held the Sword of Truth, Excalibur, boldly out in front of me.

The beast's eyes glazed crimson and leapt back at the presence of the great sword. He realized its power immediately and I sensed he had perhaps done battle with Excalibur before. The creature motioned from side to side but stepped back almost respectfully. A low growl rose from his inner belly. He was afraid!

Celine had managed to slip beside J.P.'s Pendragon and I could see her hands motioning as she applied the healing signage over him. The beast was, so far, unaware of her presence.

In a sudden jolt of supernatural cognitive consciousness, I could feel the energy of the entity before me and it had a name.

"Jean Paul", I whispered. The beast's head startled and a bewildered hiss emitted from his mouth. He edged back a step further.

Yes. The creature had a name.

The vision ran like a film in my third eye chakra.

There were two boys, Jean Pierre and Jean Paul. They were twins! I saw their early development, growing up, side by side, in the lavender hued fields of the estate of Chateau de la Breyeres. They shared the same bedroom until well into their teens, sat beside one another at the family dining table, many times wore identical clothing and most startling of all, they were identical in appearance.

Upon closer inspection, as if my focus was being directed to it, I noticed that although the two boys were impossible to tell apart, there was one slight difference. Both boys, like my daughter Christina, possessed one blue eye and one green eye but they were in opposition to one another, like a mirrored image. Jean Pierre had a blue left eye and a green right one, while Jean Paul had the opposite; left green and right blue. Yes, just like a mirror, I agreed.

In their youth, the twins shone with equal exemplary behavior. Both were excellent students, both morally and religiously respectful. Both honored their parents. Both were solid citizens of their country and both were interred as soldiers.

Jean Pierre was the eldest by several minutes. By the age of twenty-five he had been prepared for his role as Imperator to follow in his fathers' footsteps.

It was during World War II when Jean Paul was captured that the 'changes' began to occur. The Gestapo reasoned they had captured Jean Pierre de la Breyeres, the prominent figure in the resistance movement in France, and had tortured him unmercifully. Had it been the real Jean Pierre that had been held prisoner, he would have been able to cope with the 'techniques' of the Nazi brutalizers, but although both boys had been schooled in the teachings of the Order, it was Jean Pierre who had received the higher training as he had truly shown the more intrinsic spiritual attributes necessary for the Grand Imperator training. He came by the gift naturally. He also happened to be the elder.

Jean Paul could not protect himself spiritually from his tormentors. I 'saw' the impossible event that occurred and threatened humankind from that point on.

Jean Paul had the spiritual training to release himself out of his physical body. It was when he expired from the pain as the nail hammered through his hand that his spirit rose and left his body. I saw it lift up as if in a jump and hover over his head in the torture room.

Then it slipped out of the vaulted window to escape the pain and trauma and seek solace in the cosmic shelter of his inner sanctum for a brief reprieve.

It was during this brief interval that it happened. Jean Paul's 'shell', his physical body, was left unguarded and open. The maleficent spirits that assisted and guided the Nazi realm were observant of this circumstance and one of them, a particularly insidious and powerful reptilian energy from an alien environment, seized his opportunity to invade and slide inside Jean Paul like a filling into a cavity.

I witnessed the scenario through my spiritual screen as Jean Paul's' soul returned to the scene and attempted re-entry into his body. Jean Paul's soul immediately leapt out of his form in horror and tried to fly off and out to a safe haven but it was not to be. The reptilian spirit pulled him back in. Jean Paul's spirit fought valiantly and their battle resembled an ethereal dance, much like the way a fire appears as the ribbons of smoke of various colors (in this case violet and white being enveloped and choked by black and a fiendish hue of gray) whipped in and out of one another. Finally, with an audible and resounding hiss, the ebony/gray ether puffed itself up into an enormous balloon and wrapped itself completely around the violet/white hue (of Jean Paul) and literally squashed Jean Paul's spirit until he gasped. He was overwhelmed and was pulled back into his own body but with another captain at the helm.

Although it was more than challenging to be sympathetic toward the fiendish being facing me, I also realized that this energy was not Jean Pierre's' brother Jean Paul. Yet it was Jean Paul because Jean Paul *had* to be somewhere within that being. If I could connect with that soul energy perhaps, just perhaps, I could divert the attention away...

Whoosh! As if picking up and interrupting my thoughts, the thing swung his entire neck at me, attempting to dislodge the sword from my hand. It succeeded but not quite as he had planned.

The Sword of Truth, Excalibur, escaped from my hand and flew on its own volition, straight up into the air where it turned over and over, just as it had when the Lady of the Lake first handed it to me. The reptile positioned itself as if ready to capture the sword. Upon Excalibur's descent however, the sword angled itself in strike pose in mid-air and parlayed its own handle as if taunting the creature. The reptile froze for an instant as Excalibur danced in space over his head and then when the sword pulled itself back like an arrow ready to strike, the reptile turned and ran into the mist that was just settling on the mountain range.

Excalibur chased the beast until he was out of sight and then turned in my direction and delivered itself back into my still open hand, for I had not moved from my original position throughout all of this action.

"Thank you", I uttered to the magnificent metal, now returned to my hand. While clasping Excalibur, I beheld yet another truth. It was the realization that when one possessed Excalibur for any length of time, one is given the gift of prophecy and the perception of deep secrets of the cosmos and its beings. Centuries of global and cosmic events were imploded in my pineal gland in seconds of Earth time.

It was then that I heard the Lady calling. It was nearing Her time and I was to go immediately.

Pulling back the hood of J.P.'s cape so my vision would be clearer, I ran over to Celine and the Pendragon. Large as the Sword of Truth was, it was remarkably light to carry and did not hamper my speed or progress in the slightest.

Moving into the light yet enveloping mountain mist that surrounded Celine, I saw her sitting with her legs curled under her, administering to J.P. The Pendragon was no more.

J.P. lay on his back on the mountain green, his sweater torn open by the reptile beast's tail. I moved closer to view the full extent of the carnage and discerned the red gash that ran from the middle of his chest all the way under his right arm. There had been bleeding but it had stopped now. Luckily the wound had occurred in the ribcage; otherwise he would have been spliced in half. His chest was still swollen from the damaged ribs but he was healing exceptionally well and Celine's intent was very focused and intense.

At first I thought him to be asleep but as J.P. opened his eyes, he smiled in my direction forming the word "Excalibur". The sword, which had remained held upright in my hand, tilted forward toward J.P. in a nod of recognition. Or was it a salute?

I was sure I heard J.P. speak to the sword and say, "How are you, old friend?" Then his eyes closed and he appeared to be at rest.

"Will he be alright?" I enquired of Celine.

Celine did not break her concentration in her healing focus on J.P. and without turning her eyes from him, said simply, "He is accepting the energy well but he cannot be moved as yet." With her right hand she made a signage of completion, then turned to me and said, "Everything that can be done is being done. You must go to the grotto now."

As I began to protest, she held up her hand in the position that in any language relays stop and said softly, "You can do no more here. You must hurry. Serge will go with you. I will remain here with J.P. Let the Life Force be with you."

Serge moved up behind me and motioned in agreement. They were right of course. I would be of no further use there and my staying would only disobey the Lady's request, which I knew I must not do.

As we approached the helicopter, Emile turned the ignition. We ducked and shielded ourselves from the big blade. Realizing Excalibur would be awkward to carry in its manifested state; I focused on the crystal in its handle and turned it back into the crystal gemstone that had come with me from the labyrinth garden at Chateau de la Breyeres.

Just as I turned to embark the helicopter, an object like a huge royal blue butterfly began flapping its wings in the distance.

"Wait!" I called out to our pilot Emile and quickly made my way over to the large shrub that held the butterfly captive in its branches, grabbed it up and loosed it from its captor. It was Jacey's cape. The cape had fallen from the black helicopter's windshield yet was untorn and unmarked. After retrieving it, I quickly moved back to J.P. and Celine.

I removed J.P.'s cape and returned it to him via Celine. It took only an instant to wrap Jaceys' cape around me and embark the helicopter, just prior to lift off. As Emile ascended us higher and higher over the Pyrenees mountain range, I observed his head wound had completely healed over leaving barely a thread of a line where a gash had been. Knowing J.P. was in good hands with Celine, I sank back into my seat beside Serge in the back of the vehicle and tried to relax by engaging in some yoga breathing exercises.

"You are calmer now, oui?" queried Serge.

"Yes. Yoga always helps to relax me". After peering out the window at the ground beneath, I turned to Serge and asked, "Where did Jean Paul go?"

"You know about Jean Paul!" Serge's eyes darted at me. It was the first time I had ever seen him appear truly surprised. "But how…?"

"When my hand held Excalibur, I beheld the Truth", was my humble reply.

"Ah, of course…" Serge acknowledged. He knew no information had been given me about Jean Paul's' history.

"It must have been very difficult for my grand pere when his brother was spiritually captured like he was." I empathized aloud. "How did he find out?"

"Ah … it was more when he discovered it", Serge offered. "And that is a very apt description of what occurred … a spiritual captive indeed."

"Your grand pere and his brother were very, very close", Serge emphasized. "It nearly destroyed your grand pere when he realized the truth of what had transpired. Of course, he blamed himself." Serge shrugged in that matter of fact way that only the French can do.

"Had he not let Jean Paul go on that truck to rescue the resistance party members, he would not have been captured and the case of mistaken identity not been made. He would not have been tortured… and you know the rest."

"So it was grand pere who was supposed to have been on that mission and he let Jean Paul go instead?"

"Oui. And, of course, the unimaginable happened. A monster returned in Jean Paul's' place yet went undetected for quite a time."

"How long a time?" I asked.

"Let us say, almost long enough for Hitler to have won the war."

"My Lord!" I gasped.

"There are some things you and most of the world, are unaware of about Hitler's regime." Serge interjected, leaning toward me in order to be better heard over the helicopter's vibration.

"During the 1930's, Germany was in a very unfavorable circumstance. Her economy was down and her self-confidence was low. The German people had no sense of national pride. Then, along came Adolf Hitler, a seemingly self-made organizer who promised to breathe new life into the homeland again. Basically, he could be likened to a kind of a union organizer who was very efficient at bringing Germany's economy up and in keeping his promises. All seemed good in the land."

"So ... what happened?"

"Well, essentially he went bizarre ... ah ... coo-coo ..." Serge searched for the appropriate English term.

"Oh ..." I postured. "You mean he went nuts?"

"Ah ... oui ... he went ... that way", Serge gestured with his index finger making a circle near his head.

I laughed at Serge's miming. "Why? How did he become crazy?"

Serge leaned back and took a deep breath. "This is a fact that is not generally known and the reason will be obvious. Monsieur Hitler studied mysticism for a time and he became quite an interested student of a very knowledgeable mystic, from whom he learned many things arcane. We chose to call what he learned the 'profane arcane', for he chose to use the teachings to his own end and went the way of the ego. He went so far into the profane arcane that it overtook him and he became the monster he was. The reason he turned upon the Jews was because he was aware of the spiritual mystical power they possessed within their religious culture because the teacher he studied under ..."

"Was a Jew", I finished.

"Exactement." Serge nodded. "But", he postured, holding up his right pointer finger, "It gets better. Hitler was merely a pawn in the Second World War. The real culprit was greed in the form of a very high profile banking family in Germany. Wars, ma cherie, make money and the banks were out for urban renewal for the depressed cities of the motherland. What better economical way to achieve it than through a war? Also, if one owns the arms, then one can also sell to both sides and make even more money. Yes, there was a far bigger culprit than Hitler in that war, a far uglier monster. At least Adolf had the excuse of being ..."

"Nuts?" I offered.

"Oui. Une bizarre noisette." Serge tittered, rolled his eyes and continued. "But the head of the banking family that was really at the root of World War II knew exactly what he was doing. He had set Adolf Hitler up to take the fall. He backed him with arms and money to make war on a religion and a culture, not a country.

"Bizarre as it sounds, Hitler himself was part Jewish ... And the head of the banking power that put Hitler into power and allowed all the genocide to occur was a true Jew... And an aristocrat; a baron."

"They turned on their own, in other words. That's quite diabolical when you think about it. I mean, everyone was convinced the Germans were to blame for World War II and the genocide but it was a Jew behind it all."

"A German Jew", Serge pronounced as if reading my thoughts.

"Okay ..." I acknowledged. "I can see the banking demigods seeing a war as a cheap technique for urban renewal and if they owned all the arms everyone would be buying from them ... But why would they have supported Hitler? He was just a painter's son with no particular connections and no real education. I read he hated the Jews because they had all the money and all the influence to get into the academic world that he could not attain to. What would entice a high ranking world figure to back a... well... a nobody like Adolf Hitler?"

"Not exactly 'a nobody', for one thing", Serge answered. "There was somewhat of a noblesse oblige situation involved here. Apparently Hitler's mother was in service at the baron's estate at one point and it has been speculated that Hitler was the baron's illegitimate son."

My mouth dropped. "You're serious, aren't you? Of course you are!" I was stunned and amazed. "Okay ... so the baron backed his son ... but how did he know his son would cooperate? I mean Hitler started a war to take over territory and the genocide came along after he started touting the superiority of the Aryan race. How would the baron know he would do that?"

"Let us say it was possibly the baron who guided him into the study of mysticism, but guided him only toward the viewpoint he had for his own mandate."

"So he led Hitler toward the profane arcane?"

"Hitler studied the full spectrum of mysticism but only used it to obtain power and power only begot more power and without the benefit of a spiritual focus of unconditional love to assist the heart in controlling the ego, the mind cannot handle the chaos of the ego so it goes ..."

"Nuts." I answered. "Two questions ..." My ever inquiring journalistic mind needed to know. "Why did the baron make war and persecute his own people?"

"Money." Serge replied without a blink. "The Jews held most of the money in Europe. Destroy them and take away their wealth and you would basically own Europe."

"Number two: How this man, this baron, could have turned on his own culture is one thing ... But how could he have done that to his own son? Had he no ethics... no heart?"

"From all accounts, no." replied Serge.

"I have a third question." I confessed and held up my hand like a school girl before a teacher. Serge nodded to proceed.

"How do you know all of this?"

Serge paused thoughtfully. In a tone that accepted responsibility, he spoke. "The baron and his son studied mysticism at our order at one time. The baron was always more interested in the business side of it. You know the type I mean. Their motto: Every road leads to wealth."

"Why was he allowed to have this knowledge then?" I asked in amazement.

Serge sighed and went on. "It was believed that the higher knowledge would bring the enlightenment that would shift his thinking to a higher level. It did not." Serge continued, "Many other members of our order were businessmen and materialistically minded." Serge shrugged again. "It did not seem so big a problem. The baron was a powerful businessman with many connections; financial connections; that brought great wealth to our order through members he sponsored. No one could have perceived the extent that his greed would take him."

"Or ..." I pondered aloud. "Was it really the baron ... or one of those things that crawl inside people?" I shuddered at the thought of the vision I'd had of Jean Paul's body invasion.

Serge gazed into my eyes silently for quite a while. Finally he offered, "There are many things we do not know for certain. This circumstance you speak of however could be entirely possible."

I sat in silent contemplation for the duration of the flight to Lourdes. What Serge had informed me about Hitler and the unknown circumstances of World War II seemed even more unbelievable than everything I had seen in the mountains earlier. My conscious mind struggled to take it all in and accept it. It was too much information at one time and my brain felt as if it was swimming in spatial waters. Yet, if I sat in a spiritual place within myself, it all made perfect sense and I understood the great, if improbable, power and force of good that the universal consciousness demonstrated here on Earth.

On Earth we are sent harsh, even devastating, lessons in order to bring us closer to the unfathomable and infinite Love of our great Creator. How? By creating circumstances that are so horrific to us that we finally are able to tear through the transparent yet most of the time impenetrable veil of our own illusion. The world of our own creation makes it all but impossible for most of us, with the exception of those who decide to go off and sit on a mountaintop in Tibet, to be connected to our highest spiritual guides and the magic and mysteries of our great universe. (It could become a rather dangerous situation to be driving along the 401 in 5:00 P.M. traffic and have a spirit entity plop itself in our passenger seat and begin to engage us in a dissertation of our past and future lives and the reasons for the necessity of our evolution.)

So we remain all but immune to our true reality, which is that we are all things, at all places, at all times; except for those odd moments (or in dreams) where the veil is momentarily lifted for us to view our future or relive our past (lives) and get a sense of the true wonder of what we truly are. We are infinite, like our creator. We always have been here, always will be here... and we never, never die.

"Ready to land." Emile's voice brought me out of my reverie and back to J.P.'s helicopter. It was 6:02 P.M. and the Lady had advised she would appear at 7:00 P.M.

Staring at the second hand ticking away time on the Roman numeral face of my Cartier wrist watch, I remembered with a pang that shot through my solar plexus. Jacey had given me this watch on my last birthday that we were together. I knew by heart, without having to look at the inscription on the back, the words that had wrapped themselves around my heart and still touch me more than any written or spoken words ever have.

> *My Angel;*
> *With love we live forever.*
> *Until forever,*
>
> *Jacey*

Tears were sliding down both cheeks before the realization came that I was crying. Jacey had died out of dedication to what my mission involved. Emotion beyond the largest tidal wave welled up inside of me and I felt helpless to override it. "Jacey. My light... my love... my life. How will it be possible to go on without you?" I sobbed softly to myself in the darkness of the back seat of the helicopter. Just when it felt that I couldn't go on, I knew that I must.

Suddenly, The Lady came into view standing on the small balcony near the steeple of the church by the grotto. When She realized I had seen Her, She extended Her arms and smiled up and out to me and uttered my name. *"Angelique ..."*

I heard her! Her voice sounded through my ears with an energy that was both wind and light and through Her voice, my being was transformed. My body seemed to lift off the leather bound seat and I felt that it would be possible to fly by my own volition down to the grotto!

The Lady's warmth and light effused out to a radius of about fifty feet around Her and lit up the sky above the church. My great love for Her filled and expanded my heart with what seemed like a huge ball of light until I became light, suspended in mid-air and surrounded by the light majestic until the helicopter landed down in Lourdes.

Chapter 2 - *"The Return of Caliburn: The Sword of the Pendragon"*

Emile swung the helicopter around and circled the area where we were to land. A gathering of tall cedars hid a clearing in the centre of the trees that was ideal for the small landing pad.

The area contained the entrance J.P., Celine, Serge and I had driven to earlier from Chateau de la Breyeres. The helicopter dropped softly down onto the landing pad and we immediately unbuckled our seatbelts, eager to enter the hidden cave that would take us once again to the underground area of the church of the grotto.

My right foot had just hit the ground when we heard the blade sounding from another helicopter. In seconds it was circling and hovering directly over us, readying to land. I blinked back the dust and endeavored to identify the passengers. It was not possible to see the pilot but I recognized the passenger immediately and ran with my heart toward the helicopter. It was my grandfather.

"Grandpere!" I called out, rushing to embrace him. While waiting for him to alight from the helicopter so as not to be blown to smithereens by the blade, I observed J.P.'s lithe body as he disembarked the vehicle. He had changed clothes and was now wearing a black bodysuit that zipped up the front to the neck. His movements were so agile, unbelievable for a man of his years, especially considering he had just been severely wounded. Celine had done wonders with him.

As I attempted to put my arms around him, he turned his face away and instead took my arm and motioned to the cave, saying crisply, "We need to move quickly."

My feelings were somewhat hurt by his lack of response but I attributed it to his concern for time. As we approached the hidden door, Serge signaled it open and we entered the underground abbey.

As we stood in the entranceway that opened to several hallway tunnels, J.P. seemed confused as to which tunnel to take. My empathy went out to him, assuming he must have been struggling just to maintain equilibrium after his previous encounter. He stood motionless, just staring at the tunnels.

Finally I offered, "We need to take one of these tunnels to the anteroom." Observing his uncomprehending face, I went on, "This is where we will make preparation for the Lady. It's time." Pointing to the tunnel on the right and taking his hand as if he were a child, I led him gently through the dimly lit stone passage. J.P. didn't make any sound as he walked upon the stone slab floors. Listening to my own clicking sounds upon the gray stones, I envied his light step.

We wound through the tunnel to the recognizable door where I turned the antique latch, opening the room for us. Lovingly, I led J.P. to a large chair with a very high back. He must be tired, I thought, and helped him sit down. He seated himself with such agility, it was impossible to tell he had even suffered a wound at all, which made me marvel again at Celine's healing ability.

"Close and lock the door, my child", spoke J.P. in a low, almost hushed, tone. I acquiesced and returned to face him. The room was dimly lit by the white monastery candles that were situated at several different stations upon pieces of ancient furniture.

"Remove your cloak, child", J.P. spoke, again in a voice so low.

Once again I obeyed his request and placed Jacey's cloak over the back of another high back chair, similar to the one on which J.P. was sitting, situated against the wall adjacent to him. Beside the chair was a long high table decorated with side inserts of the most exquisite rose pink marble and topped with a three inch slab of the same marble. J.P. observed me admiring the beautiful table. "It is an admirable piece of antiquity", he commented in the same low monotone.

"Child", he spoke. (Child? I wondered why does he call me child? Why does he not call me by my name? Then I realized he may not even remember my name momentarily because of the trauma of the injury.)

"I want you to go and lay down upon the marble table, my child."

After stepping over to the identified table and lifting myself onto the marble surface, I lay down flatly upon it. The marble was cold against my back.

"Close your eyes, child."

Immediately as my eyelids closed, a light lifting energy surrounded me and the peace of the innocent filled my being.

J.P.'s energy felt close beside me. "Grand pere?"

"Yes, my child."

"My name is Angelica." I spoke lovingly, my eyelids still closed and filtering out the flickering light of the abbey candles. J.P. echoed out a sound that was a either a sob or a deep sigh. It was difficult to tell. Whatever it was, that sound was so unexpected and poignant, my eyes flew open instantly and beheld a sight as impossible as it was extraordinary. Standing over me was J.P. holding a dagger by the handle with the blade pointing directly down at me!

With everything witnessed so far however, I assumed this was part of yet another ritual and was not daunted by the situation.

"What a lovely dress", J.P. commented, slowly drawing his vision over my lapis gown. His hands held the dagger and remained motionless in mid-air as his eyes flowed up my body and focused solely on my face.

"Such a beautiful woman", he spoke in a voice that cried.

He stood motionless, tears rolling down his face. It was upon looking into his eyes to offer him comfort that I noticed something was different. The colors were switched. His left eye was green and his right eye was blue. The realization of the situation clicked into my brain in an instant of horror. The man standing before was Jean Paul!

Before my mind was able to utter another thought, a mistral flew into the room and held an invisible energy within it. It was an energy I knew. THIS energy was my grandfather's!

J.P. was wearing the masters' cloak that had been returned to him earlier. One arm peeked through the air and drew the cloak away from him so he was in full view. His other hand held a long sword beautifully embellished with jewels on the handle. I knew that sword; had seen it in folklore books and in replica at the museum while doing research on the Celts. This sword was the Caliburn: The Sword of the Pendragon.

"No, Jean Paul", spoke J.P. "I cannot allow you to do this. Your fight is with me, not with this woman."

With Caliburn held high, J.P. knocked the dagger from Jean Paul's hands as it teetered dangerously toward me. Instinctively I rolled to the opposite side and off the table.

With a delft hand, J.P. flipped Jean Paul in the air and landed him on his back upon the table recently occupied.

"Angelique!" emoted J.P. forcefully. "Go to the grotto immediately. I will handle this."

J.P. stood over Jean Paul, just as he had over me, and held the sword Caliburn at his throat. Surrounding J.P. was an energy force consisting of a montage of colors, some of which were indescribable. It was J.P.'s energy that held Jean Paul at bay and it took considerable power to generate it to still the powerful dragon from transforming and flying at us.

I ran from the anteroom of the grotto to the shelter of The Lady.

I knew J.P.'s energies could hold the reptilian beast's energy from surfacing in Jean Paul but the sword Caliburn may not have the strength to kill Jean Paul and eliminate the spirit that bound him.

While running through the long passageway en route to the church entrance, my mind clicked with thoughts that glued themselves to my brain.

While peering into Jean Paul's eyes, even as he held the dagger over me, I knew that Jean Paul would not harm me. Although the other energy that was enclosed within him would have run me through in a mini second, Jean Paul held the reptilian energy back as long as he could. That was why he cried out as he had. 'He', Jean Paul, would NEVER hurt me. Of that I was certain. Intuitively I felt that there was a particular reason why he would not but precisely what that reason was, I did not know.

Chapter 3 – "The Lady Speaks Again"

My heart was pounding while running along the ancient gray stones to the church doorway. Stopping to catch my breath, I closed my eyes for a second, leaned against one of the stone walls in the passageway and just breathed. I breathed easy shallow breaths, releasing all tension and stress; in and out slowly and easily.

Upon reopening my eyes, a luminescent light was bidding me forward, down the passageway toward an open doorway. The light emitting from the chamber eclipsed everything except the central figure which was the source of the light.

The Lady stood in the centre of the room, aglow with the same radiance that caught my attention from the sky. She was, in truth, clothed by the sun.

"Come in, Angelique." She beckoned. Her voice vibrated through the room softly but with a strength that was of the very Earth herself. It was so, my mind reasoned, because She was its mother and queen.

"My Lady", I spoke and entered obediently. As if reenacting an ancient custom, I bowed before her on one knee and lowered my head. The Lady extended Her right arm and placed Her hand directly upon my crown chakra. When She removed Her hand, both Her and the room were plainly visible. She still emitted a luminescence about Her but She had quickened my consciousness so that it was possible to 'see' Her and raised my vibration level so it was also possible for me to visibly 'see' the angelic energies that surrounded Her, where at my normal vibration level they were only felt. They were extraordinary and beyond beautiful! Unearthly... like light having taken on the form of blossoms.

For the first time I saw the celestial hierarchy with my own physical eyes instead of my spiritual eyes: The Seraphim; those fiery wheels and wings of red gold and The Cherubim; with their tiny exuberant faces, plump apple cheeks, fiery cherry lips and wings of golden light.

I observed the Virtues, the Principalities and the great Archangels, with Mikhail at the helm; appearing most spectacular with his silver armor and flashing shield and sword. Gabrielle was feminine and dressed in the sky and ocean just as The Lady was dressed in the sun. Uriel held the golden lamp of knowledge over his white sleeve and Raphael, the communicator, stepped forth and with a welcoming bow, extended forth his emerald arm to me. While surrounded by the heavenly realm, it occurred to me how amazing that they could all fit into this small room!

The trio energies of Light Love Life spilled into and around me and the energy literally lifted me off the ground. Rising higher and higher off the floor, it seemed so easy to fly; just like the angels must feel. As I floated in the room, the angelic realm and The Lady watched me with smiling eyes, like parents watching a baby walk for the first time.

"Am I one of you now?" I asked in a thought.

"You have always been one of us", replied Raphael.

"You were simply placed in a different location to do your work. You are of our universal branch; one of the planetary messengers. That is why your work is here, on earth."

"I always thought angels and people had different energies; that people couldn't become angels as angels were messengers from God and didn't have physical bodies." Bravely put, I thought, under the circumstances.

"That is quite correct", answered Raphael again. "People don't become angels... but angels can, and sometimes do ... But become is not the proper word ... Angels can preside over a physical being. *You* are able to do this because your vibratory level is of a higher degree than that of the majority of the Earth beings."

"All of the time?" I queried, still extended in mid air, which I quite enjoyed.

"No." smiled Raphael, "Not all of the time. You are still human." Raphael glowed with an emerald luminescence. He was crystalline in his energy, representing the healing crystal energy of the earth.

Surrounded by her celestial court, The Lady stood centrally in the room, glowing so brightly it was like being under the noon day sun on a tropical island - and just as warm. Had the Lady not quickened me, it would not have been possible to bear the intense light and heat of Her energy and I wondered how the masses (of people) awaiting Her appearance would able to do so.

"Those who can see will see", answered Raphael to my unspoken mind question.

"Yes, Angelique, you are not to be concerned about the receptivity of my visit. Everyone who comes to see me or watches via electronic media will receive the illuminated answers that their individual consciences allow them to receive at this time of their evolution – and more. Their energy will be quickened, just as yours has been. All because it is the time for humanity to perceive and receive guidance at a higher level. Everyone on Earth will be quickened because the planet itself is being quickened by the Creator. It is Earth's time to be illuminated and your race of beings will receive even more after the millennium. The true millennium actually begins in 2012, in your years."

The Lady's voice softened with a more somber tone and her eyes saddened as she spoke next.

"I have brought you here first, before I appear to your world, because there are certain occurrences I want you to be aware of, even though they may be unavoidable.

"In the year of your millennium, the numbers 9 & 11 will hold great significance in Earth's memory. Also, great destruction will come to a believed impenetrable area on your planet that will shock your world and may set into motion a situation that could threaten the survival of your planet as you now know it.

"Another war is not the answer to your planet's future challenges and yet there are those individuals who are being affected by unseen forces of the universe to perpetrate violence and vengeance instead of the energies of Love and Forgiveness. I encourage you to unite your Earth with the energy of Peace, for it is this energy that holds the answer to the positive future of this planet.

**"There is also a possibility of a marriage between England's future king and his confidante. If this is allowed to happen, the future of this hallowed isle is in great jeopardy.*

"The king, or ruler, of this land particularly was sent to represent the God presence on Earth and embodies a role of essential significance to your planet. It is imperative his life be exemplary. His princess was sent to him by the Goddess Herself, representing one of Her own priestesses. She was sent as a visionary for your world, one who by her very purity and willingness to serve the Goddess was to help transform humanity to a higher state of beings. It was the Light that shone through her that affected and illumined the human soul, for that was her mission on Earth. She was necessary and her early departure from this planet threatens to slow down its evolution.

"Should this king be aligned with and marry a woman who was not sent by the Goddess for this same purpose (of Love and Evolution of the planet), then the Light intended for the Earth at this time will be unable to be effused throughout humanity as her soul vessel would not be capable of holding this Light. This situation could, in effect, realize the ultimate destruction of this planet, as your humanity will not be able to sustain the enlightenment given to it and by so doing, destroy itself.

"The significance of this situation holds more importance than the beings in question have realization of. The queen of this land has this knowledge. She will try her best to dissuade her son from this action, but it may be of no avail.

"And..." The Lady cautioned, *"If the king to be does not heed his personal conscience and his assignment to duty and instead exercises personal choice, he could not only ultimately destroy his familial relationships but he could bring about his own ruin. This would affect his sons as well.*

"Worse yet, assassination could follow and a future war eminent as the traitors responsible for this act would be colored to have sympathies to an eastern nation.

"The king to be does have freewill and free choice in this matter, as all humankind has freewill in their personal choices. However, because of his station in life, the forces of the universe who wish Earth's destruction have been and will continue to influence the king to forfeit his duty to humanity and make a personal choice.

"Can nothing be done?" I queried, both alarmed and concerned by The Lady's warnings.

Her eyes, both serious and loving, smiled warmly to me. *"It is his choice. Let us hope he chooses wisely."*

Sadly, I realized the seriousness of what The Lady had expressed. It was entirely predictable the king to be might actually marry his mistress, in time, after the memory of the princess had subsided in the Earth's conscience. Her words disturbed me because neither of the parties involved had any realization of the magnitude that their personal actions could have, not only to their own families but to the world at large. Were they incredibly selfish and insensitive people, caring for no one but themselves? Hardly so, yet it was very likely they had no idea of the global consequence of their liaison. Was what The Lady said true? Were they under the influence of 'unseen universal forces' that were bent on humanity's destruction?

"I will tell you one thing more", The Lady spoke again. *"As in all things cosmic and mortal, there is a duality; an alpha and an omega. It was first so with the Bringer of Light and Truth that your world knows as the Christed One. For in truth, this being was actually two; the man named Yehoshua that you call Jesus, was born with a brother. Information upon this, some false and some truth, will emerge to the Light in the millennium of Light in the future. This knowledge could cause great mistrust in your world's religions in the future but it need not be so. This information can guide and unite humanity in peace and brotherhood in the true nature that your beings were brought forth for.*

"Now it is time to go." The Lady informed.

"What can I do to help you?" I reacted. "I will serve you any way I can."

"Yes, you will, I know, my dear one. Just as the princess obeyed and served, so will you. Worry not, for I will give you the words to write to express the vision the princess was sent to deliver. Your service in this way will greatly assist in uniting and evolving humanity for this planet's true great future.

"All will be well, little one. Now, go up to the grotto where I will soon see you and I will deliver my message."

As my body lowered itself to the floor, the image of The Lady and Her magnificent court dispersed but the room maintained ablaze with light. Drawing in a deep breath of The Lady's ethereal energy, I almost 'lifted off' again but maintained my footage on the floor by grounding myself with inner meditation.

As I turned to depart for the grotto, the door was suddenly thrown open, almost off its ancient hinges. Jean Paul stepped into the chamber and headed toward me. The energy of The Lady invaded him however, sending the reptile within him shrieking and flying down the hall. What was left facing me was a man whose last breath seemed to have been taken. His eyes closed as he expelled a gasp and fell to his knees on the floor in front of me.

"Angelique!" The voice that implored from him sounded like, yet couldn't possibly be, J.P. Still...

I approached him cautiously and kneeled down over him. He opened his eyes, looked up at me lovingly and smiled as much as his strength would allow.

"Quickly, my child, there isn't much time." He tried to get up, but could not. I put my arm around his slender shoulders and rested his head on my lap.

"My name is Angelica" I told him again, softly. His energy wasn't cold or inhibiting now. This was the true soul of Jean Paul lying before me.

"I know your name, my child ..." He breathed in and out, reviving his own energy. "You see ... my dear one ... You are my grandchild, cherie."

"How can that be?" Amazement overtook me.

"Your grandmother and I had a ... relationship ... and your mother is my daughter."

"But... J.P. said he was ..." I stammered.

"Yes ... yes, I understand. You see... your grandmother also had a relationship with Jean Pierre. She had a relationship with both of us... but did not know because we were... are... identical twins. Jean Pierre and I did not realize we were in love with the same woman because we never spoke of our individual involvement with her to one another."

"Then, how do know YOU are my ..."

"Because she told me ... before she left. We were very close... but you see, she called us both Jean (our Christian name) and never knew we were twins... Never realized we were two men until much later ..."

291

"How extraordinary!" What I was hearing was incredulous.

"That is why, as you realized, I could not harm you." Through his eyes, Jean Paul smiled love out to me that connected with my very soul.

"You are the beautiful granddaughter I always wished to have and now know I do. It is enough to hold you just for a moment."

Jean Paul's voice was cut off by the sounds of the shrieking reptilian form waiting in the hall.

"Alas, my child, we do not have much time together" Jean Paul continued as he stroked my hand. "There is something you must do ... and you must do it quickly ..." Jean Paul implored as tears filled his eyes.

"What can I do?" My own eyes brimmed with tears as well.

Jean Paul spoke the words clearly and succinctly as he looked into my eyes without blinking and said, "You must kill me."

"What!" I gasped.

"Listen to me ... you must kill me NOW!" he ordered, grasping my arm and looking at me with searing earnest. "Angelique, the Lady has entrusted you with too much knowledge. If you do not kill me now, when that thing returns - and trust me, it will - then it (within me) will kill you and everyone in the world that it can. DO YOU UNDERSTAND ME!" he added emphatically.

Tragically, I knew what he said was true. That 'thing' as he called it, would eventually re-enter Jean Paul when the Lady's energy in the room diminished and there would be no power Jean Paul would have that could stop it. He may as well be dead for the kind of existence he had.

I looked Jean Paul steadfastly in the eyes and said simply "How?"

"Get ... use ... Excalibur", Jean Paul expressed.

Closing my eyes, I held the stone and activated the Sword of Truth. Excalibur revisited me, appearing in my right hand where the stone had been.

"Take the blade of the sword, Angelique, and point it directly over my heart, please", implored Jean Paul.

Grasping Excalibur by its handle, I held it just as Jean Paul had ordered.

"Now ..." Jean Paul swallowed dryly as he continued. "Take the sword, push it into my heart ... and lean on it, HARD!" he finished.

Kneeling beside Jean Paul, Excalibur between my hands with the blade point just above his heart, I breathed in a deep breath but made the mistake of looking into his eyes once more.

"I can't! ..." Loosening the sword, "I can't kill you!"

"Angelique, you *must* kill me!" cried Jean Paul.

I had not noticed what he evidently had: The Light in the room was getting dimmer and dimmer, while in the distant hall, the cry of the shrieking reptile spirit was becoming louder and closer. It would not be long before...

Suddenly the room was dark and the blackish gray swirling energy tore through the doorway and whistled about Jean Paul. Jean Paul's body rose up and convulsed in mid air as it fought to keep the spirit from entry but it was no use. The eyes looking up at me at that moment were no longer those of Jean Paul and they threw out a poison dart arrow of hate that narrowly missed me. That mistake could not happen again. So I was fast.

One thrust of Excalibur and it was done. The shrieking reptile echoed out a dying shudder, releasing its spirit in the form of a putrid stream of grayish smoke that rose up and out of the chamber's high cathedral window.

After standing up and stepping back to avoid the blood that oozed out of Jean Paul's fatal wound; drawing its own stream on the stone floor; I studied Jean Paul's lifeless face which now at last, had found peace.

Another image now stood beside Jean Paul; one I recognized from her painting. It was the Maid d'Orleans. She held her own sword at her side by her armor and said simply, "It is gone ... For now", and dissolved in front of me.

**There is prophecy that the king to be would have an opportunity to meet with a holy man whose spiritual energy was one of the highest the world would ever know. This man would have the spiritual strength to intercede with the Creator to heal and clear this situation, thereby enabling the king to marry his beloved. England's king to be met with Pope John Paul II in 2007, just prior to his marriage.

Chapter 4 - "The Lady Appears"

I was silent within while treading my way down the hall passage that led through the church and out to the grotto of Lourdes.

As I walked, I heard no footsteps, as I moved I felt no wind, as I pushed one foot then another before me, I sensed no pressure on the ground. It was indeed as if my physical body as well as my spirit and mind simply and easily flew toward the grotto where St. Bernadette first saw her Lady of Lourdes.

The camera crew spotted me and immediately converged in my direction. The first man coming toward me was the director of the show The Lady Known as 'O'. He wanted to know where *She* was, The Lady was to be here at 7:00!

Calmly, my body mind and spirit floated over to him, "Where is 'O'?"

The director looked at me strangely for a few seconds but calmed his energy and pointed his right arm at the tiny grotto and said," She's over there ... praying."

Silently I walked through the gaggle of onlookers, all awaiting the presence and the appearance of The Lady of Lourdes. It was an event that had not occurred since 1858, when Bernadette had her visions at the grotto.

Several celebrities had made the pilgrimage for the visit. Some being personal acquaintances, I acknowledged recognition with a smile or a nod. Most of the crowd however consisted of ordinary devout looking individuals of all ages. Walking toward the grotto, I noticed small children accompanied by expectant parents, senior citizens of all nationalities, veterans of World War II; some standing and some in wheelchairs attended by aids or relatives and teenagers reverently praying with their rosaries. The crowd was large; too many to count; extending to the stone fence above the mountain stream that ran by the church.

At last I was at the sacred site. There, at the mouth of the grotto, 'O' knelt and faced the small cave formation. Her face was in profile to me, but it was also in rapture. 'O's face was luminous and beaming with refracted light all about her. She wore a pale blue dress with a matching sheer scarf draped over her head and shoulders. Never had I seen North America's favorite television icon appear more beautiful than she did at that moment.

'O's lips opened and moved a bit, speaking words into the grotto. Then I saw 'Her'. The Lady stood over the glass plate that covered Her stream. She was speaking with 'O' and giving 'O' a message, one I felt She wanted 'O' to bring to the world in her own way. It was curious because although a few of those in attendance at the grotto caught the vision of The Lady, so many did not. It was not yet time for Her global exposure.

'O' nodded her head in abeyance and made the sign of the cross; possibly because The Lady asked her too for I wasn't sure if 'O' was catholic. She then stepped away from the grotto. Observing my approach, "O"opened her arms in an embrace.

"Angelica ..." she whispered, hugging me to her. "I saw *Her* ... I saw The Lady ..." Tears filled her large green hued eyes. "She gave me a message. My God ... I got a message from the Holy Mother!" A combination of humility and awe painted her face. "She told me something She wants me to relate to the world, but later ..." she spoke on, crying joyous tears.

"Right now I have to cue the camera crew ... *'She's'* ready ..."

'O' stepped over to her director and the crew arranged themselves, facing the grotto. 'O' faced the camera and began to speak.

"Good evening everyone. I have been given the privilege of hosting an extraordinary event at the famous grotto in Lourdes, France.

"This is the location where one hundred and forty years ago, a young peasant girl named Bernadette saw a vision of a beautiful lady. 'The Lady', as she called Her, advised Bernadette to tell her priest that She was the 'Immaculate Conception'; a description that brought honor as well as controversy to the little village of Lourdes and to the girl Bernadette herself.

"What did She have to tell a poor young peasant girl that many of the villagers believed was half-witted?

"Bernadette received many messages from her Lady, many of which were recorded and sit in the Vatican archives. Some, but not all, have been made open and available to the public.

"Significantly, two years prior to the millennium, The Lady has again chosen to make another appearance at Her grotto in Lourdes. This time, She has advised She will be visible for all to see.

"So, please stay tuned for an experience that I can assure you will be extraordinary for all of us."

Chapter 5 – "The Call For Peace"

The camera focused on the area just above the stream, as 'O' had directed her cameraman. The Lady stood steadfast on Her perch, just as She was when 'O' had prayed with Her.

A great gasp offered up from the crowd gathered around the grotto. The Lady was now visible to all at the site... and to the world.

The camera focused on The Lady's form and then moved to the right for another angle and then to the left, keeping a respectful distance, which The Lady's majestic presence demanded. Flashbulbs resounded and then the lights flew off everywhere around the grotto, yet The Lady remained still and motionless.

Allowing them all to take their photographs and adjust their 'electronic networking' as She called it, The Lady let the crowd and the world view Her freely and openly in this manner for a good ten minutes.

It was an orderly crowd. No one got 'out of hand'. Some people climbed up on the stone fence for a better view but most in attendance simply and almost automatically dropped to their knees and began to pray. Others just stood, or kneeled, and listened, hearing a voice meant for them alone. Some people hushed those praying to be quiet, for they were receiving private messages of their own.

The Lady raised Her right hand in the air; a universal signal indicating Stop and Silence. Immediately, all voices went silent, all camera flashes ceased and everyone's attention was focused upon The

Lady, shimmering in Her clothing made of the sun, as She stood in the little grotto.

The air was eerily quiet, waiting. Suddenly, a klieg light lamp fixture belonging to the crew, exploded and frightened a baby resting in her mother's arms, spraying her with shattered glass and dust. The Lady held up both hands, sending light beams throughout the crowd and said, *"Your lighting equipment will not be necessary. Turn them off to avoid further accidents."*

The crew 'killed' the lights. The grotto was bright as a sunlit afternoon.

The baby was covered in broken glass and crying.

"Bring the child to me." The Lady bid.

The mother didn't hesitate and carried her child up to the grotto and handed her to The Lady. The baby was cut and bleeding from the broken glass, scared and hurt. Yet immediately as The Lady held her, the little girl, who was about two, ceased her cries and began to coo and smile and talk her baby language to the beautiful Lady holding her.

The crowd smiled and cheered. The Lady blew the offending glass and poison dust off the baby's head and touched her hand to the child's facial cuts, healing them upon contact. The child's mother fell to her knees before The Lady and put her head in her hands, crying with heart rendering sobs.

The Lady spoke tenderly to the young mother.

"You are not alone, my child, nor is your baby. Your husband died honorably, thinking only of you and your little girl. He does not wish you to mourn for he will always be around you to guide you and extend love to you both.

"In a very short time, you will meet a new love and the two of you will share and build a wonderful life together for your child and future children.

"This man is a doctor of alternative medicine and you as his nurse will create a healing centre in one of the remotest areas on earth where your efforts will be greatly needed and blessed.

"Get up and take your child." The Lady held the baby girl out to her mother.

The woman took her hands from her face and stared in awe at The Lady before her.

"I *am* a nurse!" The woman uttered in amazement. A beam of vibrant white light shot through the woman's heart chakra from The Lady's hand and the woman stood up and smiled, reaching out her arms to receive her cooing, laughing child.

"All who have come and all who see Me will receive a blessing." The Lady began. *"I am here so all may receive love and hope and healing within themselves. Mostly, I am here so you all will know that you can give all of these things to yourselves and to one another. This is the purpose of your being: The reason you were created upon this planet at this time was to receive this knowledge.*

"An evolution is now in process on Earth, as well as in all of the heavens. At times, this evolution is evident; at times it is not as clear. Yet it is the time for the Light of the Cosmos to move closer and infuse more into Earth's consciousness for a greater universal and interplanetary good. We are all beings beneath one roof, one Energy and it is time to create a newer crescendo of Light that can allow the galaxies to manifest as they were intended to.

"Therefore, dear ones, you as well will be invited to raise your consciousness levels so your energies are quickened to accept the new Light energy that will be flowing through the cosmos. You will feel this subtle change happen at the time of your approaching millennium, known in the cosmos as your Millennium of Unity.

"There will ensue not only a sense of unity with one another and a resurgence of the energy of the brotherhood of mankind and a genuine love and caring for the welfare of each and every being on your planet, but also a silent connection with the energies and beings that exist in the universe.

"Our cosmos is alive with energies so far unseen at your level of consciousness. Relatively soon, this circumstance will change on your planet and awareness of your of connection with the entire 'whole of existence' will be evident.

"I am here as your Mother. Some call Me the Holy Mother, or the Queen of Love and Compassion, some know of Me as the Goddess. To others I am the Virgin, representing the purity of all Earth and humankind. In truth, I am all of these. But mostly, I am your Mother, for I gave birth to you all with my thoughts, my ideas and my love. So, dear ones, I hold every being's energy and essence close to my heart for you are all from my heart. I know you all. I love you all.

"As your true Mother, My message for you all is simply this: Forgive and release the anger and pain you hold within you for one another and clear your karmic inheritance. Then, you will be able to create the lives you wish to have. In so doing, you will enable Earth to become the destination she was meant to be in the universe; the planet where the soul comes to learn to create and manifest its true desires.

"You are all souls within a body temple. As souls, you are spirit and essence. When you incarnate in physical form, you become 'real' manifestations of the creative thought forms of the High Creator; or God /Goddess. That God is also the God of your heart and the God of your own creation, just as we are the creations of the one true God.

"The one true God resides within every one of you, for you are all Gods or Goddesses in the making. You create, and recreate, yourselves until you achieve the perfection of the Divine.

"So take warning when you pollute your temples with negative thoughts and activities as you lower the vibration not only of your own souls but of the very creator that manifested you! Remember, you are in the Divine as the Devine is in you. Careful, least you create a faulty God.

"Such a circumstance has already been in evidence. Thus, the thought forms that have emanated from the Creator have, at times, been detrimental to the universe. On your planet, these situations include wars, carnality, financial greed, devastation and cruelty in overt and unnecessary manners. When such atrocities are exercised upon the human psyche, it only exacerbates and creates further trauma within a sea of already existing chaos of the mind.

"This need not continue to occur on your planet if you release the negative forces that have inhabited your consciousness and forgive one another. What has occurred was not of your making but of cosmic conditions and interference.

"Keep your temples pure and the exterior energies will no longer be able to penetrate your auric shields. Build the energy strongly around you with your thoughts of integrity and worth.

"By setting examples of such behavior for your children, you will set the energy in motion for generations to come and create on Earth the race that was meant to be.

"I bid you Love and Peace for now and a promise to return."

Chapter 6 – "The Lady Bids Farewell"

The Lady's physical form very slowly dissolved before our eyes as She bid her earthly farewell. Just before She eclipsed from our view, however The Lady raised Her right hand and held out a luminous red rose, which She threw out to the crowd. As the rose left Her hand, it flew of its own volition to a space in the sky, about thirty feet above the crowd and magnified its appearance until a formation a thousand times its original size appeared in the Pyrenean night sky above us.

In an explosion of color and essence, the sky rose burst apart, sending wafts of rose scent accompanied by thousands of beautiful red tea roses, identical to the original held by The Lady. The bomb of roses fell lightly and gracefully, seemingly in slow motion, down upon the crowd of devout onlookers.

The hand of one pilgrim reached up and a drifting rose fell into it 'right on cue', as they say in the media.

The mother of the little girl The Lady had held felt a full blown rose fall upon her shoulders before she saw it. Her baby girl shrieked in delight as an identical bloom toppled down her forehead, nose and mouth and into her tiny fingers.

I circled about and breathed in the rainfall of exquisite tea roses, which scented the air with heavenly aroma and essence as they poured and delivered themselves into each and every hand of every individual gathered in the crowd. Watching in amazement as people seemed to sense which rose was for them and reached out to grasp 'their own' with joy sketched upon their faces, I noticed not one rose fell to the ground.

Every rose found its owner... including mine, which caught in my hair on my right shoulder. When I turned my head to see it, the rose blossom seemed to reach its petal face out to kiss my cheek. As it did so, the divine energy of The Lady infused itself into me with Her message of the most profound Love and Peace imaginable.

This simple act had more impact upon me than anything seen or felt since my journey to France (and to myself) had begun several days ago. The transformation from that moment may continue to last a lifetime.

All of the crew members received their blooms. 'O' had her flower land upon her clip-on microphone, located on the cowl neckline of her ample bosom, directly at her heart chakra. She cried as she clasped the rose to her and turned her eyes upward to the night sky and mouthed words of thanks as the tears escaped down into her ears.

The crowd reacted in silent acceptance of their divine gift and quietly, one by one, began to disperse and climb back up the hill by the church into the night and their own worlds.

Realizing that everyone was leaving, I began to panic as there was no way of returning to the chateau without my guides.

"Angelique!" Celine's voice called out. Standing on the left side of the grotto where The Lady had appeared, I heard my name called out again. This time it was Serge's voice and came from the other side of the grotto.

I tried to focus on the opposite side of the grotto but the energy of The Lady continued to light the area to a degree that it was quite blinding to look into it, which had to be done to see the other side. Finally, a form headed toward me, took my hand and guided me around the grotto to a hidden underpass located on the opposite side of the hill.

The hand belonged to Serge. As we entered the narrow passage, Celine and Emile rushed up to embrace me. Celine glowed with the essence of the illumination of her rose which she held sacredly in her hand. Only her eyes showed the ghost of sadness within her. Holding her close to me as she cried with joy and the pure lightness of being, she was even more beautiful to my eyes than ever.

Emile held out his strong agile arm and I felt his heart against mine as we embraced and silently acknowledged the God and Goddess within us both.

"Where is J.P.?" I asked in expectation, wishing so to share this moment with him as well.

It was then that I understood the reason for the cross of sadness in Celine's great hazel eyes.

"J.P...." she began slowly, "... he did not make it, cherie", she finished.

"Grand pere... "I uttered weakly... and collapsed into Emile's strength and arms.

Chapter 7 – "It Is Done"

The ride back to Chateau de la Breyeres was a haze in my mind, like a surreal silent movie where lips moved and people spoke yet my audible facilities seemed to be switched to another channel.

What I heard, while being lead, lifted and driven with my small party to our destination, was likened to a kind of indescribable concert; a music of the spheres. It was as if the cosmos were executing a direction to my mind at that time, that was for my subconscious yet I felt and heard it all in full physical consciousness. I was hearing my own 'song' being sung by the great choir of the angels; *Angelica's Song*. I then sensed that every being on earth was at that time 'hearing' their own special song with their own special message that included the very meaning of their existence for every individual one of them. In other words, the Lady in Her wisdom was affecting a separate message for every being out of the same intent. Everyone would hear Bernadette's messages in a different way; a way very personal to them; a way that they would understand it. In that way it would be impossible to intercept billions of messages and the dominators would be thwarted in their attempts. How very clever of Her!

I also realized I was an audible witness to a great soul passing. J.P. was ascending.

All about this little village of Lourdes, thousands of people were departing in their cars, taking photographs of the grotto, journeying by foot back to their fulltime or temporary residences as part of their personal pilgrimage. The camera crew of 'O' dismantled their spartan equipment and the fringe media of tabloid publications began their descent upon the villagers. Kept from the original proceedings by a government by-law that Celine had organized and had put into effect, the renegade journalists were now apt to be prowling all night for their own particular 'stories' of the evening's proceedings.

Curled into the backseat corner of J.P.'s helicopter, a part of me was aware of the happenings below us in the village. Yet, within me, my spirit had risen to another place. The soft voice beckoned me; I was being 'called.' Recognizing the voice of the Lady, I flew to Her shining light and heard Her sparkling celestial choir once again.

His energy flew by me before I saw him. The handsome profile, the lithe form dressed in the white spiritual essence that sparkled all around him. The man turned his face toward me and then to The Lady. The Lady bowed Her head affirmatively and he turned and walked toward me.

The face was strong with its illumination, as his eyes glowed and smiled love out toward me.

"I have been allowed to say goodbye to you, dear one, before I leave your earth dimension. You need to know you are forgiven the release of my soul. This circumstance was cosmically ordained and you were merely the instrument. A duty you actually shared with another, for it was she who pushed the sword. You on your own would not have had the heart for it."

He turned to his left and my eyes followed. There stood the figure of the woman with the shield and sword who had appeared earlier beside me in the abbey. It was Joan of Arc, the Maid of Orleans.

"You helped to slay the evil out of me, cherie." He spoke softly, as he held me with his luminescent eyes, the right one blue and the left one green. It was the soul of Jean Paul.

We lovingly held each others energies with our eyes and he allowed me to view the scenes of his life as he fell in love with my grandmother. Viewing the movie of love they had made together on this planet in their time together, made me realize I belonged to their union somehow.

The music began again as the Light beckoned him.

"It is time for me to go now", Jean Paul voiced mentally to me. Then he turned and flew toward the great Light and The Lady at the centre of it, awaiting him with outstretched arms.

The choir sang a ceremony I sensed was called The Welcome Home. I listened intently at a distance, realizing I would not be allowed to proceed further, yet also knowing that at the time for my own soul release and departure from this earthly realm, I too would be serenaded once more by this spiritual choir.

Chapter 8 ~ "The Light of the Goddess"

Newspapers around the world raced out midnight editions of their publications announcing the message from The Lady at the grotto in Lourdes, France. The media played and replayed Her vision and Her words to planet Earth over and over again that night, as it would continue to do for days and weeks after.

Her message was as extraordinary as Her Light was spectacular. There was no doubt in anyone's mind who saw and heard Her that Her predictions for the future of our planet were eminent and Her appearance was very, very real and not merely some projected image in the sky (as was suspected to be the case in early so-called visits from the Holy Mother).

Whoever this 'Lady' was, She was not a fake and the world realized it. That fact alone diminished the power of the dark universal forces that tried to pervade Earth's atmosphere. Her very appearance strengthened a belief in the force of God's existence in our universes.

I knew I must reinforce this new and positive energy that the planet's population was feeling about itself and the very reason for the existence of humankind. I knew I must write and relate to people that it mattered not whether there had been a bible fraud or that the church had misconstrued historical facts for their own purposes and their own fortunes.

What truly mattered was that, yes, there *did* exist in our cosmos and our own consciousness a very real God; a true Creator of all of the universes who loved us and created us so that we could have the lives we all wanted, but primarily created us to learn *how* we can create these lives we wanted for ourselves *by* ourselves.

That is the secret of our existence; the mystery of the cosmos and of life. We have created ourselves just as God and Goddess, for the Creator is a beautiful duality, created us. Yes, we all had a very real part to play in our own reality on this planet. We decided before we came back here what we wanted and needed to do and learn. In effect, we wrote ourselves a loose script which our manifested reality, or physical selves, has option to edit at any time.

We did not come here to suffer; unless we chose to once we got here out of ignorance to the knowledge that we create our own reality. That is why two people occupying the same space at the same time with the same family and same lessons can exercise two completely different worlds of reality. It is all about our perceptions. However, these same perceptions can be colored and influenced by our lifetime(s) experiences, particularly if they are challenging.

Coupled with our lack of memory of our true (soul) self realities once we (again) recreate ourselves, may cause a totally different equation, one that can prevent us from seeing the truth of our 'real' selves. That, dear ones, is our true lesson here: We are not to be influenced or taken off the path of our true and beautiful reality; that we are Gods and Goddesses in the making. And, yes, we do create the God we worship, so keep positive to our true selves with positive thoughts of love, forgiveness and most of all, peace.

I trusted The Lady to somehow infuse me with the right words to write in the future to further direct and guide Her message to us all. Guide me well, my Lady, to help me to bring Your (and my) gift to the world in Love, Light and Peace. Amen.

Chapter 9 – "What Did You Learn: How Much Did You Love"

Laying in bed at the Chateau de la Breyeres that night, my mind resisted sleep. It still needed to reason; to 'logic' the recent past events.

What had been learned from the past several days through all the extraordinary events that had ensued for me? What was I meant to learn? Was it possible to complete the destiny these events asked of me?

I knew I was intended to come to terms with my family programming - "Curse! Go on, call it what it is!" - My mind tossed to me. I sat up in bed and turned on the bedside lamp in reaction. "Yes, curse! Unseen forces ..." The words went on. I got out of bed and walked across the floor as if physical movement might move my mind to uncover its own answers.

The floor, even with its thick carpet, was stone cold at that hour. The crystal mantle clock chimed twice. It was 2:00 A.M.

I slipped on the butterfly yellow ballet slippers that were by the bed and drew on the matching silk robe over my nightgown. Turning, I caught sight of myself in the gilt mirror across from me. While perusing my reflection in the soft light, a vision of a woman from another era appeared. It was me, same hair, same face but... I looked around me at the decor.

I was in a different world! I didn't even know what it was like to be my own person anymore! Looking into the mirror and feeling myself get drawn in again, I fought the pull.

"No!" I said aloud. "I need to feel like ME again!"

Running over to my own suitcase, I pulled it up onto the bed, opened it, withdrew my own nightgown and wrap and hurriedly pulled off the yellow silk ensemble. Although shivering in the spring evening air, I carefully drew on my own blue silk negligee. Exhausted, not even bothering to take my suitcase off the bed, I collapsed into the sweet lavender scent of the bed sheets and fell fast asleep.

Chapter 10 ~ "The Visit"

It was not the wind that awoke me as much as the whistle. It was like one belonging to a very old train car and it was travelling right through my bedroom! Sitting up in bed, I reached for the down comforter folded at my feet and spread it over my shoulders like a shawl. The room was freezing.

"You must return one more time", the voice commanded. Reaching over to turn on the light, I peered into the darkness to ascertain from where the voice came. It was a man.

Suddenly, the large gilt standing mirror moved swiftly across the floor until it stood about three feet from the edge of the bed. From behind it emerged Jean Paul. I gasped aloud at the shock of his appearance but felt no fear accompanying it.

With a gesture, Jean Paul beckoned me to face the mirror.

It was the scene of the Romanov destruction. The truck, the rain, the blood... Aghh! I could smell the human blood, not yet rotting and still containing the vital life force of its recipients. It was a scent that was most profound.

"Why must I go back?" I protested. "The clearance on the cellular DNA programming has already been done. Why return me to that awful place again!"

"For closure, my child; for final closure", Jean Paul assured. "You will soon know why." Staring clearly into my eyes, he commanded me to look into the mirror.

Covering my face with my hands to prepare myself for the scenario ahead, I took the preparatory breaths for meditation and opened my fingers to face my destiny.

The transportation truck bumped and rolled its way from the slaughter house at Yekaterinburg. The rain was unrelenting. Were the angels crying or was God washing away the sin from this land?

My spirit self hung above 'my' body of Alix, the grand daughter of Queen Victoria and Empress of all Russia. I knew who 'I' was. 'I', my soul, was preparing to go through the veil.

"You must not go yet. Not before you connect with your youngest daughter, who will survive and carry on your dynasty. It is imperative that she not carry the guilt of your execution in her heart."

I nodded in acquiescence to his guidance, realizing the importance of this circumstance. Anastasia's body was draped over that of her sister Tatiana, the most beautiful one. I perused the bruised head with blood matted in her lovely auburn hair; her fine pristine features outlined against the severe covering that lined the bottom of the trunk. Tatiana, the most spiritual of all 'my' daughters, now was with spirit. She had crossed over immediately and without effort as Brother Gregory's hand reached out to bring her over. I breathed a deep sigh. Tatiana was at peace.

Olga, Marie... both had ascended as well and waved to me. "Mama!" The fragmented voice echoed out to me. "It's beautiful here, mama. But we can't find papa." Marie's voice expressed anxiously.

"He won't be able to come just now", Brother Gregory's voice explained.

'I' knew immediately what Rasputin only hinted at. Nicky's soul needed intercession. Without it, all the cellular clearing and soul connecting with Anastasia would do nothing to release her guilt and clear my family.

"Nicky." I spoke to the male figure upon the far right side of the cart. "Hear me, Nicky!" I pleaded.

"Alix?" His voice was low and foggy as if he was between asleep and awake, which indeed he was. "Where are you?" he called.

"Nicolas, last Tsar of Russia", I commanded. At 'my' call Nicky's soul appeared before me. Unlike those of our daughters, whose soul energies were very light and shining, Nicky's soul was like gray fog and quite faint. I knew he had not the strength to enter the Light and if he tried would be singed and burnt.

"He needs to be quickened. He needs your help for this, little mother."

"Nicky ... ", 'I' sounded, in a strong clear voice, for he needed to 'awaken' and be alert.

Nicolas' image became stronger upon hearing his wife's voice.

"I am here", he responded clearly. Nicolas needed to be cleared by the intercession of prayer for his soul redemption or he could not enter 'heaven' and his soul and those of his descendants would be doomed forever more. That was why Jean Paul sent me back here, I realized. It was to help Nicolas!

"You must align yourself with the God of your heart and the Holy Mother in prayer and beg for forgiveness for yourself and all of your family. Pray, Nicky", I pleaded. "Pray very, very hard!"

As Nicolas' soul energy went into silent connection with the higher powers, 'I' asked Brother Gregory, Olga, Tatiana and Maria to join with me in an intercession to the Holy Mother for the soul of their father; 'little papa', as Rasputin named him.

As we all prayed in silence for Nicolas' soul, tremendous power emitted from Rasputin.

"Little mother", he offered humbly. "You must tell the little papa to ask the Holy Mother and Her Son to surround him with the white light of the Holy Spirit to remove the dark energy and any evil that resulted from his actions and replace it with the pure love of the Holy Spirit. Do this with love and ask him to make his request with love and purity in his heart. Then, tell him to prepare for the Light." 'I', as Alexandra, Tsarina of Russia and wife of Nicolas II, Tsar of all Russia, did as Brother Gregory had requested.

What followed was a cacophony of heavenly display. As Nicolas prayed for his soul's forgiveness for his family and himself, the energy about him changed from gray to bluish green and progressively lightened. The stronger the energy became, the lighter his soul color. Finally, it became the opalescent pink hue of the inside of a pearl.

"It is time, matroushka", encouraged Brother Gregory. "Ask him to prepare."

"Nicolas!" I declared, in a full strong voice. "Prepare yourself to go into the Light. No matter what happens, do not be afraid."

Nicolas's light body began to shift its shape and seemed to pull apart, as millions of tiny 'fireflies' surrounded and infused him. His light body grimaced as if in pain as the miniature orbs continued to invade his soul energy until finally, with a last gasp and sigh, his light became iridescent white and I knew he was purified.

"He is free now", advised Rasputin.

I thanked Brother Gregory profusely for his help for without the assistance of his powerful energy, the mission would have been impossible. Brother Gregory simply closed his eyes in acceptance, saying only, "Now, go to your daughter."

The scene changed. It was nightfall and Anastasia's body was not where 'my' and the others had been laid; beside the horrific pit that was dug for our grave. I saw the scene of her rescue by the peasant women and could visualize her now, safe in the farmhouse, lying in her new bed.

Anastasia was with fever. She was mortally wounded and it would be a miracle if she survived. 'I' went to her in the speed of thought and sat by her on her narrow bed. The look on her face told me immediately that she did not want to live. 'I' held my youngest daughter in my arms and kissed her forehead, letting my lips stay planted there while rocking her in my arms.

"Anya", I whispered to her soul as she slept. "You must want to live! It is so very, very important that you live on and bring the Light to the world. Otherwise, the darkness wins and humankind is doomed.

"Do not carry any guilt because you lived and the rest of our family died. It was ordained by God for it to happen that way. Papa and I paid the debt, as we should have, and died for the sins that were committed. It was our belief that it had to be so and for us it was necessary, but not for you, Anya! There should never be guilt in the living for those who are dead.

"Such was not your destiny. Nor do you need to be haunted all your life by guilt that you survived your family. You were born to survive, my rosebud... For that is what you are, a bud of the rose of creativity... a flower of God, sent here to bloom and bring forth seed that will spread light to other lands .. new worlds... and help create the world that The Mother and Her Son designed.

"Live, Anya!" I spoke as I released her from me. "Live and LOVE. When you love, the darkness cannot win."

I brushed another kiss on Anastasia's bruised forehead before standing up. Then I prayed to the Holy Mother to surround Anya with the white light of the Holy Spirit and clear her karma, so her cells would carry no residue of negative programming of the slaughter or of any survival guilt.

A myriad of firefly light descended upon Anya, permeating her being and her facial expression shifted from one of pain to one of peace. I left her with the glowing light of The Lady surrounding her.

Once again, my spirit felt the pull back through the sideways tunnel and I was back on my bed, staring at my reflection in the gilded mirror. My own aura glowed clearer and brighter than I had ever seen it. Staring back at myself, I blinked in astonishment.

"You see, my child", smiled Jean Paul.

I was speechless.

"How do you feel?" he asked.

"Just like light."

Chapter 11 - "My Gift"

"There is one thing more that I have come to you for", Jean Paul continued, seating himself upon my bed. "You do not need to decide immediately, but when you are ready to do so, you will be equipped with the 'techniques'.

"You must choose a gift to give yourself. It must be something you truly want above all else because it is your desire that brings its manifestation.

"First", he began his instruction, "Sit upright and place your feet flatly on the floor." He beckoned me to the side of the bed. I removed the quilt and slid over beside him. Surprisingly, the floor did not feel cold.

As guided, I sat up straight with both feet on the carpet.

"This exercise is best done outdoors, so imagine yourself on the top of a mountain on a warm summer day. Next, do your three breathing exercises three times, beginning with the neutral, then the negative and followed by the positive breaths." I followed suit.

"Now", he continued, "I want you to focus your attention at your second chakra, the chakra of creation. Clear this chakra with the same breath techniques. When you have finished, keep building your power by repeating the positive breaths, imaging white light energy flow in and out with your breaths."

I continued and did what was instructed.

"Next, picture in your mind what it is you truly desire and make that image as clear as possible. Remember that the clearer the image or intent, the easier the manifestation."

I thought for a moment on what I wanted strongly enough for me to achieve the required energy to make it happen. My thoughts went to Fluffy, my Himalayan cat, and my normal life back in Toronto. Closing my eyes, I focused on my life in Canada being stable and happy as it was several days ago, with my cat being safe and content, purring on his favorite sofa in the living room. From what Rose had told me about the break in at my condo, the place had been left in quite a mess. Visualizing the condo just as it had been left; I mentally took a 'snapshot' of it.

"Once you have the picture of your desire clearly in your mind at the sixth chakra, that of intent, take a very deep breath down into the second chakra, hold it there for a count of three, then pull that energy up through the body, through the other chakras and up to the sixth chakra of the mind. Then, utilizing your fifth (throat) chakra, which has already been energized by your desire, release your breath with a sound as you do so."

Filling my second chakra with white light energy, I affixed the picture of Fluff on my sofa in my neat clean condo and pulled the energy up to my temple, allowing it to hit the different chakra points on the rise up to the sixth chakra. The process seemed to energize my body and fill me with power.

Envisioning the desired image as clearly as possible, I released the white light energy through my communication (fifth) chakra and out my mouth with my sound.

To my surprise, the sound was incredibly loud and powerful as I sent it out into the night air and viewed my 'desire picture' rocketing through space into the universal cosmos for its realization.

"One other thing", advised Jean Paul. "Place no judgment or restrictions on how your desire is manifested and let the universe bring it to you the way it knows best.

After pulling my spirit off the mountain and back into my bedroom, I turned to thank Jean Paul but all that remained was the standing mirror at the edge of my bed.

At 8:00 A.M. the next morning, a knock on my door was followed by Celine poking her golden brown curls into the room. "May I come in?"

"Entree!" I invited, smiling enthusiastically while bounding out of bed to greet her.

She edged into the room sideways, like a crab, carrying a tray that held lovely edibles. Strawberries, cheese, croissants, cafe and one perfect red rose.

Celine noticed me eyeing the blossom and said, "Fresh from le jardin."

"Oh." Remarking, "I thought it might have been from last night at the grotto."

"No.", Celine smiled. "Your rose from The Lady has been specially packaged for you to take back home with you."

"Ahh ..." I said, pulling on my blue robe while Celine placed the tray on the coffee table which sat between two wingback chairs positioned in front of the fireplace.

After settling down on one of the wingback chairs, Celine's gaze focused on my robe. Catching sight of the yellow negligee folded over the arm of the other wingback chair, she picked up the ensemble, folded it and placed it in one of the drawers in the antique dresser. I hoped her feelings weren't hurt by my change of clothing. They weren't.

"You need to be in your own things", she smiled warmly, "after last night."

"Yes, it's true, but that doesn't mean I'm not grateful for everything you've done. Thank you so very much!"

Celine sat down in the wingback chair opposite me and poured me a cup of the delicious smelling cafe au lait.

"Mangez, cherie", she commanded softly. Gratefully, I reached out to receive the coffee cup and saucer.

After completion of ma petite dejeuner, Celine leaned forward and said softly. "Emile will fly you back to Paris this afternoon so that you can connect to your flight to Toronto later today."

"Oh?" I uttered, a bit surprised.

"You were not aware your return flight was today, cherie?" Celine inquired.

"No ... I mean, yes ... I knew it was today but thought it would be best to stay on longer because of the circumstances ... with J.P."

"It was J.P.'s suggestion that you return to Canada as scheduled. Because of the media and your own personal situation with your break in and invasion of privacy, it could become complicated if you were to remain longer."

Sitting back in the jade hued wingback chair, savoring the last of my café, my feeling was much like that of a child afraid to ask for a toy that's too expensive.

"I had hoped to stay a while longer and pay my respects to J.P." I managed at last.

"Ah", Celine smiled, got up, opened the gilded antique white door and beckoned me. "Why don't you do that right now?"

Celine lead me down the hall, stopping at a small alcove. Behind royal blue velvet drapes hid another gilded door which Celine opened and nodded to me to enter.

The room held a simple yet elegant blue and white toile country design on the walls, bedding and drapes. The window was half drawn so the room accepted only half of the sunlight beaming into it.

"Bonjour, ma cherie."

I was startled by the familiar voice that emitted from the blue velvet canopy bed. Supported by several pillows, J.P. was sitting up in bed and smiling at me.

"Come sit with me, cherie", he invited.

I ran to him and held him to me, raining tears down my cheeks and his.

I thought you were ... gone!" I finally managed, holding back sobs.

"Yes, cherie", J.P. proceeded in a serious tone. "I *had* gone."

"Then how?" My mind was puzzled.

"It was because of the courage of the brave heart of Jean Paul ... And you."

Sitting up straight, I wiped away my tears with my fingers.

"You see, when Jean Paul asked you to release his spirit with your sword, he gave up his own vital life force so that I might live. At the very moment that his spirit was released, mine was rejuvenated. Sometimes", J.P. shrugged in that French way, "it is 'allowed'."

"The Lady 'allowed' it." I muttered.

"Yes. I believe She did", agreed J.P.

I examined J.P.'s face in the partial morning sunlight. His color was good, the same pink toned skin, but he appeared fatigued. He continued on, nonetheless.

"For now, cherie, your work here is done. You will be needed back in your own country soon... by your family and by Jacey's."

Jacey. In all the activity of the past several days, I had certainly not forgotten him; that could never be possible; but the realization that I would not be alone in grieving him had not occurred to me until now.

"Yes, of course", I acquiesced softly, lowering my head in silent honor to his memory.

"Do not forget; the world will need you now, cherie, to help them make sense of all that has occurred - and will occur - and give clarity and assurance when the tabloids, backed by the negative energies, begin to try to create chaos and fear out of this message of hope and love. You need to be in '*your* world' to reassure '*the* world' that all is well in the universe. Help show humankind how to create their own lives, their own realities, as they were meant to do."

J.P. stopped talking and closed his eyes. Knowing he needed to rest, I stood up and kissed him on his forehead. He was alive yet he was old and had been through a great deal in the past few days.

"Bonjour, grand pere", I whispered and tiptoed out the door with Celine.

Chapter 12 – "The Return"

After a quick shower, I found my own newly dry cleaned raw silk black pantsuit lying on my bed along side a small shopping bag; a piece of lavender note paper jutting out of the top.

> 'Cherie: Your suit has been pressed and freshened. I have also enclosed a souvenir from Chateau de la Breyeres.'
> Celine

Within the pretty floral bag was a long silk scarf the color of the yellow butterflies that frequented the area. The background was patterned with exquisitely hand painted heather blossoms and a large bouquet of heather sprigs hovering in one corner.

It was so perfect, I thought! This was a perfect present and a perfect complement to the simple, elegant pantsuit. With the jacket's mandarin line and collar, its only other distinct feature was a tie belt. The scarf would add the necessary color and French 'chic' to return home in.

I dressed quickly, applied spartan makeup for the flight consisting of minimal heather toned blush, amethyst eye shadow, black mascara and heather lip gloss; no base to clog the pores. My unruly locks were held in a low ponytail with my faithful black scrunchy. My jewelry consisted of the drop pearl earrings and my filigree pendant.

Emile piloted me via helicopter directly to the Paris airport to connect me to my flight. Serge had gone ahead earlier to ship my luggage from the George V on to the Charles De Gaulle Airport. Celine remained behind to attend to J.P.

Sitting in the front seat beside Emile gave us time to chat intermittently throughout the duration of the flight. As well as J.P.'s grandson, Emile was a certified pilot and organized rescue missions when necessary. He was quiet, charming and unassuming for such a handsome man.

Carrying my bags, Emile took me through the airport as far as security allowed. When we bid each other goodbye, he hugged me to him with great feeling.

Looking into his strong yet gentle face, I could see J.P. in those deep green eyes and curling brown hair. He kissed me on both cheeks and then I turned and walked down the ramp with reminiscent tears in my eyes.

Once on board, I sank into my business class seat and made some attempt at magazine leisure reading but my mind kept returning to Jacey. Finally drifting off to sleep, I dreamed of Jacey and me flying through space together, visiting the different planets and discovering what lessons they all offered the human soul.

Chapter 13 ~ *"Where The Heart Lives"*

The limousine ride home was uneventful, except that the driver couldn't angle his way into the narrow driveway of my building and I had to carry my luggage from the sidewalk around to the side door; the one closest to my condo.

The driver offered to help, but Rosemary was waiting for me and insisted on taking the largest bag up the staircase. Rose placed my suitcase by my door and returned to her condo to retrieve Fluff. She carried my semi-abandoned Himalayan over to me and deposited his furry self into my arms, where he immediately purred his hello and licked my hand.

"He still remembers me!" I laughed.

Gathering my resources, I inserted the key into my door, flicked on the hall light and half closed my eyes at the sight that might await me. To my amazement, the interior was picture perfect! Fluffy wriggled himself free and headed right for his favorite perch; the arm of my sofa.

"What happened, Rose? I was expecting to find debacle when I returned!"

"I'm not sure exactly who they were", offered Rose, "But after the police were through, some people who looked like a cleaning crew came in. I thought they may have been sent by the building management", she shrugged and smiled.

"Remember ... Do not place any judgment upon how your desire is executed", Jean Paul's words came back to me.

I thanked Rose for all she had done and assured her the police report would be made out; even though it was evident everything was intact.

After putting my luggage in my bedroom for unpacking later, I undressed and slipped into the shower to wash the airport scent off me. My lemon scented soap was perfect for its cleansing effect. Desiring to be in my 'real clothes', I slipped on a pair of clean jeans and a favorite shell pink cotton pullover, accompanied by my well worn pink ballet slippers.

"Now this feels like me!" I said to my reflection on my mirrored closet door.

Desperately feeling the need to do normal things to ground myself after all the extraordinary events that had just transpired, I retrieved my mail which contained mostly bills, made a grocery list, petted Fluff on my lap and checked my answering service. Several mundane messages, then...

"Hi mom! It's me!" sang Christina's lyrical voice. "I saw the 'O' special last night. It was awesome! Hey, by the way, you didn't have anything to do with that, did you? Call me when you get in."

Smiling to myself, for I had long ago surmised Christina had the gift of the Goddess, I was not surprised in the least at her intuition picking up my connection to The Lady.

My building manager had left a few messages regarding my whereabouts. There hadn't been time to contact anyone before leaving for Paris and inform them of my schedule. Ah well, there would be time enough to catch up.

"Hi Red. I can't tell you how much I've missed you and am looking forward to seeing you again. I love you, Angel and I always will. See you soon."

It was Jacey's voice! He must have left it after I'd left for Paris and before...

"It's funny how that message got on the service *after* Christina's message from this morning. The fool machine must be acting up again, Fluff. I'll have to get that checked out."

Fluffy looked up at me, purring adoringly as if I were his God - or Goddess. While stroking him absent mindedly, thoughts and memories of Jacey flooded through my mind again.

"I need to get busy, Fluff", I said tearfully, kissing my furry friend on the top of his head and lifted him off my lap.

"Meow", he protested mournfully, as if phrasing, "You just got here, don't leave me!"

"I'm not going anywhere, honey." Reassuring him and moving over to sit at my computer, I got into Word and began to write. It was my only reprieve.

"*Healing Aphrodite*", the title spilled out. I made notes on the computer for over an hour, trying to draw the words from the air but my concentration wasn't there. My mind could think only of my love for Jacey.

"Focus your mind on what it is you truly desire and image it as clearly as possible." The words filtered through my consciousness.

Last night no thought would come of what I truly desired other than Fluff's safety and my stability reestablished. Now, realizing what was truly desired more than anything was for Jacey and me to be together, I wished for Jacey to be alive and with me again, impossible as that seemed.

I looked around the clean organized condo that I had 'pictured' and against all odds, had returned to a picture perfect condo. It was so simple.

Heading for the small indoor atrium in my enclosed balcony, I sat down on the wicker queen chair and began breathing slowly. I had to try.

"Remember not to put any judgment on the outcome." Jean Paul's words again. "Build the power in your second chakra ... and picture the image of your intent clearly."

After focusing hard and picturing Jacey in my mind, his face became so clear; the blond wavy hair, the sapphire hued eyes... even the tan leather jacket he'd worn just before he flew off in the Cessna into the Pyrenean sky.

"You are the love of my life, my darling", I spoke, his image clearly in my mind. "I want more than anything for you to be alive and healthy and for us to be together again. Please God, let it be so. I agree that there be no judgments on the outcome."

In my mind's eye, Jacey walked through my atrium door over to me, lifted me out of my chair, held me in his arms and kissed me passionately. I pushed the passion back out to him and could feel an orgasmic energy happen between us before we even consummated.

At that moment, I released the power breath... "Ahhhh ..."

The sound of the condo buzzer awoke me. I looked at the clock on the glass topped side table in the atruim. It was 4:05 P.M. The buzzer rang again.

"Yes, hello", I echoed into the intercom.

"Is this the home of the dragon slayer?"

After slapping the enter button on the intercom, I raced through my living room. My heart pounding and my hands quivering, I threw open the front door.

"Jacey!"

Epilogue

"With Love We Live Forever" ~ Jacey's Story

"Jacey!"

My cry exploded into his face as I threw my spirit and my body out to him. He caught both in his electric embrace and we enjoyed our soul reunion as it lifted our energies skyward in my condominium hallway.

"You're here!", I cried, burying my face in the fleece collar of his leather flight jacket; the one I'd given him for his birthday years ago when we were still together. It was an authentic World War II fighter jacket from the costume department of a film I'd worked on. Jacey had admired it so a deal was made with the costuming people after the film wrapped up.

"It's been quite an adventure", began Jacey.

I looked up into his heaven blue eyes. "All I care about is that you're here with me now." The tears were flowing out of the corners of my eyes and tickling my ears. Jacey smiled that irascible grin of his and wiped my ears with his handkerchief.

"You'll mat your hair at this rate, Angel", he laughed.

I expected Jacey to lift me up and carry me to the sofa, his usual maneuver when we hadn't seen one another for a time. Then, noticing his left arm was in a light sling, I realized his hesitation.

He caught me eyeing his sling and explained, "Yes; wounded a wing. Had it not been for the healing you gave me, flying here as soon as I did would have been impossible."

"You flew here!" I exclaimed. "When?"

"About the same time as you", Jacey smiled. "I wanted to be here to greet you. Do you like the clean up?" He switched the topic and let his eyes wander over my living room. My people did a pretty good job", he nodded as he checked out the place, moving through the bedroom and bathroom.

"You arranged for this?" I queried.

"None other!" he smiled. Jacey stopped mid living room and lowered his gaze somewhat sheepishly. "Angel", he began. "I can't lead you on and let you think my being here is a miracle."

"Oh, but it is Jacey!" Running over to him, "I meditated and focused my intent ... and created and manifested you back ... somehow!"

"You did that for me?" he eyed me quizzically. "I understand the technique ... yet ... Perhaps you should be filled in on the details of my crash flight."

Jacey put his good arm around me and we headed out to the atrium to catch the last light of the day. Once seated upon the white wicker settee, Jacey began his story.

"After leaving you at the Lavallee farmhouse, I tuned in the French equivalent of a police radio scanner and heard that the courier on the bogus pick up of the diary from the George V had been intercepted and the 'jig was up', so to speak. Another plan had to be worked out. It was a spontaneous idea so contacting anyone to inform them of it in that short a time span was impossible. Yet something had to be done, so I ..."

"Faked an accident?" I queried, in disbelief.

"Exactly", Jacey sighed. "If I crashed the Cessna into the side of a mountain, it could activate an explosion that would completely camouflage my existence. Of course, it meant being non-existent to the world from that point on: In other words dead, my girl!"

"Jacey that was a very dangerous stunt to try and carry off as you really could have died!" I admonished.

"Quite right, my love", Jacey kissed me on the forehead. "And not a feat I'd want to try every day."

"I don't understand how you made it so convincing." I said, curling my feet up under me and leaning into his good arm.

"Well ..." Jacey went on as he sat back comfortably, sticking his long legs out in front of him. "It was tricky. I had to make a real sacrifice." With that statement, he pulled up the right pant leg of his jeans and exposed his Tony Lama snakeskin boots.

"One of my best loved boots had to be left behind, as proof that I was the pilot of the plane. No one who knew me would fail to recognize my 'signature apparel'. This one was retrieved when my remains were picked up by Serge. So J.P., Serge, Celine and Emile are the only people besides you who know Jason Christopher is still alive. I think I'll keep it that way for a while."

"So, I didn't resurrect you or change history then with my 'technique', as you call it?" I replied, snuggling further and more comfortably into his chest.

"But how do you explain the bones they found? I saw them myself at the crash site."

Jacey crossed his left leg over his right and tilted his head over mine as he proceeded with his story.

"Well, realizing the situation necessitated faking a crash, I pulled open my trusty tote bag and withdrew some of my archeological findings that hadn't been cataloged yet, figuring they would serve the purpose of representing my skeletal structure when the plane was discovered. They'd be burnt and charred by the fire, therefore impossible to identify, but they were bones and who else could they belong to? Then, to cinch my I.D., I pulled out one of my Lama boots and threw it out over the mountain after parachuting out of the Cessna."

"You parachuted! That's how you did it!"

"Yup. A chute is always kept handy when I'm flying. This time it paid off. So did those jump lessons I took - and tried to talk you into, remember?"

"Hmmm ... I remember." I went once. That was enough for me. Great heights have never been one of my favorite things.

"Luck was with me. When the Cessna crashed, it fell down onto a cliff ledge, exploded and burnt up beautifully."

"It was unrecognizable!" I interjected.

"Indeed. So, with my one Lama boot zipped inside my jacket, I jumped and landed a safe distance from the crash."

"How did you hurt your arm?"

"On the way down, I bumped into the side of a mountain. The mountain won. I was unconscious from the pain by the time Emile and Serge found me."

"How did they know where to look for you?"

"While you and Serge were at the crash site, I flashed him a Morse code message with a small mirror that is kept with my chute in case of such an emergency. Fortunately he picked it up and later flew back with Emile."

A sense of the ominous spread over me and I asked without wanting to hear the answer.

"Will everything be alright now?"

Jacey sat up straight and pulled his long legs together in a seated position. Leaning forward, he looked off into space before replying.

"I don't know, Angel. I wish I did. It can't be determined at this point. It's over for *now.*" Jacey turned to face me, his heaven blue eyes holding a new depth as he continued. "But there is something coming, of that you can be sure. When it does, it will rock the very foundation of North America and if not handled carefully, might prove to be our destruction. The impact of this event may cause us to destroy ourselves. And that seems to be the plan."

"Oh, Jacey..." I put my arms around his neck, hugging him to me. "What can we do?"

Jacey sighed. "Just try and enlighten the world as much as possible in the meantime."

"Does this event have to happen?"

"No. No, it doesn't. If the nations of our world accept the philosophy of love and peace, we can avoid the destruction of the entire planet. And humanity can become what it was intended to be..."

"The tenth level of Angels."

For he hast made them
Just a little lower than the Angels
And hast covered them
In glory and honor.

The End

Afterword

It was twelve years ago that I began writing *"Angel of the Tsar": (Part I of the Gemstone Angel Trilogy)*. Although this book is a work of fiction, I was inspired to weave this odyssey like a tapestry, through a mystical love story and an intriguing tale about the Russian Revolution. It seemed that*Anastasia was directing me in order to put closure to an extraordinary, albeit tragic, episode in our history and to honor the lives that were sacrificed: Those of her family, the royal family of Tsar Nicolas and Tsarina Alexandra Romanov of Russia.

On the following pages, Anastasia will 'relate' the circumstances of her family's last hours together on that fateful night of July 17, 1918. She will also share with us the happenings that could have made it possible for her and her brother Alexei to have survived this ordeal.

"Angel of the Tsar" is foremost a story about healing and it is my hope that all who read this book will be healed and inspired by the Light. It is believed that the angels hold that all things are possible for those who believe in the Light and Love that brought us to this dimension.

With Love and Light to all,

The Author

*(The original working title of the book was *"Healing Anastasia"*.)

A spiritual blessing was spiritually requested upon this book to Pope John Paul II, the Dali Lama and the Lord Abbot of Thailand, that all who read it may be blessed, protected and guided on their spiritual voyage to their highest enlightenment.

In Anastasia's Words

"It is hard for people to understand how we; Alexei and I; could have survived such an ordeal as the execution at the Ipatiev house in Yekaterinburg. Yet it is not so difficult to understand when you know the circumstances.

"No one in our family unit, including Dr. Bodkin and mama's servants, knew what was about to happen to us that night, especially papa. I remember his cry of 'What! What!' when Commandant Yurovsky, our head executioner, read the official document that condemned us all to death. I still recall papa's last words: 'Forgive them; they know not what they do.'

"On July 17, 1918 Commandant Yakov Yurovsky informed mama and papa that we were all to pack our belongings and prepare for travel as it was no longer safe for us at the Ipatiev house because the White Force was moving in and would be in Yekaterinburg in twenty-four hours. In truth, it was the White Force that was coming to rescue us and had they been able to arrive sooner, we could have been spared that terrible fate.

"Mama immediately gathered all of the women together in the room my sisters and I shared and told Olga, Tatiana, Marie and I to each get two of our corsets. Then she opened a large chest filled with her clothing and removed all of her dresses until the chest was empty. She then pushed down on one side of the false bottom of the chest until it opened, revealing five large red velvet jewelers bags, all knotted with gold braided silk. Mama handed one bag each to my sisters and me. They were quite heavy, nearly ten pounds each. Then she set us to work.

"We each got out our sewing boxes and, as mama directed, proceeded to sew our two corsets together using tiny stitches and making horizontal rows of about two-thirds of an inch apart across the corset, totaling about twelve rows each. She then instructed us to open our jewelry bags. They were filled with hundreds of diamonds and other precious gems. She showed us how to fill the rolls we had just sewn in our corsets with the gems and stitch both sides closed so they would stay intact within the corsets. We were then instructed to put our corsets on and dress.

"Mama said this was part of the Romanov fortune and when this ordeal was over, we would need it to live on wherever we were sent. She said we had sympathizers who were ready to make their move to save us even as she spoke. 'They could come for us at any moment, mes cheries', she and papa would say encouragingly.

"Whilst we sewed our corsets, mama made a vest for Alexei from the fifth bag of gems. For her, mama fashioned a belt about five inches wide made entirely of pearls and sewed it into her corset to hold the pearls as ours did the diamonds.

"We were kept waiting all that day, sitting in that stifling heat, with those heavy corsets on. Olga and Marie became rather grumpy, so Tatiana read mama's favorite prayer. Alexei didn't complain. He never complained.

"The delay occurred because Commandant Yurovsky was waiting for the telegram to arrive confirming our fate. It did not arrive until after midnight. Then the truck, that would ultimately carry our bodies to the burial site, arrived. That was when we were ordered to come downstairs and issued into the semi-basement room that would be our execution site. We were told we were going to be photographed. Commandant Yurovsky had been a photographer before the revolution so we believed him.

"It was Yurovsky's decision to kill us there instead of boarding us on the truck and taking us to the mock trial that had been arranged by Superindent Ermatov. Little did we suspect but papa and mama were to be given a mock trial and hanged. My sisters and I had been promised to several of the officers for their amusement and were to be killed after they were finished with us. It was not unusual in times of war and revolution to torture and hang the men and to dishonour the women. That would have been the other option fate offered us. Commandant Yurovsky was aware of Ermatov's plans and because he sympathized with us somewhat and seemed to actually like papa, he made the decision to kill us there in the Ipatiev house and transport us afterward. Perhaps to him it was a kinder and more honourable way to die.

"Alexei had been ill, so papa carried him downstairs. Alexei was actually very strong and athletic when he wasn't bleeding. His blood would not clot properly so if he received a bruise he would be in excruciating pain. Several times the priest had been made ready to give him final rights, but he always recovered.

"It was because of Alexei that papa abdicated. Alexei's illness was kept a secret from all but those trusted and close to us. 'For the sake of the monarchy', grandmamma would say. She influenced papa a great deal and was very strict and traditional in all things. 'The future Tsar cannot be seen to show weakness. It would be the fall of the Romanovs'.

"Papa suffered watching Alexei in his pain almost as much as Alexei did and finally he could take it no more. Papa felt that if he signed the abdication papers, he could then be open about Alexei's condition and finally get his son some real help.

"There was one other reason papa signed that document. Mama would have been tried for treason for her heavily rumored affair with Brother Gregory, also known as Rasputin. All of Russia talked about it and nasty drawings of my mother, the Tsarina, and the monk appeared on public walls throughout Moscow. You see, everyone from St. Petersburg to the Urals seemed to be aware that Father Gregory was granted entrance to the Winter Palace and our main home at Tsarscoe Sela and was allowed to roam freely any time he wished, but no one knew why. No one realized it was because he could heal Alexei and that was the only reason for him being in our homes. Due to his vile reputation, it was simply assumed that he was mesmerizing mama right under the nose of the Tsar. So, you can imagine how people talked about the kind of rogue and scoundrel Rasputin was, but also what kind of fool and cuckold papa must have been to have allowed it. Talk about a Tsar showing weakness! It would have been far better to have been honest and revealed the truth about Alexei's illness and perhaps have gained public support and even sympathy. Hiding the condition of the Tsarovich made papa look weak and also impotent. Grandmamma had been right: A Tsar appearing to be weak was ultimately the fall of the Romanov dynasty.

"The semi-basement area we were directed into was very small. Mama complained there was no place for her and Alexei to sit. Mama had weak legs and could not stand for very long and Alexei was still not well so Yurovsky had two chairs placed near the far wall for them. My sisters and I, papa, Dr. Botkin and the servants all stood in two lines, facing the camera (which interestingly enough belonged to mama).

"We stood there for several minutes. Yurovsky took the photograph and then quite suddenly and simultaneously withdrew his pistol from its holder and a document from his jacket pocket and started to read papa our death sentence! Mama gasped and grabbed her heart, crying 'No..no!' Papa was in utter disbelief as he spoke 'What! What!' (This would be the second time papa would utter these words. The first time was when he witnessed his grandfather, Tsar Alexander II, being assassinated outside of a church). He turned to mama and my sisters; we were all crying; and said his final words, 'Forgive them, they know not what they do.' These were the same words Tsar Alexander II had spoken before he died.

"Commandant Yurovsky claimed in later documents to have been the one who fired the first shot and killed the last Tsar of Russia, but in all the confusion it was difficult to tell who actually fired that fatal shot as a dozen or so guards suddenly appeared at the door and all began shooting at once. As the doorway was very narrow, many were shooting over the shoulders of the guards in front and actually burnt their hands doing so.

"The first shot hit papa who covered Alexei as he fell. Mama was shot in the head and the doctor and the servants were killed quickly. The bullets kept firing and firing at Alexei, my sisters and me but they bounced off of our corsets because of the diamonds we'd sewn into them. Alexei and all of my sisters and I were alive when we were loaded onto the truck. Papa, mama and the others were dead.

"The truck had to stop at a station along the way as it got stuck, over heated and required water. It was here Yurovsky, Ermatov and the guards left the vehicle.

"Nearly all of the guards were drunk by the time of the execution. Many of the guards had no stomach for shooting women and children. Several of them, upon hearing of our impending death sentence after the telegram came in to the Ipatiev House, quickly sent a message to the church. The nuns there had shown us kindness by bringing us eggs and milk and washing our clothing. It was through the nuns that arrangements were made with the peasants in the area to rescue us while the truck was abandoned. That was how Alexei and I were carried off and hid away.

"Whilst they were still on the truck, some of the guards came around with bayonets and ran them through my sisters who were moaning in pain. Alexei and I kept very still and quiet so they let us be. I'm sure this is what saved us.

"When Yurovsky and Ermatov returned to the truck, no one noticed we were missing as all the bodies were covered by a tarpaulin.

"It was once said by Winston Churchill that Russia is a riddle within a myth inside of an enigma. My family's legacy is proof of that."

Anastasia

Angelica's Song

A story here unfolds,
A story never told
But now the dove will sing
And the bell can ring.

A love so fine and true,
Begun so long ago.
A fire in the night
And then the angel's flight.

Where was I
Where were you
Since that lifetime
We once knew
When our hopes
And our dreams
Were torn apart.

But here we are
In a world
Where our time
Is now the same
And the love
Of our past
Can live again.

The story now unfolds,
The visions coming clear.
The angel draws them in,
Hidden all these years.

Noble Tsar and lovely queen,
All this time unseen
But right before our eyes
Their spirits make us wise.

Where was I
Where were you
Since that lifetime
We once knew,
When our hopes
And our dreams
Were torn apart.

But here we are
In a world
Where our time
Is now the same
And the love
Of our past
Can live again.

Little do we know
Where our spirits go
When we leave this realm
And start anew.

But this much I know,
Wherever we must go
With love we live forever
In our soul.

Where was I
Where were you
Since that lifetime
We once knew
When our hopes
And our dreams
Were torn apart.

But here we are
In a world
Where our time
Is now the same
And the love
Of our past
Can live again.

———————————————————

"*Angelica's Song*" will soon be available on a music CD.